C000154748

DYLAN BYFORD was
Northumberland. He has
now lives in the foot of the Yorkshire Dales with his family.
A prolific playwright in his early writing career, Dylan has
since turned to science fiction. Airedale is his first cyber-
punk novel, a crime thriller set a near-future northern England, riven with corruption, social unrest and urban decay.

Follow Dylan on Twitter @dylan_byford

AIREDALE

DYLAN BYFORD

Northodox Press Ltd
Maiden Greve, Malton,
North Yorkshire, YO17 7BE

This edition 2021

1
First published in Great Britain by
Northodox Press Ltd 2021

ISBN: 978-1-8383430-3-3

This book is set in Sabon LT Std

For Anita, who led me here, and Elsa, Harris and Isaac, who arrived soon after.

Chapter One

——

Despite the rain, I still stank of dead sturgeon. It wasn't a smell that let you forget its presence. I wanted to stick my hands deep in the pockets of my parka, but then the coat would stink for weeks. I'd not washed it since I'd bought it two years ago and I wasn't about to start now.

I nudged the fur-lined hood over my head with an arm and stepped up onto the pavement, letting the depot car trundle off and park itself a few metres down the road. I didn't envy the person catching a ride in it tomorrow morning or the person who was supposed to be rolling home in it in the next half hour. After they'd dealt with this shit, of course.

I looked up at the building to see four shriekers nail-gunned around the entrance, their proximity sensors flashing red. RapidRez had been to seal the scene. Looked like they had only done the front entrance. A guess, based upon what I could see of the place, but if you could get around the back of this dump, you were a frigging gibbon.

An industrial storage facility was glued onto the right-hand side of the factory as if it'd been thrown together in the modularist style or dropped from a crane. Depending on your view of modularism, it could mean the same thing. On the left of the unit was a no-man's land of glass, razor-wire, and pathogen effluent, leaking out of green-black polystyrene

1

barrels into the brownfield real estate opportunity beneath. Some wrong 'un may have made their way through there but I would bet a year's credit that no responder would have bothered.

These were the Sheds, which ran along the lowest point of Keighley Basin, parallel to the canals. At least, I'd been told they were parallel to the canals. It was difficult to tell, as the canals were two storeys below us. The Sheds had once been busy with life. Human life, that is. And, if you call what twitches in the meat vats life, then, yeah, they had plenty of that, and all. They had once been the epicentre – the birthplace, some jokers had said – of the vat-growing industries in the dale. Now they just housed a few bespoke bioengineering brands, still riding customers too apathetic to switch to cheaper imports.

The rest of the Sheds were decommissioned units. Much like this heap.

I'd been told this hadn't been a meat place. I was glad. Even when they were operational, meat vats stank enough to make you vegetarian. A decommissioned meat place could have any biologically-possible strains still flopping about in its dark corners.

'Just hold her hand, Hasim,' the DI had told me.

And that was why I was here. I didn't normally do this kind of shit. I was digital. This was forensics and biohazard. Gilbert McKenn was the analyst who handled all the biohazard cases. He had clearance for the Sheds and authorisation to poke his fingers in every rotten little meat-hole in Airedale. Probably had done, as well. He was a dirty little shit. I'd seen his vidz collection – a couple were proper specialist.

McKenn worked for a different DI than me. Whole different set of cases. He didn't do bodies. But this was bodies and biohazard. We'd got category bleed. The system couldn't handle that. His DI had prioritised McKenn elsewhere, so mine had been desperate, and didn't want forensics operating alone. He was desperate enough to call upon whoever had been the closest. I was on my way back from a loft full of dead fish, so he called me in to do him a favour. I was making up the numbers, really. You weren't supposed to send an analyst in alone. And it wasn't in RapidRez's contract. Basically, I was here to stand around and watch forensics get on with their job. Make sure they didn't mess up.

Forensics was Carrie Tarmell. She seemed to be doing OK and already had the owner on the phone. His little head floating in the top right of my peripheral vision. Carrie had a nosebead installed, which was projecting the image of the owner directly onto her right eyeball. Had I stared directly into her eye, I would've seen the tiny reflection of the person talking to her. I wasn't about to do that, mind, but she hated you getting in her space.

I've never wanted any metal in my body, so I wore the standard AJC cap, which shot the dazzle back onto my eye from its rain-soaked brim. I preferred the cap, liked to think it made me look a bit younger, and hid my bald patch.

'Ten years,' said the owner. I could see his metadata, floating around his image like balloons tethered in a breeze. It told me he was a Mr Bhagwat based in Chennai.

'I've had it ten years, I told you. All this is on my file. I can zip it across to you if you want?'

Carrie ignored his offer. 'But you've not been here since sixty-four?'

'That is correct,' said the owner. He was a wiry-looking man, with a pencil-thin moustache, and a small, retro goatee. I'd already tried to get access to the files which would have told us all about the factory, its floor plans, security, history and the like, but all I could find was it had once been used for manufacturing textiles. Nothing more specific other than that. Go back a few years and this wasn't uncommon in the

Basin, but nowadays it was odd; everybody else was still trying to grow steak. At least, those who still had credit.

If you had a factory like this and if it had dropped off the public data mountains so completely, it meant you'd once paid serious cash – as in high denomination pre-load – to hide it. I was interested, even though I wasn't supposed to be here tonight.

I cleared my throat. 'You'll have seen the vidz though, yeah?'

'Who is that?' snapped Mr Bhagwat.

'Haz Edmundson, sir,' I said.

'Who? I can't see him. Why can't I see him? Are you listening in to our private conversation? Who are you, sir, please?'

'Digital analyst, me,' I mumbled. I realised I hadn't enabled my camera. I twitched my cheek and the ghost of my LED-lit face joined the virtual conference with a pop.

Mr Bhagwat's moustache loomed a little larger in my display. He frowned. 'What is a digital analyst doing on this case?'

Carrie looked at me, her eyebrows suggesting she was as interested in knowing this as Mr Bhagwat. I struggled to find an answer. She frowned and shook her head.

'Standard procedure, sir,' said Carrie. 'DI likes us to work as a team.'

'You're not the DI?' asked the owner, his voice squeaking with incredulity. 'Who are you, then?'

'Carrie Tarmell. Forensic analyst.'

'I see,' said Mr Bhagwat. He busied himself offscreen for a moment. 'I am calling my facilities manager. I think it's best that this continues with his input. On my behalf, naturally.'

'We just need you to tell us that we can go inside, Mr Bhagwat,' said Carrie. 'We don't need your FM. You need to give us access. Confirm this place isn't carrying anything hazardous to the environment and that.'

'Well,' said Bhagwat. 'I'm not certain what might be

inside… it's better that you talk to Vep. I'm afraid that it's often difficult to locate him, though. I will confirm when he is available to answer your questions. He will help you with your… ha, ha… with your analysis.'

The tiny round head smirked, shrunk, and popped out of view. As it disappeared, I wondered whether I should try a retro goatee. I was that kind of age when you got desperate.

'Yeah. I've got better places to be, too,' muttered Carrie.

'Sorry?' I asked.

'Nowt.'

We waited in the darkness, rain slowly, inevitably, working its way through the waterproof fibres of our coats.

'Fuck this,' said Carrie. 'I'm not waiting here for him to rustle up his FM. There's a Dommies around the corner. You want to get a coffee or a chocolate or summat?'

'Yeah,' I said. 'Good idea, yeah.' My med-handler tended to caution me against taking caffeine so late. But then I tended to ignore it. So the situation balanced out. Also, I hated Dommies. However, there was no knowing how long it was going to take for Mr Bhagwat to wake up his facilities manager and get him on a camera. I wasn't getting any drier or warmer standing here.

We set off down the street towards the centre of town. The middle of Keighley Basin was lively of a night but was fairly safe unless you decided to go via the canals. The weather was making this more tempting than usual. But not tempting enough.

'You going to charge for this?' My left eye was twitching, ready to shut down the clock. I was a contractor, like Carrie, like all analysts. All contractors worked the clock. Only DIs were permanent.

'Of course,' said Carrie. 'Not going to a Dommies in the Basin at eight o'clock at night on my own time, am I?'

'True, yeah,' I said, and let the timer icon sink back into its semi-transparent rest at the edge of my vision.

As we walked, she stuck her hands deep in her pockets and glanced across at me. 'Why're you here, Haz?' Her tone was dangerously flat.

I'd been waiting for this. 'You know why. Gilbie McKenn couldn't make it. He's working down at Shipley tonight. They got the riots moving through down there.'

'So DI sent you?'

'Yeah,' I muttered. People said you had to go careful around Carrie. Not wind her spring.

'Right,' she said. 'You were closest, were you?'

I shrugged. 'I guess.'

'DI didn't trust me to handle this?'

'Look, Carrie,' I said. 'I'm helping DI out, yeah. He just asked me to be here.'

'Just asked you to be here?' she sneered.

I had to think on my feet. I knew DI Ibrahim Al-Yahmeni – technically our client although it always felt like he was our boss – thought the sun frigging-well shone out of Carrie's arse and I guessed he didn't want her slashed in the face by some canal rat off his head on pseudo. He could've asked for an Enforcement operative to come down and make sure Carrie didn't get hurt but they were all busy in the middle of the Basin tonight. More rioting. Plus, they were expensive by the hour. Too expensive for a hand-holding mission. A digital analyst, however, was cheap.

Besides, I was already en route back from the Crosshills Road, so he must have decided it was the easiest thing to do. The DI just needed to divert my car from the Airedale Main Duct and dump me here. He knew I wouldn't argue, knew his analysts, and knew my problems. Carrie was one of the few people I could talk to these days. Kind of.

The one major pain was that I had to pay the childcare overtime rate at this time of night, and Greg always got pissed off if I dropped it on him last minute. I just hoped Asha and Ali weren't pissing him around like they usually did on a Tuesday.

'He told me it might be of interest,' I lied. 'Possible digital angle.'

'Really?' asked Carrie. 'It's a stiff, in't it? You don't do stiffs, do you?'

'I've done a few, when there's a digital angle.'

'Yeah,' she muttered. 'Whatever, Haz.'

We turned the corner at the end of the industrial zone and saw the faux-Brazilian greens and yellows of the Dommies outlet. Automated samba beats were just audible over the thrumming of the rain. Inside was dry and fairly empty. A few bot technicians from the old Washington place were drinking margaritas and swaying to the music. Three women, their hands dyed brown from the meat tanks, were chatting loudly and whooping with laughter at odd moments.

As we entered, they were about to crack a joke at our sodden appearance. However, I deliberately pulled back the hood of my khaki parka to reveal the cricket cap underneath. They shut up when they saw the AJC logo. Even though we were subcontractors, not directly commissioned like the DI, they knew we still had delegation. And delegation meant something.

We sat and waggled our fingers at the table's order sensor. I asked for a chocolate instead of a coffee. Even so, the med-handler had popped up on my display, trying to get my attention, but I killed it with an eye twitch.

I felt I should try to re-start the conversation, while we waited. Which was proving difficult. When Dali had been around, she did all that shit for me. I realised, looking around the tired décor and gappy lighting, I hadn't been in a place like this for nearly two years. Even if I'd been out with the kids, I'd tend to drop them into the managed facilities and make myself scarce. I'd found tricks to avoid getting stuck into these kinds of scenarios. Subconscious anxiety or some bollocks like that. I knew all about that crap. My med-handler would tell me all about anxiety until I told it to close itself down. I knew. It hadn't told me that I'd been avoiding company, though. Piece of advert-riddled shit.

Carrie saved me. In a manner of speaking. 'Why'd you stink of fish so much?'

I sniffed my hands. 'Just this case I'm working.'

'Oh, yeah?' she said. 'Illegal vats? Fish and that?'

'Not quite. It's not the fish, like, that were the business.'

'Oh? What then?'

'It were only...' I paused for effect and glanced sideways, checking the vicinity. 'It were only fucking caviar.'

She laughed. A great snorting eruption. 'For honest?'

'That's right,' I said, smiling. 'Bit different, yeah?'

'Yeah.'

'Some old ex-farmer had been harvesting it up there on the Crosshills Road. Stuck a couple of plastic swimming pools in the loft of his old place. It proper stank. And he was total amateur about it. No idea what he was doing, so he'd killed the lot. Kiddie pools full of dead sturgeon. Weird, yeah?'

The waitress brought over our drinks, half-heartedly trying to smile and wiggle her arse. She knew she was on camera. Some algorithm somewhere was evaluating her sense of ersatz Latin vibe. Truth was, she wasn't even Brazilian. There were enough in town but perhaps they didn't dare come into this part of the Basin anymore. She looked a lot like Dali, but older.

After we'd thanked her for the drinks and zapped off some credits, we sat back and sipped. I wrapped my hands around the ceramic beaker. Despite it being summer, the rain had started to chill me.

'But why'd DI send you up to a vat-growing scene?' said

Carrie, after she'd sipped the cream off the top of her drink. 'You'd not normally do the meat cases, would you?'

'Counterfeit case, in't it,' I said. 'This guy were passing it off as real shit. Been getting some encrypted authentication codes sent through from his buddy in Murmansk.'

'Ahh,' said Carrie. 'I see.'

'Spent most of the morning tracking down all his memory slivers. Cheeky beggar had been hiding them all over the building. Then I wasted most of the afternoon trying to dig through his server.'

'Owt juicy?'

'Couldn't get into it,' I said. 'All locked down. Going to read the metapattern later on.'

She grinned at me. People always asked me that. They think any wrong 'un is going to be sitting on a pile of filth.

'Still don't see why you had to go there, though,' said Carrie, the grin subsiding. 'Mind you, I don't see why you're out here tonight. What's the story, Haz?'

Thankfully, a message flashed up on our screens before I was forced to squirm any more. The FM had been located. He was going to be online in about five minutes, once he'd finished having his shower.

We necked our drinks and stepped back into the rain. I was thankful for the break. Airedale weather was easier to bear when you'd had chocolate.

'You got the code for those shriekers?' I asked, as we approached the large double doors.

She nodded, pointing to her nose. Then she flicked her hand, squeezed her fingers, and cast something in the air across to my head. I saw the zipped-up codes appear in my screen and sink from view. I twitched my cheek and dropped the huge files into my beacon. I didn't want those shriekers going off by accident. Paully Zappers had forgotten to drop the codes into his lapel bead three months back. He was off work for four days. Still couldn't hear you on a busy day, the stupid twat.

The red LEDs of the shriekers dimmed as I approached the door, turning from red to orange, then yellow, and finally green. The ancient padlock had already been ground away by the responders, ready for the analysts' arrival. I waited by the door, impatiently cracking my knuckles, waiting for authorisation to enter. The facilities manager appeared on my display as I was cracking through my second hand.

'Good morning.' He was a young man, clearly in a bed. 'Call me Vep. How can I help you?'

'Hello, Vep,' said Carrie. 'We're with the Airedale Justice Commission analytical team. We're outside a facility in the Keighley Basin area.'

He grinned. 'I have no idea where that is. England, is it? By your accent?'

'Your boss not tell you?' I asked.

'He's my client,' said Vep. 'Not my boss.'

'Of course he is,' said Carrie. 'We're in Europe, alright? Pennine Region. East Pennine.'

'Very good,' said Vep. 'My parents have been on vacation there. It's very nice!'

Carrie flicked the Vs towards her nose but remained expressionless. 'Well, that's great to know, Vep.'

'What's in this place, buddy?' I asked. 'There's no meat-vatting in there, yeah?'

'Mr Bhagwat is in textiles,' said Vep. 'He is not a flesh engineer.'

I shrugged, no longer caring what shit-awful backroom stewed biohazard might still be festering inside. I just wanted to get out of the rain.

'Have you been in yet?' asked Vep.

'Nobody's been in,' said Carrie. 'Our first responders have secured the entrance. But they wouldn't be able to enter. This facility has an intermediate biohazard contamination risk.'

'You can't just kick down the doors?'

'Not with a facility that has an intermediate biohazard contamination risk,' repeated Carrie.

'Sure you can!'

'Yeah,' said Carrie. 'If course we can. RapidRez could already be in clearing up all the blood and shit. But then we'd be liable if owt went wrong, you understand?'

'You need it to be my problem, you mean?' said Vep, smiling.

Carrie sighed. 'We need your clearance to let us through. Are we going to poison half of Keighley Basin by going in there and kicking over a poly-drum?'

'Let me see,' the young man said. He ducked out of view of his camera. When he returned, his attention was taken up by something off-screen. I could just see his finger flickering away. 'Mr Bhagwat has just the one unit in the Keighley Basin. It went offline about three years ago but was retained as an asset.'

'The output?' I muttered.

Vep laughed. 'Textiles, like I said!'

'Is it safe for us to go inside?'

'Yes, of course, but–'

I kicked open the door and stepped inside.

'Before you enter,' said Vep. 'You should probably tell me. Do you have any phobias?'

Chapter Two

Our first responder sub-contractors, RapidRez, had been called by some suburban family up on the West Daleside. Their kid had been given a camdrone for Christmas. Little thing about the size of a satsuma. You could pick them up by the dozen from any trade portal. Kid had been taking his new toy out on his bike, around the western suburbs and then into the Sheds, testing the range. I'd seen the vidz on my way back from the High Dales earlier in the day. The drone's camera was low quality. It was a child's toy. But the hole in the roof of the old factory was pretty clear. And the shape that lay within, a startling off-white amid the blackness, was clearly defined. At the time, on the vid, it was unclear why the floor was so dark. The pale shape had been surrounded by a sea of black.

Now it was clear.

My eyes tried to penetrate the darkness. The sensor on my shoulder lamp must have gone bust. I gave it a slap with my hand. We crunched over the carpet of dried carapaces as soon as we entered. The abdomen of each body about the size of a chestnut. There were piles of them, thousands.

Carrie could hardly put the entirety of her foot down, balanced as she was on the ball, shivering. 'Are these ricos?'

'Yes,' said Vep.

'Fuck,' hissed Carrie.

Rico spiders. Brazilian-bred, spliced for their silk, easy to farm, and exported across the world. I wasn't expecting them in Keighley Basin. Turns out it's a small world.

'How'd you keep them alive?' I asked. 'Airedale's not warm enough.'

Vep shrugged. 'Solar heaters, I think. It was before my time.'

'They're not venomous,' I said, trying to reassure Carrie. After the fourth strike, my lamp had started working properly. I swung the beam around the walls of the room.

'Yeah,' said Carrie, staring at the floor. 'Little buggers are dead and all.' She shuddered visibly.

'For the best,' yawned Vep. 'It's true that they're not a problem with a couple of bites. But if you get more than twenty… well, let us say, things become more complicated. There was a cleaning technician in Yangon, and we found–'

'Shut up,' said Carrie. She experimented with shuffling her feet forward, kicking away the bodies as she went, stepping deeper into the gloom.

'You got a gecko?' I asked.

'Yeah,' she said, looking pissed off, as though I was getting in her face. 'You got a frigging processing block?'

'I mean… I can't see the case for it, that's all.'

Forensics usually carried their geckos around in a special flight bag. To keep the lenses clear of dust and the expensive motors clear of other muck.

'Oh right,' said Carrie. 'Yeah, I lost the case.'

She dug in the pocket of her large duffel coat and pulled out a handful of used tissues and sweets wrappers. She carefully picked away the detritus, revealing a grubby plastic device about the size of a finger. After giving its many cameras a gentle and ineffectual blow, she crouched down and dropped it onto a relatively clear patch of the floor.

Her left hand twitched in the air and the gecko scuttled

off at speed, heading for the nearest wall. It was coded to gain height, to get into corners. Then it was supposed to take a continual stream of hi-def pictures, all of which could be used to virtually recreate the room, down to fingerprint clarity. It started to flash, intermittently, revealing more of the room and more of the spiders.

'I believe there was an accident,' said Vep. 'Is that correct?'

'Dunno about that,' said Carrie. 'But there's a body.'

'In which room?'

'Further in,' I said. 'Towards the back of the building.'

We advanced carefully. You weren't to destroy evidence before the gecko had taken its pictures. The device was now relaying to Carrie where she could tread. She'd found a sweet along with her gecko. She popped it in her mouth and sucked it thoughtfully. 'So, what you doing tomorrow?'

I could hear the tension in her voice. 'Just finishing off, mainly,' I said. 'Get started on this caviar thing tonight. Assuming I can get into the slivers. Then I've got to meet up with Clive and get Modlee upgraded.'

'Clive?' she said. 'He creeps the piss out of me, him.'

We watched the gecko scuttle from corner to corner. Our faces were lit by the flashing lights.

'Well, I got to be able to work,' I said. 'I got to get Modlee up and running again.'

Carrie stuck her sweet in her cheek. 'Glad I'm not a digital. That Modlee needs more upgrades than my nan's forehead.'

'Yeah, it does,' I said.

Carrie stepped forward. 'What's the problem this time?'

I followed her. 'IG,' I said. 'East Pennine changed rules again.'

Carrie got the signal that we were all clear. We stepped forward, deeper into the room. Now it looked more like a loading bay than anything. Back here, the ricos were less numerous. It seemed they'd been trying to escape out into the Basin and had piled themselves up against the double doors. In the furthest corners there were a couple of cabins for admin and packing and the like. But we were more interested in a second set of larger doors which looked like they led deeper into the factory.

A sign above the doors read: 'Spinning Room.'

We heaved aside the long since de-powered doors and swung our lamps around into the shadows. The gecko skittered over our heads, down the wall, and underneath the lintel. It started to flash in the room ahead of us. We stepped through.

Inside, we found the rotting remains of a large number of vertical tubes, possibly two hundred of them, about the diameter of a dinner plate. They had the familiar compost tang of some kind of vegemer. Vegemer that had got wet and old. It degraded after about five years and when it went, it properly stank. By the odd nibbled crenellations, it looked like a colony of mice had found the tubes as well.

Although it was supposed to be delicious – if you liked that kind of vegan thing – vegemer was also toxic in high concentrations. At least, until its complex chains had released the cocktail of inorganic compounds that were required to keep it so rigid. Poor things must have been munching on the stuff before it had fully degraded.

It would have been cutting-edge when this place had been kitted out. The best material to house insects or whatever spiders were supposed to be.

'What were these?' I asked, waving at the tubes.

'Hmm?' Vep had been distracted by something elsewhere on his bed, watching something on another screen.

'These pipes,' I said. 'There're hundreds of them.'

'Oh, those,' said Vep. 'They're spinning columns. Would have sent air down, or something. That's where the little critters would have hung out, catching their false-fly bait.

16

Spinning away! Making their silk.'

I looked at the ceiling. There was a large array of circular couplings attached to some kind of air conditioning unit.

Vep chuckled away to himself at the end of the screen. He was definitely watching something else at the same time. It pissed me off. Wouldn't have been surprised to find it was a RandoPorno, probably featuring him and Carrie. Might have featured me, I suppose. I liked to think people stole my ratios for that kind of thing and that there were a few RandoPornos out there featuring me. It would have been worse to know that nobody had bothered at all.

'What you watching?' I asked.

Vep looked at me and smiled. 'Nothing, officer.'

'Analyst,' I muttered.

Carrie was now at the other end of the room, trying to get through another door. She had managed to scrape it open a crack.

'She's in here,' I heard Carrie say. 'Can see a body. Come give me a hand, Haz?'

I stepped forward, my peripheral vision caught movement in the vegemer tubes to my right. I wasn't sure whether it was a trick of the flickering light from the gecko, or something else. I thought, at first, it may have been mice. I stopped and leaned in closer to the tube.

At the other end of the room, Carrie had managed to wrench the door open, muttering to herself. She pushed through and the gecko followed her, leaving me alone with my dysfunctional lamp.

I felt an immature drench of fear, being left alone in the dark. I wanted to jog – possibly sprint – to catch her up, but the movement still seemed to be there, inside the tube. I stepped closer and flashed my lamp so that it came in from the side of the tube.

Ricos. Hundreds of them. Moving. Running up and down

the inside the tube, crawling over each other. They must have found something to eat. Perhaps it was just Basin flies. But they were fast. And this was just one of the tubes.

'Carrie...' I started to say, but she was already through into the other room.

I ran, making absolutely sure not to touch any of the spinning columns. I could hear a muffled grunt or possibly a strangled retch ahead of me.

Carrie was in the middle of the room, standing in front of a column of rain drops.

I saw the body laying directly beneath the ruin of the roof. Beyond the ragged hole was the brown haze of a Keighley Basin night. The noise of sirens had grown louder. I consciously avoided breathing through my nose, the canal stench now mingled with the aggressive reek of the decomposing woman.

Carrie advanced on the body, illuminating the face. She swore under her breath I took a closer look. There was something wrong with what I saw. Then I realised.

At some point at university, a friend, Mohammed, had explained to me some old experiment conducted on Congolese tree spiders. They had fed a control cohort with beetles, moths, and flies, insects that were considered to be the standard food for the species. Alongside the control group, they had also fed another cohort with prime cuts of the best vat-grown beef. Apparently, within a few weeks, the tree spiders in the beef group had doubled in size. At the time, it wasn't the fact that the spiders had doubled in size that had made me suspicious. It was the fact that I knew spiders didn't eat raw meat like that. I knew that they ate flies and flies only.

Seemed I knew shit all.

A swarm of the ricos had reduced one cheek down to a few scraps of connective tissue, revealing the girl's expensive dental work. The teeth glimmered an eerie white alongside the black bodies which climbed over them.

'Fuck,' I whispered, forgetting to double-blink the mute signal.

'Yep,' said Vep. He was staring at the feed on his own screen. 'That's pretty disgusting.'

Carrie remained silent. I could see her shaking slightly. I should've put an arm out to steady her or something but it seemed wrong, not because of the moment, but because it was Carrie.

A forensics analyst had little to do at this point, so she cracked open a packet of menthol sniffs and stuck one up each nostril. She offered one to me but I shook my head. The gecko was doing the hard work for her, gathering appropriate data. Officially, forensics were supposed to poke around and start to try and build models about what events could've led to the death, based upon the immediate data. Carrie didn't give a shit about all of that. I guessed she knew what events had caused the death. The clue was the massive bastard hole in the roof.

'Vep,' said Carrie. 'Can we get the ricos to stop eating her face?'

'No,' said Vep, no longer so jolly. 'No, I don't think so… no.'

'Haz,' she said without turning her head, but I knew what she wanted.

In the general course of a day, and especially these days, I'd wrapped myself in a fog of something, possibly psychological, possibly narcotic, but comforting. This had been shredded by the sight of the girl's body. There was something in the overall crumpled form that had done it for me. She had been a flyer, clearly. The wing apparatus were all smashed up and torn, mostly buried under the spiders. They were as broken as their owner. One arm flung out behind her at a disjointed angle, the other beneath her, legs spread, bent forward at each knee. Her eyes were closed and had been left untouched by the ricos, thankfully. It was something about her pose, the pose of an object which had been dropped by forces more powerful than could be imagined. Discarded with zero care.

And, at that precise moment, I thought of Dali. And then things started to go proper wrong.

Chapter Three

I watched myself from a distance. My other – much younger – self was ordering a hot chocolate, depth-charged with a mint-and-coffee bombe. In one hand, a large cup of some exotic tea. Jasmine, probably, as that was her usual order. My younger version took the drinks and walked between the busy tables, the light of early dusk low in the sky, casting long and dark shadows. It was a familiar, northern midwinter scene. Somewhere on the coast. I knew exactly where. We had visited that coffee shop many times.

The Memro metapattern handlers had chopped together a good reel this evening, with plenty of varied content. The machine entities had dug out a half-forgotten piece of personal security footage from the franchise in Morecambe. Although I knew where it was – I could even pull a manual zoom straight to the cafe on a dynamic map – I'd no idea when the scene had taken place. There were a few clues. I was a younger man and neither Asha nor Ali were there. They could've been with their grandparents, but I doubted it. My other-self had much more hair, standing out on my head in porcupine quills.

Dali radiated happiness. No algorithms recognised any form of warning pattern in Dali's eyes. Even second-generation. No human handler ever saw anything in Dali's eyes. Nobody saw anything wrong. Only her happiness.

The view switched momentarily from the security feed to an external view. Possibly a passing car – insurance camera watching for crashes, flogging its content for anonymous lawyer pre-load – on its way south, to the west Lancashire sprawl. The angle was wide. It slowed down and zoomed in on the couple as they sat at their window seat.

My favourite song from that year started up, the opening rhythm in time to the slow clicking of the external camera images. That placed it before the kids had been born. Before the wedding. It had been on the wish list. IndusSun rhythms and a contralto vocal, accent somewhere midway between Alabama and Georgia.

Then back to the coffee-shop security footage, a different camera this time, panning across the crowd, before a long fade to a photo taken on the sea-front. Memro pushing the boat out on the timing. This was still taken from her camera with me gurning at the lens. I've never been able to take a straight photo, so says my mother. She always blames my father. I think she's right. Next an image from my camera of Dali's hair blowing across her face, her left cheek bright in the late afternoon sunshine. Early December, possibly late November. Nothing wrong.

Memro zooms in on another car-camera feed of the happy couple larking about with their engagement ring cameras. Before beads were ubiquitous. The music starting its rhythmic crescendo and the voice running through a litany of trite ill-doing in Spanish. I realised I really loved this song.

Nostalgia flooded my system and I was just conscious enough of reality to realise I'd groaned. The memories were vivid. Memro-made dreams. It had data access that must have bled through to some of the stricter authorisation protocols. It found new ways of showing you your past. It gave new perspectives, touched every sentimental chord in your brain.

People had found that you could ride these dreams best on vizchannel. VC was a powerful little fungal strain from some parasite of a plant you had to dig for in the southern Colombian rainforest. Of course, they'd synthesised it within three days of its discovery and now any kid with a fast-breeder tank and a solar array could knock you up a litre of the shit in a week.

Unlike a lot of the spore-based adjusters, VC was in legal limbo in the EP, so I felt safe using it. But it really messed with your perspective. It temporarily strengthened associative memories, reducing the dampening effect of normal thought, so that all memories sparked from your original sensual burn were also sparked - and, in turn, sparked others. All were remembered in vivid clarity. Not necessarily accurate, but you really felt you were there again. When you combined it with a specialist past-reconstruction service like this, it properly took you there. Although the Memro service would never dare to suggest you enjoyed its wares best on an artificial adjuster like VC, everybody still did it.

So, tonight I was on vizchannel and on Memro.

I watched as the bright flares of the winter sun disappeared over the southern Lakeland fells and the tune faded away. That last shot had been from some tourist camera. Possibly on a totally different day, different year. Might even have been some Morecambe district marketing fluff. Still, it cut itself in perfectly. I couldn't believe these things were automatically generated. It was seamless. That should have been a good one. And yet throughout all the cut scenes and the music and the wash of the VC, I was unable to fully erase the persistent after-image of a dead woman.

A digital analyst doesn't see much death. Nobody hands you menthol sniffs in my normal line of work. Of course, I'd had cases where I'd had to brute force my way into an in-situ house server or some locked-down layer of a washing-machine's memory, crouched in a dirty utility room a few centimetres from a mess of meat being photographed in queasily high resolution. But actually paying attention to the stiff – well, that had always been somebody else's job. And the corpses, they had always been other people. People whose trajectory was set years before, from the moment they'd walked through the wrong door, been smiled at by the wrong person, or failed to smile at the right person.

There were algorithms designed to follow these people, to warn them what was coming, to warn us and the world that they were coming. And yet, despite all the warnings, despite all the machine-learning, the feedback, the counselling, the interventions, these stupid fuckers would still be found laid on the concrete of their utility room, skulls disrupted. And all that they'd achieved in life dribbling away to nothing more than an insert-row command on a crime database and a minor calibration to a Prevention analyst's model.

But tonight hadn't been like that. No matter how you tweaked the variables, Meri Fergus wasn't supposed to be dead on the floor of that warehouse unit. There were some people who weren't supposed to die like that. This was bothering me and Memro seemed to be making it worse.

So, as sometimes happened at that time of night, I pushed deeper. I pulled up the Memro menu and finger-clicked in some date parameters. Recent dates.

The opening song from a concert recording I'd bought five years ago started to play. A scene faded up of low-lying hills, peat bogs, overcast skies, and bleakness. A single track road surrounded by mirror-like pools. I knew where it was. We pulled across a causeway, the sea off to our left and sea or a lake to our right. The view was from the front of the car, low to the ground. An insurance camera, footage sold by the company who had rented the vehicle. We had picked the car up from the port at the bottom of the island. We were going to drive all the way up the western side and drop the car off at the larger town in the north. The kids had been so excited by the ferry ride. They loved standing on the exposed upper deck, letting the spray and wind blow their hair back. They spent the whole journey trying to see dolphins.

The car drove north, swerving into passing places to let others through from the other direction. I was waiting for another camera angle. Just a shot of me and Dali in the car, perhaps. Something with the two children in the back seat.

Memro was messing with me.

I knew this would have been the time when Dali was starting to show the signs. Signs that I was too self-absorbed to notice then. But now, having scoured all the possible Memro cuts of her, I could see it all. Deep in her facial lines, the rising flood, the twitching, the anxiety around her eyes, the flashes of terror, quickly quelled with a laugh and a grin. Signs that her shit-useless mood-handler had ignored. That everybody else, especially me, had ignored.

I remembered on that particular holiday, I'd noticed she'd turned off her VitalZine health monitoring bracelet as well. It wasn't uncommon. We all hated being watched so much. Dali especially hated to be a string of data items on some company database. She said it was her religion. She turned off her health monitors, her security alarms, her locational tracking. She hated her locational tracking the most and it hadn't been switched on for at least a year.

This was why it'd taken us so long to find her.

As I watched the slowed-down footage of a road pass beneath me, the persistence of a memory heaved into view once more and flicked me the Vs. Meri Fergus' body. Then Dali's body. Dali's body had not been so destroyed. Yet, she had been in the same distorted shape. There were shapes that human bodies weren't supposed to make, weren't configured for. To see anybody in such a shape fired off neural pathways that were best left untrodden. And, for me, they had been too much.

* * *

I was ashamed Carrie had seen me lose my shit. Thankfully, she'd understood exactly what was going on. She'd dragged me out and got the responders back from their work with Enforcement down in the Basin. They'd shot me with some tranq as soon I'd started hyperventilating. She'd stayed with me and convinced them to take a detour via my place in Saltaire. They just wanted to get up to Arches and drop the body and move on. But she must've given them the Carrie Tarmell glare. Nobody messed with that.

She'd left me a note floating on my display and dumped me on my doorstep, letting the anti-tranq work its way through my system. I knew she didn't want to come up to the apartment. Greg would be there to look after me, in case something happened when I was coming up. She'd done more than she needed to, anyway. I was ashamed enough without having a work colleague strip me down and put me in a hot shower.

I'd hacked up my hot chocolate onto the steps of the apartment block and staggered upstairs. Greg was out of the door faster than an off-the-clock contractor. Thankfully, the kids were both still asleep, so they didn't see their screw-up of a father washing chocolate vomit from his Chennai Super Kings shirt.

I'd been able to slink into my VC and Memro comforter as soon as I'd stepped out of the shower and into my dressing gown. This particular show had taken little more than fifteen minutes, but it felt like hours.

The song finished its final, trickling notes and the view from the car's bumper turned the corner into the ferry car park. I pulled myself back to the present. It seemed as though something was trying to get my attention. This was the problem with vizchannel. It tended to let your mind wander. Something was nagging at me in the now moment, memory still firing images of the ferry arriving at... limbs contorted... Asha and Ali eating ice creams on a bench... a body on concrete... all four of us watching the boat.

I resurfaced.

There was an insistent noise. The close sound of a siren. Many sirens. Emergency squeal peaking above the general background buzz of the dale.

My apartment block was tucked into the eastern hillside opposite the old village of Saltaire. The heritage park itself had been encased in a series of domes about twenty years ago. Nobody lived there now but it was open during the day, guarded by a few sombre UN specials. A pair of billionaires out of Mumbai had come to visit, back when Airedale was attracting their credit, but nowadays it rode on a dying income stream of ageing American tourists and whatever subsidy the greys in the EP would be willing to throw at it. I looked out on the polymer-encased sandstone and heritage floodlights every night. It was pretty, of course, but it seemed to exist outside the dale, an ancient visitor sternly returning to watch over its ragged grandchildren.

Around the park itself, beyond the old mill and the twee terraces, there were some mid-century eco-blocks. These had been built in the time of prevention, when the world still believed something could be done. They were beautifully engineered, curving geometric shapes, which required no energy input and recycled all the waste. They had cost a lot to construct, so only the rich lived in them. Proximity to the heritage park helped. From my balcony window, I could see right down the valley side, across the rooftops of the narrow strip of bijou vat-growing industry that Old Saltaire still supported – at a loss – and then into the bedrooms of the rich and the lucky. I could see the floodlights from the mill reflecting on their parties and, on days when the wind came up the hill, I could hear their laughter.

Tonight, the rich were getting pelted with abuse. The disturbances were louder than ever. The rioters were working their way through the industrial strip and bearing down on the eco-blocks. I could see a few street fires and the occasional dark shape running in and out of cover.

I heard a crash outside the window and pushed open the blinds a little wider. All the outward-facing apartments in our block had a joke balcony, where you could sit with half your arse out of the window and the other half still inside. I sat myself on the sill and leaned out, trying to see what was happening below.

One of the Brazilians was running down the alley that separated our block from the industrial strip. A masked figure, small and quick. At least, I assumed it was a Brazilian. They tended to be, although they had joined up with a Venezuelan contingent recently, who also had non-specific grievances. Nobody was quite sure why these particular groups had aggregated or why their general sense of injustice had now erupted into fourteen months of street-to-street battles with the Airedale Enforcement officers. I thought that somebody was probably working on it. The Prevention analysts, no doubt. Modlee would probably be able to tell me.

Lit by the multi-coloured floodlights, I could see a cloud of Enforcement camdrones rise above the distant bulk of the mill. They scattered in a seemingly chaotic though perfectly choreographed manoeuvre, covering all streets as quickly as possible. Their tiny propellers generated a nerve-shredding whine. Behind them, I could hear the deeper hum of the shockdrones. This bass hum only ever lasted for a few seconds, warning you that they'd taken off. Once they were airborne, the Enforcement drones were as shrill as any other and they hid themselves in the background drone-shriek. Until they released their payload of smartdarts into your pitiful backside.

I turned my attention to the figure below. It had stopped. It must've heard the drones. Perhaps it was deciding whether to double back. To hide somewhere. Where, mere seconds before, it had moved with intent, it now bobbed aimlessly around on the pavement beneath like a random pixel in a broken model.

It looked small.

Without knowing why I did it – later, I told myself it was because I wanted another adult to talk to – I stuck my right arm up behind me and lazily weaved the open-block-door signal with my finger. Then patched my mic down to the doorway to the block.

'Get in,' I said, quietly but clearly. It must have been the VC still in my system but I realised I was enjoying the drama.

The figure hesitated. Rather than looking at the door, it immediately turned to look up at my balcony. Dark eyes in the gloom of a peaked cap, a bandana across the lower half of their face. I thought I could make out the distorting effects of eye-extensions. They looked homemade. Even so, it was effective, as it had properly knackered their facial ratios. This person was trying to avoid the law.

'Your choice,' I said. 'The door closes in seven seconds.'

I could see the vanguard of the surveillance drones whine their way across the rooftops in front of me. I smiled at them and waved. They had my ratio in their servers now, I had nothing to hide as long as that idiot below could get through the door. I kept my eyes up, looking into the camera retina of the tiny machines, forcing myself not to draw attention to whatever was happening below. I knew the door would've closed by now.

As the drones swept overhead, I realised, with a sickening jolt, that I'd not updated the default gesture command for the block door. That might've been picked up. It could've involved some tricky questions.

I turned and stepped into the room, telling the balcony doors to close behind me. Thankfully, I still had the beaded blinds that Dali had chosen for the apartment. I dragged them across and tried to clear my head of the remaining vizchannel. I had to get this person back out onto the street without the apartment block servers triggering an alarm. They had cushioning for strangers, of course, or nobody could have visitors, but strangers with badly-made eye-extenders and a handkerchief over their nose were probably somewhere over the threat threshold. I had nearly two minutes before the algorithms would try to analyse, choke on the facial ratios, and escalate to a human handler. If I had real eyes on this scene, I was out of luck.

Not long after Dali and I'd moved into the apartment, the residents had agreed, via our neighbourhood Servant, that we'd be setting the risk appetite to low when it came to strangers in the building. This meant a load of parties for college kids had been continually disrupted and that fast-food delivery meant a trip to the ground floor.

The risk level had been reset after a while, so people could get their pizzas delivered. I needed to move fast, bringing up the apartment server settings panel with a snap of the fingers and dragged the projection onto the dining room table. I killed all the incoming and outgoing comms and set the server to manual with a few jabs of the virtual controls. All the while, avoiding the food still not cleaned up from around Ali's place at the table. I dropped a general maintenance message to the apartment server and asked it to archive all my vidz. That would slow the system down. Hopefully it would give the stranger time to work out where they needed to go.

I went to the door and opened it by hand which felt odd.

'If that's my burrito I ordered,' I called out, trying to make my voice lower and threatening. 'Should have been here five minutes ago!'

The stairwell was quiet. There didn't seem to be any movement on the floors below.

I shrugged and went to grab a carton of Hombre, thinking it might help to clear the VC. I would regret it later, if I was still awake at the four o'clock birdsong chorus, but I wasn't going to make a bollocks of it by drifting away if anything interesting happened now. I managed to find one behind the rotting haunch of Venezuelan beef that Greg – the wrong 'un – still hadn't dealt with. I knocked back a couple mouthfuls and walked back out of the kitchen.

The stranger was there in my front room.

Immediately, I realised she was a woman. Possibly a girl. Her baggy clothes had hidden her shape. I hadn't recognised it from the window, but now she was close it was obvious.

I moved to close the door by hand, checking the stairwell for anybody else. As I came back into the room, she remained standing there, breathing heavily, the bandana rising and falling in front of her mouth. She was a foot shorter than me and perhaps ten years younger. Her black hair was tied with an intricately braided plait running from ear-to-ear around the back of her head. It looked like it had been artificially speed-grown. The eye-extenders clung to her face like bizarre swimming goggles, giving her an alien appearance, as though from a retro-virt.

'I've turned sensors off,' I said quietly. 'All comms are down, alright.'

'What?'

I waved at the arrays clustered in the corners of the room. 'They're gone. You can take off that bandit outfit now, OK?'

'Oh,' she said, reaching a hand to pull down the bandana

and eye-extenders, letting them hang around her neck. She was attractive, for a vat-worker, so I was momentarily flushed and unable to think. Flashes of Dali surfaced in my mind. Disconcertingly, as did images of the flyer's body.

'You want a drink?' I asked, offering her the can of Hombre.

She shook her head, still unsmiling, and trotted over to the window. There was no noise of the camdrones from outside. She leaned her head forward, moving the beads aside to get a better view, covering the lower half of her face with the bandana as she did so. Her eyes swept the sky.

I clicked my fingers to activate the doors to the balcony. Nothing happened so I leaned past her to push them apart slightly. She jumped back nervously as I did so, almost ready to leap at me. I could hear the skittering noise of the smartdarts and the deep thumping whoosh of the drones pass away to the north-west.

'See,' I said. 'They've moved on.'

'Looks like they have,' she said, carefully enunciating each word.

'I'm Haz. Hasim, really, but you can still call me Haz. You want some food?'

'No,' she said looking, around the apartment, eyes coming to rest on the pictures of the children. 'I should go.'

'I'd give it a while,' I said, taking a swig from the carton. The sweet synthetic taste of the Hombre seemed to be clearing my head a little.

'Thanks for letting me in.'

'No bother. If you're hungry, I've got plenty of food.'

She shook her head again.

'You've put yourself at risk, allowing me in here.'

'Depends what you've done, in't it?'

'What do you mean?' she asked, on the defensive.

'I mean, I don't think you've done anything wrong... you don't look like the type that would. Am I right?'

'Right? I don't know,' she said. 'Some people would say we're doing bad things.'

'And what do you say?'

She didn't answer me at first. Then, after a moment's thought, she stuck her hand out.

'I am Luana.'

I could smell the scent of ethanol on her clothes. I didn't want to think what would've happened if I'd lit candles in the apartment. When I shook her hand, it was still slightly cold. She must have been handling some of the fuel before she had come up the stairs.

'The block server shouldn't have picked you up, by the way. I gave it another job to do.'

She nodded. 'You some kind of hacker?'

'You could call me that, yeah,' I smiled. I hadn't heard the term spoken outside the retro tech media.

'Haz... is that right?'

'Yeah.'

'You have children?' She was looking at the pictures of the children.

I knew some people at this point would probably have lied. But I was an idiot. I didn't even think about it. 'Yeah. That's Ali, and the older one... there, that's Asha.'

'Beautiful name,' she said, as if to herself.

'I like Luana, and all,' I said. Then hurriedly added. 'The name, like... I mean I like the name.'

She laughed. 'What do you do?'

'I'm a coder,' I lied. 'Well, a designer, for meta-class systems. I work further up the dale.'

I could see it meant nothing to her.

I blurted the first thing that came to mind, to break the silence. 'I saw a dead body tonight.'

'What?'

'Saw a dead body.' I felt seven years old but, I was committed

33

now.

'Where? Did you see an accident?'

'Don't know,' I said. 'Got to find out.'

'Find out? What kind of coder are you?'

'Well, I'm an analyst, really. Not really a coder. I mean, I do coding. But my job, it's actually being an analyst, and that. I was helping somebody out. Somebody in Justice.'

She was immediately suspicious. 'You with Justice?'

'No, no! I'm a contractor, yeah? I were helping somebody out, in't it.'

'Why were they showing you a body?' She narrowed her eyes.

'There was a digital angle...'

'There was?'

'Just saying, I saw a body.'

She watched me warily. Neither of us moved. Then she nodded slightly. 'Right. First time?'

'Yeah.'

'It's a shock, isn't it?'

'Yeah.'

'I saw my first when I was twelve.'

'You did?'

'Yeah,' she said. 'My Grandfather. We were visiting him and my Grandmother. Sailed out to Puerto Rico for it, which was a major thing. I realised afterwards it was because he was dying. There was this big party. We stayed a few days. One day after the party, we all thought he was outside having a siesta. I went out to the garden to call him in but he was lying in his chair under a fig tree. I couldn't see his face because he had this massive hat, you see. It was over his face. I touched his arm, trying to wake him up quietly, but it was cold, of course.' She paused with a self-conscious frown. 'It happens. I wasn't worried. I just went and told my mama.'

'What did it feel like?' I asked.

'Eh?'

'His arm,' I repeated. 'What did it feel like?'

'Meat.' She looked at the floor. 'Anyway... your body? What did they die of?'

'She... fell through a roof. That's what killed her.'

'Was she pushed?'

'She fell out of the sky.'

'Touching the sun, was she?'

I half-smiled. 'No. She were a flyer.'

Luana nodded. 'That's touching the sun.'

'It were night.'

She laughed shortly, then leaned in close enough to stare into my eyes. 'You think somebody killed her?'

'I don't know.' I was about to shake my head and scoff, but I froze. 'Something must've happened, right? People don't just fall out of the sky, do they?'

She looked at me for a few moments. 'Well, accidents happen. Perhaps people just fall out of the sky. But you're an analyst, so you can find out what happened, yeah?'

'That's not my job. I'm just there for digital crime, you know?'

'Digital? What's that mean? As you can probably tell, I don't know much about Justice,' she said.

'Doesn't matter,' I blurted. 'What do you do?' As soon as I spoke, I whispered a silent fuck behind gritted teeth. But it didn't seem to trouble her.

'Synthetic-biologist,' she smiled at my surprised expression. 'You were expecting me to tell you I'm a vat-worker? A grunt who stirs tanks of pork loin chunks? Well, I am that as well... but I was once a synthetic-biologist.'

'You worked in the dale?'

'A few places, yes. Last job was for Caines Meats. God, screw him!'

I'd heard the name. Caines was up the dale a little way.

Gilbert McKenn, our biohazard analyst, had spoken about him. Said he jettisoned his waste directly into the Aire. Never proved it, of course. Time yet.

'And now you...' I trailed off.

'Now I firebomb the capitalists.'

I stood still with a neutral expression. I was never sure what a capitalist was, I'd missed that part of school, I think. It was something the New Democracy was supposed to have solved.

'Is that why you're... is it the capitalists... why you...' I found I couldn't finish the question, unsure what I was asking.

'What?' she said.

'I mean,' I tried again. 'Why are you doing this-'

'You opened the door for me.'

'Not this,' I corrected. 'Why are you doing this-'

'The arson? The attacks on the factories?' she finished the question for me.

'Yeah.'

'That's not for me to understand.' She shook her head a little.

'What?'

'Does a firing synapse understand torture?' she intoned solemnly.

'I'm not...' I ground to a halt. 'I don't really do that kind of thing.'

'Well.' She smiled. 'The correct answer is that no, it doesn't understand. Like a cash till doesn't understand a bank run or a snowflake an avalanche.'

'OK.'

I could see something in her eyes, a flicker of excitement, like she was going to tell me that she had seen God, or discovered El Dorado or something.

'Except,' she went on, not listening to me. 'I think I have found something that might help me.'

We were interrupted by a deep booming voice, carried up from the street below through the half-open balcony doors. I realised I'd also left the curtains apart slightly and there must've been some light spilling out into the night.

'You there Haz?'

It was Jonah Manusdottir, a work colleague. I suppose I would even call him a mate, back in the days when I used to hang out with other people. He was also an Enforcement officer. He must've been down by the eco blocks. It was oddly comforting to hear his voice, if not a little annoying.

'Yeah?' I shouted back.

'Why you gone dark, man? All your comms are out.'

'You know him?' whispered Luana.

'He's a friend,' I whispered back, approaching the balcony and shouted down. 'Quiet night in, Jonah. What you up to?'

'Me?' I could see him now. He was alone, although he still had all the Enforcement gear, making him look like a UN special who'd lost to the marketing function. 'Been tangling some vat-monkeys, I have. What about you? You got a woman up there?'

'Not saying,' I said, trying to make it sound like I did.

'He's with them?' Luana whispered behind me. 'He's with Enforcement?'

'Good for you, man,' Jonah shouted. 'I'll be getting on, then.'

I heard a crash from the kids' bedroom and sighed. Asha falling out of bed again. It was fairly common at this time of night.

'Sorry, Jonah,' I shouted. 'Gotta go. It's one of the kids.'

I stumbled back into the living room. The vizchannel flooding back into my system. It had this effect. It would come and go in waves. The scene before me now seemed as though it was from my past. My mind was trying to swamp itself in nostalgia for the time when Luana had arrived at my flat. And the sight of Asha, standing there at the end of the short corridor which led to the bedrooms, brought to mind all those times she'd fallen out of bed when Dali had still been alive.

'You OK, sweetheart?' I asked her.

'Why are you crying, Dad?' Asha asked me.

'I'm not,' I choked. 'It's just some...'

'Yeah,' said Asha. 'You are. Who's this?'

She pointed across to Luana.

I tried to say something but the VC had got me powerfully and my stomach was knotting up inside. I couldn't help but stagger to the side and slump onto the couch.

'Hi,' said Luana, who was now looking at me strangely. 'I'm here to deliver–'

'Haz,' came the loud voice from outside the window. 'You alright, fella?'

'He's crying,' shouted Asha. 'Is that Jonah?'

And then Ali was also there crying as well. He'd been having a nightmare. I remembered all my nightmares as well. The ones I'd had when I was six had been the worst. Great waves drowning me. And Asha was talking to Jonah out on the balcony. And Ali was crying in the middle of the room. And I was hugging him.

Luana was no longer there. The door was closed.

Chapter Four

————

Nobody knew Clive's surname. He had fortified his data behind a restricted access barricade. Even Ibrahim was uncertain. I guessed accounts payable would have known; they knew most shit.

Of course, he was a contractor like me. He could've hidden behind a RandoBiz firewall, then even his name wouldn't have been important. It would've been Clive's style to do something like that. Some of the cleaning firms I'd called out for the flat were often operating under monikers such as JackFishGrunt and ToeOliveGoo. This was the kind of branding RandoBiz pulled out from its algorithms on a second-by-second basis. The reason people used RandoBiz was usually related to specific legal or tax issues. And creative types liked them because they thought they were witty.

Although everybody knew Clive would never stoop to playing games with the law. He was cleaner than a nun and about as paranoid as it was possible to be, without dropping a whole phial of black pseudo. This meant he had to be in control of his inputs. He needed to know his context and made it incredibly difficult for anybody to find him when they needed to get some sodding authorisation codes.

'Destination please,' the car asked. This one had been fitted with a faint Ulster accent. It felt somewhat incongruous.

'I just want to follow the canal up the dale.'

'Which dale, please?'

'This one, of course... Airedale, you know?'

I closed the door and settled into the front seat. The AJC only ever travelled via autocar. It was known to be much safer than manual. If this had been a manual, there would've been a dashboard and a large steering-wheel graphic. Possibly even a steering-wheel itself, if the car was old enough. If anything went wrong you were supposed to take over. Start dusting off all those neural pathways last trodden when you were seventeen. I'd never driven. Only retrothusiasts liked to drive all the time and you had to be proper insured.

'Thank you. Which canal, please?'

'Main one... you know, old Leeds-Liverpool.'

'Thank you,' said the car. It started up with a tinkling chime and reversed back out of its parking space. I flicked the controls and waited for the slightly scratched window to retract into the door frame. Outside, it was still a bright day and I wanted to feel the sun. Going up via the back roads was going to be a good ride. I wanted to enjoy it.

It took us about an hour to navigate around the lower end of Shipley, through all the small streets and alleys that ran alongside the canal. At some likely-looking junctions, I asked the car to stop and let me out to check under bridges. I'd picked up a muffin from the house which gave me a chance to eat. I tried to not to get too many crumbs over the upholstery; the autocar leasing firms had some aggressive contracting lawyers.

Knowing that if only I'd had access to Modlee, this could've been achieved in half the time, was irritating. I could've pulled all the narrowboat activity down the entire length of the canal, pin-pointed suspicious behaviour boat-by-boat, identified all instances of single white males leaving and returning to their boat, lifted any available security-cam footage and fed it manually through an identifying service, linked back to when I'd last spoken to Clive. All this would've helped me pull a shortlist of locations, which would've speeded up the process.

Then again, Clive already knew all about Modlee. He was probably one of the meta-designers and would know all about the security footage, which bridges were dark, where was off-grid. The pattern of behaviour of the boat would have been precisely calibrated to match the behaviour of a Mumbai tourist, the most frequently occurring category of boat-user on the canal. Which meant I had to do it the long way. Taking the long way gave Clive time to scope you out. He always knew exactly who was looking for him, without anybody having to communicate directly. Suggesting that Clive make use of a communication device would have been an incorrect move.

As I moved north of Bingley – thick with the once-futuristic but now slightly dated and shabby residential pods – I thought I recognised the familiar bald head at the back of a boat. This section of the canal rode the hillside below a series of old locks. As the area was full of pods, rather than the apartment blocks, the views were better. There were even some of the old lime and ash trees lining the towpath.

'Park here, yeah.'

'Yes, sir.'

The car pulled over and parallel-parked expertly within millimetres of the two other vehicles. I tucked my cap into my jacket pocket, pulled up the hood so that the fur-lined cavern encased my features, and stepped out of the car. Clive didn't appreciate too public an approach, especially one that advertised your contractor status. We were alongside the towpath, so I traipsed down the road a little way and found a couple of steps up to the level of the canal itself. If Clive had seen me, he hadn't indicated as such. He was still leant against the tiller at the back of the boat, staring ahead at the distant locks.

'Morning, buddy,' I grunted as I approached.

He turned and nodded a welcome.

'Coming aboard?'

'Yeah,' I said, stepping over to the small deck at the back of the narrowboat. I noticed the water was more stirred up and muddy. He had moved recently, getting himself into position.

'What you seen?' I asked, turning in the same direction as his gaze. 'Spotted some aliens or something?'

'Grow up, Hasim,' he said primly and looked directly at me. 'I was appreciating the Rise.'

'Eh?'

'The locks there. Magnificent! Over three hundred years old and still working. That's engineering.'

'They're great, yeah,' I said. 'Do you want to go inside?'

'Why? There's no need for that, I know exactly why you're here.'

'Thought you would... It's just a standard upgrade, in't it?'

'It's not simply a standard upgrade,' he winced.

'What?'

'There's a significant spike in the political indices.'

'Eh?' These parts of the work were always difficult. Clive liked to talk over your head a lot of the time.

'In the pond, in the delicate pattern that our friends in Durham weave. I'm surprised that the DI hasn't given off more hints to this end. They've indicated that the IG taps are being tightened even more.'

'So... it's not just a standard upgrade?'

'It's an upgrade, but it's being driven by broader systemic concerns–'

'–Look, Clive,' I interrupted. 'I just need to be able to get to work, really.'

He sighed deeply through his nose. 'I thought you, Hasim, of all the analysts I serve, you would have looked at the wider context.'

'Sorry,' I mumbled again. 'I just make Modlee do the thing,

really, in't it?'

Clive reached up with both hands and scratched hard at the scraggly line of red hair that ran around in a band above his ears. 'You say that, but you don't believe it, young man.'

Carrie had told me that Clive used to be an analyst. He'd seen a lot. He'd done politics, too. Been a Servant of the People, at one point, until the scrutiny had given him panic attacks. He'd nearly made it to DI but the pressure had got to him again. All that compromise had given him ulcers. He'd been forced to do this job. Access authorisation and IG controls. It would've paid him very little, really, the number of hours he logged. I knew he was cheap or the AJC would have gone with a different contractor. One who wasn't such a complete wanker.

'So,' I said. This was an opportunity I should try to use. 'You heard about business with the flyer, then?'

'Of course.'

'What you heard?'

'I heard nothing about you losing your shit and having to be taken home by RapidRez.'

I sniffed. 'Good. Because that sounds like a load of bollocks, right there.'

'Why were you there?'

I shrugged. 'DI asked me to. Think it were the spiders.'

'Spiders?'

'Yeah,' I said. 'There were a few spiders.'

'Oh, ricos!' said Clive. 'Of course. I'd forgotten they used to use them. Kind of quaint, really, isn't it?'

'Yeah. Quaint.'

'Good job you held it all together for the DI, then.'

'Piss off, Clive.'

'Something messed you up, didn't it?' He looked at me closely. 'No.'

'Yes, it did. I heard about it, Hasim. It's important that I know.'

'Why? What's it got to do with you?'

'It's my job.'

'It's nowt to do with your job!'

'Well,' he said, smiling. 'Not directly. But it's connected.'

I frowned. 'She didn't deserve to die like that, that's all.'

'Nobody does.'

'What does that mean?

'Nothing, I was just saying something meaningless and inconsequential in a kind tone of voice to make you feel a bit better.'

'You've changed, you know.' I couldn't help but laugh.

'So people tell me.'

I hesitated. 'What have you really heard, though?'

'Hmm?'

'About the flyer?' He watched me like a well-fed cat: curious but without need. I carried on. 'I mean, has DI posted anything? Who got the case and that?'

'There is no case,' said Clive.

'What?'

'Have you not seen the coroner's report?'

'No' I said. Shite. I should've checked before I even got here. 'Didn't realise they were working so fast these days.'

'Bermuda, Hasim. Basic geography. The movement of the sun and all that. They're five hours behind us, remember. They were working on the case the moment RapidRez were called. Ms Tarmell's initial report and the path's narrative from the Arches would have closed off the work.'

Airedale had a reciprocal legal agreement with Bermuda. We shared the same legal framework. Half a dozen lawyers and a rack of algorithm-heavy servers processed the whole dale. Probably from the beach. It could've been Kinshasa, apparently. Bermuda came out cheaper. Somebody had earned themselves a yacht.

'So,' I snapped. 'What were the result? Don't tell me it were open verdict or some shit like that?'

He shook his head. 'No. They recorded it as accidental death.'

'No way, that weren't no frigging accident! That girl were murdered! I was there.'

He raised his hands. 'Hasim, do I look like a lawyer?'

'Who has an accident at a thousand metres?'

'Was that the altitude?'

'I don't know! I was just saying... people don't just fall out of the bloody sky.'

He regarded me carefully. 'No. I guess they don't. Unless they hit something.'

'Is that what the coroner said?'

'Hasim, Hasim! You never learned this, did you? It's not the responsibility of the coroner service!'

'Yeah,' I muttered. 'Is that what the pathologist said, then?'

'Watch the report.'

'OK, yeah, will do.'

'It's very short,' he said, adopting an earnest tone. 'I'm sure it will hold the attention of a young man like yourself.'

'Give over. You say she hit something, because something could've hit her...'

'I like your thinking, Hasim. Causation theory, is it?'

I ignored him. 'What's DI going to do? He could still investigate, couldn't he?'

'Not really the kind of thing I discuss with Ibrahim, I'm afraid.'

This was nonsense. I knew he and Ibrahim talked all the time. 'Yeah, sorry. But it's possible, in't it?'

'In theory, he's perfectly capable of investing resources in an investigation that hasn't been formally commissioned. But it would be risky for him.'

I was watching Clive carefully. I was an idiot for trying to read his expression, but I tried anyway. 'OK. Might ask him, yeah?'

'You'd need forensics to back you up. You'd need to get Tarmell to agree to it.'

I agreed, but there was no way Carrie was going to work with me.

'Yeah, yeah. Need to do that.' I turned away to look up the canal and asked him casually. 'What do you think, though? After seeing the coroner's report and that?'

'I think,' he said, after a long pause. 'That there was a lot going on in Airedale that particular evening. I remember a lot of activity.'

'Owt specific?'

He turned his head towards me and leaned in close. 'Hasim, you know better than that.'

I smiled. 'Worth asking, in't it? Right... I'm ready when you are, Clive.'

What followed was the standard question-and-answer session, recorded for audit trail purposes and possibly run through the twitch-monitors back in Durham, mainly to tell if my eye movements had done the equivalent of crossing my fingers. It was very similar to the taking of the Socratic Oath, back in my grad days. I had to promise this and that, not to do this and that, la-di-da and all the rest. Clive took this stuff seriously and I knew, as all the analysts did, that you weren't to mess him around. It did take an age, though.

'Authorised,' he said, once we'd finished. 'Well, at least until you get the DI to drop in his A-codes. Don't check your bead until you're back in the car, please.'

When I'd returned to the car and pulled on my cap, I could see the change in my status. There was a new little puff of smoke on my display and the tiny Modlee logo pulsed briefly in the middle of the view. I was now able to do my job again. I just needed to convince the DI that the death of Meri Fergus was a proper case.

'Where to, sir?'

'Justice and Reconciliation Division headquarters, Shipley.'

Chapter Five

_____

'Good morning, sir.'

'It's madam.'

'I'm sorry.'

'No, it's sir, I were just screwing with you.'

'I do not understand. Are you visiting today, madam?'

'No. I bloody-well work here, alright?'

'Identification, please.'

'What? It's there. You can ping it, just go ahead.'

'Identification, please.'

'You're kidding me... wait there a sec...'

'Thank you, Mr Edmundson. Justice Division is on the fifth floor.'

'Yeah, I know. I work here.'

'Please be aware, Public Health have disabled the lifts again.'

'Wrong 'uns.'

'I must kindly remind you that this security module retains audio as well as visual evidence to mitigate against acts of abuse.'

'Well, retain this, yeah.'

'I'm afraid I cannot interpret all sign language variants, Mr Edmundson.'

'Doesn't matter.'

'Have a nice day, Mr Edmundson.'

I was a contractor and my client was Detective Inspector Ibrahim Al-Yahmeni. He was working out of the Justice Delivery Branch of the AJC. As well as contracting out for his Justice analytical service, he was also in charge of the facilities for the entire division. You had to wear a few different hats these days. Ibrahim had negotiated an excellent deal with our commissioners – the Airedale Justice and Enforcement Board – and had got the Justice and Reconciliation Division seventy-five percent of a floor of a converted mill on the banks of the River Aire at Shipley. These were commonly considered to be right classy desks for an unfashionable public service such as Justice. The DI had made a lot of friends, as well as a few enemies, with the deal.

The remaining twenty-five percent of the floor was taken up with the mezzanine area of a trendy bistro and cafe. The floor below Justice housed the remainder of this same bistro together with a hotch-potch of independent design agencies. It was accessed via a number of circular staircases which seemed to have been dropped into the building with a perverse randomness. The rest of the building contained various small service offerings. I knew that one of the floors above the division's open-area workspace was securely locked-down. This floor was wholly occupied by an outpost of East Pennine's robotic military programme management. Nobody had ever been up there.

Ibrahim had also bagged the floor with some of the biggest windows, permitting views west, across the valley bottom, to the old railway line that snaked its way east and then south into the centre of Leeds. The railway line had been cut-and-covered years ago and the old ground-level track had been converted into a long, leafy public park. The park ran from Stitsils down to the outskirts of the Leeds end of the Northern Belt. Towards the upper dale end, parts of the public space had drifted out of political jurisdiction and become a temporary encampment for artists and revolutionaries. Further down the dale, in poorer areas, it had simply been used as a means to dispose of unwanted biohazard. Local Servants had been too skint to do too much about it.

Thankfully, there was still sufficient money in Shipley itself to maintain the wild willows, shaped lime trees, and the dense avenues of London planes. If you walked alone along the path which weaved through the middle of the park, and it was an especially quiet time of night, you could hear the deep hum of the trains pulse beneath you and sense the sigh of the outlet vents as the displaced air escaped.

Our branch, Justice Delivery Branch, was headed up by Chief Inspector Jaime Ogarde, Ibrahim's superior. She was a tough bottom-liner, with a badgery buzz cut to match. She'd been in Enforcement for most of her career, mainly over the far flanks of the Pennines. She was nearly seventy-five and so not far from retirement. Ibrahim could smell that retirement coming like a dog in season. He was essentially her second-in-command, handled all the Servant negotiations; ran the show.

There were two other DIs, Winters and Husane, who worked alongside Ibrahim in the Shipley Branch, but they were junior players. Further up the dale were five other inspectors and their teams. They handled sexual offences, thefts, and assault. Winters handled the environmental crimes, chemical leaks and that. Husane had been given counterfeiting and petty fraud. She wanted Ibrahim's job; he had all the high profile cases, like significant corporate fraud, anything that might spark a media storm. And the murders, of course.

For the crimes that came under Airedale's jurisdiction, this was it. This was the Justice team. Sure, the DIs had all their analysts and subcontracting service providers doing their leg work for them, but when it came down to the hard business, it was them talking to the lawyers. On average these seven DIs each had a population of near two hundred thousand under their wings. With contractors numbering close to a hundred. They had to get their shit together and turn cases fast, which was why Modlee was so important: though nobody liked to admit it, it did all the work for you.

I liked working for Ibrahim and so did Carrie. Unlike DI Winters, Ibrahim hated getting into the detail. He was a politician, a technocrat, a player. This was why he'd taken the lead on the office contract; he knew it would impress the commissioners. The Board loved him and Ogarde allowed him the freedom to essentially run the Branch. Although DI Husane desperately wanted the cases he was assigned, they got on well enough for it not to be an issue. Winters didn't care either way, as long as he was allowed to get on with his work.

'Have a mocha,' Ibrahim drawled, as I trudged up the last of the steps. 'I got the guys here to start making it the moment you hit the entrance sensor.'

'Yeah? Sensor hasn't made a complaint, has it?

'Not yet. Why, what d'you do?'

As was generally the case for any of his meetings, he'd commandeered a little nest of tables from the bistro, right next to the window. The weak sun filtering through hazy clouds, creating a grey brightness which seemed to get deep into your eyes without actually illuminating anything very much.

'Nothing,' I grunted, sliding onto one of the hemp seats. They were fresh from some North African bazaar, the hottest fashion, and really – seriously – hurt to sit on for too long.

'So, what're you after from me?' asked the DI. 'Feels like I've not seen you for weeks.'

'I've been up to see Clive,' I said. 'I need your A-codes for Modlee. New upgrade, in't it?'

'A new upgrade?' said Ibrahim slowly.

'And, as well as that, I'd like to talk to you about authorising some more access... on a possible case, as well.'

'Two sets of A-codes in one visit?' said Ibrahim. 'You ask a lot, Haz.'

'That's right,' I clammed up. This was hard.

'Are you well, Haz?' he asked, after a long pause searching my expression.

'Yeah,' I nodded, pulling the mocha in front of me, contemplating the esoteric symbol cast in chocolate dust on its surface.

'Sorry about last night,' Ibrahim said. I must have looked up too sharp, because he narrowed his eyes and smiled. 'I mean about the spiders and Carrie and all that business.'

'Oh,' I said. 'That.'

'You had a difficult night?' he asked.

'Yeah,' I said. 'Ali wouldn't sleep. Nightmares again.'

Ibrahim nodded. I knew he had four children. The eldest son had been married now for a few years and had just had twins. 'I know what it's like, Haz. I've been there.'

I grinned back and took a sip. Although I liked working for the man, he still made me nervous in a meeting. Despite his age, he kept his hair jet black and left it to grow long, above the line of his shoulders. He liked to keep it out of his eyes with a thin steel hairclip, which had the effect of making him look a little like a schoolgirl. His eyes never rested on you for long, always searching the room for more data, something else to process.

'So,' I said. 'Really, I just need your authorisation for both of those things ...you know... the A-codes.' I trailed off and waved in the general direction of his hand. Ibrahim had a load of expensive rings across his knuckles. One of these housed his bead. I was never certain which one. This could've been why he had so many.

'So, it's Modlee again, is it?' he laughed. 'I swear that's the only reason you come down here to see me, these days.'

'You're keeping me busy,' I said, trying to make a joke of it, but when it came out, it just sounded rude. 'I don't have any time to be in the office. You keep sending me out and about with the car.'

'I do, Haz,' said Ibrahim. He looked serious and leaned in closer to me. 'What did you find last night?'

I paused a moment. 'You should've had Carrie's summary this morning?'

'I did,' said Ibrahim. 'I wanted to know what you think. I appreciate your insight in these things as well.'

'That's good, because I wanted to... I mean, that's the second thing I wanted to–'

'Thank you, by the way,' interrupted Ibrahim.

'For what?'

'For stepping in. For helping me out. I knew it would be hard for Carrie in there by herself.'

'You did?' I asked. I fell silent for a moment. 'You knew about the spiders?'

'I wasn't sure,' said Ibrahim. 'But I know a few of the old textile gentlemen. Family businesses and the like. For years, they've been telling me about a load of abandoned facilities up the Basin where they brought in ricos. There was always the chance that this one would have been one of those.'

'Carrie could've handled it,' I said. It sounded false in my mouth. I was never good at standing up for the team. This happened when you started subcontracting.

'No,' said Ibrahim. 'I've got her file. She wouldn't. Let's just leave it at that.'

'Understood,' I said, and sipped my mocha.

'That was shared under paragraph twelve, naturally.'

I nodded again. Ibrahim rarely operated outside strict IG protocols. Although he'd only hinted at personal details from Carrie's medical record, he knew it was still nearly a breach.

I was flattered that he clearly trusted me enough to even let something slip through like that. Too many of those slips and he could lose his job.

'Yeah, course.'

'So,' said Ibrahim. 'I'm interested to know what you found. Besides the spiders, that is.'

'It were a body. Female. Just like in the kid's camdrone footage.'

'A flyer, wasn't she?'

'Yeah,' I said, taking a sip of my drink.

'Did she have her wings?'

'They were trashed, but, yeah, she still had them.'

'I'd love to be able to do that,' said Ibrahim, turning to the window. At that precise moment he looked like he was watching a pair of flyers riding the updrafts of the Shipley business district. Even I believed him.

'To fly?'

'Yeah,' said Ibrahim. 'Of course. Wouldn't you?'

I wrinkled my nose. 'It's a lot of sacrifice, in't it? You know, with your muscles?'

'Yeah,' said Ibrahim, instantly professional again. 'Anything suspicious around the body?'

'Nowt around it, no. Looked like a collision though.'

Ibrahim looked at me carefully. 'Is that what Carrie said?'

'No,' I flustered. 'Just, it must have been, mustn't it?'

'Carrie doesn't think so.'

My heart started beating a little harder. 'No? What did she say?'

'Says she wants to do some more digging.'

Wrong 'un. 'Yeah?'

'Why did you say you thought it was a collision?'

'Well,' I laughed. 'People don't just fall out of the sky.'

'Let's not start building the models just yet, Haz,' said Ibrahim.

'Building models?' I said. 'Well, there's no point in doing that now, is there?'

'Why do you say that?'

'You not seen the coroner's vid?'

He nodded. 'I have.'

'Recorded as accidental death.'

'I know.'

'You think it were an accident?' I asked.

He narrowed his eyes. 'That's what we've told the parents.'

'Yeah? You've been to see them, then?'

'Of course.'

'Are they close? In the dale?'

'Yes. They live somewhere expensive up in the middle of Stitsils. She's a doctor, I think.'

'How did they take the news?' I asked.

'Now that,' said Ibrahim, talking very slowly, as though to a child. 'Is beyond your authorised access levels for this case.'

I fell silent. This was the moment. I knew I had to drop the question as carefully as possible. If I came across as false, he would shut me down.

'You know, Ibrahim, about that...'

'Hmm?'

'I think it's time to... you know, I'd really like to expand my experience beyond digital. I've been doing data for so long now.'

'You know what I've always said, Haz,' said Ibrahim. 'You should've been a DI years ago!'

It always hurt to hear him say that. The truth was I nearly was, although Ibrahim wasn't to know it.

'Bearing that in mind, Ibrahim, you said Carrie was doing some more digging. Could I help Carrie out a little more on this one?'

Ibrahim raised his Turkish ristretto to his mouth and sucked the last dregs through his teeth. He peered into the depths of the small cup as though he'd lost something in there. 'Something of digital interest in the case, Haz?'

'No, fairly open and shut, if I were to jump to simple conclusions. As you say, we don't want to start building models too soon but, it looks... maybe like the girl damaged her wings? Maybe got caught in turbulence or something. Might've been a collision, who knows?' Then I dropped in my line. 'I just want to keep my interest in the day job, you know?'

This was the sucker punch. Ibrahim looked from the cup to me, a concerned furrow on his forehead.

'You're not thinking of going somewhere else, are you? I need you, Haz!'

'No,' I said. 'Not at all... it's just ...you know...'

'Well,' he thought in silence for a while, contemplating my face. 'I've got nothing else on the books, beyond you wrapping up that farmer and caviar story, so why not? If something big comes in, you're to drop it, though. I want Carrie off it within a week, anyway, as she needs to finish off that double-murder from Five Locks.'

'That's great,' I said, trying to be effusive. Somehow, it wasn't the lavishly supportive Ibrahim I'd come to expect. He seemed guarded.

'You want me to drop you the A-codes for the case?' he said.

'Yeah, why not?'

It was too casual. He hesitated, seemingly troubled by something. His right hand caressed the rings on his left, a visual tic of his. I'd concluded it meant he was considering a tricky decision.

'Let's get Carrie in here,' said Ibrahim, at last. 'Give her the good news.'

'Sure,' I said. Then I checked my display and realised it was still mid-morning. 'Actually, she'll not be out of bed yet.'

'She'll not?' said Ibrahim. 'What does she do? She's billing me for this time.'

I fell silent. I thought everybody knew Carrie's working pattern. If I'd dropped her in it with the DI, she'd have my nuts.

'Nonsense, Haz,' said Ibrahim. 'She's been joking you around. She just wants to be left in peace this time of day. We'll get her online.'

He placed his left hand flat on the table in front of him and let his bead seek out his eyes. Just visible in the dust motes that were swirling around the bistro were the projected beams of light from his hand to his face. Having a ring bead was a pain to use like this. People often took them off if they were using the inbuilt projector rather than a wall screen but Ibrahim liked to pride himself on his manual control. Well, either that, or he didn't want people to see which ring it was that held the bead.

On my own screen, I could see Carrie's icon pop up. I pulled the peak of my cricket cap a little lower to bring the projection into sharper focus.

'I wish you'd replace that awful hat,' said Ibrahim to me. 'It looks like it's housing worse strains than a Manaus floating breeder tank.'

'Yeah,' I laughed, a little weakly. 'It is that.'

Carrie answered quickly. I couldn't see where she was but it seemed to be outside. Possibly a street somewhere. She was walking.

'Hiya, DI,' she said. 'You got my site summary?'

'Morning, Carrie,' said Ibrahim. 'I did, thank you. Very interesting. Carrie, listen… just here with our digital whizzkid, Haz.'

'Hiya, Haz,' said Carrie. 'You got home OK, then?'

'Yeah,' I hated being called a whizzkid, but I guessed Ibrahim was softening Carrie up.

'We were just talking about last night's case,' said Ibrahim.

'Yeah,' said Carrie. She was crossing a road. 'I'm working on it, you know? I'll get it done.'

'It's OK,' said Ibrahim. 'I trust you. Look, what I'm saying, is we think... well, we think there's a digital angle here.'

Gutless bastard.

'Is there?' Carrie asked, failing to hide her irritation.

'Isn't that right, Haz?' asked Ibrahim.

I kept my face totally still. 'Yeah. A digital angle.'

Carrie grinned into space. 'So, what's the angle?'

'That can't be discussed just yet,' said Ibrahim. 'Just wanted to give you a call and let you know Haz is going to be accessing the files as well. Going to give him the authorisation now.'

'Well,' said Carrie. 'I appreciate you telling me. Have you spoken to Frank as well?'

Frank Pears was our resident corporate analyst. He tended to get involved when there was anything to do with the factories or if we'd been speaking to the business guys.

'Of course,' said Ibrahim. 'But you're leading on this.'

'Whatever.'

'Great,' said Ibrahim. 'I'm dropping the authorisation codes in now.'

Carrie looked straight into the camera. 'You really want to do this, Haz?'

'Sure,' I said.

'Fine,' said Ibrahim.

A little message popped up on my display explaining the new levels of data access that the DI had just granted me. This would still need Servant authorisation but that was generally just a cursory piece of admin. They never questioned Ibrahim's requests. Especially Ibrahim's latest pet Servant, Kaz Furness. He had her eating out of his hand.

'Catch up with you later,' said Carrie.

I grunted an affirmation and she signed off.

'There,' said Ibrahim. 'I hope you guys can wrap up a solid

little narrative for this one... for me, you know.'

'We'll do our best, DI,' I said. 'I promise you.'

He smiled and reached across to shake my hand.

As my client, the DI had no direct management of my work, beyond what was stipulated in my contract. His entire team of analysts was drawn from the usual agency. I worked, on a freelance basis, for an outfit that specialised in providing services for Justice cases across much of Europe. At the time my contract was signed, the agency was called GHJI but it tended to reconfigure itself every few months. Either that, or my contract could've swapped hands with another agency. Contracts were a valuable asset and highly tradeable. Technically, I'd worked for a private investor based out of Perth, Australia, but give it two months and it could be a pensions zaibatsu from Kyoto. It didn't really affect anything, who it was. The details on the contract remained the same.

My contract meant I had to take the cases the DI gave me. He needed the hard content in order to do his job, which was to wrap up a solid narrative file on any judicial infringement. My job was to provide him with a suite of suitable models, based upon the data available, ranked by its relative level of robustness. Official protocol for a justice analyst was that you gave between three and five models for the DI to consider. When I first started working for Ibrahim, I'd presented him with the full five models on every case but this had only lasted for the first few weeks. We had a short conversation and both came to the conclusion that it was wasting our time to fuss with options. We still had to tick the boxes for internal audit, but now I knew I had to give him the one model, the model that reflected the reality, and that he had to trust me to deliver.

He'd just put a lot of trust in one digital analyst.

I was itching to get Modlee fired up and start on the case. However, Ibrahim still needed to drop me the Modlee upgrade A-codes.

'Thank you,' I said. 'So, just the other authorisation, now.'

'Hmm?' said Ibrahim, looking over my shoulder.

I turned as well. The DI had been distracted by a small group of people coming up the stairwell into the middle of the cafe. They seemed a mixture of uniformed Enforcement operatives and some well-suited political types. These could well be the commissioners, although what anybody from Enforcement was doing down at the Justice offices was unclear.

'Welcome all,' Ibrahim said, leaping to his feet, scampering between the tables to shake hands and clap various members of the crowd on the back. 'We are honoured!'

I picked up my processor block from the table, dropped it into my coat pocket, and followed the DI. Even if I'd wanted to slink away now, I couldn't. Hovering around the periphery of the buzzing group and tapping the bead in my cap like an idiot still didn't make the DI remember he needed to give me my second set of A-codes. In fact, it had the unfortunate effect of making me look like I was trying to join the party. Ibrahim beckoned me closer as soon as he spotted me. He was talking to a woman around my age, possibly younger. She had a flattened nose and widely spaced-eyes that made her look a little like a shark. A shark with a blonde bob. I knew who she was Ibrahim's pet politician.

'This is the new Servant for the Waters Road neighbourhood,' said Ibrahim. 'Kaz Furness.'

'Pleased to meet you,' she said, shaking my hand and bumping knuckles lightly. It felt oddly formal but I guessed Servants had to follow certain procedures.

'Kaz is also the new chair of the Enforcement Board,' said Ibrahim.

'Congratulations.'

'Thank you. It's an honour and I'm very pleased for all the support we're getting from Justice.'

'Quickest elevation from neighbourhood Servant to regional Servant in the north,' said Ibrahim. 'You move fast, Kaz. You'll be in Durham before you know it.'

'And then London?' I asked.

'No,' she demurred. 'I wouldn't go near Westminster. It's a wasteland these days. Although I wouldn't say no to Durham.'

I smiled and nodded. I'd made myself look like a proper melon. Of course nobody wanted to go to Westminster these days.

'Ibrahim,' I murmured, resisting the urge to tug at his sleeve. This was an idiotic situation.

He ignored me, all his attention still with Kaz. 'What are you doing down here?'

'We're meeting the Chief, thought I'd put in an appearance.'

'Jaime's here, is she? Haven't seen her yet.'

Though he delivered this query like he was asking whether Kaz wanted milk in her chai, I could see he and the Servant exchanged a glance. There had been a good few afternoons of chat that had preceded this single comment, but why had they been talking about the old Chief Inspector? I logged the transaction. Like a good analyst.

'Give her ten minutes, Ibrahim,' said Kaz. 'She's busy saying hello to her old Enforcement friends.'

'Easy on the "old", Kaz,' stage-whispered Ibrahim, winking.

Was he doing this all for my benefit? What was he playing at?

'You know what I mean,' said Kaz, waving an index finger in front of Ibrahim's nose.

They must have had something on the Chief Inspector.

'You got the entire Board here?' asked Ibrahim, glancing around the various faces.

'Nearly,' she said. 'We're still waiting for some.'

'Brian here yet?' I heard somebody titter. There was a chorus of gasps and some whispered chuckles. The Head of

Enforcement Operations, Brian Fallin, was going to appear at some point. Usually he never left the depths of the Trench, the Enforcement offices were up the dale where they beat the law into you, but if there was going to be a meeting of the Board, it would mean an appearance from the ogre.

Upon hearing these comments, I could see Ibrahim's enthusiasm subside a little. He'd had a few encounters with Brian Fallin in the past. They never ended well.

Kaz seemed to have been scanning the crowd too, but when I looked more closely, I could see she was checking her display. She was wearing some hyper-thin spectacles, hardly visible on her face, but they betrayed some activity, reflected on the whites of her eyes. She suddenly turned to me, making me jump.

'You're the analyst?' she said. 'Who has just been put on the flyer case?'

'Yes,' I said.

'That's right,' said Ibrahim. 'I've just put Haz on that one. How did you know?'

'It's just dropped into my messages.'

'You been given the validation request?' asked Ibrahim.

'I have,' said Kaz.

'Great,' said Ibrahim.

'I should give it the nod?' asked Kaz. 'Should I?'

The air suddenly seemed very tense, as though all three of us had been dropped into a game where nobody fully understood the rules but where we knew that the wrong move would be fatal.

'Yeah,' drawled Ibrahim, after a pause. 'It's just routine.'

'Fine,' said Kaz, crisply. Her hand twitched in front of her. A few moments later, I could see the authorisation notice pin itself to the bottom left side of my display.

'Thank you,' I said. And then felt ashamed for having said it.

'No problemo,' she said.

'DI,' I began. 'Just one last thing and I'll be out of your face.'

'What is it, Haz?'

'Sorry, I still need my other authorisation codes.'

'I've given it to you,' protested Ibrahim.

'No,' I said. 'Not for the flyer case… the other ones, for the upgrade. For the Modlee upgrade.'

'Oh,' said Ibrahim. He laughed and tapped me on the shoulder. 'Totally forgot. You're really chasing down the authorisations today! Here you go.' He flicked his fingers. The icon spun on the screen and then sank into my bead's temporary memory. 'By the way, how is Clive?'

'Oh, you know.'

'Yeah,' said Ibrahim. He looked out of the window, his mind elsewhere. 'I need to catch up with him properly.'

I nodded my goodbyes. Kaz was already stuck in a different conversation, this time with a thin-faced white guy, who seemed overly twitchy, like he was riding something strong. But before I'd time to study his face properly, I could hear the buzz in the room. People started to clear out.

And, sure enough, when I turned around, the DI had slipped away into the crowd as well. Message had got out. Brian Fallin, Head of Enforcement Ops, was on site.

Time to hide.

Chapter Six

———

I dropped the car at an AJC depot south of Bingley. I'd decided to walk back to my flat. Although it was difficult working when the kids came home from school, I was worried that Ali wasn't settling into his new class. This was one possible explanation for the nightmares. There was also the fact that he was of an age when he was more likely to get them. Of course, there was always the obvious, but I didn't want to think about that. I just wanted to be at the house when they were there, really. The signals I was getting from Greg weren't good and I wanted to keep half-an-eye on his work. I was close to considering whether to dump him for new childcare. Greg was turning out to be a piece-of-shit care op.

I crossed over the Aire near Salts, ignoring the flock of shockdrones which rose into the sky as I passed outside its dome. Ahead of me was the ancient village green, still intact with the cricket pitch and the children's play area. Soon after we'd moved into the area, I'd signed up with Saltaire fifths and had played numerous matches on that wicket. Dali had taken both the babies along to watch their father stand out in the field and throw down a few easy-to-smash medium pacers. Even got into double figures a few times.

There was nobody there today and, anyway, now I'd other things on my mind. The Modlee service was up and running. I pulled up the white panels on my bead display, noting the exquisitely chamfered corners that came with the new upgrade, and sent the command to fire up the processing block. I could feel it buzz slightly in the outer pocket of my jacket. This portable tech was cooled by environmental input, so letting it run full in a confined space would probably be a bad move. It had already started to generate its own internal heat. I lifted it out and felt the buzz in my left hand.

With my right hand, I started to twitch and click my fingers. Beyond the re-tooled cosmetic design, the interface seemed to have been unaffected by this latest release, for which I was thankful. There was a long text file explaining the changes. I ignored it. I could also have sat through a dull vid file of some goatee-sporting geek from Vancouver, but that would've taken up too much time. And made me want to stab anybody who hadn't shaved lately. I liked to jump straight in and feel my way around the changes. So I did.

Teasing myself with delay and the anticipation of the flyer case, I turned instead to old work. I updated the sturgeon-caviar-farmer model using some additional data which had been released by the IG folk in eastern Turkey. Modlee was going to do all the hard work on this for me. It'd already tracked the source of the product verification codes and saved an evidence trail that would be sufficient for court. Verification codes for this kind of high-end foodstuff took a while to be generated.

They involved heavy maths and so tended to be cranked out by the server farms that sat alongside a natural energy source. The hydrothermal centres in Iceland and Kamchatka had once been a good bet for these, but now that the Saharan solar arrays were starting to recover from the war, more and more of this kind of rig was getting plugged in along the north Med coast.

Modlee had traced the codes to a packet which had been

silently duplicated from a deep sea cable running from Tunisia to Malta about seven months ago. Modlee had also traced the bank transfers from the farmer to the middle-man in Milan, who'd got the codes hand-delivered from a known mafia courier. The Italian police had just released their interpreted mafia tracking files. There was a lot of fudge in there – and Italian fudge was the worst – but it was still a rich source. It was plugging a lot of gaps for us.

As I turned the corner to my street and started to approach the block of flats, I stopped arsing around and dived right into the meat.

What had happened to Meri Fergus?

I created a new model and started work. First, I retrieved the A-codes from the flyer case which Ibrahim had given me in Shipley and dropped them into the access parameters page. Immediately the orphan data links started flapping on the screen like miniature kelp strands. Modlee had made a series of judgement calls on the rest of the associations, some based on international protocol, some based on human user feedback. It always left the user to plug in the last few. I still needed to make the final call on some of them. This was an intricate task. One which could have significant repercussions later on if I started wafting at them without thinking first.

As I was about to start flicking through the array, Carrie's face popped up on my screen. An icon told me she wanted to speak. I grimaced and clicked her call through with an eye twitch.

'Hiya, Haz,' she drawled.

'Hi,' I said, still a little guarded, unsure whether Ibrahim's message had been too successful at winning her over.

I was right. 'I can see you're in the data now,' she said. 'Just don't mess with the forensics stuff, OK?'

'No problem, Carrie.'

'I don't know how you talked the DI into it… but, anyway,

just don't mess around in my space.'

'I got it.'

We stared at each other warily.

'What are you doing, anyway, Haz?' she asked, after a moment. 'Why are you doing this?'

'I don't know,' I said, hoping I wasn't whining. 'Just something about... that flyer, you know.'

'You know it's just some girl.'

'Eh?' I said, trying to force a stupid laugh.

'It's not what you think it is.'

That was completely off limits. I felt my face redden. Carrie must've seen the change, or her facial handlers had waved a trigger warning flag, because she immediately started to backtrack.

'Sorry, Haz... didn't... mean it like that. Look, if you need any help with stuff...' She trailed off.

'I'm just coming to my block, Carrie.'

'Alright,' she said. 'I'll let you get on. I was just saying... you know.'

I took a breath. 'There's one thing...'

'Yes?'

I stopped outside the door of the apartment and looked up at the clouds. 'Do you know why she fell out of the sky?'

I thought I could see Carrie relax a little. 'Yeah. Been working on that this morning. Once the bastard gecko'd finally downloaded, of course. Playing up again.'

I realised I was trembling a little. I passed the now seriously-hot processor to my other hand. 'Well?'

'There was some kind of major impact to the left cheekbone. She'd been hit face-on.'

'The path had picked that up,' I said. The processor trembled in my palm like a terrified pet. I passed it back to my other hand. 'That's just the roof, in't it?'

'No,' she said, shaking her head. 'For anybody being

filmed off a nosebead, like Carrie, this movement had to be artificially generated. They'd never got it that natural and it was always unnerving to see the disembodied head swing in front of your eyes like that.

'She hit the roof coccyx-first, shredded her back and thighs. The back of the skull took most of that impact. The cheekbone was definitely impacted earlier, it was a clean and isolated strike. I think it may've broken her neck. I've extracted a specifically shaped indentation from gecko pix. It's like a curve or summat.'

'What?' I asked. 'I mean, a curve from what?'

'Dunno yet,' she said. 'But working on it.'

'So,' I said, talking slowly. 'High probability that she was knocked out of the sky. That means the probability that this is a case worth running a few models for–'

'–has just increased significantly,' completed Carrie. 'If you want to help me, I'd check out the flyer angle. I'm going to try and track down what impacted the face.'

'Are you going to the hospital?'

'No point,' she said. 'Coroners filed their vidz, haven't they?'

At this point, the pathologist would've probably released the body back to the family. Unless the DI had put in a request.

'Yeah,' I said. 'Just a thought.'

'Plus, Ibrahim said he's told the parents it was just an accident.'

'Yeah. He told me.'

'What else was he going to do? He's only got that report to go on, hasn't he?'

'But,' I started to say. 'We're telling him that it's...' I stopped talking.

Carrie laughed. 'Yeah. When you put it like that, makes all the difference, like.'

'OK,' I said. 'I'm just going to see what Modlee gives me.'

'Whatever,' she said. 'I don't know what that freaky app

does and I bet you don't, either.'

I produced a weak grin. 'See you later.'

Her face disappeared as I entered the block of flats, waved for the lift with the hand holding the processor, and prepped up the service with my other. There was some housekeeping which had to be done first. I had to create a new workspace, give it a few names, categorise it, set the system boundary parameters and suchlike. All could be changed later on, automatically, but I liked running through the routine. It was soothing. Finally, I set the access rights. Default was purely the creator. Not even the DI was given access. I selected default.

I walked in through the door, which recognised my ratios and let me in. Greg wouldn't be here for at least two hours, so I'd a while to properly immerse myself in the work.

I settled back into the ragged old chair I liked to work the data from and dropped the processor onto its cooling tile. The right-side armrest had been inexpertly hacked out to give me more space. It had been a present from my father when I'd still been at school. He liked to economise. Dali had hated the thing. She'd told me to buy a proper code chair or something but I knew those were over-designed affectations, with a price tag calibrated for the gullible. I just needed some airspace, somewhere I wasn't going to break my wrist pulling together a complicated algorithm cluster.

The white panels, with their expensive corners, started to flutter in the view before me. I turned up the contrast, until the apartment beyond my eyes was virtually unseen. Then I started to play with the shapes.

First I started to link in the data feeds I'd been given from the case. All the history of the factory and all the data on the ricos. This was interesting but wholly unimportant. If Carrie was right, which particular roof the flyer had fallen through was essentially random.

Next I checked the vidz. It seems I'd been given extended security footage of the entire Keighley Basin. Depending on the case, all analysts got the standard tax-funded and commissioned cams but this stuff had PBs of corporate footage. Looked like there was even some private footage in there. Private stuff from those weirdos who like to drape their house in cameras like a Uruguayan drug lord's hacienda.

Then I got the darker stuff. The stuff that made me itch. All the flyer's private affairs: her comms, her diaries, her pix, her vidz. This was the kind of stuff that an analyst could sell to the black market for millions. Many had done so and made a packet. So had the marketeers. Which was why we had the Oath. If I did that, and got caught, I could kiss goodbye to ever working with data again. Probably never be let within one metre of a processor and certainly land up on an island somewhere with the puffins.

There were other wrappers in there as well. Links to financials, political stuff, the background noise of Airedale on that night. Usually I would have ignored these, but I was starting from nothing. No gut instinct, no hunches – so I threw it all in.

Clive's comment preyed on my mind. There was a lot going on in Airedale that particular evening.

Modlee could represent data in many different modes. It had so many charts, diagrams, every known data, communication theorem, and the latest work from academics all over the world. It had to do this intuitively, though, as the service designers knew that their user base were simply idiots like me. No real professors of statistics used Modlee, not even data scientists like those geeks up at Prevention. It did too much of the heavy-lifting for them. It was a bit... well, random. It had a mind of its own. Wrapped in its black box. No self-respecting journal would ever publish a paper that had the taint of Modlee. It was too meta. Coders coding the codes that built the codes that ran the world. And the professors could smell it.

The reason Modlee was a popular service was because it was right so often and it was right in the most unexpected of areas. There were few contexts in which it couldn't play. It had that many connections. And its connections, its associations, were so deep, so tuned – so right – that it was the fastest service of its kind.

I pulled out a three-dimensional map with a swipe of my hand. It was a good starting point when you had absolutely nothing to go with. I'd have donated a kidney to have as much as nothing-to-go-with at this moment.

I started dropping in the usual stuff.

There were data mountains all over the world. In the old days, they were concentrated in certain parts of the network. Like the verification code farms, they'd be where there was cheap power. Now the data mountains were dispersed and speed was not the issue it used to be. Some of these mountains were stacked in rusting office blocks in downtown Lagos. Some in cutting-edge carbon spirals in east coast university towns. Others were plugged into the necklaces of storage satellites, or on the moon, or simply dispersed thinly across every processor block in the world. And you'd never know they were there. All the data that ever been produced, up to and including the twentieth century, could be etched onto a cheap sliver and dropped into a crack in a floorboard. Storage was that cheap.

The difficulty with working these ranges of data was their size. The smallest parameter would totally screw up your models. Modlee was a clever service but it wasn't clever enough to spot when something felt wrong. At least, that's what all its users liked to pretend. I wasn't so sure. I thought it probably knew when something felt wrong. At least, I thought it was damn close to feeling it. Modlee had millions of users, all plugging their results straight into the servers. Algorithms twisted and transformed under the weight of their feedback data, like an insect held too close to a flame. Some days it simply didn't like you and wanted you to fail.

I knew that Those-You-Shouldn't-Even-Think-About had complete access to the data mountains. Nobody knew whether it was nonsense or just urban legend. Analysts liked to scare each other by whispering – out of electronic earshot – that they had adapted Modlee and had developed algorithms that could tell you what somebody was thinking. At least, thinking within a high degree of probability. They did so simply by knitting together their dynamic facial ratios, medical and family histories, comms, and your reading matter. Real black IG stuff. It was terrifying to think some frigging know-nothing Servant could've had the whispers from them and given them the nod. All it took was sufficient access.

I tried not to think about them. They would be watching my face, had probably already clocked the expression that screamed: 'I wonder what the spies are up to about now?'

My data choices for the three-dimensional map were always the same. I liked it to scroll through the locational vectors for all persons of interest in the dale, as well as those from outside. Then I lifted some meta-data from security cams, running through different categories, highlighting suspicious, aberrant, outlier-type behaviour. The weighting on this could be calibrated but I set it to be a simple colour gradation. If a car pulled into a parking space in a Lower Skipton office block that'd never been seen before, it would flare out for me in a deep crimson. If Mr Almara from Stitsils had thrown a fit and chased a cat off his front lawn, it would be in a lighter pink. A random dog would flicker grey. The meta-comms activity was always available, and, though it never told you much, I liked to have it in there. Unless they were named individuals from the A-codes, to get at the actual comms would have meant my crawling to Brussels and pleading like it was the end of the world.

I wiggled my index finger and the representation flickered into life. The map started to pulse with movement. There was a concentration of activity in the centre of Keighley. More of the rioters. I hadn't realised there had been so much activity up there as well. In rhythm with the locational markers, the security metadata started to flash red as I'd expected. This noise was going to obscure everything. I took out all data associated with the Enforcement operation in Keighley that night. The centre of the Basin immediately went dark. A few flashes remained. I took out all known cases that were in operation. These would be cross-referenced in a different representation.

The map flickered lightly until the time hit the following day. There was still nothing which caught my eye, so I retraced my steps and removed all the exclusion flags, watching as Airedale's criminal activity flooded the display again in flashing reds and ambers. Just a normal day.

This was where I had to try random stuff. Get a flash of inspiration. I ran back the time variable in reverse, watching the rioters disperse. I was still dully taking it all in, unable to form any models, yet. I was just looking for a hook, something suspicious. Arsing about, really.

Then there was something odd. A comms flash at a moment earlier in the evening. It was scattered across the entire dale. I ran it again. All perfectly in time. All of that comms activity would suggest a conference call. If it was a conference call, then the placement suggested each district of the dale was somehow represented, approximately, with a few tighter clusters in the high industry areas as well.

I'd seen this pattern before in a few simulations. Representatives from each area meant only one thing: neighbourhood Servants. The Servants of the people, like

Kaz Furness.

I tried picking out names but the detail behind the comms data was restricted. This meant they were all outside the access rights given for the case. I re-ran the same time period, watching the comms flash again and again, flicking a few flags on and off, trying stuff, prodding the data. Suddenly, I realised I'd managed to turn the flash off. I checked the flag I'd selected: Enforcement.

The flare failed to happen when I'd excluded the rioting activity and the Enforcement operation. I took a log of it.

And then Greg had been there. And he had already brought back the kids, prepared the evening meal, and left. And I was awoken from my work by a small hand tugging on my sleeve.

'Dad! Dad! Dad!'

'Yeah?' I muttered, lifting myself from the weight of patterns in my eyes and cutting the service. The room suddenly re-appeared in front of me.

'It's teatime, Dad.'

'Is it... oh, thanks for that, love.'

Chapter Seven

_____

'My name's Hasim Edmundson. I'm an analyst working for the AJC. Justice and Reconciliation branch.'

'Oh, right. Hi… erm, I'm Lani. Lanoba, I mean. Lanoba Ghar. People call me Lani, mainly.'

'You're a flyer, yeah?'

'That is correct. With the Langstrothdale Club.'

'I'd like to speak to you today, if that's alright?'

'Well… I'm up in the high dale today.'

'That's no problem. I can come up from Shipley. I'll take a car.'

'Right… erm…'

'Yes?'

'Can I just ask? This is about Meri, isn't it?'

I work with a lot of abstractions, I use the abstractions to try to pin down the truth, capture it and keep it. Whatever truth means, of course. When we had analyst training, we were told the truth meant the reality: what's taken place. It's more clear-cut in some areas than others. When you worked in the digital end of things, reality and the abstract started to get a little blurry. Numbers on a screen were already an abstraction of transactional activity. Somebody somewhere decided that changing the information in the abstractions was a crime. When you change the numbers, you break the law.

But all you're doing, all you're really doing, is changing the abstractions of reality.

That always messed with my head.

When it was a case like this – a proper, old-fashioned case – the work ceased to exist in the realm of numbers of patterns and fuzzy logic. The models suddenly meant something. You really understood that behind all of the narratives, behind your rock-solid primary, your lower probability annexes, your crazy left-field guesses, behind them all was always the reality.

In this case it was Meri Fergus. That was the truth and I could reel out the facts. She'd been twenty-three years old. The only child of Fredrick and Dani Fergus. Just graduated with an excellent degree in aero-flux dynamics. She'd wanted to go and help the Kiwis design their new floating power rig off the West Coast. Possibly work on the mega-sails. She was just waiting for the right funding to come through. For the right opportunity.

The Ferguses lived up the dale. He was now retired, something to do with imports, and she was still a Triage Practitioner, working out of her front room. She'd taken an extended work pattern so her retirement was delayed. A lot of people do it these days. I knew Ibrahim had already been to speak to them. That was a role of the DI. You couldn't delegate that shit. I might get to interview specialists. Since they'd changed the protocols, I'd started to interview the suspects themselves. But analysts like me were never to go near the relatives of the dead. That called for specialist training. It necessitated a gravitas of position and I was proper glad about that arrangement.

Fifteen minutes after I'd ended the call to the flyer, I'd passed the Fergus' house. Modlee pointed it out, tucked into the little twee detacheds that ran north from Stitsils to Cononley. I was reaching the end of the fast-flowing stream of cars on the conduit and was about to hit the little roads.

The curtains were drawn. Possibly a grey-haired old man in the garden. Then we'd moved on.

The northern end of the Airedale MC17 dumped me right in the middle of Lower Skipton. The car weaved its way through the carefully managed industrial estates that spread out like waves from the centre of the town. These were mainly high-level-handler development firms. Cream floating to the top of the dale. Skipton had just managed to cling on to some of the market, unlike the rest of Airedale. It was one section of the dale that hadn't put all its credit lines into the meat vats. The town had concentrated on the coding side and still housed a large population of meta-designers, emergenticians and semanticists. These were people who knew how Modlee worked. They could've taken it apart and put it back together again with sodding bells on.

If they'd have given me the time of day, that is. This wasn't a place for a lower dale PO-chaser like me. They didn't like the Saltaire types up here. If I'd stopped the car and wandered about these streets for too long, with my big hoodie drawn up and my baggy pants showing underneath, I'd have sparked off at least a dozen private alarms. Thankfully, I was just passing through.

Despite the wealth of this end of the dale, I could still see the odd moth-balled premises scattered amongst the lawns, canals, and trees of the estates. Even the two Skiptons couldn't totally survive the crash that'd dragged down their neighbours.

Then I was through the estates and out onto a proper country road. Heading up towards the northern end of the fat dog-leg of Wharfedale Citizen Park and then east into Langstrothdale Wilds. I had never been to this part of the hills. I imagined it was like all the others. And I wasn't wrong.

It was thick with unkempt heather and clusters of gorse

just coming into yellow flower. Tangling this mess further were the weaving stalks of thick briar, looking like one of the more esoteric visual reps that Modlee might have churned out. The car passed old, abandoned farms, their rectangular order now disintegrating under the onslaught of the annual spring greenery. Once or twice, I also passed ghostly patches of cleared earth, where the surrounding wilderness had still to colonise. These had once been a building, a farmhouse, an outhouse or one of the many remote residences which were ubiquitous in those days. Sometimes, it was possible to see the odd remaining drystone wall, which hadn't been knocked down when they'd brought the Act in.

As soon as I left the buzz of the city, I asked the car to run with the top down. I thought this was something that was supposed to make you happy. I could see that there was a pleasurable sensation in the feel of the sun on my skin and the wind on my face. But there was also the alien smell of feral sheep shit mixed with the coconut tones of the gorse, a combination that made me feel queasy.

On top of this, the selected approach-SFX was locked on 'rustling bamboo'. You couldn't turn off the approach-SFX on cars like this – pedestrians would get knocked down in their thousands – but I thought there must be other sounds that didn't get into your head as much as that damn bamboo. Despite pleading with the car's control unit, it was adamant that there was nothing that could be loaded without breaking some insurance nonsense. So I waved my hands to pull back the windows and the roof, before sitting back, arms crossed, trying to work out what I was supposed to be doing up here.

The problem was, I'd never done something like this before. I'd interviewed plenty of people about their data and locked-up encryption. I'd enquired as to how it was that they'd happened to forget all their numeric keys. What were they doing with a server farm under their bath. Why they'd tried to hide data slivers in the arse of their pet cat.

But I'd never interviewed anybody about a death. I wasn't sure where you even started.

All I could think of was the sight of Meri Fergus' face being eaten away by ricos; the distorted shape of her limbs as they lay flattened, white across that black floor.

I stuck on some loud music.

It took me about an hour from Upper Skipton to get through the tangle of backroads and to reach Langstrothdale. The last part of the journey had been along a valley bottom, and the heat from the sun - and my general exhaustion - had lulled me into a drowsy mood. There was something tugging at my mind, with an insistent dread. Something that I had to do today. I wasn't sure if I was dreaming it or whether there was something I'd forgotten. It made me nauseous, though. The ting of the arrival message shook me awake and I rubbed my eyes, wishing I'd brought coffee.

Lani met me as I stepped from the car.

'Hello. Haz, was it?'

'That's me,' I yawned. We clasped hands and knocked knuckles.

We were in a car park on a high saddle that looked down into Wensleydale to the north. Further to the west, it was possible to make out the shape of distant peaks, wreathed in the smog which rose up from the Lancashire levels. To the east, a monstrous slug of mountain was dark under passing cloud. I should've known what it was called. But I didn't really care.

As well as Lani, other members of the flyers club were already parked up and starting to get into their gear.

'Sorry to have dragged you out here today,' he said. 'It's just, I run the club and I need to be here … you see?'

I grunted, still trying to work out what I was going to ask him.

'It'll be quick, buddy, don't you worry,' I said, stalling for time. 'You going up right now?'

The other man grinned and checked the clouds above him. He shrugged.

'Wind's good,' he said.

Lani was shaped, in the manner of all flyers, like a small, starved, and stringy adolescent. Just one who'd had the thighs of a rhino grafted onto them. You had to have exactly the right body shape to be a flyer, a body shape that had inherent lightness but also incredible muscular strength.

'Not everyone can fly.'

That'd been the moral of a story I could still remember from primary school. It'd been a story about a flyer and a fat kid. I guess he was supposed to be average, probably fitter than me, but we all knew him as the fat kid. The fat kid had to learn that he'd simply never be able to fly. It was supposed to teach you that, although everything was theoretically possible, you might find life easier if you managed your expectations a little. I remembered that the teacher had only begrudgingly extrapolated the meaning of the story. Even an emotional cripple like me had realised that she'd not totally agreed with the sentiment.

It seemed to have upset a lot of other kids in the class as well. But it was what the commissioners had asked for, and, well, she was getting paid, wasn't she? It hadn't bothered me. I never wanted to be a flyer. And I knew I was never going to be. Of course, if you paid your money you could get plastic in there to compensate for your shitty physique. Replace your femur with something out of a printer. But then that would be a life of specialised physio and all that rubbish. Followed by early cartilage deterioration, spinal problems, and so on and so on. They found the best flyers were the ones who were born for it.

There weren't many who could, despite years of

experimenting. When they'd made proper gossamer for the first time, somebody had done the maths and had realised that this was, at last, the material that could make human beings fly. As in, really fly: flap your arms and run and actually take-off. Naturally, you needed the suit and all that. You needed to strap yourself into an arm rig of struts and poles. And when you were taking off, you basically flew with your thigh muscles. That was the power. It was the thighs that got you in the air and your arms just steered. Which explained the mutant rhino effect.

'Hey,' said Lani. 'Check it out there… behind you.'

I turned and saw a woman in her late twenties come into land. It was, I had to admit, an act which was beautiful to watch. The rectangular-shaped wing which you often saw in the sky, designed to catch the thermals, had to change shape when it came into land. I watched the woman release the finger mechanisms which unfurled additional pockets of stretched gossamer. She curled her arms out and brought them beside her head, snapping the full landing wing out and bringing her speeding form to a near perfect controlled halt with only a small stumble as she landed on the uneven tussocks. Then she raised her hands and shivered the wings back into their folded position.

'Sweet,' I said.

'That's Tirana,' Lani said. 'She's nearly the best we…' He trailed off.

'Nearly?'

'Well,' said Lani. I turned and could see tears in his eyes now. 'She's the best now, isn't she?'

I don't know why I said it but it came out anyway. 'Meri was the best?'

'Yeah, she was up in the air nearly every hour. Whatever the weather, no matter the wind, or whether it was light or dark.'

'She went up at night?'

'Of course.'

As I was about to ask some more questions, Modlee caught my attention. It'd registered the ratios of Lani, Tirana and the two other flyers and had been doing some work in the background. It'd picked up some interesting patterns: there seemed to be a significant link between all the flyers. As another flyer ran and swept up into the sky – which took attention away from me – I twitched my hands surreptitiously in front of myself, disguising the fact that I was also plugged in. I expected to be told they all drank together, all went to the same college, or happened to have downloaded the same vidz series on flying. I was wrong.

I should've trusted Modlee. It always came up with insights like this. East Pennine IG normally stopped all fishing trips. You can't walk down the street and let your bead scream out names of your fellow citizens every time it recognises them. We've got laws against that kind of invasive crap. The law only allowed you ratio-linkage if it fell within the scope of your access codes. These lot were all tagged to Enforcement, somehow. I followed the tag and quietly found my way through some comms sites to a minor reposting-server. It had originally been registered out of Bradford. Reposting-servers were semi-autonomous comms-handlers that could be bought as a service. They were configured to post messages, churn out copy, and upload pix and vidz across all sorts of media. There were billions of them, of course. Anybody who wanted to advertise themselves, or something they believed in, all made use of reposters. But this one was close to home and familiar.

Airedale Enforcement // Violence Without Limits

It was a name I'd heard many times before. Jonah had mentioned it a lot. The Enforcement boys and girls were very pissed at this particular reposting-server and the people behind it. I'd never got involved, as it didn't have much to say about Justice and I didn't give a shit about comms-chatter on a normal day.

I felt myself shiver. The stunt Modlee had just pulled was only possible because of the kind of data mountain access I been given by Ibrahim. Associations between facial ratios and reposting services were deep layer. Any personal comms was highly contentious stuff. Everybody was allowed to be able to be as radical as they wanted without the state prying into their musings. It was a key plank of the IG ruling which had been passed nearly half a century before. You don't bloody-well mess with people's comms. And tread carefully around ratios. Even getting the rights to log ratios off your bead was way off the IG scale. Normally you'd have to ask permission with your sad little spiel. I'd never been on a case like this before, but it seemed murder got you access.

'Tell me about your reposter,' I said to Lani. 'Violence Without Limits.'

He grimaced. I'd asked the right question.

'You tell me,' he said, glancing at the logo on my cap. 'You're AJC. You know what's happening.'

'I'm Justice and Reconciliation side. Don't get involved with Enforcement end of things. I know they do a bloody straight-up job, mind. Every night they're out there keeping people like you and me safe on the streets. It's a tough one, in't it?'

'And what? You're also going to say...'

'What?'

'Especially nowadays.'

'Well,' I said. 'We all know it's getting worse down the dale.'

'Is it?' asked Lani. 'Is it really?'

'Look at the metrics,' I said.

He sighed. 'You're all commissioned. That's what you've got to say...'

I raised a hand. 'Just tell me about this server. Was Meri involved in it?'

'Yeah,' he said. 'She was the one who set it up. She was furious at what was going on.'

'She got you involved, then?'

He shrugged. 'She was convincing. It's not just us flyers, there are people all over the dale who don't like what's happening. There're lots of us.'

'I know, I've got access, Lani,' I said, tapping the peak of my cap. 'I've got the data, I know everybody on this moor has submitted material to that reposter.'

'Of course,' said Lani. 'That's why Meri came to us, she needed the flyers.'

'Why?'

'Bird's eye view, man!' he said, spreading his arms as though they were wings.

I frowned. 'You mean aerial footage?'

'That's right. We've posted some excellent footage of your colleagues in full action.'

'Why not use a camdrone?'

'That would be useless,' he said. 'Any type of drone would be intercepted within seconds. They would have taken it offline as soon as it was in the air.'

'They would?' I asked. 'Who is they?'

He closed his mouth and looked at the ground. 'You know, man. You know exactly...'

One of the other flyers, an older woman, slight and short, had shrugged off her wings and sauntered over to join the conversation. She saw the logo on my cap and I could see a frown tighten her face.

'This about Meri?' she asked.

'Sorry,' I said. 'I'm just trying to interview this gentleman here. Can you please give us a minute?'

'Why?' she said. She had an Indian accent but must've lived in the north for a while. 'You can interview a hundred people with that processor rig you've got.'

'You are?' I asked, sighing a little.

'You tell me,' she said. 'I'm not hiding my face, inspector.'

She was correct. My display had her ratios logged as Puja Jaffrey. She was registered as a freelance media consultant from Bradford. There were quite a few like her, who made their details public. Transparency nutjobs, the lot of them. They'd post pix of their kids' faces online if they could. Proper militant.

Still, sometimes it saved time when people had nothing to hide and it seemed she'd nothing to hide. She'd no other associations that Modlee could tell me about, beyond the reposter.

'Analyst,' I muttered.

'Analyst,' she repeated with a nod. 'DI didn't want to come up the high dale, did he?'

'This is standard procedure, you know,' I said. 'DIs don't get involved during the initial data gathering rounds.'

'Does he not?' she asked. 'So what's an analyst doing up here talking to a bunch of flyers?'

'He wants to know about Without Limits,' said Lani.

'Of course he does,' she said. 'AJC are always very interested in that. As they should be.'

'Look,' I said, raising my hands in a conciliatory gesture. 'I'm here to help understand what Meri might have been doing the night she died. I've got nowt to do with Enforcement, so can we pack in all this defensiveness, alright?'

Lani agreed, looking relieved. Puja seemed more guarded but she was the first to speak.

'She was recording.'

'For this reposter?' I asked.

'Of course,' said Puja. 'There was a war going on down in the middle of Keighley Basin that night.'

'She were streaming footage?'

'No,' said Lani. 'We never stream while we're flying. It's too easy to intercept over a wireless channel. And it's too slow and expensive to encrypt. We have to do it later.'

'Can I see what she filmed?' I asked. I was thinking about what Modlee had shown me on that night.

Puja looked at me like I was an idiot. When she spoke, her voice cracked with grief and rage. 'Are you listening to us, son? Or are you just reading comics on your bead?'

'We haven't got it, Hasim,' said Lani gently. 'She died that night.'

I frowned, fell silent, and blushed. 'Yeah, right, of course.'

'Your forensics team will have picked it up, probably,' said Puja. 'It would have been on her...'

She broke down and turned away. Lani followed her and put an arm around her.

'I'll give you a minute,' I muttered.

Keeping an eye out for any other flyers coming into land, I walked back to the car and called up the forensics data files. I ran a quick search and found nothing about a camera. Without thinking, I hit the icon that called up Carrie. She refused the call immediately, which irritated me. But a few seconds later she buzzed me a message.

What do you want?

I dictated a quick question, my fingers drumming out a staccato rhythm on the bonnet of the car.

Was there a camera found with the body?

There was a pause. As soon as I'd sent it, I regretted it. It was a question that could be interpreted as a potential provocation. It suggested that she was keeping something from me. Or she was incompetent at her job. However, she wasn't going to let me know if she was upset. The response was short and clear.

No.

I sent a quick thank you message and returned to Lani. Puja had gone to talk with the other flyers. Even from this distance, I could see that she was now furiously weeping.

'There was no camera recovered,' I said to Lani.

'Really? She was definitely filming that night.'

'What kind of camera was it?' I asked.

'It was professional equipment. Like for a professional cameraman. I think it had long distance, night vision, heat, the works.'

'Not small, then?'

He put his hands up to indicate something the size of an apple.

I nodded. 'OK. Did she ever say she'd been bothered by anybody?'

'No, not really.'

'You'd never had direct threats made about the reposting-server?'

'No,' said Lani, slowly. He frowned. 'Do you think they took it from the body?'

'That's unlikely,' I said, pausing to think. What did Modlee need? 'When she flew over the Basin, did she always take a particular route?'

'Yeah,' said Lani. 'We all took the same one. You get the best updraughts from the Conduit, the MC17, you see, and then there's a huge meat vat place just on the Flatts side, where you can get easy height and come back north. The Caines' place.'

'Caines?' I asked.

'Yeah,' said Lani. 'You know it?'

'Can you show me?' I pulled up a map of Keighley Basin and the northern edge of Keighley Flatts on my display then took off my cap. I threw it over to Lani, which he caught and put on, before started to trace a line in the air in front of him.

I checked my watch. It was nearly eleven. I'd the rest of the day to track down this camera. I was sure I'd the rest of the day. Yet, there was still that subconscious itch reminding me about something. Something that I needed to do today. It had something to do with Asha. I couldn't remember which annoyed me, but I tried to ignore it.

Lani finished tracing the route in the air before him. I took back my cap and thanked him. Then headed out of the hills and back to civilisation.

Chapter Eight

―――

My diary handler waved cheerily to get my attention during the second retch, which I ignored. At the third retch, I gave up fighting the urges and allowed myself to purge the semi-digested contents of my stomach. To be fair, this was probably for my own good. It was a bean-and-rice wrap I'd picked up from some alt affair on the outskirts of Upper Skipton on the way back into the dale. It'd tasted funny when it had gone down and still tasted pretty funny on the way back up.

Whoever had coded the diary handler, they hadn't accounted for the facial proportions of somebody vomiting. It kept up its ting-a-ling as my diaphragm convulsed beneath my ribs and bruised my internal organs. As the second wave hit me, an arc of sweat surged along the brim of my cap and I felt it start to bead up my forehead as well. I retched for the third time. As I put a shaky left arm out to steady myself against the concrete pillar, I flicked my right in the correct configuration to turn the thing off.

The ting-a-ling stopped.

I was never any good at this shit. I took it badly, envied my friends at school who seemed to relish the opportunity to regurgitate whatever cheapest-on-display alcohol they'd slung down their necks at blood-poisoning velocity. To them, it was a rite of passage, just part of the evening. But for me, it was a full body punishment and I hated it. I leaned forward for another dry heave. We were beyond the bean wrap now. Into darker territory.

Then I remembered.

The alarm was reminding me that I was supposed to be chatting to somebody in under fifteen minutes, Sadie McManus. She was thirty-three and she lived on the Isle of Bute with her one child and the child's pet guinea pig. Her interests were reading, painting, and going on forest walks. Divorced. The guinea-pig was called Gerald. For whatever reason, the MoreThanSum service had selected her from all the other single women within a three-hundred mile radius.

It'd been a bad day when I'd selected that particular parameter.

I'd come to the conclusion that the MoreThanSum service had suffered some kind of exponential glitch in its mathematical models. The single women it'd selected for me had been so direly inappropriate, I'd even started to joke about it with some work colleagues. The problem was, my subscription to the service had been a present from Asha. She'd, no doubt, been put up to it by my mother, who had certainly given her the credit line for it. But when she'd handed me the birthday card, with the authentication sliver carefully taped inside, she'd smiled with such hope in her eyes that I'd had to try and stamp down the cynic.

And I'd tried, many times. Sadie McManus was my last chance. If I turned her away, like the others, they would cancel my subscription. Then I'd have to find some way of explaining this to Asha.

The call I was supposed to make in a few minutes was going to be the first time Sadie McManus and I had ever chatted face-to-face. In the shock of seeing the dead flyer and the craving to take on the case, I'd completely forgotten that this was supposed to be my afternoon off. That I was supposed to be tucked up at home, with appropriate background images of happy children and clean furniture. Clean-shaven, a fruit juice in my hand. Happy and smiling. And with no pictures of Dali in sight.

In between hawking up and spitting out the last of the vomit, I muttered a command to the bead. 'Next appointment. Create message. Reply to attendee. Message content: 'So sorry, having trouble this afternoon. Can we do this evening?'

'Confirmed.'

The bead sent the message and I straightened up, wiping the last of the bile from my mouth with my grubby parka sleeve. I retreated further from the heap in front of me, avoiding looking at it.

It was at these moments that I wondered what'd happened to the desk job. I knew I only had myself to blame.

On the way back down to Airedale from Langstrothdale, I'd called up the high-end satellite images of the river and dropped in a few likely shape vectors for the camera Lani had described. There was no telling where the thing might've been dropped. If it had been dropped at all. I started with the general area of the industrial units where Meri's body had been found. This was Keighley Cutt, the northern end of the district.

This had returned nothing.

I tried scrolling down further down into Keighley Basin itself and got nothing of interest. Getting bored, I told Modlee to go through the entire length of Airedale. The processor block had to come out of my pocket at this point.

But still nothing.

When I expanded the pix search vector to include anything white or shiny or clearly unnatural, I immediately got a few million hits, so that was a waste of time. I'd tweaked a few shapes but this got me nowhere. There was a human visual-recognition service I could've dumped the images to but this would've cost me. Plus, I never really trusted that kind of operation. These days, they tended to be housed out of Indonesia or Argentina, either aircraft hangars of students earning their way to a better life or dispersed across the suburbs of Nigeria or Jakarta to bored parents trying to earn a little pocket-money. It wasn't a quality service. If you wanted quality, there were also the east coast military outfits or the Murmansk labs, but you didn't dial up an order for them like you were ordering pizza. And the DI wouldn't have liked the bill.

After I'd stopped in Skipton for the fateful takeaway, I set Modlee looking across the technology exchange and second-hand buyers. There was always a chance it'd been found. There were a few well-known reposters that handled this kind of activity, so I set it to prioritise them. Plus a few more in specialist areas. There were plenty of that kind of camera doing the rounds but the nearest was Berlin and that seemed a little tenuous. With a little exploratory research, in between bites of bean-and-cheese mix, I even tried to track down the vidz signature that would be associated with Meri's camera. Unfortunately, she must've bought it offline or via some black-market currency, as there was no record of her ever owning one. It was going to be an outside bet, anyway, as I doubted anybody who might've stolen it would've started posting vidz with an old signature.

As I was finishing the last of the bean wrap, I concluded the camera wasn't laying out in the open somewhere in Airedale, nor was it being sold or exchanged, and nobody was using it. Which meant a number of scenarios: somebody had picked it up from a field or the river and sat on it, or it had been taken from the body and hidden, or it had exploded in mid-air, it had never been taken in the first place, or it had been dropped at the point of impact and had somehow got into the sewers.

The thing was, I knew that anything that hit the sewers in Keighley only ever went in one direction. This was the Aire. And if didn't it had washed up on a bank somewhere in the upper dale, it was going to end up in the Keighley Flood Levels.

* * *

The Keighley Flood Levels boasted an installation that been commissioned from the South-West Keighley Environment Services about twenty years ago. It was still maintained, on the cheap. I'd heard that they were thinking of ripping the whole thing out. That would've cost the taxpayer, of course. Decisions like that weren't taken quickly.

We called it the Grid. Some people called it the U-Bend. This wasn't because of its shape; mainly it was due to the kind of things that got stuck there. It was a huge graphene mesh that'd been strung across the entire length of the southern exit of the Basin flood levels. At some point in the last few decades, the lower inhabitants of the dale had complained to the Servants in the Keighley area that the river was depositing the – sometimes still twitching – contents of meat vats from up the valley into their back gardens. Tighter fines had no effect, so they were forced to invest in the Grid.

I never liked visiting the Grid, but you found your stuff there.

I was two floors beneath the Keighley Basin retail zone. The flood levels, a warren of concrete basins and sink chambers, were on the same levels as the canals. Designed to disperse the water when the river was in spate. A hundred years ago, this used to take place further up the valley, across the fields of sheep farms. Of course, these were now residential parks and coding villages, so the water had to be deep-channelled further down the valley where they wanted it and where they could make use of it.

Keighley Basin had need of the water. Once the upstream downpour reached these flood levels, every meat vat in the town would sink their pipes into the muddy mess, sucking up as much as they could. The nutrients in the flood waters were some of the best in the world for vat work. You could try and synthesise the same effect using a slurry of nitrogen and silica but the meat just never responded as well as it did to the natural stuff. It was part of the secret of Airedale's success.

Of course, once they had topped up their vats with the good shit, the factories needed to find somewhere to dump their waste. It was better not to think about the waste product from meat vats. I was working very hard not to think of it. Or to look at it. Or to smell it.

It was illegal to jettison this kind of biohazard into the Aire but then "illegal" was a flexible term to some industries. Despite the collapse in the meat vat industry, the flood levels were still terrible places to be. Especially after a dry spell. Then the slurry really backed up.

Today was a bad day to be here. It was hot, starting to come into summer, and we'd had a half-spate river about two weeks ago. This had picked up all the waste and spread it across the levels. I was regretting having made the decision to come down here.

I'd left the car in the seven-storey public car park that dominated the skyline in the middle of the Basin. I'd been to the flood levels many times before so I knew how to get access. For a normal citizen, it was difficult to find your way down there, but if you'd the right clearance and the right delegation, you could get anywhere. Technically, I didn't have the right clearance, but I did have the authorisation codes for the security booth that had jurisdiction over the south-west corner of the Joyful Shopping Arcade. I'd done some work on a security guard who'd been using footage to blackmail people and had been given dynamic access to the booth. Nobody had the wit – or the audit trail – to know I still had the A-codes. If you flashed your AJC badge at security guards, they tended to keep quiet anyway.

It'd only taken a few minutes of scurrying through the shoppers in the Joyful Arcade and I was at the door to the booth. As I approached, the codes in my bead signalled to the door and it slid back. Behind was a small antechamber that led to the monitoring station and a small canteen. There was also a small door stuck in a corner. I walked across with the confidence of an Enforcement operative, trying to bulk up my shoulders. If anybody had challenged me, I would've protested that I was undercover. This was a little offset by the logo on my cap, but I hoped the security guards would keep quiet about this aspect.

The small door opened onto a tight spiral staircase. A close inspection of it would've revealed the small water seals that ran around its edge and its solidity. This was designed to take some pressure.

The flood levels didn't need artificial lighting, as the architect who had designed them also had the foresight to install the light pipes, so in the middle of the day there was a permanent ambient light. This had proved unfortunate when I'd finally reached the Grid, however. It meant you could see everything. Scraps of protein, rotting and fatty, were all balled up, clustering around more solid artefacts. A trio of torso-sized grey protein plugs were lined up like ship's fenders. A rusting bundle of barbed wire, embedded with pink and green flesh. A cracked bucket, fragments of vegemer, scum, and scum, and scum. Fizzing, popping and fermenting in scattered pools of foam, where bergs of flesh chunks slowly writhed.

Of course, wherever there's dead flesh, there is also life. Continuous movement unnerved one's peripheral vision and the distant sounds didn't help. I could hear the skittering of the rats, sometimes loud, sometimes quiet. There would've been feral cats down here as well. Possibly dogs. But it was the smaller creatures that held dominion, burrowing their pale bodies into the gelatinous mounds in front of me.

I'd kicked a tree branch free of the goo and broken off a stick. Using this, I was able to work my way along the line of Grid. I'd managed to get over halfway before coming across a full side of beef. It was larger than me. I'd poked it accidentally and it had ruptured, releasing a writhing mass of maggots onto the concrete floor, causing me to retch.

It took me half an hour more – after I'd sent the delaying message back to MoreThanSum – of poking the stick into piles of sludge, some of it still clinging to life, before I hit something that felt like what I was looking for. The stick was an effective prod and it allowed me to disentangle the solid object from its moist home. Unfortunately, it was a terrible tool for cleaning off the muck and I had to kick the thing along to a shallow pool nearby to actually check that it was what I was looking for.

After it'd been dunked and sloshed a few times in the puddle, the last meaty remnants fell from it and the shape emerged. A camera, matching Lani's description.

I picked up the device carefully between forefinger and thumb and dropped it into an evidence bag. Although I'd a few dozen of these stashed deep in my pockets, they were usually called into service when I visited the bakers and had forgotten to bring my bags from home. It felt good to actually use them for something other than samosas and churros.

The security suite, previously quiet, was now manned by a couple who seemed interested in what I'd been doing in their patch. There was a large woman, possibly European by her accent, although it might've had traces of Joburg, and with her a small man who looked Central Asian. Their English wasn't perfect but not necessarily a handicap in a job like security. You essentially carried out the commands issued to you by the relevant handler code and these could be in whatever language they needed to be. Of course, it helped when they came to demanding answers.

'What are you doing?' the man asked, jabbing a thumb towards the sealed door.

'I'm with the AJC,' I drawled, pulling my hood back a little to show the cap. I used to have a little card with my photo on it but lost it some time ago. I suspected Ali had placed it in the kitchen bin when I wasn't looking. Hard copy ID was for show, these days, so I'd never bothered with it too much. You were supposed to use the electronic ID in your bead.

'Correction,' said the woman. 'You have a hat with the letters AJC on it.'

'I'm a subcontractor for the–'

She ploughed on. 'I have a jacket at my house with East Coast USA Nuclear Unit on it.'

The man laughed. 'She does. I've seen it.'

'However,' she said, and paused for effect. 'I'm not a nuclear scientist.'

I stared at the floor, ignoring her laughter. This was annoying. I could've simply dropped them my AJC codes and got on with this without any fuss. But that would've sparked me up online and I wasn't sure I wanted to be so visible just now. The business with the pattern Modlee had found was making me a little edgy.

'What's that?' asked the woman, jerking her chin towards the evidence bag. I noticed although she was pushing the bravado and the jokes, her left hand was fingering the little spray can on her belt. If she got jumpy she might whip the beggar out and fill this little – and unventilated – room full of whatever messed-up concoction was inside. I didn't want to see the effects of that. It wouldn't kill, of that I was certain, but it would certainly slow me and probably put me off my tea for a good few days.

'It's evidence,' I said. 'I'm with justice and reconciliation.'

The shorter man narrowed his eyes a little and looked closer, under the brim of my hat. 'Hello! You're the one who put Gerry in exile, weren't you?'

I couldn't read his face. Gerry was the name of the security guard who'd been blackmailing concession holders. I nodded slowly. 'Yeah, that were me.'

The little man reached out a hand. 'Well done, mate. Gerry was a total... what do you say... a total wanker!'

'No problem,' I muttered. The woman relaxed and her hand slipped from her canister.

'Go on' the man said, stepping to one side. 'Let me get the door for you, sir. That shit's beginning to stink up the place, yes?'

I nodded and grinned at the bag. 'Yeah.'

I got myself to a public toilet as soon as I could, dunking my arms to the elbow in soapy water. I also took a moment to clear out my mouth and palate of the few remaining specks of regurgitate. The old gentlemen who were in there at the urinal eyed me suspiciously from behind their dicks but didn't comment.

While I was in the toilets, I also took the opportunity to try and get the data out of the camera. I could've hacked into the device remotely, but if it was a high-res vid then it would've been slow and heavy to process. Plus, I liked the idea of being able to hide the content. There were too many snoopers on the wireless.

Using some toilet paper, I wiped off the sludge from around the waterproof seals, and snapped back the catches. It looked like the machine had hit something hard, its lens was fractured and one corner of the plastic casing was pitted with gravel. It was so light that it could've travelled quite a distance, with enough water to float on and a little help from the wind.

Once I'd found the sliver, tucked it into my cap and re-sealed the evidence bag, I wandered out into the shopping centre.

It was wall-to-wall with people trying to reclaim some hope from their hopeless lives by zapping out credits from their beads. Credit they were never going to re-pay but that some unnamed algorithm in Helsinki had decreed they could spend anyway. Just to keep some other algorithm in Zurich happy. The world was a messed-up place.

I found myself at a retro piemaker's place which did coffee, along with the dinky curry-crusts and pork-strata. I got myself a large glass of water with an espresso and settled into a table by the wall. Turning my security up to high and plugging myself into the sliver.

I was above a town, I guessed it must've been Keighley. There were the bright lights of the central Basin area; further down the dale were the darker, more linear shapes from the Flatts, and over to the left, the swirling whorls of the residential Vale estates.

A voice provided some kind of voice-over.

'There they are,' it intoned. I guessed it was Meri's. She was trying to adopt a sombre tone but her voice was too light and came across as a little false. 'These are the lights of freedom, the flares of the rebellion beneath me.'

The view zoomed into the Basin. The screen showed the glowing orange grid of the centre of town. Making their way into the western villages were a few brighter pinpricks of light. These must've been the fires from the riots. The camera zoomed in, with a juddery amateurishness. We were immediately in among the fire. About a dozen people were dragging what looked like industrial, hand-operated low-loaders down the middle of the street. On the low-loaders were wire baskets full of flames. I couldn't see any wood there, so I guessed they must've doused some textile with fuel. That kind of combustible material was difficult to get hold of.

They would've raided some chemical depot down the valley.

The voice-over continued. 'Here are the vanguard warriors of the new age. Here they come to recover what they have lost. Together, they form a conflagration that will light up this region, this country, this hemisphere.'

At this moment, she had trouble with her wings, the view swerved off to the left and the filming stopped. When it was switched on again, the angle was higher and she'd gained altitude. It took a moment to focus on the action and then took us back into the action. Something was happening in the streets near the centre. A small shield wall of Enforcement operatives was making its way towards the caravan of flaming loaders. I could see that they were downhill of the rioters and knew immediately what was going to happen next.

'Now the oppressive ideology is smashed by those who have never tasted...' Here, the voice-over dropped off a little. Perhaps she'd lost her thread or perhaps it was the sight of the loaders barrelling their way into the shield wall. The Enforcement officers went up in flames. They immediately deployed their localised extinguishers and the flames went out. The camera adjusted immediately to the decreased illumination.

The flame attack was clearly an act of transgression, as the moment it hit the group of operatives, an officer towards the rear of the group chopped her hand in a command signal, and started talking into her bead. Although the focus of the filming was still on the front-line tussle between the operatives and the rioters, I was able to watch the officer on the side of the screen. She was looking up at the sky. Almost directly at the camera lens. She turned to a colleague and leaned in to shout in his ear, waving at the sky. Her colleague also looked skywards.

Then I heard a high-pitched shriek and could see every rioter flinch. Most of them were trying to pull something out of their chests, legs, or necks. I guessed these must've been the smartdarts. Very quickly, I could see the rioters turn to run, some already stumbling uphill.

'Legal in all oppressive regimes… people treated as though they were game to be brought down. The police now little more than well-paid hunters or military generals, calling in airstrikes on unarmed civilians.'

The camera view juddered a little, as though Meri had lost her concentration. There was a roaring noise and a wet thunk. The camera view flickered away and the view faded to black. I assumed it'd turned off but I when I looked closer, I could see the faint outline of orange-tinged clouds. This was the view upwards from a falling camera.

Then the vid stopped.

I drank my coffee, about to re-play the footage when I saw a call come in for me. I waved it through.

'Yo,' said Ibrahim. A little peremptorily, I thought. 'I've just been passed this interview request for Kaz Furness.'

'Yeah,' I said. My mind was still on the footage. 'It's just a lead I was following up on.'

'You want to interview Kaz?'

'Yeah. Like I said, it were a lead.'

'What kind of lead?'

What was Ibrahim's problem? 'There were a pattern I saw on the night the flyer died. She's Chair of Enforcement Board. I need to interview Enforcement people.'

'All based on a pattern?'

'There were some association.'

Ibrahim breathed through his nose and twitched his lips. 'How strong a pattern?'

I laughed. 'You know how this works, DI. You see the patterns and you follow up on them. I haven't weighted it. Even Modlee doesn't do that.'

'You must be able to say how significant a lead it is, Haz. Or you could be chasing butterflies!'

'You give me the parameters for the significance, DI, and I'll run a scenario for you.'

'Haz,' he said, with a sudden grin. 'I'm not being difficult. I'm not here to question your judgement. You've got the commission because you're the best, of course.'

I regarded him solemnly for a moment. 'What's the problem, DI?'

He laughed again. 'It's nothing, really. It's just, I'm not sure what all this has to do with the Enforcement Board? Remember, Ms Furness is a Servant of the people. She demands respect.'

'It were a pattern, DI,' I said, speaking slowly. 'That's all I'm following up on. I wanted to understand what the communication was that took place between those people. By working the parameters, I was able to tell it concerned Enforcement-related operations. So, I'm putting in the request to speak to a Servant who has connections to Enforcement about what happened that night.'

Ibrahim stared at his bead camera for a moment. 'In your professional judgement, Haz... as our top analyst, you believe this is worth following up on?'

'I do.'

'Right,' he said, smiling. 'No problem. Just thought I'd check first. Come into the offices tomorrow, OK? I'll get it to you then.'

'Cheers,' I said.

'Catch you for a coffee,' he said, waving as his image flickered away.

Ting-a-ling.

There was a little message icon in the corner of the screen from MoreThanSum. I dragged it into the middle of my display with trembling fingers. The message was fairly short.

'Perhaps another time, then. So sorry to catch you at a bad moment. Sadie.'

Chapter Nine

———

Carrie called me as soon as I'd dropped her the link to the vidz.

'Where'd you get this?' she asked.

You never expected pleasantries with Carrie but this was professionally abrupt.

'Hiya, Carrie,' I said. The car had picked me up from outside the Joyful Shopping Centre about ten minutes before and I was on my way home, south along the MC-17. The conversation with the DI had left me in a bad mood. He was being transparently protective of his reputation and I shouldn't have expected any other response from my request. I knew the interview request had been a contentious ploy on my part. I'd never got on well with Enforcement. And now I wasn't sure why, but there was something about what I'd seen on the vidz which had only strengthened my views.

'Where did you get this?' she repeated.

'Found it in the sewers. In the Basin.'

'You watched it?'

'Of course.'

'You know what it is?' she asked.

'Yeah, it's our Enforcement buddies, in't it?'

'You seen the reposting site that this usually gets fired off to?'

'Course I have,' I said. 'Spoken to other people who also post to it as well.'

'Wow,' Carrie said. 'You've been busy.'

'Do my best. So, what did you make of it?'

She fell silent for a moment, then shook her head and looked down, as though she'd lost interest. 'Where are you?'

I looked out of the window of the car. Rain streaked the glass. 'Not sure. On my way home, anyway.'

'Roughly,' she said.

'Just left Keighley Flatts.' I thought I could make out the familiar rusting gas hulks passing me on my left. The rain was creating such a sheet I didn't recognise the place. 'Why? Are you tracking me now, or something?'

'We need to talk,' she said. 'Like… immediately, Haz.'

'What about?

'Face-to-face.'

'Oh,' I said. 'Where are you, then?'

'Centre of Leeds, at the 3D modelling place.'

I shook my head. 'Leeds? No way, Carrie. I gotta get back to the kids. My care help is not going to be happy if I'm late again.'

The small face on my display grimaced. 'OK. No bother.'

'What you found, Carrie?' I asked her.

'Nowt,' she said.

'Then why'd we need to talk?'

'People I've been talking to,' she said darkly.

'Like who?'

'Not going to say. Not here.'

I thought she must've been smoking too much. This was proper tinfoil-hattery. Only a few people would've had the IG clearance to intercept a line like this. Still, Carrie was known to be a bit paranoid when it came to tech.

'How about first thing tomorrow?' I asked. 'I'm going into the office. Got a meeting with the DI.'

'With the DI?'

'He'll be there, yeah. He's going to give me some interview authorisation.'

She wrinkled her nose at the thought. Then she did something off-screen. After a moment, she nodded. 'You know he's stuck in a commissioning meeting all morning, though?'

'Who with?'

She checked something off-screen. 'Don't know. Don't recognise the names... Kellis, Arathan...'

Trying to show off a little, I also dragged up the DI's diary on my screen and dropped the names into Memro. It came back with a direct associate pattern.

'They're all Servants,' I said. 'Makes sense. Commissioning and that.'

'Servants,' she spat. 'They're like spiders... you're always within a metre of one, or summat.'

'Yeah,' I said, trying to laugh. I noticed something about the location. 'Oh hell, Carrie!'

'What?'

'He's having that meeting in the bloody Trench, yeah?'

'Enforcement? He never goes up there.'

'Well, it's in his diary. He's not got a virtual invite or anything like that. He's going to be there in person, I reckon.'

Carrie thought for a minute. I knew she hated going up to the Trench. 'You said you spoke to him?'

'Yeah.'

'He were going to give you some A-codes?'

'That's right. For an interview.'

'Perhaps he just forgot,' she said. This was unlikely. Ibrahim's diary was as carefully managed and presented as a bonsai tree. 'Are you going up there, Haz?'

'Gonna have to now,' I said. 'I need that authorisation.'

'OK,' she said. 'I'll meet you there. By those Justice desks, yeah?'

'Alright,' I said. She seemed to be lost in further contemplation, eyes a little unfocused. I cleared my throat and laughed, harshly. 'You sure you've not found owt yet, Carrie?'

Her tiny floating head stared at me. 'Yeah I'm sure.'

* * *

The person who signed off on the facilities contract for Enforcement clearly didn't have the same negotiating capabilities as our DI, Al-Yahmeni. As long as I could remember, the force had occupied three levels of this fibreglass monstrosity sunk into the Bingley Trench. What had once been a deep, meandering curve of the Aire was identified as prime land, and some construction firm had concreted over the course of the river, using it as the foundation to build upwards, eventually reaching the level of the old road bridge. Enforcement had been allocated the bottom three floors. The rumour was this gave them the ability to dunk people they didn't like in the mucky ooze of the river that passed below.

It was a sombre place, even on a spring day like this. Natural light bled into the floors through erratically cleaned sunpipes and the odd transparent polymer column, but these only ever let in a weak glow. This meant artificial light was the norm. I guessed it must've explained why Enforcement were always out-of-the-office. To add to the grimness of the place, it'd suffered significant flood damage about five years previous, which left the place with a dank scent and stained walls. I never enjoyed coming here.

Justice and Enforcement were supposed to work closely together. Different steps in the same process. Different sides of the same coin. We were all about the law, but everybody knew that we didn't see eye-to-eye on things. True, we were both more cynical about human nature than the smiley, clappy bunch in Reconciliation and the geeks at Prevention, but we still couldn't see each other's worth. Enforcement thought Justice wasted time messing about with pointless investigations and fussy details while we should be working harder on putting the wrong 'uns behind bars.

And Justice? We just thought they were thugs.

The reputation that Enforcement had in Airedale had been carefully cultivated by previous commissioners. They could see that the threat of the shockstick was more effective than that particular tool's deployment in action. Taxes had been gradually increased in areas of drones and surveillance, with the explicit endorsement of Prevention. They needed that shit as well, the whole division was now tooled-up to such an extent that commissioning experts from places as far away as London and Lisbon had dropped by to understand the success.

I stepped out of the lift and onto the uppermost of the three floors, where the senior members of the force tended to work and where all key meetings took place. The level was vast, curved into the walls of the surrounding valley, with greenish, transparent columns jutted up from the floor, carrying light down from the surface. They'd scrimped on the roof space, which made it feel low above your head.

Despite hanging around the five Justice hotdesks all that morning, I'd not seen Carrie. I was infuriated and knackered, as I'd been awake most of the night wondering what she wanted to speak about. Insomnia was becoming a normal part of my life. I'd tried some pills and the like from the chemist but they never seemed to work. I'd failed to mention it to my med-handler. Purposefully. It tended to drop me little questionnaires now and again, but I needed to be careful about what I told it. During a weak moment, I'd revealed the fact that I'd been crying every night for a week; it sent the paramedics around. Terrified the kids and took me a month of sloping off to the GP to convince them that I was fine. Nobody really told their med-handler the truth these days, except for those people who no longer had anybody to talk to. I guessed that the public health algorithms took that demographic into account.

The DI had been stuck in his meeting all morning as well, as Carrie had suspected. It was definitely something to do with Enforcement commissioning. It can't have been the main Board but was possibly a sub-committee. Probably something linking in with Justice, given the DI's involvement, but then the algorithms that recommended attendees at these gigs went crackers now and then.

Despite craning my neck from my desk, I couldn't see who was chairing.

The meeting was taking place in one of the central pods. The architects hated the meeting areas being called the pods, so had called them the 'questing space' or something, but Enforcement just called them the pods anyway. Surrounded by alternating bands of transparent and opaque curves, you could see clearly into the pods, but only a small portion. If people weren't using their own displays, you could never see the public screens but you could see a lot of the faces. Ibrahim must've spotted me nosing around, because he sent me a smiley icon.

I wouldn't be able to make the direct connection, not with my level of access, but I could guess some of the people in that room were those who'd had the brief burst of communication activity on the night the flyer died. Not that this was any use to the case. I couldn't put any of this stuff into a model. It was an educated guess based on the parameters and the pattern. Ibrahim would nod and smile if I told him, but it would go nowhere. Somehow, I needed to get something more.

'Ah, you twat!'

One of the Enforcement admins turned towards me and frowned at my outburst, looking a little concerned.

If the comms flash was truly a bunch of Servants all connected, then it would be public domain. All I needed to do was filter down the likely group.

As a reward for my brilliant insight, I decided to treat myself to another mocha-strike and scurried over to the Enforcement canteen, virtually drop-kicking the order ahead of me. It was waiting for me by the time I'd strode the significant distance through the snaking desks.

'Thanks. I'll take it away.'

As I made my way back to my desk, I called up the Modlee front-end and scrolled back to the last map model, looking for the comms flash again. I noted the time and used it to filter against all possible public meetings which could've been taking place in the dale. It returned five covering a broad range of services. There was a public hustings for a new Servant for Giggleswick, audit hearings on Environmental Services, something called the Airedale Regionale Board, the northern Spinal-Contract Board, and a weekly public health forum. There was nothing specifically associated with Enforcement, even with Justice or the AJC itself.

Deflated, I put in a request for Memro to gather in all the linked docs for these meetings. It would've been tedious to trawl through them myself. Memro would do it much more efficiently. I selected random pattern searches and tried to think of another angle.

As I pondered the problem, sipping my fresh coffee, the small rational man at the back of my head started wagging his finger and admonishing me for not working systematically. He always came out at moments like this. He was telling me that I'd no evidence that justified all the attention I was paying to this comms data.

I ignored him. I knew that this weird comms flare meant

something important.

The key was the fact that the comms indicators had disappeared when I excluded Enforcement activity. Which meant the particular conversation must've been tagged. Somebody – technically it would've been a bit of code, some handler – had classified each comms data as having association with Enforcement. The classifications would be owned by the AJC, specifically the Enforcement meta-designers. The link between the tags and the comms data was probably owned by a subsidiary of the network corporation. It was the law that this kind of data was firewalled off in another virtual organisation. It was only for IG purposes. Nobody could get to that.

However, I knew enough about how the flag at the AJC end would've been assigned. I'd worked on plenty of cases and I knew some of the data designers in Bradford who had tweaked the last release. Basically, it primarily went on the metadata logged on the diary handler. If the event was tagged as 'Enforcement', then it would tag the conversation as 'Enforcement'. If no metadata was logged – which was frequently the case, as people were lazy when they set up diary events – it did a trawl of the outputs of the meeting. If there were no outputs, or the outputs were restricted, it went on the role data of the attendees. I couldn't dig any further into the tags without the IG authorisation needed to access that data mountain at the network subsidiary. And I didn't want to go there yet.

I realised I was back where I'd started. There were too many variables involved. This was too slippery to hold.

I finished my coffee and went over the logic. Why did I think the pattern was important? There was nothing specifically. It was just temporally associated. Plus, it was Enforcement related, which meant it had some higher-level association with Meri and what she was filming.

Then I remembered I'd guessed the meaning behind the locational patterning; it was a Servant pattern. My hunch had been based upon the patterning of that flare. The Servants were the important part of it. If I couldn't get anything from Enforcement, perhaps I could just ask the Servants? There were enough of them in the pod. Some of them must know something about it.

Having watched enough detective vidz, I knew the format. You just needed to ask the people in power some impertinent questions. Get ballsy with them. Inevitably, they got the huff and threatened you with being fired. But they always revealed something.

I had about half an hour to get my questions in some kind of appropriate order. As I was rehearsing them for the third time, I noticed three Enforcement operatives come up the stairs by the cafe. One of them was Jonah.

'Alright, Haz,' he called out and wandered over, clapping his two buddies on the shoulder as he left them.

'Morning,' I said. 'Going well?'

'Yeah,' he said. 'Just about to pick up the commander.'

'He's here today?' I asked.

Jonah pointed his nose at the pod in the middle of the room. 'In there.'

'Oh, aye,' I said. 'So is the DI.'

'Ibrahim?' said Jonah. 'He puts himself about a bit, doesn't he?'

I shrugged. 'As long as he leaves me be. What they doing in there, then? I never seen that lot before.'

'New sub-committee,' Jonah said, yawning. 'Some bright idea of that new Chair of the Enforcement Board, Kazza, or something, in't it?'

'Kaz.'

'Yeah, her. Anyways, she wants to create stronger links between Enforcement and Justice. This is supposed to be about that, I think.'

'How do you know that?' I asked.

'Commander told me.'

'Oh, right.'

'He thinks it's stupid,' said Jonah. He rolled his neck and massaged his shoulders. 'I feel broken.'

'Been on night shift?'

'Yeah, trying to save up some proper leave, like. But it's costing me. Hitting the streets of Saltaire and Keighley every night for two week snow.'

'Shit. You on risk money?'

Jonah grinned. 'We're all on risk money, Haz. That's why we do it!'

We spoke about the kids for a few minutes, until the time came for the meeting to break up. Jonah scooted off to catch up with the two other operatives. I'd started hovering by the doors a few minutes before the scheduled ending, hands dug into my trouser pockets. I could see them clicking their fingers, picking up their messages. Some were stretching and chatting to their neighbours. I chose my moment and went for it. Pushing at one of the many doors, I bustled in and strode up to the front of the room.

'Sorry about this, everybody,' I said, raising my voice. I could feel my face turn immediately red. My med-handler had spotted my heart rate and was jumping about like a jack-in-the-box at the end of my display. I ignored it. The finger clicks would be too obvious.

'Haz,' said Ibrahim, frowning. I could see he was concerned, a little alarmed.

'Won't take a moment, DI,' I said. 'While you're all here–'

'Are you with Ibrahim, young man?' asked an older gentlemen. I thought I recognised him as Arathan. He was quite a senior Servant, representing our dale in London.

'I'm with Justice, yeah,' I said. 'I just wanted to ask a couple of questions how... How many of you are representatives? Servants of the people? Quite a few, right?'

There were nods. A few of the Servants were still in discussion with their colleagues. There were two impatiently waiting at the door. Ibrahim had frozen behind his chair, knuckles white against his dark skin. He was trying to smile but I could see a new look in his eyes. One I hadn't seen before which might've been terror.

'Excuse me,' said an Enforcement officer from the back. I recognised him as Jonah's commander. He looked quite old, only a few years from retirement. He also looked tired. 'Is this protocol? These people have got other meetings to go to, son.'

'This isn't protocol,' said one of the Servants. She turned to Ibrahim. 'What's going on, DI? Is he one of yours?'

'Haz,' said Ibrahim gently. 'I think we'll wrap this up later, yeah?'

'Just a minute,' I said. I could feel the heat in my face transition into sweat. I was conscious of it on my forehead. 'It's about a board meeting... or something that you would've had on...'

I struggled to remember the date. I punched it up on my display and gave the date that Meri had died. Most of the Servants, those who were still packing up their things in the pod, shrugged and shook their heads. Some of the more polite ones, who clearly felt a little sorry for me, made an effort to check their bead displays, but they also shook their heads.

'Not us, son,' said Arathan.

'What about a reposting site?' I struggled on. 'It's called Violence Without Limits.'

'We know all about that,' said the Enforcement officer.

A few of the Servants also nodded and some smiled, in a knowing but sad manner.

'DI Al-Yahmeni,' said the Enforcement officer. 'Who is this

guy?'

Then things got a little dizzy and I needed to sit down. I felt some hands holding my shoulders and keeping me upright. I thought I could see Jonah and then the commander and a couple of admins.

I heard a voice in my ear. It was the DI. 'Let's go get some air, Haz.'

* * *

We walked out of the building into a light rain. Directly in front of us, raised on its concrete stilts, was the humming ribbon of MC17. Beyond it, grey cumulus chunks had started to stud the blue sky. It was getting warmer but it felt like the rain could get heavy any minute.

'You feeling better?' asked Ibrahim.

'Yeah,' I muttered.

'Why don't you get yourself home?'

'I'm here for the codes.'

'The codes?'

'Yeah,' I said. 'To interview Kaz Furness.'

He looked at me seriously. 'I've thought about that, Haz, and I'm not authorising it.'

'What? Why? You agreed.' I was whining. I hated myself.

'Get yourself home, Haz.'

'Need to be here. Waiting. I'm waiting for Carrie.'

'Is she coming in?'

'Said she was going to.'

'No,' said Ibrahim. 'I didn't think she was going to be in the office today.'

'Why?' I asked. Suspicious and paranoid.

'Well,' drawled Ibrahim. 'I spoke to her first thing. She was going to be at home, she said.'

I stopped in the street and looked at him. 'She spoke to you today?'

'Yeah,' he said. Then he forced a laugh. 'Before I lost three hours of my life in that pod!'

'She didn't say anything …'

'What?'

'Doesn't matter,' I said.

'I spoke to her about the case,' said Ibrahim. 'We both feel that... well, we both feel that you probably ought to be working on something else now.'

'What?' I said, ears pounding. I angrily killed my now frantic med-handler with a noisy wrist slap. My movements were so uncontrolled, I nearly ending up punching Ibrahim in the stomach. 'You spoke to Carrie about that?'

'I spoke to Carrie about a lot.'

'About what hit Meri?'

'That the victim got hit in mid-air,' he said. 'Yeah, I spoke to Carrie about that.'

'Something hit her,' I said, my voice hot. 'Isn't that sufficient, DI... isn't that enough for a murder investigation... at least, for some deeper analysis?'

'We need to do some more work on the collision, yeah. But that's Carrie's area. Not yours.'

'What if it were deliberate?' I hissed.

'There's nothing in this for you,' said Ibrahim. 'There was a mid-air collision, that's all.'

'The flyer was making vidz for a group's reposter... she was investigating the riots and that.'

'I know,' said Ibrahim. 'I've been reading your notes, Haz.'

'You've seen the vidz, then?'

'Nobody's bothered by Violence Without Limits,' said Ibrahim quietly. 'We live in a free, democratic country. It's the New Democracy. Enforcement welcome reposters like that... Jaime was talking about it the other day with some journalists. She name-checked that exact reposter. I was there when she talked about it. Check the vidz, I'll send you the links. Reposters like that prove that we're in a different place politically. Nobody wanted to see that poor girl hurt, let alone killed. The fact that she had the freedom to do the filming she was allowed to do. That's evidence which the commissioned service and the Servants here are all operating in our New Democracy.'

I was silent for a moment, my head reeling. 'But what about the communications that took place earlier... the one nobody seems to know about?'

Ibrahim held me by the shoulders and turned me to face him. 'Listen to yourself, Haz. You've got to step back from this a bit. Get some perspective. You're seeing stuff that just isn't there.'

'They were Servants...' I trailed off, hearing what I was saying. I felt sick.

'Go home,' said the DI. 'Get some sleep. I'll send you over the new case tomorrow.'

Chapter Ten

I slept well, which surprised me. I'd dreamed of waves of human flyers above the dale in V formation, heading north from Africa. Then I'd been one of the flyers. There may have been something about building nests under the arches at Stitsils. Maybe not. The more I tried to grasp at the threads of the sequence of events, the fainter it seemed. But I'd felt happy in the dream. It'd felt good to ride the thermals and to be buffeted by the winds. The feeling of satisfaction in positioning oneself with accuracy alongside your companions. I hadn't dreamed like that for a long while. It may have been the fact I'd avoided Memro and stayed clear of the VC. The thought of snorting spores made me feel ill.

It was Thursday which meant, by general consensus, that the evening would be the start of the weekend. Although Admin Friday was supposed to be about clearing out your messages, tidying up your outstanding paperwork and the like, people mainly used it as any policymaker should've guessed it would be used for – an extra-long weekend.

The Friday Act had come about mainly because of subcontractors like myself. My dad always insisted it was because of all the email crap he'd had to deal with in his day – manually, as well – but I'd read convincing arguments which pointed to the boom in subcontractors. We were supposed to have been given the additional time in the week to handle our invoicing and timesheets and follow up on new work, market ourselves and all that stuff. Nobody ever did, of course, but the Act had proved so popular no government had had the nerve to roll it back.

I was planning to take the children down to see their grandparents in the SLS the following day. Normally the children would be at school on a Friday but I could see from my messages that they'd also be off. Something to do with their incomprehensible study plan. Opportunity to let them see their grandparents and give me a bit of time away.

It was a dry and warm morning, so I decided I'd work at the park rather than the office. While I was making my way past the Saltaire ground, I dropped a message to Greg to tell him I would take the kids on Friday. I got a rather curt reply to confirm he'd received the message. Wrong 'un.

The New Saltaire Park ran up the eastern side of the dale. It'd been knocked together by a subcommittee of the Amenities Board within the last year and the trees were still bedding in. The area had come up as available for development following a land dispute between the planning guys and a construction firm out of Dundee. Dundee lost. The decision was to knock down their partially-built nest of modular builds and let the Amenities guys turn it into parkland. The actual trees and turf I was walking over were a mashup between a park that had been ripped out of the middle of Bradford and whatever they could pick up wholesale from a forest in East Sussex. It was a good park. I liked it because it gave you views of the mill.

I found myself a dry enough patch of dirt under a sweet chestnut and plugged myself in. This was a good spot. I was pleased. One of the few free trees in the busy park.

If a stranger from another time had dropped in on that slope of grass and trees that morning, they would've assumed the human population of the world had become afflicted by some condition. All around the grounds, on benches, under trees, lying on the grass, there were people alone, twitching their hands and talking animatedly to the air above them.

I worked through the morning. There was a lot of finalising of the caviar case to be done, so I concentrated on that first. The box icon for the new PO Ibrahim had sent me over first thing pulsed quietly on my screen, reminding me what I needed to deal with next. It had a little name tag floating beneath it: 'Grahams-Flint'. It glowed a satisfying green. The little box with the name tag 'Sturgeon Farming' was glowing a bright red. I was late with the caviar case. I was first to admit it: I had an erratic working pattern.

Once I'd packaged the caviar case narrative, linked all the evidence and causal justifications, I dropped it back into the AJC server files. It was a solid piece of work. The story I'd built was well-evidenced and elegantly argued, I thought. The DI would be alerted to its upload once it hit the servers. Sure enough, I received a congratulatory note from him almost immediately. No presentation needed. This was a relief but not a surprise. It was his style to simply kick it along to the prosecuting advocates, so I expected the courts would book it later in the day.

Then I turned my attention to the new case, slapping at the green box. It unfolded its contents. I skimmed the summary and a readme file which I checked this time. Thankfully. If I hadn't, I would've wasted a lot of time. There was somebody I needed to ring. I blinked up my contacts and twirled a finger to find the name.

Louie Daine.

I twitched a cheek and the calling tone sang in my ear.

A face appeared on the display. Staring up at the sky, it looked as though the face was superimposed upon the clouds. Like the face of God. Although Louie looked nothing like a god – I assumed – it was an image he would've loved to cultivate.

'Hasim Edmundson! How're you doing? Thought you were dead.'

Louie liked to talk a lot of nonsense. He once told us he was part Chinese. We all knew that he was part Kazakh. He worked as a digital analyst in the Central Manchester Justice Branch by day. By night, he liked to boast that he sang songs online to billionaires from New Delhi. Naked. Which was probably rubbish as well. We'd trained together for six months in Bradford which seemed a long time ago now.

'Hello, Louie,' I said.

'You know something, Haz... I sensed you were going to call me.'

'I know.'

'You know everything about me,' Louie sighed. 'This isn't a personal call, is it?'

'Afraid not.'

'You phoning me about the Grahams-Flint thing?'

'Yeah,' I said.

Louie squinted at me from his clouds and looked serious. 'Haz, you're in a bad way, pal.'

'I'm fine,' I said stiffly.

'Rubbish! Look at you, look at your face! You should get yourself over here. We should get a drink. I hadn't realised–'

'Realised what?'

'Nothing,' said Louie. 'But seriously, try and come see me. Stay round ours. I'll get Barry to make noodles.'

'Thanks,' I said, trying hard. 'Yeah. That, would be great.'

Louie paused again, concern in his eyes. 'Anyway, the Grahams-Flint thing. Where do I start? They're a smallish company, based in Stockport. They're a vat making place, bespoke and all that. Family-owned, three generations. Current CEO is Jenni Flint. She's been doing the job for years, now in her late fifties. It's been ticking along fine. Now, have a look at this.'

A graph flashed onto my display, squeezing Louie's face into a comedy miniature at the top right corner. The graph showed sales by time, across a three year period. I knew the corporate analysts loved this kind of stuff. Fred Dancuk – our busiest business-fraud analyst – was forever cornering me in the cafe, trying to explain that a graph could tell a story, that it had drama. Even I could see the tale behind this one was a classic. The jagged-edged line started with a sharp increase for the first six months and then plateaued for about two-and-a-half years. This was a company launching and doing reasonably well. Then it got interesting: three months ago, it'd started to increase again, sharply. In the last couple of weeks it had dropped off again, creating a huge spike.

I highlighted the increase from a few months ago. 'That's what we're interested in, is it, Louie?'

'That's the monkey,' he said. 'Look at that spike – that's a moneyshot! Only, Grahams-Flint had done nothing, according to Ms Flint, that is. They had no change in operations, no big marketing spend, nothing. They were busy, sure, they kept taking in the orders, but they'd not caused the demand. She's claiming ignorance. Said she was happy for the business, of course.'

Inside, I was sighing. I'd seen this same story about a dozen times. I'd been hoping Ibrahim had been kind and given me something interesting. 'You got the testimonials rating?'

'You're ahead of me,' said Louie. The image flickered and another line superimposed itself on the graph, matching over time but a different vertical axis. This was the testimonials rating. It was supposed to provide some kind of aggregate index of positive comments from reposting agents. I didn't know where it came from – somewhere in Dallas, probably, they tended to – but it habitually correlated to sales activity.

And it always coincided with this kind of content farming crime.

The DI was a wrong 'un.

'False testies, in't it.'

Louie nodded. 'Straight up, pal.'

It were a crime to knowingly provide false testimonial. The law had been that way for years now. Back then, thousands of businesses had ridden the development in AI by releasing viruses that filled every available messaging site with positive reviews of their products. It'd been an exhausting but straightforward task to test the validity of these basic postings. You had to find evidence of other posting activity, parse the comment through a variety of academic groups, in some cases prompt for follow up.

Then things became more sophisticated. Whole sheds of kids had been found in suburbs of Cairo chatting away to grandmothers in Chengdu, telling them that this particular shampoo was the best they'd ever used. As ever, analysis got more sophisticated as well and the international community understood their markets were going to rattle out of control if they ignored it. The sheds got closed down. Then the problem started to disperse.

Which was when they started hammering on the doors of ordinary citizens, demanding evidence that they'd, in fact, bought and enjoyed a particular album of Kurdish ambient. Meaning nobody posted any reviews, so only trusted reviewers received any airtime, and the AI viruses pretended to be trusted reviewers. And so businesses started to go down the pan which was when they whined to the European government and it was officially criminalised across the world.

'What's the Airedale connection?' I asked.

'You know a place called Oxenhope?'

'Course,' I said. 'It's an estate outside of Haworth, in't it?

Up on the moor.'

'Well,' said Louie. 'That's where we picked up the last of the reposting activity. That's in your dale, Hasim. We need you to go and see what you can find.'

A servicedrone spotted me from across the park and banked sharply in the air, heading in my direction. It was a lurid little green-and-yellow number. I recognised the colours. Must be a Dommies outlet around here somewhere.

'Sure, I can drive on up there.'

'Sweet, I'll wrap up the leads and throw you the whole package.'

The servicedrone whined to a halt in front of me. A tinny samba sounded and then it spoke. 'You want any coffees or chocolates, man?'

I tried to wave the thing away with my free hand. 'I'm OK. Thank you.'

'High five for partnerships, brother,' said Louie.

'No problem,' said the servicedrone. 'What can I get you, man?'

'Yeah, high five,' I said weakly. I was fairly certain that Louie was joking but you never knew with him.

'High five, man? We don't have any high five, I'm afraid. Is there anything else you would like?'

'Just go away, alright!' I hissed at the service drone, muting my mic.

'You alright, Haz?' asked Louie. 'Looks like somebody's give you trouble.'

'Damn machine wants me to order a coffee,' I said.

Louie laughed. 'Oh, right. I'll let you sort it out. Chill out, Hazzie. Take care of yourself. And get yourself over to see us, yeah?'

'Yeah… I will.'

The connection closed and Louie's face disappeared from the space in front of my eyes.

'Is there anything I can get for you, man?' asked the drone again.

I raised myself from the grass and tried to land a kick on it. 'Go away, sod off!'

It whizzed away, leaving behind an unconcerned rattle of drum. 'OK. Have a nice day.'

Around the park, other workers had raised their heads and were staring at me. I tried to ignore them and turned to the package which had appeared on my screen. I opened it and started to read. It took me about an hour to fully understand the leads the Manchester analysts had tied together. They'd done a good job tracking down locational positioning of the messages. There was enough data in the bead's positioning signals to fill a few servers. There was also something about the company in there, as well as background on Jenni Flint and her management team. I started to read.

At about midday, I got a call from Greg. He looked upset.

'Morning Greg,' I said, mind still tracing associative paths. 'What's up?'

'Sorry, Haz,' he said. 'Gotta call off this afternoon.'

'Oh, why's that?'

'Stinking cold, man.'

'OK, sorry to hear that. Have I had it?'

He rattled off a long code. I never remember the bloody things but it didn't sound familiar.

'What about the kids?'

He shrugged. I guessed it was going to be one of those conversations.

'I'll pick them up, Greg,' I sighed, gritting my teeth. 'You take the afternoon off. I'll see you on Monday, yeah?'

'Thanks. Bye.' He cut the call.

It shouldn't have upset me, but there was something in his abrupt manner which annoyed me. I spent the rest of day fuming.

* * *

The South Leeds Sprawl was generally referred to as the SLS. Unless you were a Servant from one of the old towns and then you hated any acronym. They were still trying to carve out a Unique Urban Presence. They did this by clinging onto the old names: Batley, Dewsbury, Wakefield, Normanton. Everybody knew they were now just another mega-burb of Leeds, though. No amount of branding contracts or media stories could hide that fact.

I'd grown up here, trudging the endless kilometres of houses, riding the flyover cycle tracks at night, watching the laser displays from the city centre light up the cloud base with advertising slogans. It'd seemed so glamorous to me, the centre of Leeds, at that time. Of course, you hit a certain age, and the level of glamour – previously seen in places and people – swiftly became proportional to their accessibility. I came to realise that Leeds, Manchester, even cities further afield, were just towns of people trying to survive like me. Who probably thought Airedale was an edgy spur somewhere in the north. Where they lived exciting lives and had exciting jobs.

No accounting for idiots.

I'd toyed with the idea of popping both the kids in a car and sending it on its way. Then I could have a bit more time on the case. It would've been perfectly safe. Other parents frowned on stuff like that but sod em. I was a single dad. Single dads get special dispensation when it comes to people telling you how to look after your kids. You get to say shut up.

In the end, I felt like I wanted the journey as well. The Grahams-Flint case was clearly going to be more tedious. It was all clear-cut narrative – proper copy-and-paste – bar tracking down the actual wrong 'uns. And then, after the weekend, I would take a car up past Howarth and check out Oxenhope. Wrap it all up and give it to Louie with a bow.

During most of the journey, the kids watched vidz and I dozed. But as we got near, I asked them to turn them off. The noise was bugging me. This meant, unfortunately, they started asking questions.

Asha was interested in what had happened to Greg.

'He was fine yesterday,' she said.

'Why do we get colds, Dad?' asked Ali.

'Dunno,' I said. 'Study at school and you can tell me.'

'I know why,' said Asha.

'Do you?' asked Ali.

'Not telling you, though.'

'You don't know!'

'I do,' Asha gloated.

'Dad, why do people get ill at all?' asked Ali.

'Nobody knows,' I said.

'You don't know why Mummy got ill?' asked Asha.

'Shh. We're here,' I said. The car was pulling up on the kerb. 'Be good for Grandma and Grandad, OK?'

'OK, Dad,' said Asha.

'What's Grandma done to her hair?' asked Ali.

My mother was about the same height as me and my dad. She was thin in the face, which made her look taller. She'd never willingly given into old age and had, I noted with a bit of a groan, clearly requested a tufted style at the last visit to her hairdresser. This was what the teenagers had been going crazy for over the last few months. It made you look as though a toddler had been let loose on your head with a razor. As usual, she had continued to eradicate the few greys with viral-dye treatment.

Dad had started to get fat, I thought. He had always been active – cycling, swimming, parkour and nonsense like that –

but his ankles had started to suffer. I was beginning to see the old age catching up with him.

'First we're going to the park,' said my mother. 'Then we're all going shopping. Then you are all going to help me shell some peas. How does that sound?'

For the rest of the day, I sunk into my habitual semi-conscious state. There was something about home life that allowed me to do this. Nobody really expected you to perform, beyond domestic chores. You needn't even communicate fully. I'd spent much of my teens and most of my twenties grunting and shrugging my way through the house and the park.

Also, as well as the mood of being at my parents' induced, I realised I was still furious at Ibrahim for what he'd done to me on the flyer case. Despite trying to stop myself, I was running scenarios in my head on how to get back on the case. How to resurrect it. I knew it still had life. I knew there was a crime there. It couldn't have been an accident.

I kept spotting women in the market who looked like Meri Fergus. One of them caught my gaze and coolly returned my stare with deadening animosity.

Late in the afternoon – tired of watching the children dust my parents' kitchen floor with Uzbek flour – I went looking for my father.

Dad had been a coder, then a meta-designer, then he'd tried to be an entrepreneur and had lost it all. He did odd jobs now, tweaking bits of code here and there. He'd got into repairing damaged beads. Nobody knew why. Beads were disposable tech. Once they broke, you chucked them out and bought a new one. My mum thought it was because it proved something for him. I thought it was daft.

I found him in the workshop, a converted attic with walls covered in hundreds of small drawers, all containing new and recovered components from beads and other electronica. He had lapel pins, cuff-links, earrings and noserings. There were integrated beads still glued to roughly-cut bits of material, retro rings, and even some colourful little numbers glazed in pinks and purples. I knew, grimly, that these were still likely to be connected to bits of somebody's cuticle.

These things couldn't be repaired by hand tools. They were too bulky. My father had bought a second-hand micro-engineering unit, a toy, really. A tragic, chrome device he had in front of him on his piled up desk. It linked into the channels of your house server and you could manipulate the various moving, cutting and soldering tools through hand movements. He slotted something into its side and flicked it on.

I peered into one of the drawers on the desk. It was hard to resist the urge to stick a finger in and rummage around the pieces, but I knew, from childhood experience, this would lead to a furious explosion.

'What are you working on now then, Hazzie?' my father asked. When he worked on the beads, he never wore one himself. He liked to use an old-fashioned screen. There was a roll-up pinned to the wall behind his desk. He still used the same old gloves, as well. Some hand-me-downs from an uncle who had done engineering at the York Science City. He liked to think they gave him more control. I thought he was talking rubbish.

I watched the screen, as the finger twitches moved the microscopic tools closer to the broken connection. 'Nothing much, Dad.'

'Can't talk about it?'

'Nah,' I said. 'It's not that. Well, can't give you names and addresses and like but... it's just not that interesting, yeah.'

'I'm always interested in your work, Hazzie. Always have been.'

'I know.'

He looked up at me, carefully pulling his fingers away from the table. 'You've been very quiet. Is it a difficult case?'

I laughed. 'I'm just tired.'

'Woman trouble, then!'

'Dad!'

'Did you… you know,' he said, finding it difficult to say. 'Did you try that service that… well, the subscription? You know, the one Asha gave as a birthday present?'

I frowned. At least he admitted it. Mum kept feigning airy ignorance whenever I brought it up. 'That's none of your business, Dad.'

'My grandchildren are my business,' he said, being slightly huffy.

'No, they're my children.'

He looked as though he was about to initiate a detailed rebuttal of my views but ended up sighing a little and turning back to the screen. 'Yes, Hazzie. They are. We're only doing it because we care about you.'

'Let me get on with my life,' I said. I felt as though I'd gone back twenty years, which only made me even more irritable.

'Don't blame your mother,' he said. 'She's worried about you. Proper worried. Me and all, if I'm honest–'

'It's a murder case,' I said, a little too loudly.

He edged the tools across the screen with the tiniest movements of his hand. There was a momentary pause. 'That's different. For you.'

'I've done similar cases before. You know, when there's a digital angle, and that.'

'Oh,' he said. 'So there's a digital angle in this one?'

I paused momentarily before answering. 'I think so.'

'You think so?'

'Yeah. I think so. I'm only halfway through the work.'

'And those poor sturgeon. What happened there?'

'I filed that one. All finished.'

'Good. So you've gone from dead fish to dead–'

'Dad!'

'Sorry,' he said. On the screen, he made the connection fuse and brought in a finishing tool.

'There's a testimonials thing as well,' I said.

'Again?' he asked. 'I hate those people.'

False testimonials really got my dad angry. Not murderers, though, it seemed. You can't choose your parents.

'Pretty tedious one, that. Going to follow that one up after the weekend.'

'Oh yeah? And what's the next move on the murder one?'

I fell silent. 'Dunno. See what turns up.'

He turned to look at me again. 'I see.'

* * *

At tea, my parents fussed around their grandchildren like attentive birds at a busy nest. Ali especially liked visiting the SLS because he got the food he liked to eat: kebabs. My mother had cooked up a large pot of Gujarati rice, little dishes of steamed carrots and peas, and my father had done his bit and filled a gravy boat to the brim with spicy dhal. I realised that I'd had this meal regularly since I was about ten. I didn't mind, as food had never interested me much, but I was beginning to wonder whether, as my parents got older and older, this might be the only meal they were able to prepare.

'This is lamb from Airedale,' said my dad proudly. 'That's up your way.'

'I know,' said Asha. 'We learned about it in school.'

'I was reading,' said Dad. 'That Airedale meat is on the up again. Winning lots of awards. There's some place... Dale Flatts, I think it's called, that's where all the good stuff comes from. That's Darren Caines, in't it?'

Caines. Who had been talking about Caines? He'd been on the news yesterday morning. A massive bull of a man, with ginger implants still bedding in across his shiny scalp. 'Yeah, they've been winning awards, and that.'

We settled down into the seats and started to eat.

I wanted to avoid the inevitable conversation about MoreThanSum and my cock-up with the last opportunity. 'So, Mum,' I said. 'How's work?'

Mum had the worst job in the world. She was supposed to encourage rich professionals from Karachi and Mumbai to jump on a plane and enjoy the cultural heritage of Wakefield, Batley, and Dewsbury. She worked for a tourism development company that had repeatedly won the contract for the combined neighbourhoods of the SLS. Having grown up in the place, I'd always found it amusing to hear her talk about it. But somehow, she'd managed to make her employers some money.

'It's wonderful,' she said, carefully pulling a chunk of lamb off the skewer and dunking it in the dhal.

'That's not what you've been telling me,' said my father.

'Well, we're a bit stressed, that's all,' she said.

'About what?'

'That rating thing,' said my father. 'You tell him.'

My mother chewed and glowered at him. 'We're being pressured for the Regionale rating.'

This word seemed familiar, but I couldn't locate why.

'What's that?'

'The Regionale? It's their new... what do you call it? I can't remember the word.' She frowned. 'Supposed to represent a region or summat.' She paused and spoke with the coldness of a judge passing sentence. 'I don't understand it.'

'Have you got enough water, Ali?' said Dad.

'What's it measure?' I asked.

'Yes, thank you, Grandad.'

131

'No idea,' she snapped. 'But it's right important, apparently.'

'Why?'

'Can I have some more dhal, please, Grandma?'

'Of course, love. Because if it's high, it means we're doing well.'

'You mean for your company?'

'Thank you, Grandma.'

'And me, Nan!'

'Ali, don't shout like that. And it's Grandma.'

'I'll get him some.'

'No, the region. Dewsbury, Batley and the like. The SLS, you know! It's the… what did they call it? I think they called it an "index". The index for the region.'

I nodded. 'Makes sense.' Where had I heard it before? I was itching to twitch my cheek and start tapping out a search on my archive. I'd deliberately left my processor at home, though. Something one of my therapists had convinced me I needed to do. Lock away the processor at weekends. I had to leave work at the door on a Friday night (or Thursday, depending on my mood). I was wishing I had it now. Any rummaging around in the Modlee system, or my work files, would've sparked off an alert to Ibrahim. I hadn't checked, but I was guessing that he'd already revoked my A-codes for the case anyway.

'Anyway,' she said, ladling more dhal over my kebabs. 'Tell us about you. How are things going with that dating service you've signed up to?'

Dad winced but I could tell he wanted to know as well.

Asha grinned up at me and nodded. 'Tell us, Dad.'

I took a deep breath and forced a smile. This was going to be a long weekend. And I'd used up all my spore.

Chapter Eleven

The rest of the weekend with my parents had been tiresome but not unpleasant. They'd not given up trying to work out whether I'd managed to arrange a meeting with anybody from MoreThanSum. They even started to question Ali about it, which I considered desperate. So, late on the Saturday night, I'd snapped and told them it was none of their bleeding business. The subject hadn't been mentioned for the rest of the weekend.

Sunday was spent working our way through the twisting snake of the pop-up outdoor market that connected Batley with Dewsbury. The children had demanded – and received – numerous trinkets. Baby elephant carvings from Iceland, leaping electronic building blocks, living paint. In the afternoon, we walked alongside the river and went to a computing museum – more for my father's benefit than the children's. We ate a big heap of Yorkshire puddings with chickpea curry.

On the journey home, with the children snoozing in the back, I started to dig around the files I'd dropped onto the processor from Modlee. I remembered the term which my mother had been discussing and tapped it into a search procedure. This scurried around my processor's files and returned a hit within milliseconds.

Airedale Regionale Board.

After a few hand flicks, I found their minutes and agendas saved and unencrypted in my temp files. I couldn't remember why. I tried to think why I would have them saved locally. Then realised they were one of the public boards that'd been in session during the evening of Meri Fergus death. This was interesting but I still couldn't see how it was helpful. There was no obvious connection between the Regionale Board and Meri's death. I ran the comms model again, freezing when I got to the spike of activity. After I'd poked around with the parameters, I was surprised to find there were also flags for 'Regionale'. I'd never noticed it before, but it seemed to be legitimate.

However, when I selected the Regionale flags, the model went almost completely blank. Just a bright cluster of activity where I guessed the Board must've taken place. Looked like it was up in Stitsils somewhere.

I checked out some of the names on the Board. It had a few Servants I recognised. I'd never heard of the chair, a Servant for Cowling. Somebody called Abi Hassan. Her pic showed her in an Italian headscarf, wrapped tight to her face. She was pretty. Reminded me of one of my cousins from Lahore. Then I spotted the name Darren Caines and his porky red face. He seemed to crop up everywhere. His factory was between Keighley Basin and Stitsils. He probably had offices up there somewhere. It may've been where the Board had met.

Still, all this was pointless off-the-clock musing. I wasn't on that case now. I needed to get on with the Grahams-Flint work from Monday and I really wasn't looking forward to it.

Chapter Twelve

—

The following morning I was up in Oxenhope and I wished I had a gun with me. But analysts weren't licensed. Not even the few analysts that worked for Enforcement – and no, nobody could explain to me what they did either – were able to carry a weapon. Not that they issued you with proper guns these days. The wrong 'uns still had them but Enforcement operatives were supposed to survive on shockstix, tanglers, and a variety of tranqs deployed from a variety of different mechanisms.

One of those mechanisms was hovering by my left shoulder as I stepped out of the car. Its tiny rotors whined like a big mosquito. Beneath its threatening carapace there hung an array of two dozen smartdarts. This thing could take down an entire street battle if it had wanted to. Except it wasn't that clever and it was as likely to put a dart in the back of your own neck before that of a wrong 'un. At least it also had a camera, so your own take-down could be replayed for the amusement of your colleagues.

I tilted my head towards it carefully and spoke gently. 'Close proximity.'

'Yes, sir,' it said, with a clipped, metallic voice. It came in so low, I could've flung out an arm and embraced it. Of course, that would've been a stupid thing to do.

The weekend's sunshine had been chased away by a cooler, northerly breeze, which had also brought in a fine drizzle. Up here, right on the Pennine ridge itself, the wind came in strong. I would've hated to live up here in the winter. Nobody who could afford to live in the dale wanted to live this far out. Oxenhope was frontier land now. Between here and the Basin were derelict industrial units and residential clusters which, although seemingly empty and dead from a distance, still managed to cough out life like grass growing through a pavement.

What little work there had once been up on the Pennine ridge had long ago moved to the equator. Anybody who was able to get work elsewhere had done so. The Servants had attempted a policy – a hated policy – of Collaborative Managed Decline. A fancy title for something that involved a shite load of taxpayers' money being spent on 'reducing the residential footprint'. The end result was Oxenhope. Huge areas of cleared, barren land, striated with rubble moraine, tangled briar nightmares and purple explosions of buddleia. And placed irregularly between were these few ancient towering blocks. Monsters built in the moulded-modular style which squatted, majestic but dark, amid their ruined kingdoms, like giants from future times.

I advanced towards one of these brutes, picking my feet carefully through the layers of glass and scrap metal. The building rose like an old-fashioned beehive into the grey. Each of the globular living modules was supposed to be snapped into the underlying superstructure, as required, and the place had thus been able to grow with demand. The theory and it worked fine when the residents flooded in.

Nobody had read the fine print of the contract, though, and so when it came to reducing the number of modules, the local Servants had found themselves stuck with an expensive headache. As I neared, I craned my neck up and saw the gaps in the structure. Modules which had been burnt out, dismantled for scrap, or had been simply blown up in a miscalculated narco-strain experiment.

The ground level was open to the elements, other than a hexagonal arrangement of pillars at either corner, each with an integrated lift, and a small central staircase. I summoned the lift and jabbed at the buttons for the sixteenth floor. So far, I hadn't seen another soul. Except an old woman in the distance who seemed to be pushing a trolley laden with meat towards the hills out on the wasteland.

Taking the lift was a mistake. In such a confined space, the security drone sounded like a trip to the dentists. I stepped out onto the sixteenth floor wanting to swat it. I was met by a circular corridor, living modules attached to both side, facing into the inner courtyard area and out to the wilds beyond. I couldn't decide which view was worse. I turned left, heading down the corridor, pursued by the drone. Thankfully, once I'd located the right door – 1623 – the thing rose to the ceiling and attached itself to the metallic struts which held the tiles in place. Its rotors fell silent.

I glued my warrant to the wall next to the door and the tiny beacon flashed an alternating pattern of purple and blue.

There was no sound coming from inside the flat. Which didn't mean there was nobody there, of course. I hit the bell icon and hammered the door.

'AJC,' I shouted. 'Commissioned operative.'

Whoever might've heard that lie wasn't coming out to check. Around the curve of corridor, an elderly couple with a toddler, hand-in-hand between them, had stepped out of the lift and were watching me suspiciously. I waved at them and smiled, pointing to the logo on my cap. Shaking their heads and muttering to each other, they turned and headed away, disappearing around the curve of the corridor section. The toddler kept peering over her shoulder, staring up at the drone which had parked itself above my head.

Once they'd gone, I turned back to the door, and twitched on my AJC beacon. 'Police override,' I said, feeling very self-conscious. 'Open the door.'

Normally, in situations like this, the use of the formal authorisation – via voice or hand signal – should've activated door lock's inbuilt mechanisms. It was a legal requirement that all buildings built in the last twenty years could be opened by this override, called the coppers' knock. It should've worked. It didn't.

But I wasn't surprised. I'd been vidding the whole thing, ensuring this had been noted for the record. Overriding the AJC codes was a criminal offence. A minor one, naturally, but you had to get the wrong 'uns for what you could. It tended to mean that beyond the locked door you found something pretty bad. Like a tankful of unlicensed koi. Or a tiger.

I rummaged in my pocket and retrieved a pocket toolkit. I'd had this since my tenth birthday. The AJC could issue you a proper toolkit for such situations but that was for RapidRez and guys like that, not for analysts like me. So I got out my toy screwdriver.

I hacked away at a panel next to the door, revealing a bundle of wires and fibres. I'd managed to dig the end of the screwdriver into my finger by this point, so I was sucking the blood off it while sorting through the wires with my other hand. I found what I was looking for and pulled the thick fibre out from the rest of the bundle. This was the data pipe between the residential flat module and the block's servers. With my non-bleeding hand, I dipped into my pocket again and found a clamp. I attached this to the wire and squeezed. A tiny probe in the device bit into the pipe. Contact.

My bead immediately started flashing emergency signals from the block's servers to my screen. These were automatically dealt with via the AJC A-codes in my bead, ready for such occasions. The server eventually calmed down, convinced I was from Justice Branch and not some wrong 'un trying to cut-and-clear the place. I started to sweat a little less. It wasn't about to call in a squad from Enforcement. Which would've made my day. It didn't help my mood to know anybody in Enforcement would've simply shoulder-barged their way in after one minute of arrival. Not pissing about with screwdrivers and all this rubbish. Reaching across my body with my free hand, I dug into my other pocket and switched on the processor. Having satisfied myself that I wasn't about to spray the inside of the corridor with blood, I flickered my hands in the air in front of me. I dropped a few commands from personal files into the processor from my bead. My processor started to work its way through the defences put in place in the flat's servers. To use the processor for this was pure brute force, but it was effective.

The door opened. The drone immediately dropped from its perch above me and swooped into the room. Then I went to work.

We digital analysts must've had a good union in the past or something. We were always on the scene looking for data-bearing tech and sweeping a room was a routine op. We all knew a gibbon could do it, of course. If you could get it to hold the sliver-detector, that was.

Once I entered the apartment, I quickly worked out nobody was at home – oblivious to the problems my compatriot in the air was having – and proceeded straight for the digital analyst's mother lode: the flat's local server. Usually these were embedded behind a light switching unit but whoever had owned the flat had ripped this out and dropped in a more portable version. I found it humming away in the back of one of the cupboards in the kitchen. It was designed to look like a tin of sardines. Given time, I could've done a soft extraction and just emptied the contents straight into my processor but

I didn't want to be in this flat too long. So I got a quick vid pulled from my bead and then picked it up and threw it into my pocket. It was warm which felt unpleasant for a tin of fish.

Then I started the sweep for other devices. These were generally slivers but there were plenty of other, more old-fashioned means of hiding data: retro disks, household items, antique tapes. Some people had even buried their ID codes in the pages of books. These were always a problem. Written data wasn't about to be picked up by the scanner. You had to be a tedious frigging analyst to capture that kind of information. It was about as much fun as reading.

The scanning device had once been a metallic-looking glove but I'd accidentally split the palm of it a few months back, so it didn't stay on my hand very effectively. Also, I was very self-conscious of the fact you had to present it as though you were offering up your hand to be kissed. I didn't want any vidz of that being discussed back at Shipley. So I held the torn glove stretched out between two hands and ran it over bookshelves and cupboards, watching my bead display for any likely readings.

I'd found two slivers already, tucked into a couple of bars of unused hand soap. I was going through the kitchen again. There were some readings from the fridge-freezer. It wasn't uncommon for wrong 'uns to drop a load of dodgy data straight into a domestic appliance. They thought they were being clever, but it was an obvious storage place. Except my bead had already scoped out the fridge and the freezer as utilities, as well as the lighting, the coffee machine, even the headphones and the foot-massager. The readings I was getting came from inside the freezer itself. After poking around inside, I worked the signal was coming from a pack of frozen mince.

Sighing, I pulled it out and slung it on the counter. Behind me, I heard a clatter. I turned, adrenalin suddenly surging.

And then I saw the drone on the floor of the kitchen.

'Close proximity,' I said. Possibly squealed. 'Status report, now!'

'I have a power malfunction,' said the machine. 'I am re-setting my system.'

Various LEDs on the machine started to flicker.

'Power up,' I said.

'Re-charge required,' said the machine. 'I'm sorry, sir.'

Then all the LEDs went out.

The panic didn't come on fast but crept up in little lapping waves. After a few kicks of the drone had failed to restore life, I gave up on it. I hurried to try and hack out the slivers from the frozen meat instead. It would've taken me at least five minutes to cleanly extract the slivers. I didn't want to wait that long. I considered defrosting it in the microwave but, despite their general hardiness, even slivers couldn't survive that kind of treatment.

There was only one option. I'd need to take the bloody thing with me. Unfortunately, I'd need the drone as well. Not that a technical fault was my problem, but for an analyst to leave a dangerous piece of kit like that out in the field would've caused trouble. Problem was, I was running out of arms.

I started rummaging through the cupboards in the kitchen, looking for a bag or some kind of carry-all.

'What the fuck you doing?' barked a voice behind me.

I froze and started to turn towards the voice. 'AJC. I'm an operative–'

Then I got a hard boot in the back and slammed forward into the cupboard. My cap was ripped from my head.

'Don't fucking move, pal,' said the voice in my ear.

I could hear a few clunks and clicks and then the whirring noise of a fan. A small crackle was followed by a chirpy ting. My bead had just been microwaved. I sighed. I thought I might be sick.

'Are you Darrop?' I said. 'If you are, there's a warrant outside your door.'

'Is there?' said the voice. 'I couldn't find one.' I could hear the sound of something being stamped into the floor.

'I've got delegation,' I squeaked.

'So have I,' he said, and poked the end of the gun in the gap between my shoulder blades.

'This is all on official record, Mr Darrop,' I stammered.

'No,' he said. 'It's not. Nowt leaves this flat, pal. I've made sure of that.'

'Alright,' I said. 'Just let me go–'

'You got owt else on you?' he said, his face close to my ear. 'More beads and that?'

'No,' I said.

'Get up,' he said, wrenching me to my feet. I could now see, in my peripheral vision, that he had some kind of assault rifle. Something that'd leaked out from the US troubles or from the African crossings. It looked real enough. His hand started to go through the pocket of my coat on my right-hand side. Being as gentle as possible in my movements, I dipped my left hand into my other pocket and deftly removed my processor, trying to palm it away from his sight. As he shoved me to the side, to get to my left-hand pocket, I hid my hand with my body and passed the processor to the other side.

'Stand still!' the man shouted at me.

'You're pushing me, buddy,' I whined, and feigned a stumble, falling to my knees. With my right hand still hidden by my body, I pushed the processor block underneath the cupboard a little way. Unless you were low to the ground, you couldn't spot it. I'd managed to place it so that one of the rudimentary cameras it carried was facing out to the room.

'You've got a lot of shite,' said the man, dumping my tools and devices on the counter top. 'You're not an Enforcement operative, are you? You just some half-cocked burglar or what?'

'I'm an analyst.'

He laughed. 'Really? What are you doing here, then?'

'You know.' I knew I needed to play for time now. The processor wasn't capabe of sending a signal to Shipley HQ. Anyway, even if I could send a message, it would be a good half hour before anybody bothered turning up. But it might be possible to get into the flat's servers. This meant somehow I had to get up to the root control display.

'What's that?' He'd finally spotted the powered-down drone.

'Shockdrone, yeah.'

'I can see that, you idiot! What's it doing in my kitchen?'

'It's broken, in't it?' I said.

The man laughed. 'Bunch of amateurs!'

Thankfully he'd still not made me put my hands up. Hidden by my body, I quietly squeezed thumb and finger and jabbed my thumb upwards in the air. If the camera on the processor was pointing in the right direction, it would've picked up the command. It was the hand signal to open a display on the local nodes. On the floor in front of me I could see the flickering patterns of the projector trying to find a human eye to focus on. I needed to get it to stop flickering about. It was going to draw attention. I tapped my fingers together and dragged the display into a fixed location.

'Listen, buddy, I can help us both out here.'

'Yeah?'

There was now a small image projected against the grubby fabric of my trousers. Unfortunately, it was upside down. I could've turned it the right way up but I knew I only had a short window to operate. I clicked and drew up a menu to access all local networks. I found the flat's functions. He'd not locked down the domestics.

'You're in a of bit trouble, buddy, you know?' I said.

'Oh yeah? Who's the prick with an AK in their back?'

After a frantic scramble through an old-fashioned navigation window, I found what I was looking for. I twisted my hand. On the reflections on the floor in front of me, the lights began to dim slightly. My hand continued to twist. The lights dimmed even more. Then I twisted the other direction and they brightened.

'What was that?'

'Eh?'

'Are you doing that? Put your hands up!'

He was pointing the gun directly at my head. I was laughing like a maniac by this point.

'Can't help it, buddy!' I put hands out from away my body. If I put them too high, they'd lose the camera on my processor. I wiggled them a bit. The kitchen lights brightened.

'Stop pissing doing that!' he screamed.

'I'm just making the lights flicker.'

Lights were a waste of time. I tried a different option. One of the movements had made a tile in the corner of the kitchen light up. Sat over the tile was an autonomous vacuum cleaner. I knew what that tile did. There might have been a possibility of moving it. I tried to look down to my leg without drawing too much attention to it. Back up the main list of commands.

'How are you doing that?'

'I don't know,' I giggled. 'Magic.'

He turned towards the microwave, raised his assault rifle, and put the stock to his shoulder. Thinking better of it, he turned the weapon back to me and snarled into my ear: 'Make it stop, pal.'

I could see the light beneath the tile in the floor move to an adjacent tile. I twitched my fingers and directed it across the floor.

The gun was jammed into my neck. I could feel the circle of

the barrel digging into my skin.

'Make it stop!'

The light reached its destination. I wasn't sure how long I would get. Depended on how much juice was required. Possibly a few minutes.

'Are you just the relay?' I asked.

'I don't understand what you mean.'

I looked towards the microwave. 'You've cooked my bead and my frigging hat! It's not recording anything now.'

'I've done nowt wrong.'

'Well,' I said. Just a few minutes more. 'Somebody in this flat's been relaying posts, that's all.'

'What kind of posts?'

'Testimonials, in't it? You know...'

He laughed. 'That's what you're here for?'

'You been writing false testimonials?'

'Do one!'

'What's in the freezer?'

'What do you mean?'

I nodded towards the pack of mince I'd left on the counter top. There was now a pool of blood forming underneath it.

'In there. You got a bit of naughty data, yeah?'

'You've got nothing,' he snarled. 'Take the lot, if you want, I don't care. I'm innocent.'

'Except,' I said. 'You've been pointing a gun at me for a few minutes now.'

'Self-defence! I don't know who the heck you are.'

'How about we play it like this, then?' I said. 'I forget you threatened me with that firearm and you leave with whatever you need from this place? How's about that, eh?'

'How about you go back to Shipley and come back with an actual warrant!'

'I have a warrant,' I said slowly. 'You saw it beside the door as you came in and–'

'I saw nothing.'

'Look, if you're the relay, you'll only need to be a witness, yeah? We'll let you off on a minor charge and that.'

'I'm not a relay!'

'We know you're into this whole thing.'

The gun was jammed in my back again. 'I'm not a relay!'

Then things happened fast. The re-charging tile had done its work. The slumbering drone came to life and whined straight up into the air. The man turned, firing the gun as he went, leaving a line of dusty holes across the wall of the flat. The noise was in instant assault on my ears, making me cower with my hands clasped to my head and I fell to the floor, curling around to face the room as I fell. I watched as the drone tilted slightly, revealing its array, and released first one, then two smartdarts. These fizzed through the air towards the man. He stumbled back and twisted to his side. The sensors in the darts adjusted the propellant flows and they changed direction right at the last minute. The first hit him in the belly. He grunted as it impacted and sank its load into his organs. The second missed him by millimetres and thudded straight into my thigh.

The pain was excruciating. I couldn't help howling. As I slipped into unconsciousness, my only thoughts were that the bloody machine was trying to kill me.

Chapter Thirteen

'The DI's sending you over to Manchester.'

'Eh?' I said, unable to open my eyes. The voice was familiar.

'Have you fallen asleep again?' questioned the voice. I felt a slap on the back of my hand.

'Eh?' I tried to raise my hand to rub my eyes and turned my head to peek out of the corner of my right eye. I was in a hospital bed. They'd made it into a private cubicle by slotting blown-plastic partition walls around me. It made me feel horribly claustrophobic. I wondered if I was having a nightmare.

'That's better,' said the voice. I squinted and a face loomed at me. It formed into someone recognisable. Carrie Tarmell. 'It's me, Haz! Wake up.'

'I were shot,' I breathed. 'Bugger shot me.'

'No he didn't,' said Carrie, shaking her head. 'The drone got him first. You just got tranqed.'

'That's what I mean – that bastard drone shot me!'

'Oh right, yeah,' said Carrie. 'We know that. Everybody's watching the vid right now in the office.'

'What? Wrong 'uns,' I said, coughing. 'You can't. That's me on there. You can't be watching it. What about the IG?'

'It's evidence, in't it, Haz? We gotta look.'

'Evidence?'

'Yeah,' said Carrie, grinning. 'After the alarm signal came through to Bingley, the Enforcement boys and girls turned up en masse to pick you two up. That guy might wake up with a few more bruises than he went to sleep with. He's going down for… well, for summat, anyway.'

'Good,' I said.

'That's not all,' said Carrie. 'DI says you've got a bonus. Friendly-fire bonus, you know?'

'Cos I were tranqed?'

'Yeah, that's right.'

'Ta.'

'Don't thank me. Thank the DI.'

She tapped her pocket, suddenly remembering something. 'Oh, they got your hat back.'

She pulled out my cricket cap. It had a large circular patch of singeing where the old bead had been.

'Ta,' I said, not really meaning it.

'They put in a new bead for you. You gonna take it?'

I shrugged and took the cap off her. 'Could've got me a new one.'

'Eh?' she said, and then patted her pocket again. 'Oh, and these are for you, and all.'

She retrieved a small plastic bag and passed it over to me. 'They were taken from some bag of meat. They said you'd been at it with a knife.' She sniffed her fingers. 'It were lamb, I think.'

'Thanks,' I said, looking at the bag. It contained three small data slivers. I sat myself up and put the bag on the small shelf next to me. The tranquilizer was beginning to clear from my head, but there was a throbbing pain in my thigh.

'Oh, and this is your processor, in't it?'

I took the little lump of tech. 'Ta.'

'Pleasure.'

'This the North Airedale?' I asked, looking around.

She nodded. 'Nice, yeah?'

'What time is it?'

Carrie shrugged. 'Four-ish.'

'Shit... the kids...'

'Dealt with. I spoke to your guy... what's his name?'

'Greg.'

'That's it. I spoke to him. He knows what happened.'

I turned to her. 'What are you doing here anyway, Carrie?'

'Wanted to make sure you were OK,' she said, checking her watch. 'Look, I've got to run now.'

'Carrie,' I said. There was something very important I knew I had to speak to her about which I was trying to remember.

'Yeah?'

'I've learned something about–'

'What?'

Then I got it. 'The night she died,' I said. 'On the same night, there were a Regionale meeting.'

'Who died?' Carrie asked.

'Meri. Meri Fergus.'

She rolled her eyes. 'Haz! Leave it alone.'

I was starting to lose the reasons why I had to tell her. 'I think... I just think it's important.'

'You do?' she said. 'Why?'

'You see, I were speaking with my mum...' I stopped talking. 'I'm not sure. But it's connected. He told me there were other things going on that night.'

'Who did?'

I spoke quietly. 'Clive.'

Carrie snorted. 'I wouldn't listen to Clive. He believes in aliens.'

'I'm just saying, that's all. That there are connections.'

Carrie narrowed her eyes. 'You still think she were murdered?'

I nodded. I felt like an idiot, though.

'Forget about it,' said Carrie, standing up. 'Now you've woken up, I can leave you to get dressed. You've got a busy night ahead of you.'

'Eh?'

Carrie pulled back one of the partition walls. 'DI wants you in Manchester, to finish off Louie Daine's investigation ASAP. They've got a massive fraud case about to hit later in the week and don't want people messing about with rubbish like this. He wants everybody to have wrapped up their work. Whatever it is you're helping them out with, it needs to be sorted in a couple of days.'

'False testies,' I said.

Carrie widened her eyes. 'What did you say?'

'Testimonials, you know. What?'

'Thought you said summat else,' muttered Carrie.

'Eh?' I said.

'I don't deal in your stuff, Haz,' she said. 'I deal in bodies, don't I?'

We both stared at each other and then she shuddered. 'Anyway, you're going to Manchester tonight. I've sorted it all out with Louie – you're staying with him and Barry.'

'What about the kids?' I said.

She shrugged. 'Take them to Manchester? It's not my problem, Haz.'

* * *

It took a while to track down Dad but he agreed in the end. I knew I could rely on him to help out. My sister's kids were forever being dumped on his doorstep. I knew he enjoyed being the responsible adult. He liked to tell me and my sister off for being bad parents. We ignored him. That's what you were supposed to do with your dad when he got to a particular age.

'How are they getting here, Haz?'

'I'll get them a car,' I said. 'Hire car, taxi, something like that.'

'Is that safe?' asked my father. He was stood in front of some kind of shrub. On the screen, it flared up behind his head like a halo of foliage.

'Yeah,' I said. 'Course.' It wasn't. People were always jacking autocars. I couldn't think about that, though. This was just one of those things you had to do as a parent.

'OK,' said my father. 'Let me know when I need to be at home.'

I thanked him and cut the call. I was still outside. Before me were the steps that led down into Stitsils station. It was a grey day. Muggy, with low cloud. Felt like it was brewing up for something ferocious later on. Above the station were the towers and arches of the North Airedale Health Centre. Their off-white facade melted into the clouds behind and the steam and smoke from their impossibly tall stacks exited into the low cloud wisps.

I delayed descending the steps. Something was making me feel sick. Must have been the tranq. If I could've found the wanker who had programmed that piece-of-shit drone, I would've battered his head in at this point. Except he was probably thousands of kilometres away. In a shittier place, if it were possible, than outside the doors to Airedale's largest health centre. And he was probably a she. And had kids to feed.

I twitched my eye and brought up my contacts list, scrolling through for Greg.

'Yo,' he drawled, answering after a very long pause. What was he playing at?

'Hiya, Greg,' I said.

'You feeling better, man?'

'Sorry?'

'Your colleague,' said Greg. 'Carrina or something like that. She called me up earlier. Said you'd been hit by a security drone. Took you down.'

I clamped my jaw down and bit hard onto nothing. 'Yeah, I'm sound, me.'

'Cool,' said Greg. 'The kids are watching vidz. They're a bit tired but they're OK. Oh, hang on.' Greg waved at somebody off-screen. 'I've somebody here who wants to give you a message.'

Asha's face appeared on the screen. 'Hello, Daddy!'

'Hiya, love.'

'Has Greg told you?' asked Asha.

'Told me what?'

'I haven't told him, Asha,' said Greg, off-camera.

'Oh, goody.'

'Well, what is it?'

'We spoke to somebody at… what's the name? At that place… MoreThanSum, that's it. For some reason they were going to stop you using it.'

'Why were they speaking to you?' I asked.

'I don't know,' said Asha. 'Why?'

'Payment's in her name,' said Greg. 'On the account, I think.'

'It is?' I almost shrieked.

'I think it was your Mum's idea,' said Greg. 'They wanted it to be her present.'

'Anyway,' said Asha loudly. 'The man said they could give you another chance.'

'Another chance?' I said, my head still too fuggy to deal with this conversation.

'So,' said Asha. 'You've got a date!'

'A what?'

'A date, Daddy,' said Asha. 'It's all set up. With somebody you've been speaking to already. She wants to meet you. In Glasgow.'

'That's lovely,' I said. 'But I'll need to check and that.'

'You'll go, won't you?' Asha pleaded.

I nodded. 'Yeah. Course. Asha, baby, you and Ali are going to stay with Grandad and Grandma tonight. Can you put Greg back on?'

'OK, Daddy.'

'Yo,' said Greg. 'What can I do for you?'

'Greg, listen. I got to go to Manchester now, buddy. My dad's going to have the kids tonight. Can you get them into a car for us?'

He narrowed his eyes and looked as though he was moving to a different room. 'Technically, Haz, that's illegal.'

'Yeah, I know. Just do it, though, OK?'

'Cars are getting jacked all the time at the moment.'

'They'll be fine,' I muttered, stomach knotting a little and precursor sweats starting to bead on my forehead. My med-handler popped up suddenly, asking if I was well.

'Sorry for asking this,' said Greg. 'But are you OK? I mean, I was told you'd just got hit by a security drone and that.'

'I'm alright!'

'What I'm trying to say is, are you OK to be making these kinds of decisions?'

I thought I might actually be sick on the street. 'I'll give you more overtime, Greg. Just help me out, yeah?'

He smiled. 'I don't want any more money, Haz. It's not that. It's the kids I'm thinking of.'

'Whatever. I'll get my dad to come up. It's not a problem. Bye.'

I cut the call and stumbled over to a small alcove set into the walls of the station entrance. I heaved up phlegm and watery froth. It had been a while since I'd eaten. A passing couple came to check I was alright. I waved them away.

Leaving the scene in a hurry, I clattered down the steps.

Chapter Fourteen

_____

The journey across the Pennines had been well spent. I'd managed to get myself a table seat, near the toilets, and had started to fill the space in front of me with the various detritus from the flat. There were the three lamb-scented slivers, the house-server in the shape of a sardine tin, and two other chunky data slivers found lying around in plain sight. I also fished out my processor block and dumped that alongside the other items. To save on wireless bandwidth – and because I'd started to get a case of the Clives – I carefully wiped the slivers clean and inserted them into the processor. It resembled a partially denuded hedgehog by the time I'd finished. There was something threatening about its reflection in the window glass and the flicker of tunnel walls behind.

If you followed the line down to Bradford and then up past Halifax, you'd never see daylight until you got out at the other end. However, I'd managed to get on a direct connection from Airedale which went up past Howarth and over the top of the Pennine ridge, so the tunnel didn't last for long. Once we were sufficiently clear of Airedale's outlying suburbs, the train burst from the tunnel, flooding the coach with natural light.

As I turned to look out the window, I could see the towers of Oxenhope, far off in the distance. I was tempted to flick them the Vs but contented myself with glowering in their general direction.

It took a while – and a little bit of online research – before I'd taken the metadata from the slivers. Whatever was held on there was so well encrypted, it would've taken Those-Who-Can't-Be-Named at least a decade to bore their way through. Justice, of course, had routed around this particular problem a long time ago. You needn't get to the data itself in order to get a data conviction. You just needed to prove sufficient secondary evidence to make a reasonable judgement. Don't fight the system, wrong 'uns, it'll always win.

I easily discovered that each sliver had been written to five days ago. I knew they'd used an encryption method commonly employed by one of the half-dozen Russian data-gangs. I called up a tool from the processor which could analyse the shape of the encryption. Although it was all black-boxed up, every piece of hidden data revealed a broader pattern. This was a recent innovation on the part of justice teams around the world. It was going to be countered at some point. However, it had been sufficiently evidential to bring in at least eighty convictions in the UK alone, which I knew the DI would support. And when it was countered, we'd find some other dirt on you, wouldn't we?

The shape of the encrypted data was similar on the first two slivers but significantly different on the last. It seemed to suggest textual data interspersed with pix. Depending on the ratio between the two, this could be an online magazine, a manual on bomb-making, or an illustrated kids' story about piggies. However, the pattern here was very regular. It was a solid match for encrypted comments. Comments you'd find posted and reposted across message boards. Exactly the kind of data you'd find in a reposting relay which specialised in providing false testimonials.

I logged the pattern and my conclusions in the case notes,

before turning to the other two slivers. These were chunked up into much larger files of differing lengths. Larger files tended to suggest currency or authorisation-codes, validation-codes and the like. But they tended to be of a regular length. Currency was very easy to match, as the file size of the keys all hovered around the same extent. It wasn't like that with these. They looked like vidz. Given the level of encryption, and the size of the slivers, they weren't massive vidz, either. It was weaker, but I noted the files could be testimonials as well. Vid testies were harder to fabricate, but there was plenty of free software out there which could take a face and make it talk.

I knew I wasn't going to be able to get anything more from the slivers, so I fired up Modlee. Once I'd got in and built a new area, I dropped in the locational data for all the vat factories specialising in lamb protein. I flicked up a map of the world and made the factories glow. There were pockets scattered all over, with the main concentrations along the Nigerian coast and Brazilian ports. There also seemed a large amount of activity in the central Asian countries and northern Iran. I dropped in locational data for known data-farming centres. There were thousands of cross-overs. I filtered out the shit, dug around, and gained access to the meat imports into the EU within the last five days. I dumped into the parameters. The flares on the screen almost disappeared but there were still too many for a solid match, mainly clustered along the southern borders of Russia, in the Caucasus Mountains.

I filtered again, scaling the imports in relation to their proximity from Airedale. I got null. So I tried seeing what kind of data access the case had given me. I was looking for traffic. It'd given me a lot, short of personalised links. I dug around for some vehicle ratio libraries. When I found them, I selected the vehicles with refrigeration capabilities, and dropped these ratios back into Modlee. I set it running through all the vehicles which had come and gone in Airedale over the last five days.

This was going to take a while, I leaned back in my chair and stretched my sore arms. The pain in my leg was back. On my way to the train, I'd grabbed a bottle of water and a packet of dried protein crunch. I'd used most of the water to swill out the vomit from my mouth in the toilets but there was enough to have a sip. I cracked open the packet of crunch and started to throw the salty morsels into my mouth.

Four seats down, on the opposite side of the carriage, a mother was trying to restrain her two toddlers. They looked like twins. They had hooked their elbows over the back of the seat and were both staring at me, watching every move I made to my mouth with the protein crunch. I smiled at them and crossed my eyes. They giggled in response. Their mother rolled her eyes at them and half-grinned at me, apologetically. She rose from her seat and hoisted them back off the headrest.

I was suddenly flooded with memories of Asha's weight at that age. Of the endless, gentle lifting up and lifting down. And the way that they'd tuck their head into your shoulder. But it was their weight which seemed most vivid for me.

Then there were tears in my protein crunch. Making the horrible salty crap even saltier. I hurriedly wiped with a sleeve and looked back down, focusing on the bead-screen in front of me. The results had come back in. I didn't have the necessary A-codes for vehicle tracking – you needed to be onto terrorists for that kind of data – but that wasn't a problem. All I needed to do was to associate two places. I already had the port locations for lamb protein deliveries. This took me to a set of distribution depots. I made an educated guess we were looking at wholesale. So I plugged in the vehicles' ratios of all refrigerated trucks entering Airedale in the last five days back into the public camera footage of everything coming and going through a wholesale-distribution depot. This took about five minutes. There were five vehicles remaining. I plotted the public camera footage on a map and watched five differently-coloured dots slowly move around Airedale. One of them had come to rest three days ago in the middle of Haworth.

I tipped the last of the protein morsels into my mouth, realising I was starving hungry. I took a sip of water and then called up the vidz themselves. It was a plain white van parked up in the middle of a grotty car park on the outskirts of Haworth. Twirling my finger in the air in front of my processor, I fast-forwarded and reversed the footage until I spotted the driver. He was making deliveries to a fast-food restaurant chain. I could've plugged Mr Darrop's face into a ratio-constructor and run this against camera footage as well. But converting raw vidz into facial ratios was massively resource-heavy. I'd have better success simply doing this by hand.

Sure enough, after a few minutes of rattling forward, I saw a figure of a man approaching the van. When he turned, it was clearly Darrop. I took a few frames for evidence and logged the time and location.

The van had transported meat protein from a factory in Ghorvsk. Previous case files on data-farming crime had multiple hits against Ghorvsk.

This was too easy.

Chapter Fifteen

———

'Problem was,' continued Louie. 'Some of it had squirted up onto the table. It was all over his bread roll!'

Barry winced. 'Louie!'

'Ugh,' I said, on cue. 'What d'you do then, like?'

Louie paused to drain his glass. 'Well, I ate his roll, obviously.'

Barry shook his head. 'I wish you wouldn't tell that story. I mean, tell it to everybody.'

'Hazzie's an old friend,' said Louie. 'You should know, Hazzie – Barry's cum tastes like nothing on earth.'

Barry was a huge man with dark black hair and broad shoulders. He was Scottish and a lawyer or something similar. He'd come up from London and met Louie about seven years ago. Next to Louie, who was short and thin, they were a comedy pairing. I always wondered why they were together. It seemed as though, every time I saw them, Louie was trying to work out some way of antagonising Barry sufficiently to get him to dump him and run.

I'd wolfed the meal quickly, and now the gnocchi was lying heavy in my stomach. I'd only been drinking water but I'd insisted they drink wine.

'Hazzie's not religious,' Louie had hissed to Barry. 'He's just a lightweight.'

The end of the meal arrived and Louie fell to telling anecdotes about sexual exploits in public places. Most of these also involved Barry who (it seemed) had very little influence over whether his privacy was going to be protected.

Thankfully, Louie had not been quizzing me about whatever he'd seen in my face the other night. Too little sleep or too much coffee and chocolate? I knew I'd been overdoing the Memro and VC a little recently, but that didn't leave shit on your face. I may have been doing the odd spore – and that left you a little heavy-lidded – but I hadn't dug out that pot from the spice drawer for a while now.

Thankfully, whatever had freaked Louie was left unsaid for the rest of the evening. I made my excuses at midnight, when they became so drunk they ceased to be coherent. I was being polite by not sneaking off earlier, to be fair. I hated that point in the evening when the person opposite you had to take a deep breath just to get a sentence out. They were never worth listening to from that point onward.

The case was still playing on my mind and I couldn't sleep. Although I was a couple of rooms away from Barry and Louie, I could still hear them get down to it. Barry was surprisingly vocal. I realised I wasn't going to be able to get any rest. At least until they'd finished doing whatever it was they were doing.

I heaved myself out of bed and padded over to the window. The house was so old, it hadn't had auto-tinted glass panes. Louie and Barry lived in one of the old redbrick houses that were rampant across the outer rings of Manchester. I knew it was expensive from the size of the garden, the fact it had a garden in the first place, as well as the sheer bustle of trees and ferns infesting it. Louie can't have been earning much as a digital analyst so Barry must've been creaming it in somewhere.

The orange glow from the cloud cover above Manchester

lit up the room. I stuck my head between the curtains and looked out into the night. Most houses in the street were quiet. A lone security-drone, smaller than a wren, flew down the middle of the road, its green LEDs flashing intermittently. A tired, balding man's face, framed by expensive velvet curtains, was at this moment being written to some data mountain. Probably in Kamchatka. I liked to think it was Kamchatka.

I dragged the duvet off the bed and hung it around my shoulders and flopped into a low chair near the window. I pulled on my cap and blinked wide so my bead could do its security checks.

The case sat on the screen where I'd left it.

In my gut, it'd felt wrong so far. Tracking down the data slivers had been too easy. Finding Darrop easier still. I was sure he was being set up as a fall guy somewhere. If the only lead was going to be a factory in Ghorvsk, I was buggered. I had to work out who was going to benefit from this. Darrop was likely to go down for a number of years. There had to be something of value at stake.

I called up the graph Louie had showed me before the weekend. Could there be something in that testimonials rating index?

Modlee's white tabs flared in the darkness of the room around me. I started working by intuition, dragging data sets into visual maps almost at random. I was letting the system do the work for me, letting Modlee make the decisions. Everything was coming out as noise.

Then I spotted a familiar shape. It was the indexed price of Grahams-Flint. One of the many indexed prices, as it was considered risky to raise credit via shares alone. This one seemed to be a newer credit system, involving nested shares. It may have been an old-fashioned hedge fund. It called itself Ghawar. Algorithms-within-algorithms would take buying and selling decisions on behalf of investors. As far as I could glean from reading the blurb on their sites, these algorithms would take feeds from other commonly available indices. One of these must have been the testimonials index.

Comparing the Ghawar index on Grahams-Flint with the testimonials index, there was evidential strength correlation, with very little time lag. This was a responsive service. But it still didn't explain the crime. Financial fraud wasn't my area of expertise but I'd dealt with some similar cases. I plugged in the transactional data in Modlee and tried to identify large trades against Grahams-Flint. There was very little, small amounts suggesting hedging and the like. If somebody was going to be betting against it rising or falling, they were making nothing but pocket money out of it. Grahams-Flint had benefited a little for the additional sales, but their rating was now at rock-bottom. The owners had not profited. Nobody else had profited. Where was the crime?

There had to be a crime. It involved a Kalashnikov and a relay link in Oxenhope. I knew the place was dodgy but that kind of set-up didn't spontaneously spring into life. I knew there was a crime here somewhere. I could smell it.

Then a thought occurred. I called up a list of other bespoke vat manufacturers like Grahams-Flint. The list was phenomenal. I ranked them by the level of Ghawar index-based trading over the past few weeks. There was some general noise but one company stood out from the others. It was a major player called SLSV, based somewhere in Louisiana. I plugged its Ghawar index into the graph alongside the testimonials index. As the Grahams-Flint index peaked, the SLSV index had started to drop. Not by much, but clearly a drop. Then I plugged in the trades. There was a huge investment in SLSV as it reached the bottom of its Ghawar index. Shortly afterwards, there was a huge sale once it had bounced back. Just as Grahams-Flint had started to fall back. Somebody had made millions.

We just had to find out who that person was. I was done.

I was starting to feel tired, at last. I took myself back over to the bed. Louie and Barry had fallen silent. Thankfully I was so plugged into the work, I'd missed their climax. Before I lay down and pulled off my cap, I thought I'd check something. It might break a few IG rules but who cared? Nobody was watching. Weaving my fingers in the air, I pulled the trades data and plugged in a new date. A very familiar date. There'd been a lot of movement that night, like Clive had said. I tried to see where the activity had been centred but it was lost in the international trading relay. Somebody somewhere was making serious money.

I then pulled up the Airedale Regionale index.

Correlation.

I wrote a short note to Carrie and fell asleep.

Chapter Sixteen

———

The vast room would've swallowed a football pitch easily. At least, I thought it could've. I'd no sodding idea how big a football pitch was, of course. Come to that, what they looked like. I estimated football pitches had fewer server boxes, for a start.

We were walking across a steel mesh floor, beneath which were laid twisted, heavy coils of optical fibres and power cables. Inside the room, it felt like being close to an immense organism. The place hummed. Stacks of hissing storage banks sprouted from the floor at regular intervals, like prehistoric monuments, taller than a man. Extraction vents, fans, and huge air pumps covered the walls, producing a deafening noise.

'We're with Justice,' Louie told the desk.

This was the North-Western European Security Storage Facility. Every second of all footage from all state-commissioned security cameras from each of the countries in the bloc flowed through this one room. There would be vidz of people throwing bottles at each other in Limerick town centre, high-def stillz of somebody having a piss in Tromsø, and zoomed-in close-ups of couples giving each other oral sex on Beach Front South, Amsterdam. Each of those faces would be captured, processed, and translated into ratios. A precise shorthand for the key characteristics of your face, which would never change. Unless you mashed yourself in an accident and lost your nose, eyes and mouth, those ratios would be logged against time, location, activity, and proximity to other ratios. And on and on and on.

Algorithms checked for patterns of fighting, stealing, and intimidation. They'd be crunching through the images and categorising the scenes. All of which would be indexed for fast retrieval. Each country who supplied the vidz could stick a pipe into the data and use it for their own security purpose. Everybody could see everybody. If I'd have fed Darrop's ratios into this particular data mountain, it would've given me every time he'd hit a quayside in Brittany to a snowfield in Finland.

Except they wouldn't have let me. Although the sheer weight of the data rushing into the facility was enough to induce a laxative effect on you, it was the weight of IG that affected me more. Simply standing here – being allowed to stand here – was making my knees turn to masala custard.

The number of legal and privacy frameworks colliding in this one room were so complex that there was another, equivalent-sized building across the other side of Manchester, full of lawyers dedicated to the problem. There was no way I'd ever get the A-codes to see everything in that room. They'd given me a taste on the Meri Fergus case. Then taken it away. Only for the serious cases were you allowed to play in this room.

Or if you worked for Those-Who-Cannot-Be-Spoken-Of.

'We're just having a look around,' Louie had told them.

As one would expect, security was set to a low-risk appetite. Gangways circling the upper floor were full of heavily-armed private security contractors. Every technician or group of sightseers like us had at least two of the security personnel tracking our progress and keeping a beady eye on our movements. Alongside the human security, there were also stationary smartdart arrays slung from the ceiling, ready to deploy at the merest hint of dodgy behaviour. You made the wrong kind of face and they were going to fill you full of tranq before you could ruin your pants.

'Pretty cool, yeah?' shouted Louie, in my ear.

I nodded. It was good of him to bring me down here. He needn't have bothered, but I'd spoken about it before, and I suppose he thought it was something he could offer as a treat. The facility was positioned under the Manchester Central Justice department, below the basement levels, so we merely had to trot down the staircase for a few extra floors. It was underneath their own offices because their Justice division had won the commission from Europe to provide an intra-national role in cross-border police. They had stuck in this facility as part of the deal and Louie loved showing it off.

'Bet you hit this baby about every day!' shouted Louie. 'The stuff you're doing.'

'About that, yeah,' I shouted back.

Yeah, right.

We had just wrapped up the last of the Grahams-Flint investigation and packed off our bundle for review by Louie's DI. It was a neat package. The primary narrative laid out was based upon discoveries from the night before. We made the case that it was a mid-level Russian mob operation to artificially deflate the Ghawar index price of the American vat-makers through the use of poorly articulated and virtually unhidden false testimonials.

On the back of the case, Jenni Flint had been released back to her job. I still had to provide some input into the Darrop sub-case – his provision of an illegal relay. His threatening-with-a-weapon was being picked up by some analyst in DI Husane's team.

Although Darrop was just the fall-guy in the whole

operation, I hadn't liked the fact he'd stuck a gun in my back. I wanted to see him in court. I was confident. The analyst had already caught me on my chocolate break, barking out a cursory interview through my bead. She seemed to know what she was doing. I hadn't suffered for nothing. The pain in my leg still hadn't gone away.

'When are you off to Glasgow?' Louie shouted in my ear.

'Carlisle,' I said.

'What?'

'It's Carlisle,' I said. 'I'm going to Carlisle now. We agreed to meet halfway.'

'Oh, right,' he said. 'When did this happen?'

'After lunch,' I said.

'You animal,' Louie shouted. 'Going for a dirty night in Carlisle.' He paused. 'I'd have chosen somewhere else, myself.'

I shrugged and smiled weakly. What was I supposed to say in this situation? 'Yeah. But you gotta take it when it comes—'

We were interrupted by one of the security operatives shouting down to us and waving us away. 'Please make your way to the exit, gentlemen!'

Louie gave him a friendly wave and started dragging me back to the airlock. I noticed the smartdarts in the nearest array had swung around to point directly at me. Despite the cool of the air-conditioning I'd immediately started to sweat. Not helped by my knowledge of smartdarts. The programming which went into those buggers would identify sweat from nearly thirty metres. Perspiration was yet another indicator that demonstrated you were a potential threat.

'What's going on?' I shouted in Louie's ear.

'No idea,' he said. I noticed he had stopped smiling and he was walking more briskly than usual.

On neighbouring gangways, other operatives had swung their weapons round barrels loosely aimed in our direction. I started to hurry now, overtaking Louie and forcing him to break into a trot to keep up with me. Had one of the sombre figures on the gangways brought their weapon up to their shoulder, I think I would've started to run.

'Steady,' said a voice from above. 'Nice and steady, gentlemen.'

When we reached the airlock and stepped out in the lobby area, we were met by further security members.

'What's the problem, Tienes?' asked Louie.

'Him,' said one of the operatives. She was in charge of the squad guarding the entrance. Her unfocussed gaze indicated she was studying something via her bead display. 'He started to come up as an AG.'

'What the hell's an "AG"?' asked Louie.

'Amber-green,' said the operative. 'He's not clean.'

All eyes in the lobby turned to me. I felt my face flush. 'What've I done?'

'We don't know,' said the officer. 'We don't get any more information than the high-level indicators. AGs aren't allowed into the facility.'

'I weren't AG when I went in, then?' I asked.

'No,' she shook her head. I could tell she was struggling not to pull a comedy confused face and shrug her shoulders at me. 'Sorry... I mean, sir, we have criteria to follow. I'm afraid you are unable to visit the facility any more. I mean... at all.'

'Sorry,' I said to Louie.

'No problem. I just want to know what the hell you did. You flick the Vs at a bunch of cameras or something? Pissed in the commissioners' azaleas?'

'I dunno, must be one of those things, you know. Glitch in algorithm, and that.'

I was trying not to think about the shockdrone in Darrop's apartment.

Chapter Seventeen

———

Sadie McManus was what my mother would call petite. It wasn't a word I'd ever used in conversation but even I could see it was a useful generalisation. Sparrow-like is what my father would've called her. But then he was into his birds. MoreThanSum had run its algorithms – rubbish as they were – and found somebody who was, like me, a little bit Asian.

I wondered, bitterly, whether I was going to find out her husband had also killed himself in a remote piece of Scottish moorland while she was reading to her children. Whether she had tucked them in, ignorant of her husband choking on a bespoke designer-toxin and the blood that was spewing up from his disintegrating throat and stomach-lining.

Whether she'd sat up a little while and then gone to bed, in mild irritation that he had caused her some mild upset to the routine. Whether she had woken up the following morning, having slept through the whole night without a care and had even taken the children to school before trying to find out what had happened to the man she had sworn her life and love to.

Whether she regretted quite a few of the decisions she had made on that night.

I doubted MoreThanSum had found somebody like that. But there was always the possibility.

'Hiya,' I said, conscious that I was being too brittle. 'I'm Haz, yeah.'

'What?' she said.

'Haz,' I repeated. 'I'm Haz. Haz Edmundson. Hasim. You can call me Haz.'

'Oh,' she said, forcing a smile. 'So sorry. Aye, I'm Sadie.'

I wasn't sure whether to shake her hands or give her a kiss. The former seemed ridiculous and to go for a kiss right at the start would be too much. I settled for an awkward nod of the head, which turned out to be weirdly slow, as though I was a samurai awaiting orders. I was cocking this up like a proper moron.

'You hungry?' I asked. 'I mean, do you want to get something to eat?'

She smiled and nodded. I wasn't hungry at all. She probably wasn't either. She didn't look like she ate much.

'Aye, Haz that would be great. I'm starving.'

People who addressed me by my name in conversation always made me edgy. It reminded me of the DI. There was something predatory about it, like they were saying they owned you because they knew your name like a spell.

'Yeah,' I said, looking up and down the street. 'What do you like eating?'

'Oh, I like anything,' she said. 'What about you?'

'Me?' I said. 'Owt, really. Never really thought about it.'

'Me too.'

There was an Austro-Malay restaurant three doors down. The signage outside suggested it would be OK. Not too grubby, anyway. As we made our way past the couples and groups of young'uns out on the town, I remembered Austro-Malay didn't always settle easily. Malay meatballs, especially, always made me a little queasy.

'You ever eaten kangaroo?' I asked, as I held the door open for her.

'Of course,' she said. 'All the time. I love it.'

I was out of conversation. Beyond plugging on with the inane questions. 'What about crocodile?'

'I prefer alligator. Can we have a table for two, please?'

'Of course. By the window?' asked the waitress.

'Unicorn?' I babbled, as we followed the girl past other couples and families.

She was about to sit down, but looked at me and laughed. 'No. That would be weird, wouldn't it?'

'Yeah,' I said. 'It would.'

They only ate unicorn in Japan.

I ordered a kangaroo pattie with simple breads and salads. She went for a fish curry. I was glad we'd agreed to split the cost of the meal. Fish was out of my league.

'You're an analyst, aren't you?' she asked. 'With the police?'

It was weirdly retro to hear that word. Cute, though. I nodded. 'Yeah. Airedale.'

'Airedale?' she said. 'That was going to be next big thing, wasn't it?'

'Was it?'

'Aye. I was reading it was once the fastest-growing region in the north.'

'North of what?' I asked, trying to smile.

'I don't know,' she said, and laughed. 'North of somewhere, I think.'

'What about you?' I asked. Sometimes I wished I drank. Whether it was because of me not drinking – or whether it was just evidence MoreThanSum had done its thing right – she'd asked only for pineapple juice with the meal.

'I work for the Forestry Commission.'

I nodded with a smile. My bead, which had been stuffed into a pocket with my cap, started to whine at me.

'Sorry,' I said, reaching for it. 'It might be about the kids.'

'Of course,' she said. 'I'd do the same. Go on.'

Rather than putting it on, I held the cap in my hand. The bead adjusted itself and found my eye projected an image. I could see the small image of Carrie's face pulsing on the screen. I sighed. With a twitch of the eye, I blocked the call.

'Anything wrong?'

'Work,' I said. 'Never stops, does it.'

'Oh,' she said, smiling. 'I don't know.'

'So,' I said, moving clutter away as the drinks were brought over by the waitress. 'It's Forestry Commission, is it? You cut down trees? You a lumberjack?'

'No,' she laughed. 'I'm not a lumberjack, although it would be fun, wouldn't it? And, before you ask, I don't plant them, either.'

'Right,' I said. 'What d'you do with them?'

'I count them.'

'Eh? I mean... pardon?'

'I count the trees.'

'One by one?' I said.

'I run the software,' she said. 'We put aerial footage through a service we subscribe to. I buy satellite stillz from the Euro military and use those, mainly.'

'Euro military? Fucki... I mean, bloody hell!'

'Aye,' she said, mock-serious. 'Military. I'm playing with the big boys now.'

'You ever find owt suspicious in those stillz? Alien landings and that?'

She shook her head. 'No. It's really dull. You see poachers now and again.'

'You report them?'

She laughed. 'Well, I'm guessing those stillz are about five years out of date... so, no, I don't bother, normally!'

I laughed as well. As we both drank, I thought about it a minute. Then something occurred to me. 'You feed data into tree census?'

'Of course,' she said.

I think my father had once been involved in the tree census. At least, he always talked a lot about it. It was probably more of an excuse to have a wander through remote parts of the country. Despite being a bit of a hoarder, I didn't have him down as one of the extreme collecting types. There have always been those kind of people who need to collect things like vehicle numbers. There have always been others – or possibly the same people – who need to see every variety of bird and discuss the fact they've seen every variety of bird with others like them. Now we had them on the trees. It had been going for years now. Something in your bead would take a picture of a tree, work out what species it was, log its position, and fire that off to the census. They were nearing the ten billion mark now.

'That's not what you're paid to do, though, is it?' I asked. 'I mean, census is just a bit of fun, in't it?'

'Yeah,' she said. 'I do it for the Forestry Commission, not the census. The Commission needs to keep track of its assets. The information I collect on the trees is used by the money guys to… I don't know. They call it leverage or something. Anyway, they can make some money on the back of my numbers, that's all.'

As the conversation progressed I'd found myself sinking into a comfortable place. Like putting on a jacket I hadn't worn for years, it was strange, yet surprisingly familiar. I realised I was enjoying myself. I was enjoying talking to someone about, well, just about stuff. The message from Carrie had nearly thrown me off. The thought about Sadie's tree numbers being used to generate money also sparked off thoughts of both the Meri Fergus and the Grahams-Flint case.

Thankfully, the meal arrived at that moment. I could safely kill any more discussions of data and money.

'Tell me about your kid,' I said. 'Then I'll tell you about mine.'

We carried on talking for another hour, about our children, a little about my job, about Scotland. I was scrupulous in avoiding any mention of Dali. Sadie was being as careful about her husband. I was feeling relaxed and was wondering what we should be doing afterwards. I'd already called up home and relayed the rendezvous details to Asha, who I was expecting to squeal with delight but who was oddly sombre about the whole thing and formally told me she hoped it all went well. My parents were very glad to keep the kids for another day and to sort out Greg and school and the like. Although they never said as much, it seemed they were assuming I was going to stay overnight in Carlisle.

Sometimes, my parents weren't very East Pennine.

I hadn't even thought about the plans for later in the evening. I was only here because I'd been forced into it, but I was enjoying it now and I wanted to spend some more time with Sadie.

'You want to see the sea?' I asked, as we paid the bill.

About fifty years ago, Carlisle had been suffering. This had been sheep and cow country. When the place had run at profit, it had run on narrow margins. When the meat-vats had started taking off, it had wiped out most of the remaining hill farmers and Carlisle was worst hit. Apart from a limp tourist trade and whatever minor industry could be cobbled together with public grants, there was nothing going for the place. This was on top of the fact that the Eden River – which flowed through the middle of the town – also had a perennial flooding issue. So, trying to solve both issues, somebody had managed to convince the European government to throw some regeneration cash at the town. They were supposed to spend it on turning the place into a holiday hotspot and stop the flooding.

Somebody had a brilliant idea. The ambition had been courageous. Some might say it had been foolhardy – that means 'fucking stupid', if you're posh. But they'd done it and brought the sea to the doorstep of town, by the simple plan of digging a great wedge of it inland. Carlisle was re-classified as a coastal resort. And Carlisle had a seafront.

The place still flooded at the merest sniff of rain, of course. But then, there was no accounting for a complex system like that.

And nobody came here for their holidays.

Sadie and I strolled along the promenade which ran alongside the estuary banks. Behind us, in the distance, the castle was lit up from below by a mixture of municipal LED arrays and the flickering campfires of vagrants. Beyond the mud flats and fields to the north, we could see the sky illuminated yellow by the New City of Torduff, Little England across the Firth.

We looked down into the brown swirling waters beneath us.

'It's not the Outer Hebrides, is it?' said Sadie.

'No, nothing like that.'

'You ever been?' she asked.

'Once,' I said. 'Just a holiday, like.'

'You liked it?'

I stared at the water, not wanting to be sad. 'Yeah. It were grand.'

She snuggled up against my shoulder. 'Maybe you'll go back? One day?'

'Yeah,' I said quietly. 'That'd be right good, yeah.'

A security drone, bristling with darts, was suddenly behind us. As I caught sight of it in my peripheral vision, I staggered and slipped on the stone, falling on my arse. I think I even released a frightened yelp. Afterwards, I kicked myself for doing so. This was exactly the behaviour they were programmed to pick up on. Sure enough, it twirled in the air and banked over to us, stopping a few feet out of reach in front of us.

'Haz,' said Sadie. 'What's wrong?'

'Nothing.' I heaved myself to my feet.

179

'Doesn't look like it.' She gave me a hand to help me to stand.

'Surprised us, that's all.'

She stared at me a second and then turned to the machine. 'What does it want?'

'Dunno,' I said.

'Are you sure you're OK?'

'Fine,' I said, finding it difficult with legs still a little jelly-like. 'I'm fine, yeah. Just took me by surprise, that's all.'

We both stared up at the camera sensor for a few moments longer. Eventually, the drone passed by, swinging its way back towards the centre of the city.

Two minutes later, I got a notification trill from my bead. I checked. It was Carrie. I could see the start of the message.

I need to talk about what killed…

I twitched my eye, instinctively, to bring up the full message.

I need to talk about what killed the flyer. I can meet you tonight. Can you be at my place in an hour?

Carrie's flat was in Shipley. There was no way I could make it in that time. My fingers danced out a reply.

Two hours?

Yes. Quickly though, and no speaking to anybody else.

'Sorry,' I said, turning and giving Sadie a small, apologetic smile. 'Kids. Gotta run. I'll call you.'

I leaned forward to give her a kiss. I hadn't even thought about whether I should. It felt right. She froze and I stopped, nearly toppling over in the air. She nodded. 'OK. See you soon, then.'

'Yeah.'

As I half-ran back down the promenade, I could hear her shout out after me. 'Hope they're OK, Haz.'

Chapter Eighteen

———

'Carlisle? What were you doing up there?'

'Doesn't matter.'

'Where're the kids?'

'With their grandparents. Picking them up tomorrow.'

The roof of Carrie's apartment block had once housed a lush garden of low shrubs, herbs and creepers, entwined around a snaking arbour of wicker. Of course, somebody's maintenance contract had expired and nobody had commissioned a replacement. Some of the residents seemingly tended to it but it was starting to look a little overgrown and the fixtures were rusting. It was generally used as a place to have parties. Or, if it was quiet and still, a place to drop yourself into some designer haze. As a result of too many accidents resulting from the latter activity, some serious steel mesh had been unpleasantly welded to the top of the waist-high balustrade which ran around the rim.

Carrie had been insistent I'd not enter her flat. Or her 'lair', as she called it. Might have been too much of a mess. Perhaps it was because she thought I was a vampire and the like. She could've had a row of chickens lined up for sacrifice. You never knew with Carrie.

So we'd come up here, well after midnight, listening to the hum of Shipley. Loudest were the throbbing bass beats from the bars and clubs, intercut with shrieking party-goers on the street, and punctuated by the sirens of passing ambulances or Enforcement teams.

Thankfully, the rioters were concentrating their efforts further up the dale this evening, so people were able to get out for a drink. I'd watched the shark-faced Servant – Kaz Furness, the one who I'd spoken to with the DI – do her thing on the media channels earlier in the evening. Watched it while coming over the Pennines and past the old viaduct. It looked like she was taking all the heat on the violence.

There were Regional Servants being interviewed as well. This was bad news for Furness. If Regionals were starting to take an interest, she was in trouble. If she wasn't able to sort the problem out, they could be sending up the N-Guard from the south or down from Scotland. That would sort the wrong 'uns out. Would've been bad for Airedale, though. To be bailed out like that. I could see this Furness woman was worried.

Having said that, I didn't care much about what kind of problems she was having.

As there were few clouds in the sky, it was a chilly night, but still warm enough to chat without shivering. We found a bench at one remote corner of the garden, as far away as possible from a couple sleeping together in the faux meadow grass.

'I started working on the gecko files as soon as I got home that night,' said Carrie. She was speaking in a low voice.

'Yeah?' I said. 'No hanging about, then?'

'No. You know the speed the DI works at. We've got to turn this stuff around in fast time. So, before I went to bed, I'd taken the pathologist's report, run my own bone matches, and got a positive ID. Messaged DI the name after midnight… or sometime. Coroner's got it a short time after.'

'Sweet,' I said. Thinking about case-turnaround, I realised

Ibrahim hadn't posted me any more POs since I'd wrapped up the Manchester angle. It wasn't unusual for the work to come in spikes, but this was still a slight niggle. I had rent, Greg's wages, and credit was a little stretched. I wondered when Enforcement were going to pay me off for having my leg shot by one of their drones. 'That's quick.'

'Would've been quicker,' said Carrie, elbowing me. 'If I'd not had to drag some loser's heavy arse back home.'

'Yeah. Sorry.'

She laughed. 'No bother. Just hope you'd do the same for me one day.'

I sat silently for a while. Then I had a thought. 'Did he respond?'

'What?'

'DI. When you messaged him? Did he message you back?'

'Course,' she said. 'Mind you, I'd drunk quite a lot by that time. I can't remember what he said.'

'He spoke to Meri's parents at some point the following morning,' I said, not really listening. 'Coroner's report had come in. He'd already made up his mind by then, hadn't he?'

'What?'

'That it were accidental death. That there weren't an investigation worth bothering with.'

'So?' said Carrie. 'I knew as soon as I'd seen that footage from that kid's camdrone, it were going to be written up as some kind of freak accident. I weren't that bothered.'

'But you carried on with the investigation. You carried on digging, yeah?'

She nodded. 'That were your fault. You muscling in on my case. Talking about a digital angle and that. You got the DI to give us the case. Don't know what kind of case it is, mind. You still think there's summat digital in this?'

'I didn't,' I said, smiling. 'But now, I kinda do think so, yeah.'

'What you found?'

I ignored the question. 'You still think it's an accident?'

'Dunno,' she said, and shrugged. 'But what you sent me last night got me thinking. That's why I tried to call you.' She fell silent.

I waited for a moment. 'Carrie?'

'Yeah?'

'So, go on then. What hit her?'

Carrie stretched out a leg and smoothed down the faded denim of her jeans across her thigh. An image was projected onto the surface from her nosebead. 'That hit her.'

I looked at the image. It was a rendered model of some kind of three-dimensional object. It spun in the air in front of me. It looked a lot like a child's beaker on its side.

'What's that?'

'Nosecone of a Type II Buzzard shockdrone.'

'Nosecone? Never seen one of those things before.'

'You'll never have seen one at all, I reckon. Least, not at night.'

'How come?'

'Because they're too high up. They have to take off from an airstrip or summat. Then they get themselves up high.'

I nodded. 'I see, yeah. How'd you find it?'

'Well,' she continued. 'After I'd done the facial ID, I crashed out, didn't I? Got up early and started analysing the gecko footage… trying to work out how she died, like. I took the path report and tried to match up with what we'd found on the scene. We had a hole in the roof. And where she landed on the floor. So, didn't take long to do the usual… you know, direction and stuff. She fell from over seven hundred metres. Direction of the fall was fractionally south-by-southwest, by a few degrees. She was travelling at close to two hundred kilometres per hour when she hit that roof. Went in arse first. That's why she did the back of her skull. But the damage to her face, to her cheekbone, that weren't the impact of hitting the factory. That were summat different. I could pull up a model of what had smacked into her. They found nowt more at the hospital. Coroner put death as being caused by collision. Impact to the head. So I knew that's what I were working with.'

'When we spoke to you,' I said. 'When Ibrahim and I called you up, did you know then?'

'Know what?'

'That a drone had hit her?'

'No,' she said. 'I were still looking. But I were close. All I needed to do was to tweak Bullbus–'

'What's that, like?'

'Bullbus is the 3D modelling service we use,' said Carrie. 'You know, for knife attacks and bullets and the like. Usually you just dump the gecko image of an exit-wound onto their servers and they'll tell you it were a Glock such-and-such fired from two-and-a-half metres. And then bill you.'

'Sounds right familiar,' I said.

'Yeah,' she said bitterly. 'A frigging monkey could do my job. Like yours. No offence. Anyhow, they didn't have nosecones of high-alt drones on the database, so I did some proper analysis. I started building my own wireframes. Began hitting manufacturing data mountains for industry specs. Took me an afternoon but I got there.'

'Where'd it come from?' I asked.

'Well, it were made in Taiwan.' Here she paused and flicked away the image. 'But, listen to this, Haz...' Her voice lowered and she checked the couple in the grass were out of earshot. 'It were designed in the East Pennine Military Drone Facility.'

That sounded familiar. Then I recognised it. 'That's our office, in't it?'

She nodded. 'Next floor up!'

'Damn,' I said. 'She were hit by a military drone?'

Carrie shushed me hurriedly. 'Hey! That's the kind of text

string they'll listen in for.'

'Yeah,' I mumbled. 'Sorry.'

She checked the roof garden again for anybody listening, then turned to me. 'So, what do we do now?'

'What do you mean?' I said. Was this all she had? 'What've you told DI? Did you tell him when you'd found out?'

'I told him everything,' she said. 'That Meri Fergus were hit by a military drone. Make, model, the lot.'

'What'd he say?'

'He said it must've been an accident.'

'Bullshit,' I said. 'We've got to talk to them. Find out who was operating it.'

Carrie nodded. 'Yeah.'

'How?' I asked.

She smiled. 'Ibrahim's in London tomorrow. I've got ourselves booked into the conference box.'

'What?' I asked. 'Can't we just walk upstairs and knock on the door?'

She shrugged. 'I guess. But they didn't want us on site.'

'Oh,' I said. 'Right.'

'It's their loss.'

* * *

When I got home, I hardly slept at all for the rest of that night. I lay in bed, too hot. The pain in my leg was intense, throbbing behind the bruise, a black-yellow sun flare against my skin.

The discussion on the rooftop garden and the pain were taking over my brain space again. While I'd been working with Louie in Manchester, I'd managed to push them away into dim corners. Squash them down flat like old rubbish waiting to go to the pit. But they only bounced back when I let my mind wander.

When I'd been chatting to Sadie, I'd almost totally forgotten about those things. That body on the floor of the factory. Those unnaturally splayed limbs. But Carrie's call and the conversation had taken me right back. To the rain falling onto the skittering forms of the eight-legged horrors. Feasting. Now I had the girl's voice in my head as well. After I'd been listening to her speak into that camera. I'd played it too many times. I could hear her speaking in death loops in my mind. Her ridiculous, affected voice, talking of riots and brutality, as if she knew what it really meant.

And the impact at seven hundred metres. A drone in the face. Coming out of the dark.

When it got around to four in the morning, I could hear the sound of birdsong outside my window. Never heard that normally. I got up earlier than I needed to, really. I could've just picked up the kids after they'd had breakfast at my parents and taken them directly to school. But I had to get out of that bed. Those damn sparrows were noisy.

* * *

'Everybody has been very well-behaved,' said my mother. 'Ali has been especially polite.'

'I got more ice cream,' said Ali.

Asha pulled a sour face and looked in the other direction.

'Thanks, Mum,' I said.

Despite it being so early in the morning, Mum had still pretended to need to go to work and was dressed with her hair made up. There was no way she had to be there at half six. She only worked around the sodding corner. Dad was making no pretence at all. He was at his bedroom window still in his pyjamas, waving at Ali, who was pulling funny faces in the back seat of the car.

'See you soon, Asha,' said my mother, kissing Asha on the

top of her head. 'Thank you for all your help.'

'It were a really big help,' I said, giving her a hug. I could feel her ribs and tried not to think of bones impacting industrial roofs.

She smiled. 'As long as it was worth it.'

I smiled quickly and then grimaced. 'Mum!'

Both of them chatted without pausing for breath all the way back to Saltaire. I tried to listen and take part but I was riding on about four hours of sleep anyway and the warm can of Hombre I was sipping wasn't really hitting the spot. I ended up dozing in the front of the car, letting the red-brick heritage terraces of the SLS segue into the sandstones of lower Airedale.

The northern city belt which ran from Leeds right through Bradford, Manchester and Liverpool was slowly coming to life. As we progressed north-west, in and out of road tunnels, we could see the signs of this happening around us. Pelotons of cyclists started forming on the major bike paths. Crowds bunched up in delta formations outside the entrances to stations. People walked clutching their coffees and their chocolates, talking into thin air. Sunglasses were being dropped onto noses and jackets were coming off. It was going to be a hot day. Everybody had come prepared.

As we hit the eastern stretches of Bradford, I pulled up MoreThanSum on the bead and checked for messages. Nothing had come in from Sadie. I hesitated, knowing I should be the one sending her something. I'd no idea what I should write. Half of me wanted to turn around and ask Asha. But it would've been idiotic. Surely this couldn't be that difficult. All I needed to do was tell Sadie I'd enjoyed the evening and I wanted to meet up again. I kept starting to write messages but then ended up deleting them. They were coming out as false, a bit half-hearted, or just too short and plain rude. I toyed with the idea of writing her a dirty comms.

I even got halfway through before I chickened out and wiped the filth from my eyes. Didn't think she'd appreciate it anyway.

By the time we were swinging through Shipley, I'd written nothing and still had no idea where to start. It was hacking me off so much I killed the service on my bead and took my cap off.

Sadie could wait.

I put on the news when I'd got the kids home. We watched it when we were having breakfast. I tried not to do this too often because the stories messed them up but I wanted to know what was happening with the riots. Where they'd moved onto.

'Clearly we are doing everything in our power.' It was Kaz Furness speaking. I watched her get interviewed. She was getting all kinds of stick from other commentators. Because she was the new Chair of the Board they were trying to drag her down for it. What were her plans to resolve the issue? Did she have faith in the commissioned officers? Were subcontractors failing to deliver? Who was accountable?

I learned that the riots had moved to Stitsils now, beyond Keighley. An expert from Prevention came on. He was a short guy with spiky hair. He looked edgy, uncomfortable being interviewed. He stood alongside Kaz, outside the Trench, barely coming up to her neck. He was very apologetic as well. They still couldn't predict where it was ever going to start or who was going to be involved. They didn't understand why it ever started. The piece cut to other experts.

Then there was some American professor from Scarborough Uni. Standing on one of the three piers. The North Sea grey and depressing behind him. Asha, who had been watching intently, recognised the pier immediately. But she was still confused.

'But he's American,' she said. 'Why's he in Scarborough?'

'Your mum was from Kerala,' I said. 'She'd been to

Scarborough.'

'Yeah,' said Asha. 'She were.'

'He's not American,' said Ali quietly. I hadn't realised he was watching. It was normal for him to have his face pressed into a screen of cartoons at this time in the morning.

'Yes he is,' said Asha. 'You mutant!'

'Asha,' I said warningly.

'He's Canadian,' said Ali. 'That's a different accent.'

Asha and I looked at the man on the screen. I listened to him talk but couldn't decide either way. Perhaps Ali had a good ear for voices though? Something I hadn't noticed.

'Whatever,' said Asha. 'You've got mutant ears and you–'

'Shh,' I said. 'I were listening.'

The professor was talking about the riots. The hovering subtitle said he was some kind of emergentician. I thought I could follow the arguments. Something about complex systems and multiple agents. Then I lost it. He started talking in gobbledegook. Upshot seemed to be it was very difficult to predict. Seemed he'd been consulted by Prevention, though. The man with the spiky hair was telling the interviewer that this professor was going to help them get Enforcement in the right place at the right time and help dampen the flames. Or something. This seemed to be the main accusation of the commentators on the various media channels. If they could understand it, if they knew who to watch, then why would Enforcement not simply be there at the start to extinguish the spark before it blew up into a big bonfire?

'Come on,' I said, my display beeping. 'Let's get to school.'

Chapter Nineteen

I was supposed to meet up with Carrie at Shipley in the morning. Thought I'd drop off the car there and go straight to the office. However, there was something about the conversation the night before which meant I wanted to approach Shipley as though it were a normal day at work. I cleared my throat noisily and told the car to take me to the eastern Saltaire depot.

The early morning heat hit me as soon as I stepped out the car. The depot was a few floors deep and the air conditioning must've broken, as it seemed had the lift. An apologetic sign hung from the door. A suspicious little part of me thought it might've been the public health attack teams doing their Disruptive Interventions again.

I found the stairs. At least they were lit and not too full of crushed shards of pseudo pipes.

At the first corner a man stepped out beside me, whipped off my cap, and stuffed it into his pocket. I choked back a yelp of terror, before recognising the red hair and the impassive face.

'Dammit Clive!'

'Good morning,' he said. Then he repeated it, more slowly this time. 'Good morning.'

'Hell!' I yelled. 'Don't go creeping up on us like that!'

'Apologies, Hasim,' Clive said. 'You know me, though. I'd

rather be discreet.'

I squinted. 'Was it you?'

'I'm sorry.'

'Did you turn off the bleeding air conditioning?'

'Oh, that?' he said. 'No. I'm afraid you only have the sub-standard service providers to thank for that.'

'And lift?'

He stared at me. 'These stairwells are discreet. I needed space to talk to you.'

'What do you want?'

'Can you spare me five minutes of your time?'

'I'm just on my way in.'

'I can see that.'

I stopped and turned to him. 'Have you been following me?'

'A little,' he said, looking very solemn.

'For how long?'

He smiled. 'Sufficient time.'

I paused and thought. 'Were you following me last night?'

'I'm aware that you visited Carrie Tarmell's flat.'

'You're creepy, man!'

He shrugged. 'Your opinion doesn't really affect me that much.'

'We weren't doing anything.'

'I know,' he said.

'What do you mean, you know?' I asked. 'You got cameras on her flat, and all?'

'That would be wholly unethical.'

'So what did you mean? You know about my own private life.'

'No,' he said. 'It was merely a throwaway comment. You could've had your tongue right up Forensic Analyst Tarmell's anus for all I care. It's not important.'

'Urgh, Clive,' I said. 'Just sodding-well get... what do you want?'

'How's the leg?' he asked.

I was surprised at the question and mumbled my way into silence.

He pointed at my thigh. 'Where the dart hit. How is it?'

'It hurts,' I said.

'I've been led to believe they can be very painful.'

'Yeah. Painful.'

'That was a significant quantity of kinetic energy discharged at close range.'

Having no answer to the comment, I nodded. 'How did you know about that?'

He shrugged. 'We all knew about it. I listen to the chatter.'

'So, how come you're so interested in it?' I asked. 'D'you know something about it? Cos if you do, I really–'

'The reason I'm here,' he said, cutting across me. 'Is a little more serious.'

'Yeah? What's happened, like?'

'Well,' he said, smiling. 'I'd really like you to tell me.'

'Me? What are you talking about?'

Clive let his cheek muscles relax. It was a little terrifying. I attempted to recall all my actions over the past few days. For Clive to put in a face-to-face, especially in such a public place, must've meant something serious. What was he getting at?

'I really don't know,' I said. 'Look, I haven't been giving out my A-codes in return for blowjobs or anything.'

He laughed. 'Oh, I know that, Hasim.'

'What've I done?'

'You tell me.'

'I don't know–'

'I think you do, Hasim!'

'Straight up, for honest, Clive, I've got no bloody idea–'

He cut across me. 'Inappropriate use of authorised data access.'

'What?' I said. 'I've done nothing like that.'

He stared around at the luminous graffiti which had been scrawled over the walls. 'Two nights ago, at four minutes past one in the morning, you drew down a query on the Ghawar index.'

'Yeah,' I said. 'So what?'

'Your manners are deteriorating, Hasim,' he said. 'You always used to be a very polite religious boy.'

'I were never religious, yeah,' I muttered. 'I made that choice.'

'Shame,' said Clive. 'Might have given you manners.'

'Let's talk about your religion, then, Clive,' I said.

'Let's not,' he said. 'You accessed the data repository of the Ghawar index.'

'Yeah, I did,' I said. 'It were what wrapped up that vat-making case. False testies and that.'

'Indeed,' he said. 'I had a little skim of the narrative behind that. Was that all your work, Hasim? It was very impressive... the thinking behind it, that is.'

I nodded. 'Yeah, it were all me. You know how Louie works. You do heavy lifting. He comes in at the end and makes it read proper and look dead nice.'

'I don't know him personally. But I've heard a lot about the young man.'

'Yeah?'

'He'll be in charge of your Justice division at some point, Hasim.'

'No doubt.'

'Whereas you,' said Clive. 'You'll still be treading water in the shallow end. Because–'

'Because what?' I snapped.

Clive got close in my face and shouted. 'Because you break the IG rules, Hasim!'

'What the hell have I done, Clive?' I shouted. This was so unfair. I was exhausted. I needed sleep.

'Approximately fifty-seven seconds before you logged off

the Modlee system, you used your Grahams-Flint access to lift additional data from the Ghawar data site. You filtered for the Airedale Regionale index and for associated activity around that.'

I kept my mouth shut. This was stupid, everybody mixed their access between cases.

I shrugged. 'So?'

'You were taken off that case,' said Clive. 'You were told to leave it alone.'

'Have you been speaking to Ibrahim?' I asked.

'No,' said Clive. 'I don't care what particular Servant he's grovelling to at the moment. The politics of the case don't interest me. He is right, though.'

'Eh?'

'Enforcement had nothing to gain and everything to lose by killing that girl.'

I shrugged. 'I never said anything like that.'

'It's what you intimated!'

Not understanding the word Clive had just used, I turned away, like I was at school. I kicked away at a step. 'Piss off.'

'You've got to listen to me, Hasim.'

'What's your point, like?'

'You broke IG rules,' he repeated. 'You used your A-codes, released for the Grahams-Flint case, to access data on the Meri Fergus case. That is an offence. I could have your analyst card taken away. You took an oath, remember?'

'The oath? This has got nothing to do with the oath?'

'You broke the rules!'

I stared at him. 'What are you going to do about it Clive? Tell DI?'

He regarded me calmly for a moment. Then looked down at my leg. 'I'm worried about where you're going, Hasim. I don't know what it is you've done. Whether you've lifted one too many stones. Whether you visited one too many dodgy reporting sites.' He looked back up at me. 'But you're starting to flash up in some hazard indicators and I think it's having other unexpected effects.'

'What kind of effects?'

'Odd phenomena,' he said, watching me carefully.

'Stop talking like that. What is it?'

He checked around him, listening for other people in the stairwell. 'A digital analyst working on a drug case in Bournemouth was shot in the neck yesterday. By a defective shockdrone.'

I froze.

'Yes,' he said. 'Coincidence?'

'Yeah,' I laughed. 'Course it is.'

'What about Hamburg? Digital analyst shot in the left buttock by a taser.'

'Shockdrone?'

'Yes,' said Clive. 'Again, supposedly defective.'

I was silent. 'Think there's a link, like?'

'I do,' said Clive.

'But you believe in aliens, buddy. Little green men, in't it?'

Clive practically roared in my face. 'I don't believe in aliens!'

'Whoa,' I said, stepping back against the handrail.

'There's a pattern,' said Clive, more quietly. 'Perhaps it's coincidence, perhaps not.'

'They checked the drone that hit me,' I said. 'It were definitely defective.'

'It was old. They gave you an old machine. In all these cases, the analysts were given old machines.'

'So, nobody gives a damn about us. What's new?'

'It seems,' said Clive, smiling. 'That some people now care even less. I'd recommend you tread carefully.'

Chapter Twenty

The conversation with Clive had shaken me. Even though he was a freak, he knew his shit. If he said you were in trouble, you listened. Plus, he never typically left that boat. If he'd bothered to leave his boat, you listened. It meant something special. He'd taken time out of his busy schedule (of raining shit on analysts' lives) to corner me in a stairwell and give me a primary-school-grade lecture on IG.

The amount of footage his face would now be on, although it was peanuts in a normal person's world, would've infuriated him. Clive never let his picture be taken lightly. You had to get it signed in triplicate with him. And, though I knew he loved his IG, I didn't realise he loved it enough to let his ratios get logged in Manchester just so he could slap me about it. In Clive's world, he'd just done the equivalent of run around a shopping precinct waving his cock in people's faces. It felt like this was some top-shelf shit.

I was sure he'd seen something. I don't know what it was, but he'd seen some new pattern. And it wasn't all this talk of digitals in Bournemouth getting shot in the neck and the like. That was all rubbish. British Isles had close to a hundred and twenty million people. You're going to get some matches with that kind of sample. Doesn't mean those matches actually meant anything. It's just fluke. I saw this kind of stuff all the time. It was just correlation, wasn't it? Not... whatever the hell the other word was.

But Clive knew all this. He was a clever lad. I was sure he knew more than he'd been letting on. Had he been warning me off the Meri Fergus case all together? Did he care what happened to me? I couldn't believe that he did.

Clive didn't care for anybody but himself.

Whatever had been screwing about with Clive's mind, the bugger had certainly messed up mine.

When I heaved myself up the last steps and into the buzzing bank of Justice hotdesks, I was jumpy. Seeing Carrie over in the bistro with a coffee calmed me down a bit. She waved and called me up on her bead.

'You want a drink?'

'Yeah,' I said. 'Chocolate. And a shot.'

'A shot?' she said. 'You didn't sleep either?'

I grunted and cut the call. I wondered whether Clive had also cornered Carrie and blasted her with his IG lecturing.

I could sense a presence over my left shoulder. It seemed patient, waiting for me to turn. There was only one person who crept up on you.

'Hasim?'

DI Winters.

I turned to give him a little smile and a nod. He was only a couple of years older than me. A DI *and so young* was what people always said. Except I knew I wasn't young anymore. This had always irritated me. Though it had always been my choice why I hadn't gone for that kind of job. Things were too complicated now.

'Ibrahim handed me the keys to the kingdom,' he said with a shrill chuckle. I could tell he was nervous, but I was unsure why. I wasn't the kind of person which made somebody like him nervous.

'Yeah?' I said. 'Where's he at, then?'

'London,' Winters said, smoothing down his hair. While most of the Justice Division wore casuals, Winters liked to set an example, always immaculately dressed in a three-piece suit with the AJC logo on his lapel. Carrie had always said it looked like his mum had dressed him. 'More training.'

'Training, yeah,' I said.

Winters coughed, adjusting his expensive glasses. Like me, he didn't want any bead in his flesh, but he was too precious to wear a hat. So he had the small exec glasses. 'Just been looking at your board.'

'My what?'

'Your purchase orders, Hasim,' he said.

I relaxed. 'Oh. Right.'

'Ibrahim hasn't posted anything for a week.'

'It's quiet, yeah.'

'You're not working on anything at the moment?'

'No,' I said.

Carrie appeared at my side, startling Winters. She handed me my chocolate. 'Shot and choc, Haz. Hiya, sir.'

'Hello Carrie,' said Winters. 'Just saying… you've not got any POs posted, have you, Hasim?'

'No, it's proper quiet, in't it.'

He looked around the room and then back at me, taking a deep breath before he spoke. 'Then why are you in the office?'

I snorted, a little too loudly. I'd been waiting for him to try and give me an awful enviro case. Not to interrogate me about my frigging life. 'Just a bit of tidying up. Admin, you know.'

'Are you claiming billable hours?'

I checked my display. A small timer was pushing through the minutes on the top-right of the screen. I remembered I'd clocked on as usual that morning. This was supposed to be just another day. I considered a little lie then realised he was probably getting me on a vid anyway – this was DI Winters after all – and it would be complicated to try and explain away that one.

'Yes, sir. Just realised I am, yeah. Oops. I'll stop it now.'

'Please,' said Winters looking edgy, as if I was about to pull a gun on him or something.

I waved my fingers in the air and clicked them to switch off the clock. 'There. All done, DI, sir.'

'And the backlog?' he asked.

'The what?' I asked.

'The backlog,' he said. 'All the hours you've wrongly claimed.'

'Oh, right.'

He squinted at me. 'You will resolve it, won't you, Hasim?'

'Of course.'

'Only, Ibrahim is a very busy guy at the moment. I don't think he has the time to check on all his staff's whereabouts. But today...'

He left the sentence hanging in the air. Carrie took a sip of her coffee and said brightly, 'But today, you're in charge, sir.'

Winters looked sharply at Carrie, trying to find some offence. 'Yes. Just covering, of course. While Ibrahim's in London.'

'Great,' said Carrie.

We stood awkwardly for a minute. Then Winters asked me the question again. 'So, why are you here today?'

I started to sweat. 'Bit of admin, in't it.'

'You told me that,' said Winters. 'Isn't that what Fridays are for?'

'Isn't this Friday?'

He slowly shook his head. 'Are you getting enough sleep, Hasim?'

I could see a couple of Sherzai's analytical team hovering around the front of the vid-conf box. It was after ten o'clock now. We were in danger of losing the slot. And our guy at the other end.

'Plenty, sir,' I said. 'Sorry, gotta run, yeah.'

'Where to?' he asked. 'Your administration?'

Carrie cut across him. 'Ibrahim's been too busy to post a PO. But Haz is helping me out.'

'Right,' said Winters. He paused for a moment, considering what Carrie had just told him. Then smiled broadly. 'That's great! Good to see some cross-specialty working. I wish my guys did more of that.'

'Yeah,' said Carrie. 'Forensics and digital work closely together.'

'What's the case?' asked Winters. I could see his right hand was itching to start pulling up the PO board for Carrie and start validating the arse off her story.

'Not posted yet,' said Carrie. 'But I know the DI's onto it. Been busy, that's all.'

Winters nodded and smoothed down his fringe onto his forehead with a delicate hand. 'You can't tell me any more than that?'

'Just some assault case,' said Carrie. I could see her eyes flicker across to the VC booth too. The two analysts were now knocking on the door. 'Nothing interesting.'

'Can't say too much,' I said. Then pulled out my trump card. 'IG, in't it? Sorry, like.'

Winters thinned his lips. 'OK. IG?'

'That's right, sir.'

'You don't mind if I check with Ibrahim on it?'

'Check?' asked Carrie mockingly. 'If you want to. Not sure what he'll make of it, though.'

'What do you mean?' asked Winters.

'Well,' said Carrie. 'It could sound like you're checking up on him not posting a PO when he should've.'

Winters thought for a moment and then nodded. He turned to me. 'IG was the reason you didn't mention it before?'

'Yeah,' I said. 'That were it.'

He thought for a moment. 'Very good. Keep up the good work. And you, Hasim, you turn that clock back on.'

'Will do, sir,' I said, clicking my fingers.

We got ourselves booked into the VC booth immediately. After Carrie had virtually shoved Sherzai's women out the way. It was a retro-designed piece of shit, supposed to look like a huge packing crate in the corner of the room. There was another at the opposite side of the floor made to look like a bale of cotton. Probably some art school project. I always felt a little embarrassed using it. The DI, of course, thought they were wild and always patted them gleefully whenever he ducked down to get inside them.

'It would be quicker to take the lift,' said Carrie, looking at the gleaming brass doors a few feet along the wall from the VC unit. 'But I guess they don't want to know.'

I shrugged. 'We could always go and knock on the door?'

She shook her head and, ducking down, slipped inside.

The guy who they'd put up for the interview looked like he was about to retire. It could've explained why he was so bloody cheerful. Said his name was Mick. Although thin in the face, he had a proper gut and thin, wispy hair. For an organisation that designed drones to kill and incapacitate people with optimal efficiency, the jolly old man seemed oddly inappropriate. After we'd made our introductions, we started discussing the fact that we had to use the VC. It seemed he found the locational nonsense incredibly amusing.

'I love it,' he roared with laughter. 'So, how many feet apart are we?'

'Not many,' said Carrie.

'The modern world, yeah?' he said. 'It's crazy, no?'

I thought he sounded a bit European. Possibly German or Polish.

'Yeah,' I said. 'It's proper messed up, in't it?'

'So, what can I do for you lovely people? You had a question about our Buzzard?'

'That's right,' said Carrie.

'One of our more modern models. How can I help you?'

'Why would there be one flying over Airedale?' asked Carrie.

'Has one been found?' said Mick.

'No,' said Carrie.

'OK,' said Mick. 'But you believe there was one in the dale?'

'I know there was.'

'You are drone-spotters, perhaps?' he said with a laugh, less easy-going now than before. I got the feeling the humorous perspective on things could get dropped when Mick wanted it to.

'One of your drones hit a flyer,' said Carrie. 'Meri Fergus. Collision at approximately seven hundred metres altitude above the northern end of Keighley Basin.'

'A flyer?'

'Yeah,' Carrie said. 'A flyer. You know, with the wings and that?'

'Oh,' he said, nodding. 'I think I know. It's a new craze, no? We never had that in my youth. It's a shame. I would love to do that.'

'There's still time,' said Carrie.

He smiled and shrugged. 'Perhaps... anyway, enough of my dreams. How do you know it was a Buzzard?'

'I ran some analysis on the shape of impact. It came back with the curve proportions for the nose cone of a Buzzard.'

'Excellent,' said Mick. 'I love all this stuff. You guys are real whizz-kids these days.'

'Well,' said Carrie. 'They give us the toys, don't they?'

Mick nodded in my direction. 'And why the digital analyst?'

'Him? Oh, he's working on the case as well.'

'Is he?' said Mick, regarding me coolly for a few seconds. 'Very good.'

'So, what would a Buzzard be doing above Keighley?'

'I have no idea, my dear. But I can tell you we only supply to two markets.'

'Which are?'

'Military, naturally,' he said. 'And Enforcement subcontractors.'

'Makes sense. Anybody local?'

'A few. Which do you want? Military or Enforcement?'

'I can't do military,' said Carrie. 'So let's assume Enforcement, OK?'

Mick bent his head over and his hands played lightly on his knees. 'Let me see... recent deliveries to Newcastle, Aberdeen... here. Last year, we supplied a company by the name of HiSkyEye-Hutchins.'

I was already onto it, fingers flickering in the air above me.

'Where are they based?' asked Carrie.

'Leeds end of the Belt,' said Mick. He read out an address just as it flashed up on my display. Not even bothering to cast my net wide and filter down by location, I simply ran a check against known subcontractors for AJC.

It produced a hit. I knew it would.

'Yeah,' I said. 'That's it.'

'I love you digital analysts,' said Mick. 'You're so chatty, no?'

'Can you tell us anything more about the contract?' asked Carrie.

'Well,' said Mick, now wincing a little. 'This is all commercial confidentiality, you understand.'

'We've got delegation,' I muttered.

'Of course,' he said, looking down at his lap. 'They specified the latest models. Buzzards are fast-moving, very controllable. They said they wanted something that was... well, it says here they wanted something "dangerous".'

'Those guys,' said Carrie. 'They're like proper out-of-control.'

'I know,' said Mick. 'They are keen.'

Carrie wrapped up the interview neatly and we bundled ourselves out of the VC booth. Winters wasn't around, thankfully. If he'd been chatting to Ibrahim, like he'd threatened to, we might be in a lot of trouble by now.

'Let's go get a car,' Carrie said quietly.

As we were heading to the car depot, I sensed something was about to go wrong. It was proper butterflies. I knew I didn't want to get in an AJC car. It wasn't about the safety. It was because I didn't want to tell anybody where we were going. Didn't want to plug in our destination.

'Wait,' I said. We had reached the street outside. 'Do you have a car, yourself?'

'Absolutely not,' she said, still walking. 'Why bother? I were going to the depot. It's only over there.'

'It's just...'

She stopped.

'What?'

'Don't want a depot car.'

'What?'

'I don't want a depot car.'

'Why not?' she asked.

'Let's keep this off servers, yeah?'

'And people call me paranoid!'

'Just being safe, and that.'

'You seeing aliens now as well?'

I jumped. 'What?'

'You're starting to sound like Clive.'

'Why do you say that?' I asked. 'You spoken to him?'

'Yeah,' she snorted. 'At some point. What is it with you today?'

'Nothing. Just tired, that's all, in't it.'

'Get us a taxi, then.'

I flicked a beacon on my bead to search for a taxi. There was one in the next street. I received a message to tell me it was on its way.

'There's one coming,' I said.

Carrie nodded. 'You paying in credit?'

I didn't answer. I could see the taxi turn the corner three streets away and head towards us. It was a battered old conversion. The driver's seat was entirely taken up with heavily secured processor arrays.

My display flashed a message to tell me that my taxi was here. Always helpful, considering that I could see the frigging thing right in front of me. I killed my beacon and stepped up to the vehicle.

The lock in the back doors clicked. Automated taxis only let you into the back. They didn't want you messing with the controls. We climbed in. I gave the street name from the address we wanted, but added ten to the number. In my pocket, largely unused, I had a pre-loaded card. I fished it out and waved it in front of the sensor.

You only paid in pre-load if you didn't want the trail. Only criminals used pre-load.

As the taxi set off, I noticed Carrie flinch in her seat beside me.

'What's up?' I asked.

She shook her head and twitched her eye.

Then I saw the pulse on my display and heard the buzz. Ibrahim was trying to call.

Chapter Twenty-One

———

I shared my display with Carrie by grabbing the air and throwing it to her head.

'What'd he want?' she muttered.

'Perhaps Winters contacted him?'

'You going to answer?'

'No,' I said, snapping my index finger against my thumb. The caller icon faded away into the background of my display.

Carrie looked at me for a moment and then turned away to stare out of the window. After we both sat in silence for a while, she spoke. 'How much trouble are we going to get into? I mean, doing all this?'

'Why? You worried?'

'No,' she said. 'Don't care what DI thinks, cos I know I'm good. But if this turns out to be nowt... well, nowt more than some random thing, I'm going to look a right twat.'

I grunted. 'Got to make sure, though, Carrie, yeah?'

'Gotta make sure.'

I dozed in the taxi while Carrie caught up with her messages. There wasn't much to see for most of the journey. other than the houses and offices built over the bones of the main arterial route into central Leeds. Standard cut-n-cover. Other cars flickered past, occasionally dissected by the blur of electronic advertising boards which formed a wall either side of the road. Calibrated to respond to the demographic of the travellers, they were constantly changing.

Once, at least ten years ago, they'd been given direct access to your identity and had targeted you accordingly. The EPIG soon put a bullet through the idea. Now their algorithms had to rely on car makes and models, time of day, and numbers in the car. Even your hair and skin colour. Hints. Metadata.

The processor on duty that day obviously thought I needed a flight to Dhaka for skin whitening cream or a new job.

I started to drift asleep.

I may have dreamed it but, as we started heading up off one of the exit slipways, I thought I caught one of the advertising boards exhorting me to move out and start a new life abroad in Scotland.

Our car pulled up and a few seconds later we exited into the rain. Thankfully, it was still warm. I liked standing in the summer rain, but this was winding itself up to be a drencher.

'Always rains when I'm with you,' said Carrie, breaking into a jog. 'Where is this place?'

Because we'd deliberately given the taxi the wrong address, we struggled to track down the building. We were in the first outer circle of corporate towers which ringed Central Leeds end of the Northern Belt. Although we weren't in the direct centre this was still a significant area of wealth. The centre proper required security checks and personalised invites. For relative scum like us, coming down from the ruin of Airedale, it was a shock. Suddenly our clothes seemed dirtier, shabbier. I felt unshaven in a genuinely slovenly way, not in exquisitely managed sort of way.

Even Carrie, normally the least concerned with appearance, must've been feeling the change. As we took cover in a shop front, I could see her edgily check her reflection in the glass and smooth down her hair. I could see the dark eyeliner she wore already starting to run a little.

I found the building. About time.

'There,' I said, pointing down the street to the opposite side. 'I think they're on the fourth floor.'

They'd surrounded the entire ground floor of the building with a greenhouse. Like some massive glass cockring. The reception area was bolted onto the outside of the greenhouse, as though an afterthought, and manned by a kid who looked like he'd just got out of school. By the sound of his accent, he'd come straight from Stockholm. Everybody seemed to be bundling out of Sweden at the moment.

I stood by the glass at reception, looking in the greenhouse, and pressed my hand against its warmth. There was a little condensation but the views inside were clear. The receptionist was telling us how it was kept clean by massive African snails. Apparently they'd been dicked about so that they only ate the crap off the glass that you get in a place like this. Or a cloche. Whatever the hell that was.

The person who came to meet us was called Joanie Grant. She looked flustered and smiled a thank you at the receptionist. 'Jan said you were with Airedale Justice...'

'We just want to ask a few questions,' said Carrie, kindly.

'Erm,' said the woman. 'Sure, I guess. Do you have any... ID or something?'

'Of course,' said Carrie, fingers flickering in the air in front of her. I also pulled out my analyst credentials and dropped them onto a temporary beacon.

The woman raised her wrist and checked her ridiculously small watch. I could see the light flicker across her eyes. I noticed her beautiful dark brown eyes. She wore formal business attire, white shirt and pencil skirt with a slit up the side to her thigh. I hadn't realised this was the fashion for office workers. Only, at least, for this end of the Belt. It hadn't quite reached Shipley yet.

She seemed satisfied with our AJC creds. 'Are we in trouble?'

'No,' said Carrie. 'We just want to ask you some questions. Are you in charge of the AJC Enforcement contract?'

She shook her head. 'No, that's Pauline. But she's out of the office. Most of them are out of the office.'

'Where are they?' I asked.

She turned to me. 'All the technical staff have gone to a conference in York. Something to do with new drones from South America. Chileans flogging new kit,' she laughed. 'We're trying to upgrade.'

'Who's left here, then?' asked Carrie.

'Just me and a few temps, really.'

'Why aren't you there?' I asked.

'Don't like York?' asked Carrie, with a smile.

'No,' she said, looking defensive. 'Somebody needs to be in charge.'

Carrie nodded briskly, giving the woman an encouraging smile, but I could see the disappointment in the slight thinning of her lips. I was already feeling very deflated. Especially now I knew Ibrahim was trying to call us. I'd blocked all his calls but the unanswered ones were starting to stack up in the bottom-left corner of my display.

'So, you're in charge, then?' Carrie asked.

'Yes,' said Joanie.

'And what do you do?'

'I'm the risk liaison officer,' she said.

'Right,' said Carrie. I was mentally working out how we could extract ourselves from this situation without looking like complete dicks. 'You have any contact with the AJC contract?'

The woman nodded eagerly. 'Oh, yes! I'm risk liaison officer for all the contracts, so I know all about that one.'

I found myself breathing out a little too sharply in relief. Carrie and Joanie looked at me. I smiled. 'Good... that's good, I mean, helpful, in't it.'

'Um,' said Joanie. 'What's all this about, then?'

Carrie looked around the reception area. 'Can we talk inside?'

We were taken through the double airlocks into the greenhouse perimeter. Butterflies, some the size of my face, fluttered around the roof. The noise in here was immense with the rain battering down on the glass. I'd immediately started to sweat, taking me back to the few visits we had made to Dali's family in southern India. The same wall of heat which hit you stepping out of the protection of the air conditioning. The feeling of being draped with a very heavy, very hot, and slightly moist paper towel.

'It's nice in winter,' apologised Joanie. 'But you don't want to eat your salad out here.'

'No,' said Carrie, with a solemn face. 'I wouldn't want to eat salad out here, either.'

We progressed through a communal atrium, with other workers lounging about on comfy chairs and at little cafe tables. I was even more conscious of my appearance. Eyes flicked up from their work and over to us. I realised that my baggy trousers had been on for a few days now, hems mud-encrusted and dark. That my hooded coat had never been washed.

'How many companies work here?' asked Carrie.

'I'm not sure,' said Joanie. 'I think possibly seven largish ones... including us, of course.'

The fourth floor was deserted in comparison to the atrium. In the distance, we could hear the sound of somebody telling a joke and the shrieks of laughter in response.

'In here is probably best,' said Joanie, showing us into a medium-sized boardroom. Apart from the huge windows down one side of the room, each wall was a blank high-def screen.

'Can you tell me about what the company does for AJC

particularly?' said Carrie.

'First,' Joanie said. 'Can you please tell me what it is that we're supposed to have done?'

'We never said you've done owt,' I chipped in.

'So, what is ... why are you here? What's happened?'

'A young woman died,' said Carrie. 'She were a flyer. In the sky above Keighley Basin, over a week ago. She collided with drone, a Buzzard Mark II. She died when the drone hit her.'

'Oh my God,' said Joanie. 'That's awful. What a horrible accident–'

'We're treating it as murder,' I said.

She fell silent at this, staring at me. 'Murder?' she almost whispered.

'We're investigating,' said Carrie firmly. 'A young woman has died. We have to investigate and try and understand what happened. We believe it may have been an AJC drone which you operate on behalf of our Enforcement Division.'

'Who does the operating?' I asked, growing impatient with Carrie's gentle approach. 'Can we talk to the operators? Or are all of them at York and all?'

Joanie shook her head slowly. 'No, not really.' She waved her fingers over the middle of the table and one of the walls flickered into a screen full of footage views and metrics.

'What's this?'

'Well,' said Joanie. 'It's one of our operators.'

We stared at her. After a moment, Carrie simply said: 'You what?'

'All our drones are autonomous, you see?' said Joanie. 'They're not controlled by any human operator, as such.'

'Who controls them?' asked Carrie.

'They control themselves,' she pointed at one of the footage feeds. 'See. That's the internal camera of one above Dundee.'

We watched the footage showing an aerial view of some cityscape running alongside a waterfront. Occasionally the camera would zoom in on some specific activity on the ground.

'Can we see the drones which were out that night?'

'Actually see them?'

'Yeah,' said Carrie. 'You know, see them. I want to see what they look like.'

'I think so,' said Joanie, hands flickering. She turned to a screen and stood up to move to a closer seat. 'Unless they're in the air. They're all in a hangar in our airfield.'

'I want to see the drone that were up that night, please,' said Carrie. 'See its nosecone.'

'What night was it?' asked Joanie.

Carrie gave her the date and she entered it into the system.

'These are the drones for the northern region,' she said. We could see a dimly lit hanger with a dozen drones lined up in a herringbone pattern.

'All those are for AJC?' asked Carrie.

'No,' said Joanie. 'About a third of them are.'

I shifted myself on my seat. 'You can tell which ones were out on that night?'

'We have the logs,' she said, hands scrolling through a list of obscure technical messages, which started popping up in the corner of the screen. She continued to run down the list until she found the right date and time.

'You see that ID there? That was the one above Keighley that night.'

Carrie glanced over to me, wanting to ask the same question. But it seemed inappropriate somehow.

Finally, Carrie cleared her throat. 'Can we have a close visual on the nosecone of that one?'

Joanie swallowed. 'Of course.'

The hangar camera's view turned and tightened on an individual drone. It zoomed in close onto the shiny alloy. The image struggled to re-focus. Eventually, it became clear. There were no dents or damage to the nose cone. But we could all see the faint line of dark brown that encircled it.

'I'd like a copy of that,' said Carrie quietly.

'Is that...' said Joanie. 'Is that her blood?'

'Yeah,' said Carrie. 'I'm guessing. Those drones are tough, are they?'

'Well, they're designed to military specifications.'

'We know.'

'Do you need the drone?' Joanie asked.

'Not sure, yet. That would be a decision for DI.'

'What about the footage from that night?' I said. 'Can we see that?'

'Oh no,' said Joanie, turning to me. 'Absolutely not. That's the client's property. We don't get access to that.'

Carrie grunted in irritation. 'Bloody contracts! What about your logs, then? Do they show summat on that night? Like an error message? An inflight adjustment?'

Joanie had to force her eyes to track focus away from the thin streak of brown. She pulled the sheet with the stacked messages to the middle of the screen and scrolled down a few pages, then pointed. 'Yes. There, you see? Something happened at thirteen minutes after twelve. It started to lose altitude.'

'And then?' I asked.

'Then,' she said, scrolling down a little further. 'It recovered from its fall. Ascended... here. And, well, carried on.'

'Just like that?' Carrie said. 'But aren't they designed to avoid collision?'

Joanie nodded. 'Yes, of course. They all have inbuilt sensors and software which makes them get out of the way!' She laughed and then caught herself. 'Sorry.'

'So,' said Carrie slowly. 'If one were to hit something in the air, what would've gone wrong?'

I interrupted them talking. 'Can we see the software

upgrades?'

'Sorry,' said Joanie. 'What do you mean?'

'Can we see when that drone's software was last updated?'

'I think so. It's not something I've ever had to do.'

She flicked through a properties screen for the drone. After a few minutes of searching we managed to track down the upgrade history. It had been upgraded yesterday, and before that, about six months ago.

'I don't think it could be anything to do with that,' said Carrie. 'That's too long ago.'

'Definitely all autonomous?' I asked.

Joanie nodded. 'We just set the location, timings, altitude, and... you know, those kind of things.'

Carrie raised her head. 'Altitude? You mean what height it's supposed to fly at normally?'

'That's right. The range it would normally fly. Unless you changed the risk rating, of course...'

'Can we check that?' said Carrie. 'Whether somebody changed it recently?'

'The altitude?' said Joanie. More screens appeared. She shook her head. 'Well, it looks like it was set at the start of the contract and never changed. There, see, a thousand metres.'

'A thousand metres?' I asked.

Carrie and I exchanged a glance. Then she shrugged and shook her head.

'No changes made to standard location?' Carrie asked. She was rattling off the questions now.

'No,' Joanie said. 'It's always been Airedale... then particular districts within the spur.'

Carrie looked at me, creasing up a tired face and then raised her eyebrows. 'What do you think, Haz? Are we done here?'

I didn't look her in the eyes. I know it couldn't end like this. I knew that there was something in these numbers. My tired mind just wasn't seeing the right associations. I kept staring at the multiple screens on the display. While Joanie had been scrolling through the software parameters, one word had caught my attention. I'd tried to store it on short term, planning to go back for it later. But, naturally, it'd vanished now.

'Haz?' Carrie asked again, standing up now. Joanie was also standing, much more slowly, as though unsure sure what the protocol was in such a situation.

'Give me a minute,' I muttered. I'd got halfway back through the conversation.

'He's very thorough,' said Carrie with a nervous laugh. From my peripheral vision, I could see her flicker her hands. She was probably checking her messages. Perhaps she also had a stack from the DI.

Then I remembered what it was.

'What was your job again?' I asked, turning to Joanie. 'Sorry, your title.'

'Risk liaison officer,' she said.

'And you said risk rating affected altitude?'

'That's correct,' she said, a little slower this time, suddenly more defensive. 'More than that, though... many aspects of the flight pattern are changed.'

I nodded. 'Can we go back to that screen... that one there on the bottom right?' I pointed to the screen. 'That thing there. You have anything to do with that risk rating?'

She looked at the numbers on the screen. The parameter was labelled 'Operating Risk Threshold'. It showed forty-five percent.

'Yes,' she said. 'I do, actually.' She sat down again slowly and hunched her shoulders over in her chair, staring at the screen.

'What are you thinking, Joanie?' asked Carrie. She'd stopped checking her messages and quietly sat down next to the slightly shivering woman.

'I don't know...' Her hands started flickering and more screens started to appear.

'You set that?' I asked again.

Joanie nodded, grimacing a little. Her mouth drawn in tightly like a child who'd just drawn an imaginary zip across their mouth.

'Is forty-five normal?' asked Carrie.

Joanie shook her head.

I leaned across the table to her. 'I'm guessing that's going to affect the behaviour of a drone in flight? Yeah?'

'Yes,' she muttered, still searching through the logs.

'I'm also guessing a drone with those kind of risk parameters is going to be flying a bit lower than normal? Flying dangerously?'

Then she froze staring at a list of messages. 'Nobody said dangerous. Why do you say that?'

'Your reaction, love,' said Carrie.

Joanie stopped dragging up files onto the screen. She sat back in her chair, staring at the screen, biting her nails.

'What's that tell us?' I asked, waving at the screen.

She almost whispered. 'It tells us that... well, it tells us that night I changed the risk rating.'

'You what?' asked Carrie.

Joanie cleared her throat. 'I changed the risk rating on that night.'

'Why?'

'Look,' she said. 'It's routine. That's my job! The client tells me what risk rating they want and I adjust the numbers. It's as simple as that. I run the modelling software for the entire squadron. I put in the risk ratings. I can tell if there are going to be problems.'

'You do it manually?' I asked.

'I'm supposed to,' she said, and then looked directly at me, eyes flickered over mine, trying to read me.

'But you've got a little code, yeah,' I said. 'Here and there, you use a little code to do your job for you?'

She didn't answer.

'I mean,' I said, opening my hands a little. 'Everybody does, don't they?'

'I'm supposed to be on call every hour of the damn day!' Tears had started to course down her cheeks.

'You do, then?' I pressed.

'Yes,' she almost shouted. 'Yes, I've got some automation!'

I jabbed a finger at the screen. 'When this were changed, I'm guessing it were code that done it, then?'

She looked at the screen and nodded. 'Look at the time. It was about eight o'clock in the evening. I'm not going to be at work then, am I? I have a social life, like everybody else.'

Carrie patted Joanie's forearm. 'Of course, love. Of course.'

'What does the rating do?' I asked. 'On an individual drone?'

'It... it's difficult to explain. Lots of things! It affects how fast the drone flies, how carefully...' She trailed off.

'How carefully it flies?' I asked. 'Its evasion algorithms, and that?'

Joanie sat rigid, staring at the floor.

'What was it set at before?' asked Carrie.

'Seventy,' said Joanie.

'Is that a significant change?' asked Carrie.

She nodded, raising her face to us both. She looked numb. 'What have I done?'

'Nowt,' said Carrie briskly. 'You've carried out a contract. You weren't to know.'

Trying to keep my voice from cracking, I asked her the question. 'Who requested the change?'

She shrugged and laughed as though it were a stupid question. 'Well, the client, of course.'

'Who specifically, though? Is it your contract manager?'

'No,' she said, wiping the snot from her nose with the back of her hand. She'd calmed down a little now. 'It's some group. Some kind of governance board. You'll know more about it than me.'

'We're Justice,' said Carrie. 'We're not Enforcement.'

'OK,' she said. 'I didn't know that... here, there's the message. It's always semantic. Which was why my code could pick it up.'

On the screen was a message. I checked the time sent. I recognised that time. It'd been sent a few minutes after the comms flash had lit up my Modlee patterns. Although the start of the message read like a legal letter, advising the contractor of the client's requirement, most of the message content read like a piece of code. It was a set of parameters. Most of the options had been set to default. Hidden within these was the risk rating adjustment.

It told me who it was from. The Airedale Enforcement Board Secretariat.

Inside my head was a whooping chorus of relieved shrieks. I spoke quietly. 'That's the Enforcement Board.'

'You were right,' said Carrie, looking a little paler than I'd ever seen her.

'What happens now?' asked Joanie.

I stood up. 'You let me have a copy of everything on that screen, yeah?'

She looked like she was about to object but then shrugged and waved her hands, releasing the files. I hoovered them up into my bead and made a backup in my processor.

While I was busy doing this, Carrie was thanking Joanie and telling her that she wasn't under arrest or suspicion and that we would be back in touch.

We were shown back through the atrium and greenhouse. The rain had stopped falling and it was oddly peaceful in there. We thanked Joanie again and said goodbye at the reception desk.

When we got outside, there were a couple of familiar faces waiting for us. The woman was a solemn, thin-faced officer from one of the Enforcement branches. I thought she was called Mahn or Hann or something like that. Never heard her spoken to by her first name.

The other one was Jonah.

'Hazzie,' he called out. 'How you doing, man?'

'Alright,' I said.

He wasn't smiling as broadly as he usually did. 'Apparently you guys don't have a car? You want a lift?'

Chapter Twenty-Two

―――――

I wondered if I could make it into a joke.

'Oh, that's right kind, that,' I said. 'Ta.'

Jonah didn't really smile, just beckoned us down the road. 'Come on.'

'I'm going to head home a different way,' said Carrie. 'Thought I might check out the centre, you know. Catch a late train.'

'Everybody's coming back to Airedale,' said the woman.

'Mo's had a call from Head,' said Jonah.

Mo Hann. That was her name. She'd once broken a wrong 'uns nose by throwing her shoe at his face. It was a fucking small shoe and all.

'Brian wants a chat,' Mo said.

'Are we under arrest?' asked Carrie, holding out her wrists mockingly. 'Do you need us lashed up in back? You got a van down here?'

Jonah glowered. I could see the conflict in his face. Being sent down to the Belt to pick me up was upsetting him.

'Come with us, Hasim,' said Mo quietly. 'He just wants to talk to you.'

'Sure,' I said. 'I've got a few questions for him, and all.'

'Are you recording?' asked Mo, pointing at my cap.

I nodded. 'This is all evidence.'

She looked over to Carrie, who had sidled a little distance down the street. 'And you?'

'Of course!'

Mo sighed and shook her head. Looking at the floor, she started to recite a familiar phrase. 'Under section three of the EPIG Act, I am formally requesting that you to cease and desist from recording me and my colleague...'

I turned my bead off immediately, then raised my hands to show that I wasn't controlling it anymore. Unless I had good reason to keep recording – and I mean a damn good reason – then that would be my license shredded.

'You stopped now?' asked Jonah.

'Yeah,' I said. 'I'm done.'

'Carrie?' asked Mo.

Carrie shrugged and nodded. She'd stopped moving now and had the slumped attitude of a teenager who had given up a fight with her teachers.

'Where's the car?' I asked.

'We don't have to do this, Haz,' said Carrie. I knew from the tone of her voice that she didn't mean it. It was for show. A bit of bravado. We were done.

'Right! Sod this!' Mo said, and stepped up briskly to Carrie. She grabbed the analyst's first two fingers on her right hand and twisted them. Swearing in pain, Carrie buckled under the pressure and found her arm suddenly behind her. Mo leaned forward and pressed her lips into Carrie's ear. 'You recording this, eh, bitch?'

'Mo,' said Jonah, half-raising his hand. He didn't look like he really wanted to get too close to her.

'Analysts,' spat Mo into Carrie's ear. 'What is the point of you?'

'Mo,' I said. I'd like to think it was forceful and loud but I knew it was a bit of a terrified shriek. 'Let go of her or... I'll start recording again!'

Mo let go of Carrie and hopped back from her before the analyst could retaliate, smiling a private joke to herself. Her thin face turned to me. 'I'm done. Now... get in the car.'

Thankfully, they'd brought a proper car. And not one with the tiger stripes. I had visions of being bundled into the back of a container van and having to sit among the piss and vomit of some wrong 'un's dirty protest from the night before. I was already feeling sick. Being in one of those things would've been like someone fiddling at my tonsils with their bored fingers.

Jonah sat in the back, between Carrie and myself. Mo was sat up front in the driver's seat. Although this was another automatic, Enforcement had to be ready to drop into manual. They always had a driver. No excuses for getting into work late when the motorway server dropped out for a morning.

Although the whole scene had shaken me up a little bit, and feeling sick, I wasn't too worried. I comforted myself with the knowledge that I'd been in worse spots the past few days. The feeling was not unfamiliar now. I still had faith that people like Jonah would be able to see sense. That we wouldn't be thrown into a lift in the Trench with a thumb on the minus five, where they took you for proper treatment. I didn't fancy having my head dunked in the Aire.

After we set off, it was tense and quiet in the car. Carrie had settled down and hunched herself into a sulk in a corner. Mo was filing her nails. I turned to Jonah and tried to make conversation. 'You still working nights, Jonah?'

'Aye,' he said. 'Lots of overtime.'

'They no closer to sorting them out?'

'What?'

'The disturbances,' I said. 'You know. Rioters and that.'

'Well,' said Jonah. 'Prevention reckon they're onto something.'

I could hear a grunt of derision from Mo.

'Oh, yeah?' I asked Jonah. 'They've got something, have they?'

'Waste of time,' said Mo, not turning around. 'Playing music and planting flowers! Only thing that'll sort those wrong 'uns out is a shockdrone formation from above.'

Jonah laughed then stopped himself. 'Sorry, Haz. Didn't mean to laugh. How's the leg?'

I looked out of the window, trying not to think of the conversation with Clive. To not give too much away. 'That? Oh, that's sorted now.'

It was when we were passing through Shipley I realised the time. And realised I was the shittest dad in the dale. The shittest dad in East Pennine. It was after school pick-up and I was supposed to be picking them up today. I'd totally forgotten.

I hurriedly scrolled through my contacts trying to find Greg. 'I'm just going to make a call,' I said. 'Sorry.'

Mo turned around and made as though to grab my cap off my head. 'Don't you dare!'

'It's my kids,' I protested. 'They need picking up!'

'Mo,' said Jonah. 'He's got kids. He's telling the truth. It'll be alright.'

She ran her tongue under her lower lip for a moment then relented. 'OK, whatever. But you'll be getting a smartdart in the other leg if you're not careful with what you say. Head doesn't want any of this getting out, mind. I'm serious… you tell anybody anything and I'll be ramming the bugger in myself.'

'Unbelievable,' muttered Carrie.

Mo glared at her but restrained herself from reaching around and giving Carrie a slap.

I nodded and hit the call icon. Greg answered instantly. 'I'm already here, Haz.'

'Thank you,' I said. 'Thank you, Greg. You're a lifesaver,

you know. Dunno what I'd do without you, yeah?'

He nodded. 'It's not you I'm worried about, Haz.'

'Yeah,' I said. 'I understand. I've been rubbish. Total rubbish. I'll make it up to them, promise.'

'You coming home now, then?' asked Greg. 'It's just that I'm supposed to be heading out tonight… that was why you were supposed to be here.'

'Well,' I wheedled, trying not to look around at the other faces in the car. 'Can you do me a tiny favour more? It's just that I've got to see… well, see a colleague first.'

'Oh yeah?' asked Greg. He arched an eyebrow. He really was an arse. I had to get new care. 'At Shipley?'

'No,' I said. 'Up at Bingley… the Trench, you know?'

Mo reached around and jabbed a finger directly into the bruise on my leg.

I shrieked in pain. 'Gotta go, Greg. Bye, buddy.'

I cut the call and breathed in fast and shallow for a moment. I thought I really was going to be sick in the car.

'You finished, you twat?' said Mo. 'Don't tell anybody you were going to the Trench. I hope the Head gives you some bother! I hope he gives you both bloody barrels.'

* * *

The car parked itself up in the lowest level depot in the Trench. It was near the end of the day now and some Enforcement administration staff were already streaming out of the lift. Like dour-faced trolls, they looked to me like they never got enough sun. Something to do with working in this arsehole of a building.

'You're still on the clock?' asked Mo.

'Of course,' said Carrie.

'Good. I wouldn't want to bring you out to the Trench without you getting paid for it. That wouldn't be fair at all, would it?'

They took us up a couple of floors and along a plain corridor. It was weakly lit by the transparent columns, bringing down the remains of sunlight from above. It was dingy but it felt safer which made me feel a little better to be on this floor, at least. To be able to see any sunlight at all was good news. These were the meeting rooms which still meant they were interested in asking you questions in a semi-controlled environment. It was better than the lower levels, better than a cell. I wondered if that was coming later, if we didn't answer the questions or answer them right.

Of course, if they'd really wanted a friendly chat, they'd have taken us to the cafeteria. Secretly, I was glad we weren't in there. The cafeteria stank worse than the Aire in mid-summer. I preferred the meeting rooms.

We pushed into Number 310, midway along the corridor and gnat small. The room had been kitted out for presentations to be displayed against the wall opposite the door. The walls to the side of this screen were set up to continually display a relaxing woodland scene. That was the intention. Like everything in the Trench, they were old and didn't seem to be working properly. Either the display needed replacing or the bandwidth was too tight. They would flicker intermittently, fading away to black and then flashing back on. The effect was not unlike a nightmare I'd had when I was child or a method of psychological torture from the last century.

'Wait here,' said Mo, leaving Jonah to keep an eye on us.

'Can I get a coffee?' asked Carrie.

Jonah made a face and shook his head. 'Sorry.'

'No drinks?' asked Carrie. 'You trying to starve it out of us?'

'Let us have a drink, buddy,' I said.

It was angry, colder, solemn, and appraising, like a fighter watching his opponent. Whatever he'd been told about the case, he was hacked off with me. As far as I could see, all

Carrie and I had done was to ask a few questions of one of their subcontractors. And I'd disrupted one of their Boards, so why were the whole of Enforcement furious with us?

'Better wait for the Head, OK?' was all he said.

There was a mixture of comfortable seats and stools, the latter clearly stolen from the cafeteria. I'd grabbed one of the stools and pushed it in a corner and I was now perched, surveying the room. Behind my left ear, the edge of the wall screen flickered between a grainy photo of an autumnal beech and an error message. Carrie, having more balls than me, was slouched on one of the comfy chairs in the middle of the room, back to the door. Jonah was stood behind one of the other chairs, fiddling with the seams on its back. We'd only been sat down in the meeting room for a few moments before Brian crashed in through the door.

Of course, Head of Enforcement Operations was Brian Fallin. He was shortish, with a round, sticky-out arse and fat, blond sideburns like a new-wave biker from the southern Appalachians. He was from Australia originally, and, though his accent had softened a little, he seemed to contain a bubbling resentment for every minute he spent in Airedale and not in Adelaide.

'What the hell were you doing at HiSkyEye?'

Carrie turned to look at me, as though seeking some guidance. I shrugged. She cleared her throat. 'Justice business, Head.'

'Yeah?' he sneered, turning to me. 'That's the truth, yeah?'

'Justice work, in't it?' I heard myself say.

'Bollocks to that analyst rubbish,' he said.

'That's what we said, Head,' said Mo. She'd taken up residence beside the door, arms crossed like it was an interrogation.

'It were my idea, Head,' I said. 'Carrie's got nothing to do with this. It's the Meri Fergus case, yeah?'

227

'The what case?' said Brian, stomping around the seats. He was clearly unnerved at the way Carrie hadn't bothered to turn around when he'd entered the room.

'Meri Fergus,' said Mo. 'You remember her? The flyer?'

'Oh, yeah,' said Brian. 'Took a tumble into Keighley, didn't she? Pity it wasn't the rest of her crew as well. Sanctimonious little–'

'That's her,' said Mo.

'Pretty straight-up case, that, isn't it?' said Brian. 'Why are you still shoving a rattler up me on that one?'

'What do you mean?' I was genuinely interested to know. Metaphorically, of course. Carrie took it all wrong, though and started giggling.

This didn't go down well with Brian. 'So you think it's funny, do you, you little idiots?'

'We were following up on a murder case,' I said. 'We were doing our job, yeah?'

'That ain't no bloody murder case,' said Brian. 'Girl got hit in the air. Accidents happen. Everybody knows that. A thousand metres like a sodding MC these days. The girl knew what she was getting into.'

'She knew the risk threshold, did she?' I asked. I couldn't help it. Inside I gave myself a slap.

'Yeah,' said Brian, who had not picked up on the word. 'She did. She knew the risk and she took it in a busy bit of airspace at a busy altitude. She got hit.'

'Well,' I said. 'It may look like an accident but we were just following up on some evidence which might suggest otherwise.'

'It's not a bloody murder!' shouted Brian.

I fell silent for a moment, looking across at Carrie for support but she'd now let her chin rest on her chest and was staring at her shoes. I was on my own.

'There're some leads, like,' I muttered. 'Got to follow up on them.'

'You're a liability,' said Brian. 'Both of you. Crashing around like that, these last few days.'

'I were just asking some questions, that's all,' I said. 'What's the problem?'

'Well, genius,' said Brian. 'Let me put it like this. I don't know if you'd noticed but we've got a civil war breaking out in this valley. You ever check the news, mate? I've got a dozen teams of knackered operatives cruising up and down the MC17 every bastard night trying keep you and your loved ones from being fire-bombed in your beds. Since January I've had three deaths… I've got so many overtime claims I'm going to break my budget by Christmas. I've got at… Mo, how many up in the burns unit in Stitsils?'

Mo cleared her throat. 'Nearly thirty, sir.'

'That's right,' said Brian. 'I've thirty of my team up in the Arches right now. Durham are starting to pay attention. Even sodding London. The last thing we want… the last thing the Servants want is Durham or London poking their sticky-beaks into Airedale's work. They'll send in the N-Guard or something and then the place will go up like a wedding in Chennai.'

'What about Prevention?' I asked. 'Jonah were just saying–'

'Shut up,' said Brian. 'I don't give a damn what Prevention say they can do. I've been in this job close to ten years now and I've not seen Prevention do jack all. That's not real police work. What's dumping a drone on a crowd playing bloody classical music got to do with police work? What's the colour of walls got to do with police work? Mirrors everywhere? No, they're messing about with their maths rubbish to justify their funding. We're the ones on the frontline here, we're the ones getting rocks and biohazard thrown at our heads! And then you…' He stepped closer to me, breath reeking. Together with the flickering hazel bush scene behind him, my head was spinning. 'Then I hear you're poking around again! Some know-nothing analyst from Justice Branch is going all rogue and spinning up some yarn about Enforcement doing this and doing that...'

I leaned my head back, stuck in the corner of the room. 'I'm following up leads,' I said stiffly.

'Shut up,' he screamed. 'Do you know how much chatter your stunt at the sub-group caused? I've not had a minute pass without some Servant phoning me up wanting to know what you were talking about at that Board meeting.'

It was probably the effect of the room or the smell of booze on his breath, but I suddenly found myself saying something a little foolish. 'One of your drones killed somebody, Brian.'

'The hell it did!'

I started to talk fast. Too fast. 'The Board authorised a lowered risk rating, the night Meri Fergus died. It issued a directive to HiSkyEye to lower the general risk rating. Which means that drone were flying more dangerously at lower altitude. Knowing this would increase the chances of an accident. That Meri Fergus were up there and their drones would hit her. Hit her and kill her.'

'This is such utter, utter rubbish!' Both fists were raised, ready to batter down on my face and shoulders.

The door opened at that point and my children were ushered into the room.

'Daddy,' cried Asha. She was eating an ice cream. Careful not to drop it, she came and squeezed in next to me in the corner.

Ali came up to me and hugged my leg. He'd clearly finished his already and was wiping sticky chocolate from his cheeks onto my knee. 'We've been looking for you.'

'Hey, how did you kids get–' began Brian, turning to the door.

'Good evening, my friends,' said Ibrahim, leaning against

the doorframe. He also had an ice cream. 'There you are Ali, Asha. I told you I'd find him.'

'DI,' said Brian. 'G'day, mate.'

Ibrahim nodded at him and smiled, taking a nibble out of the ice cream. 'You well, Brian?'

'Yeah,' he said, trying to crease his face into a smile.

'See you're encouraging some cross-working with my team,' said Ibrahim, nodding at me and Carrie.

'We were just having a chat,' said Brian.

He stepped away from me and left the room.

* * *

'I ended up calling your flat number,' said Ibrahim. 'Your care op... what's his name? Craig? Well, he picked it up.'

'Greg,' I said.

'That's the one. We got chatting, as you do. He said you couldn't get home but that you'd been taken to the Trench. He was annoyed because he'd somewhere to be so I offered to... well, here I am.'

We were walking alongside the canal, the sky still bright in the early evening. Once the DI had got us out of the building, I was going to get a taxi for myself and the kids. But he'd insisted we have a 'chat' so we decided the walk along the canal was best.

'You alright, Carrie?' asked Ibrahim. Carrie was walking directly in front of us. Ahead of her, Asha and Ali were playing tag, hopping from bollard to bollard.

'Uh huh,' she said.

'Why didn't you answer my calls, team?' asked the DI. 'I've been trying all day.'

I shrugged. 'Thought you'd tell us to stop.'

'You're right,' he said. 'But we'll get onto that. I want to know what you've been doing.'

'This and that,' said Carrie.

'That won't do, Carrie. I think, after what I've done for you today, I'm owed a little explanation, yeah? A little bit of team talk?'

So we told him about the nosecone, the indentation in Meri Fergus' face, the military drones leased to a surveillance subcontractor, the subcontractor's relationship with Enforcement, and the risk message.

'It was from the Enforcement Board?' asked Ibrahim.

'That's what she told us,' I said. 'It were there, DI, in black and white, you know.'

Ibrahim nodded, scratching at the designer stubble around his chin. 'OK–'

'Am I done here?' asked Carrie.

'Yeah,' said Ibrahim, nodding. 'I think so.'

As soon as he'd nodded an affirmative, Carrie turned on her heel and started off along the canal path. Straight back the way we'd come. 'Night.'

'Goodnight, Carrie,' Ibrahim said to her departing back.

The kids shouted goodnight as well and she waved her hand in the air.

'I need to ask you,' said Ibrahim, as we continued on our way. 'Have you retained any vidz of the encounter with our friends from Enforcement?'

I shook my head. 'No. It were all wiped.'

'Good,' he said. 'Sounds like there are still some rules you follow.'

We walked in silence for a bit. Towering alongside the narrow strip of green that housed the canal were tower blocks of flats. Families were gathered on the balconies, firing up barbecues and lighting lanterns. The smell of burning ethanol and charcoal wafted down to us on the path.

'So,' said Ibrahim, as we reached the bridge. 'I'm going to carry on here.'

'OK,' I said.

'I'm sorry about this, Hasim,' he said.

I frowned. 'About what?'

'I can't continue your contract. You understand?'

Almost mute, like a schoolboy, I shook my head and strangled out a syllable. 'No.'

'The whole thing's too compromised now. You need to take a break from Justice, I think.'

'But...' I started. 'It's all... I mean, what else...'

'Haz,' he said gently. 'You've broken the rules, man. You can't continue.'

I huffed through my nose. 'It's Clive, in't it? What's he been saying?'

He looked confused. 'No. I haven't spoken to Clive for weeks now. It's the way he likes it.'

'Oh, right.'

'No, Haz. It's your work. It's erratic and you've... well, I'm afraid you've not abided by the terms of your contract. Personally, I think you need something different.'

'Something different?'

He nodded. 'Find something else to do for a while, yeah?'

I looked up and saw Asha land the first punch of the evening onto Ali's arm.

◆

Chapter Twenty-Three

The following day was Admin Friday again. Always seemed to come around faster. I'd very little to tidy up having done nothing that week. Beyond getting shot, messing up a date, and losing my job. Although it was a bit of a hobble, I managed to take the kids to school. Greg was never normally booked in for a Friday, so I didn't have to speak to him to explain the situation. He didn't need to know just yet. I'd tell him on Monday. I knew he would only nod and simper fake sympathy behind his sneery little attitude.

In the morning, I knocked back a couple of Hombres and made an effort at cleaning the flat. Now I was just pottering around it in the daytime, I could see it had got out of hand. Greg was supposed to clean it now and again. The little wrong 'un wasn't abiding by his contract. I took a few photos for evidence. The dirt behind the fridge was awful. It took a long time to re-program Asha's eMouse so it could squeeze behind there and take some incriminating photos. It cheered me up a bit. This was going to stitch him up something proper.

I dropped into Modlee at midday, not planning on doing anything while I was there but I was curious. As I'd predicted, the system had removed all my access. This would've happened the moment Ibrahim cancelled my contract. A rolling cascade of A-code deletions across all services and subscriptions. The only links left active in Modlee were the vanilla public domain data mountains. The stuff kids have access to. I could see how many gnu had made it across the Serengeti over the past fifteen years. I could draw up models of the tax take in Reading throughout the 40s' and display them in the default dynamic ripple charts. It was all rubbish. They'd chopped off my hands.

There was a message from my agency. I ignored it. I didn't want them giving me grief. I knew I'd have to talk to them soon enough. There was also a message from the DI. I checked it, just to see if he'd relented. He hadn't.

Sorry I had to do this, Hasim. I've tried to smooth things over with your agency. Told them you still come recommended from me if you're looking anywhere else.

* * *

It was nice to be able to pick the kids up after school. I made nondescript chat with some of the other parents. The ones who used to know Dali always took pity on me and made an effort to trot over to say hi. I could never remember their names. I smiled and lied and lied.

As we walked away, one of Ali's friends shouted after him. 'See you on Sunday!'

'Sunday?' I asked.

'Oh, yeah,' said Ali. 'Bil's coming to my party, as well, Dad. We invited him.'

'Oh,' I muttered. 'Yeah.'

Ali's birthday. Greg, the bastard, hadn't reminded me.

Some people went out to shops to buy gifts. This felt awkward for me. I had an online service which did it for me. I logged on Friday night. They would deliver Saturday. I put in Ali's age, the kind of things he liked. Because I'd used this service for the last three years, Christmas and birthdays, it knew what he already had. It was great. It cost a bit but it was easier than actually shopping.

It arrived while we were having breakfast. I hid it in the cleaning cupboard by the door.

I took Ali to his swimming lesson after dinner. It was a new facility up on the hill overlooking the southern flanks of Ilkley Moor. I took Asha along with me. She had to come normally, unless my mum and dad were around. I knew she found it boring, so I'd got her some tiny earbeads to listen to music with. She'd started getting micro-credits from me – automated, of course. She'd been spending them on the music. I didn't know what she listened to. I'd have probably hated it.

Today, though, she took out the earbeads and carefully cupped them in her hand. She watched Ali and the other children splashing for a moment and then took a breath. She lost her nerve and exhaled heavily, then took another breath. 'Have you been sacked, Dad?'

I narrowed my eyes and shrugged. 'Kind of, yeah.'

'By Mr Al-Yahmeni?'

'Yeah, he were my boss, so I guess it were him.'

'That's mean of him.'

'Weren't his fault.'

She paused for a moment. 'He bought us an ice cream.'

'Yeah.'

'That were kind, weren't it?'

'Yeah.'

'It were mean of him to sack you, though...'

'Yeah.'

There was a long silence and then another little breath. 'Are we going to be homeless?'

I laughed. 'What, love?'

'If you're sacked, that means we won't be allowed any credit. We can't pay the rent. Will we live with Grandad and Grandma?'

'No, I'll get another job. Plenty of work for your Dad.'

'Where you going to work, then?'

'Not thought about it, love. Don't worry.'

'Would we need to move out of Airedale?'

'Stop worrying. I'll get a job in Airedale.'

'A police job?'

I hesitated. 'Probably not, love. But they're plenty of other jobs for somebody like me.'

'What jobs are there?'

'There'll be some, don't worry.'

'Have you not looked yet?'

'You know, you nag like your–'

'What?'

'Nothing. Just listen to your music.'

'Just asking, Dad.'

'I'll look. Don't worry.'

On Saturday evening, I did start looking. First I went to unopened messages from the agency. It seemed Ibrahim had been true to his word. There were no recriminations. They wanted to talk to me.

I settled down and called them up. They were disappointed but professional and brisk. They didn't have time for analysis and post-mortems. They had to turn a job fast or they dropped you fast.

They had a few jobs still going in AJC. The one in Enforcement was out of the question, but there weren't any reasons why I couldn't go for a job in Prevention or the couple they'd posted in Reconciliation. Except Reconciliation were only a few floors away from Justice in Shipley. They'd also posted a few jobs in some private sector organisations. A facial harvesting operation in Cowling looked interesting. The others were grunt work. The kind of thing you'd get a grad to do. I thought I was ready to move away from the AJC work. But something was making me hesitate.

I wasn't ready to commit, so I told the agency I'd get back to them. They let me know they'd like to get an answer by the end of the weekend. I knew if I didn't give them a little burst of enthusiasm within a day, their local algorithms would be dialling me right down to the 'not really interested' category, which would be worse than a temp. Then, if I didn't put in the hours, I'd be off the spreadsheet and into the archive. It wasn't the guy at the end of the phone's fault. He'd a lot of clients to process. He needed some help with this. That algorithm helped him.

The next day was Ali's party. It was at some virtz arcade stuck into the northern flank of the dale above Shipley. I'd pre-booked it about five months ago. Well, technically, Greg had booked it with Ali. I'd approved it. Ali was very excited and had invited a few friends from school. There were a few second cousins too and I'd let Asha bring some of her friends along as well. I'd not invited my parents. They usually did drop into these things but I'd had enough of the needling about my personal life. Thankfully, none of my cousins were hassling me. I'd managed to grunt a hello and disappeared into a corner with a chocolate.

I only did this crap for Ali. I couldn't stand these events. There were children running everywhere, screaming. Parents everywhere, trying to have half-conversations. I took a sip of my chocolate, stuck my cap down close on my head, and randomly selected some news casting services. Shaky, head-held footage from wars and violence around the globe started to flicker across my eyeballs. My ears were filled with the sounds of screams and gunfire. It helped to distract me a little but it wasn't really cutting it.

Then I noticed I'd positioned myself not far from a newish-looking booth. I'd not seen this one before. It had a big sign on the outside: U-Vatar... have you ever wanted to talk to yourself?

I wandered over. It seemed to be some AI-driven device which read your facials or something. I stepped inside. The screen in front of me was blank, so I waited. I saw my face appear as though rising from a lake. It wasn't a reflection or even a streamed camera shot. It was moving independently of my movements. It raised its eyebrows at me.

I stared at the hateful, puffy-eyed avatar and told it to sod off.

'That's rude, naughty,' said the avatar. It had a northern accent but I knew it didn't sound like me. Underneath, some words scrolled up: Tell me about yourself.

I started mumbling, in a cod-American accent: 'My name's Mickey Mouse. I used to be a cartoon character but now I run anonymous cartels of illegal black-market drugs and guns. I'm everywhere, man.'

The avatar nodded. 'Hello, Mickey. Pleased to meet you. That sounds interesting.' I noticed its accent had taken on a false American note. 'Do you enjoy running cartels?'

'No,' I said. 'I sodding-well hate it.'

'In order to chat some more, you need to release some credits, Mickey. Wave your credit device over the screen here.' It produced an ethereal hand and pointed to a pulsing icon on the screen. I didn't move. We stared at each other for a few moments. Then it raised its hand. 'Goodbye, Mickey. Sorry it couldn't have lasted longer.'

As the face faded back into the darkness I stuck two fingers up at it.

I sat in silence in the booth for a moment. Then I had a thought. Firing up my bead, I dug around the files for any cached image files. I scrolled through them manually, zooming out as much as possible without losing the ability to recognise the key features. Then I spotted a familiar head shot. I dropped it onto my workspace. It took a couple of minutes to take out the background. I crouched down in the footwell of the booth, ensuring my head wasn't obscuring any cameras or sensors and placed my cap on the seat. I flickered with my fingers in front of the cap, until I had managed to project the image on the back of the booth. The curtain there was destroying the projection. I tugged it away to the side, revealing a smooth, plastic surface. The image projected perfectly.

'Dad?' I could hear Asha shouting. 'Where're you, Dad?'

I considered keeping quiet. Then I thought she might barge in on me, so I crawled out of the booth. 'What's up, love?'

'Can I have some micro-credits?'

'You've spent it all?'

'I didn't have much.'

'OK,' I said, digging around in my pocket. I threw a card at her. 'Take some pre-load. Be careful with it, though. I want some of that back, yeah?'

'Thanks, Dad,' she shrieked, and ran back into the dizzying twirls of light and sound.

Back in the booth, I could see the machine's cameras had picked up the projection. On the screen was an eerie floating face. Its eyes looked around the booth. It smiled. It frowned. There was still a little message asking for a name.

It took a few moments of playing with my processor, but I managed to get to the reposting site and search the archives. It didn't take long to find the right words. They were at the start of nearly every message she'd posted. I cut out a short audio clip.

'This is Meri Fergus.'

'Hello, Merifergus,' said the face in the booth. 'Tell me about yourself.'

I played the next clip. 'I'm here, telling the world the truth about Airedale.'

'That's interesting,' the face said. 'Is Airedale somewhere which interests you?'

I hadn't any more clips lined up. It was enough for the machine to simulate her vocal range. I stared at the face for a while as it repeated the words, 'Hello, Merifergus. Hello,' for a long time.

I was about to stop the game, but hesitated when reaching for my cap. I had another thought. I'd have some time, but would need to use the processor for this. With its camera pointed at the screen and its screen projected down onto the floor, I fired up another service.

I stretched a little, starting to get a crick in my back from the position. The face asked for credit, so I waved my hand in the direction of the screen and my bead zapped across the necessary code.

I watched the display shine on the grubby floor of the booth from the tiny projector in my processor. It was a login screen. You had to give yourself up to Memro. It had to take your ratios. It wouldn't let you see anything that wasn't unrelated to your ratios. You had to be in the vicinity. It would let you spy, but only on yourself.

I kept the camera focussed on the booth's screen, waiting. This was possibly illegal in a number of countries, but I didn't care much about that. Now I just wanted to see what Memro had on her. I wasn't going to leave this booth without finding out. I just hoped she wasn't already on the system.

The login service hadn't picked up her face properly. I tried moving the processor closer, until Meri's face nearly filled the screen. The face spoke.

'Hello, I'm Merifergus.'

I played the second clip again. 'I'm here, telling the world the truth about Airedale.'

'I'm glad you're here,' said the face.

I played the clip again.

'Tell me about Airedale,' said the face.

This was enough. The Memro service took her ratios and

tried to transcribe her name. It got it wrong, so I manually entered the name. She wasn't on the system because she'd have known about the pact you made with Memro. I hadn't been sure but I guessed she wouldn't have gone near it if she were alive.

I asked the service to cut a simple reel and turned my processor's projector so that it beamed directly into my eyes. There were no dates I needed to enter so I left those parameters empty with locations set to Airedale. Events were left blank. I watched the timer icon twirl in front of me before the reel started.

I got her whole life.

The service was struggling a bit. It had decided to break up the narrative, so I got a repeated shot of her in her late teens in some form of confessional. Sly conspiratorial eyes. I heard snippets of words but Memro didn't let me learn the full extent. Slo-mo footage from demos, uploaded to public domain re-posting sites. A graduation ceremony, looked like somewhere in Germany, happy parents, must've been taken by somebody else's camera, footage too zoomed, poor quality. Then flying, endless footage of her taking off, landing, taking off, landing.

I felt like I couldn't breathe. I couldn't stop myself from watching her.

I don't know how long he was there. I sensed his face just behind me. Perhaps I felt his breath on my neck. I turned.

'The lady says they're going to cut the cake.'

'Yeah? OK, Ali, give me a minute, yeah?'

'Why aren't you sat in the seat?'

'Um... it works better this way, yeah.'

He looked at me with a solemn expression. 'Are you watching Mummy again?'

I looked up at the screen momentarily. Meri's face hung there impassively. I snatched back my cap, breaking the projection. The face started to fade away. Too slowly for Ali, though.

'Who's that, Dad? It's not Mummy.'

'Nobody, it's just work, love.'

'This is what you do for work?'

'Something like this, yeah.'

'Oh,' he said, nodding a little. 'So you weren't watching Mummy again?'

'No,' I said. 'I weren't. Why'd you think I were?'

He stared at my eyes and my cheeks closely and breathed in through his nose. He shrugged. 'I don't know.'

'Shall we have some cake?'

'Yeah.'

I climbed back out of the booth, my back now a column of pain. Ali led me by the hand back into the throng of his friends, screaming around a table in the middle of the hall.

I'd made half a decision.

Later on, when we'd had our birthday tea and I'd tucked them into bed, I started to hit the media archives. I wanted to know what Prevention actually did. Whether they would be of any use to me. Their public-facing information was deliberately sketchy. They had to do this. Any government agency had to. Give away too much information and people could start to triangulate what you were capable of, where you had weak points, how you could be played. Some agencies were mischievously inventive with actual disinformation. Border control were telling people they could spot illegal asylum seekers from a continent away.

Some, like Those-Who-Have-Never-Even-Existed-Right, had kick-started a consensual myth-generating machine within society itself, maintained through carefully calibrated feedback mechanisms. Their power was now absolute.

Prevention clearly had some serious kit. They were running some big maths. They didn't tell you what it was for. They just talked about models.

Then I found a little interview with the spiky-haired man again. Talking on some late night IT discussion forum. He'd let his guard down.

'Are these models... I mean, these models we're discussing, are they based on real people?'

'Yes,'

'Like you and I?'

'That's how we build them. We need real data.'

'What kind of data?'

'Well, the typical models we're running, they need crime categories, locational vectors, IDs and the like. We're building meta-patterns. What sort of clustering shape forms before a mugging, does this pattern suggest a brawl is going to kick off and suchlike? But those models are only valid if–'

'If you've got real data to validate it against?'

'Well, yes. I mean to say, there are a number of datasets in play, that's all. I don't want to say much more than that.'

'Of course, of course. I understand.'

I posted a message to the agency. I asked them for the Prevention job. The agency confirmed the position about five minutes later. With full references from the DI.

Decision made.

Chapter Twenty-Four

—

First day with Prevention, I caught the train up to the northern end of the dale. Their office was in the floodplains of Lower Skipton, in the middle of the Data Barons. It was a squat cube, stark and hyper-modernist, constructed from graphene polymer and glass. When you stood at the top of the steps that led down to the car park underneath, you could just make out the lumpen shapes of hills in all directions, lurking behind the corners of other buildings.

The Data Barons had built their village in the confluence of three valleys. Craven headed to the West, Upper Airedale to the north, and then there were avenues of posh mansions which lined the road over to the west towards Wharfedale.

The moors that sat above Skipton and Ilkley were almost entirely encircled by urban clutter. Though nobody had bothered to put residential sites on the rock and bog of the tops themselves, they had been used for experimental vat-growing and splicing industries. Most of these had closed down, leaving virtual brownfield sites, frantic blizzards of wind turbines and rigs of solar panels.

My first morning there, I'd been introduced to the spiky-haired man – director-in-charge of the Prevention Branch, Cordan Grene. It seemed I was going to report directly into him, at least for the time being.

He was shorter in person than on the television, barely coming up to my chin. He had a round face which looked disconcertingly young for someone in such a senior position. I found out later that he was a lot older than he looked.

I found myself uneasy when he was talking to me. He was a jittery man, who spoke in a wavery, upper-class Glaswegian accent and who seemed to have to drop meds every few hours. I could imagine his display's handler was forever popping up, telling him what to do. Drop a yellow one now. Drop a red one in ten minutes. Breathe. Breathe.

The oddest thing about the office cube was how empty it was. Prevention, for all the noise about them on the news – and the grumbles about them from Enforcement – consisted of a team of only about fifty people. This was bolstered with the occasional subcontractor – like myself – who passed through on some compartmentalised and obscure task.

I made a few friends with the subcontractors but the permanent guys were heavy work, socially. As a digital analyst, if I was pointed out in Justice as the guy who spoke in binary, this lot were shitting ones and zeroes. They were hardcore. All had some post-doctorate letters after their name, through Durham and Newcastle.

It wasn't just their training that was intimidating. Seeing them in the flesh would freak out young children and pets. They all had hardware wired into their body somewhere. Double nose plugs, embedded ear pieces, tactile feedback loops running like black lace across the back of their hands and through their palms.

Before I started working there, I'd heard about girls having storage blocks inserted in with their breast jobs; I reckoned the two green-haired ones – who always sat giggling together on the first floor – probably had a little server farm stitched into their tits. The only thing that was stopping this lot going the next step and melding into the semantic soup was the fact they worked for AJC. And doing anything like that was highly illegal.

They'd told me that they'd get me coding. Or, at least, coding in the modern sense of the word. This wasn't the stuff I'd been taught at college. There were no issues with language and syntax and memory handling and all that antique rubbish. This was grindingly necessary human input into the code previously coded by other codes. That was the meta-shit kind of coding. Theoretically, it meant attempting to apply real-world meaning to digital constructs. In practice, it meant boxing up coloured blocks inside other coloured blocks via associative patterning, all to do with little comms clippings and media transcripts. It wasn't really coding at all. It was grunt work. The stuff you give the contractor. Still, if you're hungry and you've been thrown a scrap of rotting vat-grown, you just shut hell up and chew on down.

I got on with it, not really understanding what it was I was doing. Just that it was some module inside a bigger module. Mafu, the Tongan guy who'd taken my induction, had tried to explain the whole thing to me but he was speaking in a language far removed from my area of knowledge. It was about the rioting. I knew that.

It was some high-end modelling which ate up all the processing capacity sitting in the server banks below the car park – and then some. In between punching some opponents in the eternal online game he was clearly addicted to, he had proudly explained that they had bust most of their budget burning capacity in the farms built in upstate New York – cooled by Niagara Falls no less – and the latest state-of-the-art relays in Iceland.

I could live with it. Although it was boring, it was weirdly therapeutic. I could let my mind sink into the blocks floating up in front of me and the stack of gibberish semantic messages coming in from other Prevention teams across the globe.

I tried not to think about the world outside. But I knew I was only waiting. Passing the time.

On the second day, I had to read a comms piece about Meri Fergus' funeral. This had taken place at a secular memorial about half an hour's walk from the office. There were no vidz, obviously. Lani, the flyer from the moor, had apparently read a poem. The mother had wept. The father had carried the coffin, all by himself, on his shoulder. There was no mention of any criminal proceedings. It was all a terrible accident.

These things happen.

Most evenings, I tried to read to the kids, and when they were asleep, I would diligently obey the directives of my med-handler. Except from when I snuck out and scored new strains of spores. Then I would ride the visions, paranoid that Ali would wake up and want to know why I was lying on the living room floor in tears.

On the evenings when I wasn't snorting spores, I started communicating with Sadie again. She sent me pix of her son. He looked like a happy little surfer, all buzz-cut and red-cheeked. In return, I sent her vidz of my two, playing in the park which overlooked the mill. I still couldn't quite work out whether this was making me happy. But I did it anyway. Asha kept on at me and I couldn't let her down. Sadie was keeping something back, I could tell. It might've been because I was, as well. We dropped hints about meeting up again.

I kept well away from Memro and the VC. I couldn't risk going back there yet.

I never got back in touch with Carrie. I knew it would've sparked some kind of alarm somewhere. She never got in touch with me. I guessed she'd decided to take the hint and get out while she could. Prevention were still part of the same division as Enforcement. I had to pay my rent. I wasn't about to ruin this little window of stability.

I still had a plan, though. I just knew I had to wait.

* * *

I travelled up on the train to the next station. The one which sat between Lower Skipton and the towers of the Embsassy estates. It was a short walk through the preserved cobbles in the centre of Upper Skipton. Cordan lived in one of the glass-bottomed houses sitting astride the canal. Why anyone would want to have endless views of that swirl of muck and parasite colonies had always confused me. But – according to one of the green-haired girls – it was one of the most sought-after areas in northern Airedale.

To be fair to her, she had looked a bit sick at herself for knowing all this after she'd told me.

Cordan didn't invite me inside to show me his glass-bottomed rooms. I wasn't surprised. I wouldn't let me inside my own house on most days.

We were going to see the professor. I'd heard the news that Cordan was needing to consult on some esoteric matters regarding the model. Mafu had been down as the one who was supposed to go with him. But he was stuck on a particularly challenging level of his online game and I could tell he didn't want to go. As we were leaving one evening, I dropped hints to him that I could stand in for him, if he'd like. How I knew he was up to his neck in coding work. How I now understood the modelling work they were doing (did I bollocks?) and that I could feed back to him everything the professor told us.

Mafu nearly bit my hand off. He had to work hard on Cordan but eventually the director relented. So I arranged for Greg to get the kids after school and take them to my parents. He and I were on better speaking terms now. He didn't piss about huffing and puffing like a kid who'd been told to clean their room. If anything, he seemed cold and withdrawn.

Cordan had one of the newest models of autocar, legally allowed out on the roads by itself. Beyond the taxis – which the community accepted as a useful risk – you generally had to have a licensed driver sat somewhere inside. Just in case it dropped out of a few loops and started to ram other cars. The machine pulled up and tidily aligned itself to the kerb. It was small, neat, and hittable. Even the trim Californian accent, requesting our air conditioning needs, made my knuckles itch. Cordan had made me finish my breakfast burrito outside the car. I deliberately tried to breathe as much of its dirty egg and chilli sauce onto the fixtures.

We had a quiet journey. It was spent with me doing more of my semantic associations and Cordan doing... well, something with his display. This involved muttering to himself a lot and tweaking his hair to even higher spikes. The journey was relatively quick.

I'd been on a few holidays out this side of the EP and my childhood memories were mainly of sitting in hot traffic jams. These days you didn't get traffic jams. Cars had navigation systems which re-routed you around any snarl-ups. Or, more accurately, as Cordan explained at tedious length, it predicted where the snarl-ups were going to happen and re-routed itself on the back of this. Something to do with network mechanics or some bollocks. He loved the fact it did this. It made the little bugger proper excited.

I soon got bored and called up the MoreThanSum service, checking whether Sadie had left me any messages. I kept it open, in case she came on and joined me for a chat. I also started drifting my way through some adverts for other child care workers. I'd been meaning to do this properly for some time.

We were passing underneath the southern bulk of the Moors when Cordan hit me with a question. 'Hasim?'

'Yeah?'

'You're a digital analyst, aren't you?'

'That's right.'

'You ever used Spidz?'

I shook my head. I'd heard the name, it was some network analysis tool. 'No. I tend to use Modlee.'

'Ah, Modlee, yes,' he said. Without even looking round, I knew he was trying not to smirk. 'I forgot that's what you guys used. Well... I'm trying to get you set up on Spidz. I think it would be useful for you. I've plugged in your ID and it's come back with a query.'

'What kind of query?'

'Just... it says it will need to refer up to a human handler.'

I frowned, my stomach had knotted up again. 'Never had any trouble before.'

'Very odd.'

'You want me to check on mine?' I asked.

He shrugged. 'If you'd like. I don't want to send this off and get a load of crap on my plate.'

'Of course.'

'You've not been doing any mucky stuff lately?' he asked me, only half-joking.

I laughed. 'No more than usual! Couldn't do my job if I were, yeah?'

'You check, then.'

I closed down MoreThanSum and Modlee. Then fired up the Spidz registration pages. I got past putting in my ID and saw the follow-up questions. I worked my way through these and hit the icon to pass the registration through. I paused at the final confirmation.

'Worked for me,' I said. 'You want me to put it through, yeah?'

'Wait.' After a few moments, he grunted a little. 'Worked for me now, as well. Odd.'

'One of those things, in't it,' I said.

'Yeah,' he said. 'I'm going to put this through–'

I had a thought. 'Wait up. Can I check something first?'

'Fine,' he sighed. 'You do it, OK.'

I logged back into Modlee and MoreThanSum. Then I went through the Spidz registration. I got the screen requesting human referral. I grunted. The small knot in my stomach tightened. The breakfast burrito was feeling like a mistake.

'You alright there, Hasim?' asked Cordan.

'No problem,' I said. I hurriedly closed down the Modlee and MoreThanSum services and carried on putting through my registration. 'I'm just getting it set up now.'

'Great,' he said. 'That'll be useful. Did Mafu tell you what you'd be doing for him today?'

I shook my head. 'Not really, like. Just that I were to take notes and all.'

Cordan sighed. 'I thought it would be like that.'

'Suppose there's more to it, then?'

'A little, yes,' said Cordan. He looked totally hacked off now. 'You know who we're going to see?'

'Some professor,' I said. 'Canadian, yeah?'

Cordan glanced across at me. 'You've done a bit of research then, anyway.'

'Got my sources.'

'Well, Tad's been helping us with the model.'

'What model?' I asked. I knew exactly what he was talking about, but nobody ever spoke about it. Like it was some kind of big fucking secret, except it was all over the comms channels.

'The riots, Hasim. We're modelling the riots.'

'Bloody hell,' I said with a whistle. I might have overdone it as Cordan turned in his seat and looked at me as though I was taking the mick.

'Yes,' he said. 'We're trying to prevent them. Tad's an expert in this kind of thing.'

'So,' I said, digging my hands deeper into their pockets. 'He reckons you can … what?… Predict it and that?'

Cordan shook his head. 'No, he says it's near to a statistical impossibility. But we can explore means to reduce the probabilities of them occurring.'

'Uh huh,' I said.

'What Mafu was supposed to be doing today was understanding Tad's approach. To get a feel for the patterns. You're doing the associations, now, aren't you?'

'Yeah,' I said. 'I guess so… the little blocks, yeah. And the news clippings and that.'

'Yes,' said Cordan. 'The little blocks. You know why you're doing that?'

'No,' I said.

'Because you are still faster at making those connections than all the server farms we're currently renting off Iceland and the East Coast.'

I nodded. 'True, that.'

Cordan laughed. 'And we need those links as part of the bigger model. Mafu's supposed to be working on the next level up. He needs to know the patterns. You're going to take note of the patterns, alright?'

'Yeah,' I muttered.

I spent the rest of the journey pretending to read the papers Cordan had directed me towards. None of them were really sinking in. My mind was on other things.

It was a shock when we pulled up alongside the waterfront and I stepped out, the wind from the North Sea tearing at my parka jacket, fighting my hands as I tried to pull my hood up over my head. I gave up in the end. It was supposed to be getting close to midsummer but it was grimly cold and there were no patches of blue in the sky.

I was hit by the multiple sensations of coastal nostalgia. Sure, Memro and VC made memories sharper for me, but they never captured the full thick smack of the tactile sensations like spray hitting your face, chilled cheekbones, the smell of seaweed, chips and churros. I had been on this beach at least four times. Three times as a young child and once as a teenager.

A tall, blonde girl from the Netherlands had tried to drag me away to the virtz-games hall. My parents had – a little too eagerly, I thought – waved me away with her. She had kissed me in the Jack Salt Assaulter booth. Her tongue, which tasted of doughnut grease, had ran itself all over my front teeth. I couldn't remember her name. Even the memory of her face was gappy – although I had recently successfully tracked it down via Memro using some judicious time-location filters. But the memory of that tongue pushing itself on my incisors, insistently, was always there.

'Love it here,' I said.

'Do you?' asked Cordan. He looked around, blinking a little bit. 'I hate it. It's horrible.'

'Where we going?' I asked.

Cordan pointed to the third pier.

I knew a little about the university. At one time, I'd even thought about attending. It was one of the modern-style dispersed institutions. I pulled up a map on my display and filtered for all the uni buildings. It had accumulated tutorial rooms, lecture theatres, and administration offices wherever there was the cheapest rent. As long as there was sufficient walking time between the buildings. I had attended a similar university in Bradford and the SLS. In the SLS, we had been allocated a twenty-minute walk, which meant the campus could cover a lot of ground. In the morning, I could be in a draughty industrial unit somewhere, working on something practical, then move onto a tenth floor apartment for a tutorial, finishing my day at the cafeteria that the students shared with the Christian homeless.

I supposed that Scarborough had settled on a ten-minute walk vector, as my map was sparking up nodes across the centre of town and up the older parts of the castle walls. I looked out to sea and saw the three piers. Our destination seemed to be on the southernmost one of the piers.

The pier had been built to house numerous retail concessions, no doubt selling candy floss and burrito bites, but most of these had gone. There was a burnt smell of meat too long on a griddle, mixed, not unpleasantly, with the smell of the sea. The university had rented out a few of these units and their cheery brand was stamped across the doors.

The professor's offices overlooked the sea. While on the pier I could see the waves, grey and white, sloshing between the boards underneath my feet. But inside the professor's offices, it was warm and cosy. They'd packed in some wool insulation and a heater. The pier-side windows had been darkened, to stop snoopers, but the windows facing the covered the entire wall.

The two units were connected by a modular door. By the numbers of chairs in the first room, I judged that this was used for tutorials or possibly small lectures. We were taken into the second unit which was oddly spartan, with plain grey walls, painted in faux-concrete style. A chair sat facing the ocean with an expensive-looking processor and screen rig beside it. Set along the entirety of the pier-facing wall was a bookcase, covering the old door. I'd never seen so many books in one place. The guy must've been a collector or something.

The professor was much larger than he'd looked on television. Broad as well as tall. I felt puny but Cordan must've felt like an ant. We made our introductions and he apologised for wanting to meet in person. It appeared this was the deal with Cordan. He'd insisted we make the journey. Insisting that he wasn't paranoid, merely that he'd yet to understand what it meant to communicate these ideas through a vidz-link which were a poor means of communicating. I knew what he meant. On vidz-link, you can't smell the bullshit.

The professor went to collect chairs from the adjoining room. Catching me unawares, he slid it across the floor at me with a gruff, 'Catch'. Thankfully, I managed to field it without making a fool of myself. As Cordan and the professor settled down, I sat myself near to the wind-lashed windows. And, as the low tones of the Canadian and the lighter Scots of Cordan mingled in conversation, I couldn't help letting my gaze drift out towards the sea.

'Hasim here,' said Cordan, jolting me out of one of my reverie. 'Has been working on the comms links.'

'I see,' said Tad. 'You getting it?'

I tried to read Cordan's blank gaze. Was I supposed to pretend I knew what I was doing?

'A little, yeah.'

'Well, you're doing the words. We also have the vidz. That's a whole new area you can look into. I've been watching the footage over time. I can take the noise out and leave just the salient information. If we generalise it enough, this gets you to the meat. It's difficult to explain what these bits of information mean. Possibly we don't have the grammar for that yet. They may represent something that would be impossible for us to explain. Possibly even to comprehend. Anyway, we need to get these generalised peaks of information in order to measure the whole. I've started to find true elements of dynamism here. The whole changes shape. In an ordered way. It's not a random thing.'

He stood and waved a hand. One of the walls shimmered into life. After a little Canadian-style cursing, the professor managed to navigate to the right model. A complicated graph sprang onto the wall. It made no sense to me. Looked like our kitchen table after Ali had been at the spaghetti.

'Look, if I run the pattern here,' said the professor, waving his hands. 'You can see this generalised shape, then it goes to this, and... three weeks ago, it went back to that shape. I've called that alpha state, this one here beta state, and that, gamma. Alpha seems to be the steady state. Then beta is a series of stuttering declines in violence.

'What's gamma?' asked Cordan.

'That's a spike. Correlations between the gamma state and meta-media data suggests it's when the...' At this point, he laughed a little self-consciously and sat back in his chair. 'That's when the shit really goes down.'

'That's only correlation, though, isn't it?' said Cordan.

'Of course, it's all only correlation. We don't understand why this happens. But we need to see the patterns first.' He turned to me. 'You getting all this, Hasim?'

I nodded. 'The patterns... yeah.'

'It's not the patterns we need to worry about,' said Cordan. 'That's just the abstraction. It's the measure. It's the system dynamics underneath.'

'What system?' I asked. I was beginning to sweat.

'Sheesh,' said Tad. 'The riots. Conceive a discrete riot as a system–'

'They're not that discreet,' I said, laughing a little hysterically.

'Yeah,' said Tad. 'There's an arbitrary boundary, for sure. All open system boundaries are a bit fuzzy, it goes with the territory. But try to imagine that a riot is a discrete entity, with sub-systems, rules. A system, yeah?'

'Oh, right,' I said. I thought for a moment, frowning. 'Can anything be a system?'

'Nothing can be a system,' said Tad. 'It can only be conceived as a system. Or rather, it's useful to be able to conceive something as a system.'

'Eh?' I said.

'Don't worry,' said Cordan. 'It's not important...'

Tad had started to get into his topic. He was animated now.

'Think of all those rioters forming a larger whole. That larger whole has behaviour. If there is an appropriate configuration of rioters, then it starts to repeat certain action. Sometimes there is behaviour that can be identified and we might even be able to draw up rules for it.'

'All rioters together form the... something else? A system?'

'That's correct. Conceptually.'

'A bunch of people is... well, a bunch of people, in't it?'

'Depends how they are configured. A soccer team isn't really a soccer team if you don't have all eleven players on the same pitch all at the same time. It's just a bunch of eleven men or women who share the same design of shorts. If three of your players were in Greenland and your goalkeeper was in Sri Lanka, they're not going to behave as though they were a football team. In the same way, if they were all on the pitch but half of them had their legs tied up and the other half had blindfolds on, they wouldn't have the appropriate properties to be a football team. The parts that make up the whole must have appropriate properties and be appropriately connected in appropriate configurations. Then they... well, some might say they start to have the properties of something like a machine, or an animal.'

This was it.

'Or a person?' I asked, quietly.

Tad frowned, thinking. 'Yes, I guess so. Some societies, some economies behave as though they have isomorphic similarities to the human personality.'

Cordan was starting to drum his fingers on his knee. I guessed it was time to stop. Smiling and nodding a thank you to the professor, I sat back, tapping away on my slab.

'You want to hear about the inhibitory signals?' asked Tad.

Cordan nodded. 'Yes. Let's move on.'

The talk continued for a while. We were only there for about another hour. The professor said he had a group who was going to be there at three and he had to prepare. I tried to listen to most of it. It was now necessary, but difficult not to let my mind drift away to other systems, other configurations.

Back at the car, I made up an excuse. Something about seeing an old friend. About catching the train back myself. Cordan nodded and said he understood. Inside, I could see he was punching the air and whooping like a demented cheerleader. I could sympathise; I couldn't stand being in my own presence either.

The station was about ten minutes' walk from the waterfront. I set off, consciously leaving my hood flapping around on my shoulders. I tilted my head upwards and pushed my cap back a little to ensure maximum coverage.

There were a couple of kiosks down in the underpass that led to the station entrance. One sold drinks, chocolate, and churros, the other novelties. They were both underneath the 360-degree camera array. I positioned myself in front of the novelties kiosk, standing close under its awning, to ensure I wasn't being recorded. I picked up a pirate's fancy dress costume. I still had some pre-load in my watch, so I waved some off into the stallholder's device. I stuffed the costume into one of my pockets and walked out into view of the cameras, waving my arms as though they were empty and I had no money. I shrugged apologetically at the bemused stallholder.

Then I sought out the toilets. They were down the end of a dark corridor off the underpass. People got a bit upset when they found out you were vidding them in the loo. They were a safe place. Back in the time when they drowned witches and threw urine out their windows in the morning, people would make for the church when they needed sanctuary. Sanctuary these days meant toilets.

On the wall outside the toilets, next to the little booth where the attendants would normally hang out, there was an emergency first aid pack. I checked there was nobody else coming down the corridor, then knocked in the protective glass with an elbow and lifted out the pack. I carefully lifted a piece of the glass from the floor and dribbled some sanitizer over it from the auto-dispenser by the door.

I found a cubicle and used the shard of glass to make a cut under my right eye. Sorted through the contents of the first aid pack until I found the little packets of dressings, and ripped one open to dab on the blood from the cut. Then I applied it and taped it down carefully so that my right cheekbone bulged out a little.

I dug out my pirate costume, separating a red-haired wig, a plastic waistcoat, a bandana, and an eye patch. I considered the wig, before vanity kicked in and I dumped it back in the bag. Hair wasn't an issue. The waistcoat was useless, so that went back in the bag as well. I took off my cap and applied the eyepatch to my left eye, drawing in the elastic tight to keep it in place. It was uncomfortable to wear, placing it a little out of where it would normally rest. If I looked tight to my right, I could just see out from behind the patch. The bandana went straight on. Although it wasn't necessary – I guessed – I thought of other eyes. Anyway, I hated having to show my bald patch and bandanas were cool.

After unlacing my trainers, I kicked off my left one and fished around inside for the removable sole. I doubled this over and stuffed it back in. I put the trainer back on and laced it up again. I tested the feel of it. It would be enough.

I stuffed the bag of unused costume behind the toilet bowl. Powered down my bead and stuffed my cap in one of the pockets of my jacket. I walked back out onto the concourse. With as much ease as I could manage, I trotted up the staircase that led back into the town centre.

I walked most of the way to his house – finding it was the easiest piece of data linking I'd done for a while – and lurked. The walk didn't take long. Scarborough was a small town, after Airedale. But the wait was glacial. Nearly an hour before he appeared.

He clearly didn't recognise me at first. Then I remembered I was dressed as a pirate. I raised the eyepatch.

'Hey! It's you, from Airedale... with Cordan, right? What are you doing here?' He looked unnerved.

I raised my hands. 'Look, just a quick chat, yeah.'

'I don't have time... Hasim, wasn't it?'

'Yeah, it's Haz, look–'

'I've got to get in to see my family, Haz. Please let me get by, yeah.'

'It'll only take a minute, for honest! It's about what you were talking about before.'

A few seconds previously, he had looked as though he were going to shoulder me aside and get through to his drive. Now he was more relaxed.

'OK, Haz. A few minutes only. What happened to your face? And why are you dressed as a pirate?'

The street where Tad lived had no real security cameras on display. They'd have been removed as part of the sweep that happened after EPIG. I was sure a few drones might pull a fly-by, though. I'd tried to get some cover from a large box-wagon but I'd had to leave its protective bulk while heading the professor off at his gate.

'Long story, doesn't matter,' I said. 'Look, you ever heard of Modlee, MoreThanSum, or Spidz?'

'Spidz is a service I use,' he said. 'I know some people use Modlee, God help them! Never heard of MoreThanSum.'

'Well, you're probably married, yeah?'

'Yeah, sure am,' he said. 'And she's waiting for me, Haz, so make this quick, OK?'

'OK, yeah... well, could these services be linked? Could there be some kind of connection between them?'

'God alone knows! Why?'

I explained what had happened in the car over to Scarborough, the fact that my security clearance became doubtful when I was also logged into the other services. Then I talked about the North-Western facility I had visited with Louie, and the AG rating. I didn't talk about the drone attacking me in Oxenhope. I was worried I might start sounding like a paranoid freak.

'What's your point, Haz?'

'Isn't this... I mean, what you were talking about... feedback, and that?'

He laughed. He looked like he meant it. 'That's why you've gone to all this trouble? Why didn't you ask me this in the office?'

'Weren't part of my work, yeah.'

'Well, short answer is – who knows? Sounds like there's some kind of central or third-party security rating these services' access. It could be that. Bores the hell out of me, though, Haz! Good luck with registering for Spidz!'

'Right.'

'Can I get to my house now?'

I nodded and stepped aside from the gate. He nodded at me and crunched up the gravel. I turned to him.

'Professor!'

'Yeah, what?' he said, about to wave his beacon at the door.

'You know you said the riots form a... you said it was a "whole," a thing in itself. Well... not form, you said, but... but they can be seen as a thing in itself. With its own rules and behaviour?'

'It's simplified shorthand but, yeah, I'll accept that. What's your point?'

I hesitated then cleared my throat. 'Could a place... a region do the same?'

'What?' He shrugged. 'Oh yeah, sure, whatever. Is that it?'

'Yeah,' I said quietly.

'Good evening, Haz.' He closed the door.

Chapter Twenty-Five

The train trundled around the bend onto the second rail bridge. I dug out a battered pre-loaded payment card and squeezed its corner gently. A few digits emerged from the depths of the display before sinking back again. It seemed I was going to run out of money soon. I had a couple of similar cards which I'd checked, but the numbers were much smaller.

I grunted. Once that shit was gone, and I needed more credit, my time and location would be transmitted and persist forever. I had to try and eke it out.

From the previous times I'd been up here, I'd learned not to look out of the window at this point. But I glanced across at the other bridges anyway. The late afternoon sun had lit the bridges to my right in a warm, red glow. To my left, they were a Victorian silhouette of mesh and girders. Today I felt much better about the height. I'd never enjoyed the view so much, which felt good.

I stuffed the cards back into my jacket pocket, finger tips brushing the folded piece of paper. I resisted the need to check it again. I knew it was there.

I walked through the centre of town and it only took about ten minutes to find the public information facilities. It was hidden in one of the backstreets off the main shopping square. These places always felt cavernous and smelt of damp. My

Grandad had once told me these PIFs used to be full of books. You could take them out for free. It must've been slow getting your hands on data back in those days.

I ducked my way past the cameras on the front desk and found myself a dark corner. I cranked up one of the wall-mounted slabs and started clicking my fingers in front of it. I noticed the screen had been partially cracked where the steel clasps which held it to the wall had been too tightly screwed.

In a few minutes, I'd managed to set up a small business site and got myself a comms presence. I fired off an introductory message and received an automated message in response. I was really wanting somebody in particular. I hope he hadn't gone too early. The message had made clear I wanted their business.

I had the folded piece of paper in my lap with an address on it. I'd been thumbing the bit of paper so much on the journey up, it was starting to become a ragged around the edges.

The screen pinged a response. A human response – although it was harder and harder to tell these days. He said he could meet up. I replied, telling him I could get to the company office. He responded that he was leaving but there was a pub opposite. He gave me the address.

The Metro line weaved its way through the skeletal structures along the riverfront. Although I'd visited the place a few times, I'd never been along the Tyne at this end of the city. They still made some of the best virtz up here. This was the home of the stories made especially for you. As an adolescent, I'd immersed myself in the lives of werewolves and gangsters and space junkies. They'd all been born somewhere around here.

I found the offices and the pub. It was busy when I went in, but he spotted me immediately. I congratulated him.

'Not many folk with an eyepatch in here, man,' he said. 'What's the story?'

I muttered something about a condition.

'Oh, aye?' he said. He could tell I didn't want to tell him

anything more. He was in his mid-thirties, about my age. He wore a suit, which was an oddly retro fashion. But then, that could be his way.

'So, you work with Darren?' he asked.

'That's right,' I said. 'Well, the whole Board, you know.'

'You know Abi, then?' he asked brightly.

'Yeah,' I said. I guessed that must be Abi Hassan. The Chair.

'What kind of things you trying to do?'

'Oh you know… the usual,' I said. 'Marketing the brand and that.'

He nodded. 'Getting it out there?'

'Yeah,' I said. 'We're just trying to add value and that.'

'Add value,' he said. 'Of course.'

'Thing is,' I said. 'I'm going to need something more… from you, that is. If that's possible?'

'More than the index?' he asked.

'Do you offer more?' I asked.

He laughed. 'Don't know what you're getting at, man. We don't give out free massages with every Regionale contract, you know!'

I laughed as well. 'Perhaps you should?'

'Aye', he said. 'Perhaps we should. But I still don't quite see what you're after.'

'Well,' I said. 'I mean, your business, it runs the sums, doesn't it? It does something like that, yeah?'

'We generate the indices, aye.'

'So,' I said, starting to lean in closer. 'What goes into that?'

He looked at me for a moment, suddenly less friendly. 'Are you trying to bump your score?'

I shook my head firmly. 'No! It's not that at all. I'm not asking for any of the secrets. I don't expect you could give me that–'

'The only way to improve your Regionale rating,' he said. 'Is to make your region a better place.'

'I know,' I said. 'That's in your marketing and all. But you must know some of what goes into it… don't you?'

He frowned. 'Have you spoken to Abi about this?'

I shrugged, unsure how to respond. 'Yeah…'

He continued. 'Well, I've told her all this.'

'Look,' I said. 'I'm trying to get some business off the ground. She's going out to tender on this. I'm just one of the possible bidders. I've come all this way – can't I get a little help?'

He frowned, checking the pub again. 'OK. But only what I'm allowed to tell you. You could be an auditor, couldn't you?'

I smiled and showed my palms. 'I could be… but I'm not, buddy, yeah.'

'What's your question?'

I cleared my throat and spoke quietly. 'How is the rating linked to the Ghawar indices?'

'That's nothing to do with us. Our agency manages the Regionale indices, not Ghawar.'

'But there's a link?'

'Aye, there's a link,' he said. 'But it's at their end, not ours. Nothing to do with us, man.'

'An increase in the Regionale leads to an increase in the Ghawar index?'

'If you say so. Like I said, it's not connected to what we do. They handle their own indices.'

'OK,' I said. 'So, you've spoken to Hassan and Caines about this?'

'Aye,' he said, taking a swig from his pint. 'Well, only to Abi, really. Not spoken to Darren Caines about it. She was interested in it.'

'And you told her it were nothing to do with your business?'

'That's right.'

I nodded. There was a cup of tea on the table in front of me. I realised I hadn't touched it. A tiny midge had landed on its surface and was trying to climb up the side.

'And did you talk about risk?' I asked, still staring at the midge.

'What?'

I looked up at him. 'Did you talk about "risk"? About Enforcement?'

He took a breath and stopped. 'Who are you from?'

'I told you,' I said, a little harder this time. 'Why're you so interested in that now?'

'They told me you were from a start-up. Beth told me you were from a semantic marketing start-up.'

'Who says I'm not?'

He looked around the pub, panicking. 'I shouldn't be talking about all this–'

'Sure you can, buddy,' I said. 'Have your drink.'

He took a sip of his pint. 'It's getting late. I should be going, really. Getting back, you know.' He started to rise from his seat and gather his jacket.

'Sit back down.'

He fell back into his seat, white-faced. Even I surprised myself.

'Who are you?' he hissed.

'Perhaps I'm audit… perhaps I'm Justice… hey, perhaps I'm the company director of a small semantic marketing start-up. It don't matter.'

'Justice?' he whispered.

I just stared at him across the table.

'You going to answer my questions?' I asked him.

'I don't know,' he stuttered a little. 'I don't know. I mean, you could be anybody, couldn't you?'

'I have to know what you've told Abi Hassan and Darren Caines.'

'But they're clients,' he whined.

'A girl has died.'

He clamped his mouth shut. I realised I'd probably screwed it up.

'Am I under arrest?' he asked.

'No,' I said, smiling. 'There's nothing to worry about.'

'Are they under suspicion?'

'They might be… we don't know yet.'

He started rummaging through his jacket pockets. 'I should be calling Billy.'

'Billy?'

'Aye… our CEO.'

I shrugged. 'If you want to prolong this, that's probably right thing to do… but then he might get to hear more than he should about what you've told your clients.'

He froze. 'I've done nothing wrong.'

'I'm sure that's true.'

'Look,' he said, speaking very slowly. 'I have done nothing wrong.'

'I know that,' I said. 'I trust you.'

He frowned and regarded me suspiciously. 'Aren't you supposed to have ID or something?'

I rummaged in my pocket and pulled out my cap. I pointed at the logo. 'That good enough for you?'

He shrugged. 'AJC? Never heard of it.'

I was a little deflated by this response. 'Airedale Justice Commission. I'm in the Justice Division.'

'Ahh,' he said, nodding. 'Hence Hassan and Caines. That's the Airedale account, of course.'

I smiled. 'It's all fitting together, yeah?'

He looked at the cap again. 'Still, anybody can buy a hat, can't they? Aren't you supposed to have proper electronic ID and that kind of thing?'

I had been worried about this. 'You want my A-codes?' I tried to be as aggressive about it as I could.

He was shaky. But he still nodded.

Dammit.

'OK,' I said. 'Sure.' I stuck the cap on my head and fired up my bead. A flurry of messages started popping up in a carousel of subject lines across the bottom-left corner of my display. I tried to ignore them and started trying to find my A-codes. I hoped he wouldn't realise they had a best-before date.

Across the table, he had slipped some sunglasses out of his pocket and had put them on. He looked an idiot. I found my A-codes and cast them across to his sunglasses.

I noticed a stack of missed messages from both my mother and my father.

I tried not to get distracted. 'You got those now?' I asked.

He nodded and then took off his sunglasses. 'OK. Fine. Why the start-up rubbish, though? Doesn't seem like proper process.'

I shrugged. 'Down at the AJC, we do things a little differently... devolution and that, yeah?'

He nodded. 'Aye, I understand that... we try and work with the team in London and it's a whole different country down there.'

'So,' I said, trying to concentrate. I considered turning off my bead. 'Back to Hassan and Caines. What do they know about the Airedale Regionale index?'

'A lot,' he said. 'What do you want me to do? Start from the beginning?'

'No,' I said. 'Just the money side... the effect Regionale has on the investment indices. When did you talk to them about that?'

He struggled to think. 'I can't remember. But it was only Hassan on that. I've sent her documents and the like.'

'You sent her documents?'

'Aye,' he said. He looked a little shame-faced. 'It was... well, it was part of our new client pack. We think it's a selling point of the Regionale index, you see.'

'You expect regions to start investing cash against their name?'

He looked about wretchedly. 'Not that... no, it's just an opportunity for clients... well, not even that, really. We use it to demonstrate the true power of the index. Like, the fact that it has an impact on the real world, you know?'

I nodded. 'I can see the real-world impact, buddy. What about Caines?'

'I've only spoken to him once. Abi was my main contact. She signed off all the payments.'

'What did you speak to him about?'

'Are you recording this?'

'Of course. Would you rather I didn't?'

'Aye. I get to request that, don't I?'

'You do,' I said. I turned off the recording. Some words from one of the messages floated across the bottom of my screen: *Airedale Family and Child Support Service.*

'You done?' he asked. I nodded, trying not to read my messages. 'Well, I spoke to him just the once. He'd heard there was a correlation between Enforcement risk levels and the Regionale index. He wanted to know if it was true.'

'What did you tell him?'

'I told him... I told him that, yes, there was a correlation It's something we've known in the company for a while. Something to do with the way we've linked up the algorithm.'

'You recorded this conversation with Caines?' I'd stopped listening properly and was reading my messages.

Airedale Family and Child Support Service.

'No,' he said. 'But Caines did. He said he wanted to talk to the others about it.'

'The others?'

He shrugged. 'I don't know. You're not going to use that as evidence... are you?'

But I was already running for the door.

Chapter Twenty-Six

———

'I don't know, Haz, love… they wouldn't tell us. I tried, love, I really tried.'

'Must be in the dale somewhere, aren't they?'

'I don't know. I couldn't speak to anybody. Except the receptionist. She were being helpful but she said she couldn't give me any more information.'

'What about Greg?' I asked. 'Does he know anything?'

'Love,' said my mother. She'd turned off the visuals. I could only hear her voice in my ear. She choked. 'He were the one who did it.'

'What?'

'He took them in himself… he's been telling all sorts of stories, I think.'

'Greg took them?'

'That's what the receptionist told me. Well, she told me that their care worker had dropped them off.'

'Did she tell you why… I mean, were there any reason given?'

'Oh, Hazzie,' she sobbed. 'They said it were neglect. Whoever it were… Greg or whoever, they said you'd neglected them, the little ones. They said it were neglect. Oh, Hazzie–'

I ripped off my cap and slammed it on the dashboard. I coughed out a command thickly: 'Car, stop!'

'Command understood,' said the car. We were working our way through heavy traffic, south past Washington, still in the cut-n-cover. Ahead of me, past the red glow of flickering car sensors, I could see the arch of dim twilight. The car must've fired off its messages to its neighbours, because the cars to my right parted – some surging forward, some dropping back – and left a gap just large enough to let the taxi pass through. With sharp but precise movements, the taxi swerved left, across three lanes, and came to an abrupt halt on the hard shoulder. I heard the locks on the door click and I yanked the manual release, spilling myself out onto the tarmac.

The noise outside was eerie. Hundreds of muted vehicles, all moving at speed, their tyres pulling at the surface of the road. It was like a rushing waterfall, a high-pitched roar. The smell was a dark, sharp distillation of grease and heated metal.

Leaning forward on one knee by the car, I dry-heaved. Once. Twice. Then I controlled myself. This was pointless. I punched myself viciously in the stomach. The pain distracted me. I punched myself again. It felt good. I tried hitting my head. It felt better.

I stood up, nausea gone. My stomach and my head hurt. I kicked the concrete wall of the cut-n-cover. Just above shoulder height was a small walkway, protected by a steel balustrade. I head-butted one of the metal uprights. I knew people were watching from windows of cars as they passed me. Some were pointing. Some were laughing. I didn't care.

After I got back in the car, I told it to carry on south and put my cap on again.

'Haz! Hazzie! Are you still there?'

'Fine, Mum,' I said. 'Just had to get some air, yeah. Much better now.'

'What are we going to do?'

'Coming home now, Mum,' I said. 'Going to sort it.'

'Where are you? Are you still in Scotland?'

'Just,' I lied. 'Near the border now.'

'Oh, love,' she sighed. 'Your special evening tonight. It's all been ruined, hasn't it?'

What special evening?

'It's fine. Going to sort it.'

'How long will it take you?'

'Don't know,' I said. 'Are you at home?'

'Yes.'

'Well. Stay there. I'll call the Family Service now. See if I can speak to somebody who knows what's going on.'

'OK.'

The Airedale Family and Child Service clearly all went home after six. There was an automated call-handler, who was unable to understand my request to be put through to somebody in charge. I guessed that's why they'd deployed it. Effective. They had some idiot on their messaging site who was answering written posts, but he seemed to be mainly interested in the fundraising side. Every other message posted was asking for donations from people worried about neglected children. Having read down some of the comments on the board, I thought it best not to crash their party. I wouldn't be welcome.

I checked my Modlee access. It was now fully locked, unsurprisingly.

The taxi emerged from the cut-n-cover. The red glow from the summer twilight lit and warmed the right side of my face. I'd concluded that if the taxi travelled directly across from Harrogate, it was going to be quicker than changing multiple indirect trains and approaching the dale from the south. I wasn't so sure now. The traffic was bunching up too much. This was going to slow me down.

'Car,' I said. 'Estimated journey time?'

'Three hours, twelve minutes.'

'You what?' I said. 'That's not what you said twenty minutes ago.'

'I'm sorry, I don't understand.'

'Oh, forget it. Car, what is the estimated journey time without traffic?'

'One hour, forty minutes.'

'Dammit. Find an alternative.'

'You want me to find an alternative route?'

'Yes. Go totally cross-country. Smaller roads, you know.'

'There is a higher risk of unforeseen congestion.'

'And what if we stay on this road?'

'There is a high risk of continuing congestion.'

'Re-route. Just get me home.'

'Re-routing now.'

All around me I could see other cars doing the same. They would be in contact with each other, sharing their routes, negotiating the best option. This kind of congestion was supposed to have been eliminated by all the autocars. It was strange to see it happening here.

I lost interest in where the taxi was taking me. I was grappling with Spidz now. Despite having only been on it a few seconds, I was already missing Modlee. Spidz had clearly been designed without any involvement from a user. It was a pig of a system. But after a little tutorial and some fiddling with the screens, I started to find the data. There was no way I was going to be able to design and run the simulations the system was designed for. But I could get some information out of it.

It had total demographic data for Airedale, anonymised, naturally. But they'd left enough hooks in there for me to get at the truth. I needed to find them.

I knew the family service would've a scattering of voluntary homes across the region. Each of these homes, these families, would've been carefully vetted, and had to meet some strict admin just to be considered. Short of hacking the servers directly – which was out of my league and would've sent half the nat-cybers on my case – there were other routes. I knew there'd be some indicators I could latch on to.

Spidz had all the crime data going back five years. Even minor anti-social incidents were catalogued. I pulled up all the recorded activity relating to 'neglect' and 'abuse'. These events had suspects linked to them, with actual crime IDs. You got a little less privacy once you were a suspect. I didn't know the names but the ID would allow me to link them to other crimes. I guessed that there would be scenes with parents outside the safe houses. I pulled up all the 'domestic' and 'family' coded events. The data also recorded the number of people involved. I ignored everything with only two. All I needed to do was link my list of IDs across to these incidents.

I guessed the Service would never place a home in an area that was classified as unsafe. The insurance firms had a system for rating areas. So I imported the insurance firms' locale datasets and applied this to my current list of incidents. This reduced the numbers to under one hundred-and-fifty.

A quick search of some dull-as-dishwater media articles told me the Service had been forced to install specific level of security in its houses as part of Durham directive five years ago. They had awarded the contract to a conglomerate from Bonn called HJU GmBh. A quick search of their online presence gave me the patterns and dimensions of their logo. I captured it and converted it to a ratio using a piece of software I'd stored on my processor block. Although you needed the necessary A-codes, it appeared Spidz had the means of scanning pix and vidz for ratios. Naturally.

I knew somebody in Lower Skipton offices was right at this moment running serious expression-based software on all the captured footage of the riots. Or, more probably, the two hours preceding the riots. Sufficiently frowning eyes would spark an emergency florist to get in there quick and dump a few terracotta pots or get somebody to turn on a bit of soothing classical.

Because that always worked.

There was a publicly-available vidz service, RoadEyes, which streamed all house fronts. It had all the house fronts in the world. Obviously, they wiped off all the human ratios, but they hadn't touched the logos. I connected the RoadEyes stream to the post codes I'd already filtered for and plugged it into the Spidz ratio matching environment. Then set it to search for the HJU logo patterns.

I scrunched up my eyes and felt grit crack a little in the corners. I rubbed them, looking out of the window. Ahead of me I could see the black rumple of the Pennines. We were now in the countryside proper. Around me, the crumbling walls of old stock fields and the odd farmer making a living. Some had worked hard at the soil and had managed to go arable.

There were a few of the goat farms as well: genetically-altered to produce whatever the hell you wanted. Goats were long-suffering. They'd put up with humans messing them around for centuries. Now they had to urinate antihistamine and substandard insulating material. But they would probably take over at some point. I quite liked goats. So had Dali.

Her parents had had a smallholding with three goats – and a loads of chickens – about ten kilometres out of the centre of Kochi. She had grown up with them and had made me watch hours of vidz with her as a child, feeding them, stroking them, leading them around the little dusty field on a little halter. She'd always told me that goats were a special animal, properly attuned to people, on a spiritual level.

She hated sheep, mind. Thought they were proper daft.

I rubbed my eyes again. Thinking about Dali had made me want to plug myself into Memro again. I was about to flick my way through my service icons. But, froze my hand in the air, remembering the Spidz and MoreThanSum login issue.

This is how it all starts, the moment when you become self-aware, when you know that you are being watched.

I wasn't even bothering to cover my tracks, now. Clive could do what he liked. This was too important now. They were never going to give me another job anyway.

The images of the house fronts started to drop into a screen in front of me. One-by-one, I pulled them up. I wasn't sure what I was looking for but knew I could discard a load of them.

I was about half-way through when the taxi approached a crossroads and turned left, onto what looked like the smallest of the roads.

'Where are we?' I asked the taxi.

'Approximately five kilometres north of Pateley Bridge.'

Outside the window, I could see crumbling walls and scrubland below rain and low cloud. We were coming down a steep incline, into a wooded valley.

At a rather unexpected speed.

'Estimated time of arrival?'

'One hour.'

The voice cut out and an alarm started to sound which meant the auto had lost control. I'd only ever heard it in vidz. This was when you were supposed to remember all your driving skills – last used when you were in your late teens – and drive the bastard thing. In a commercial car, your dashboard would spring to life with a virtual wheel and the like.

Converted taxis weren't compatible. If anything went wrong, you were like a rat in a cage waiting to be put out of your misery.

I was in the back seat on the passenger side. A plastic barrier between myself and the console. If I'd have pounded at the partition with a heel, I could've easily kicked the thing aside. But I knew I didn't have a minute. The car was already veering across the road, heading for the remains of a wall.

I checked my seat belt and hunkered down. The right-hand edge of the bonnet connected with the stone wall and the car immediately bounced into the air, before landing sideways on the road, passenger-side down. The closest window shattered against my head, showering glass over me. Eyes firmly closed, I could hear the sound of metal scraping tarmac inches from my ear. It seemed to go on for a while. The taxi skidded down the road a short way then hit something substantial and I was jerked violently backwards in my seat, head snapping back into the head rest.

* * *

It was the lights which drew me to the place. There were orange glows from the windows and cold bright exterior security lights. The clear shapes of walls and outbuildings shone out of the darkness. Visible from the road, I'd stumbled for half an hour to get away from the crash. I wasn't sure what I was going to ask them for when I arrived, but I'd bust up my nose and could hardly see out of my left eye. Even my med-handler had topped out, probably from hysteria. There were no nodes out here so I'd been unable to call in an ambulance. I was expecting the farm to have had some kind of long-range channel, but, whatever it was, it'd been encrypted and I'd need to be patched-in to break into that.

I was hoping it might need only a knock on a friendly door.

The approach to the farm was via a long, curving gravel drive, open on both sides to the old sheep field. It was dark now but there was enough ambient light for me to make out the boundary between the stones of the drive and the grass and nettles of the field. As I walked, my right leg started to feel worse. I'd bruised the shin badly in the crash but I'd been able to neck a couple of painkillers, allowing me to walk on it for a time. The knee was playing up now. Not only was it painful, but it wasn't working as it should've.

I was startled by a movement ahead of me. Something had just ducked around the corner of the main farmhouse. I stopped on the track and crouched down, swearing at the pain now coursing through my knee. My eyes searched for more movement. I could now clearly see the windows of the farmhouse, light escaping from curtains or blinds. I waited a few moments more, hearing more movement.

As I neared the house, I could see the farm was in a run-down state. I wondered who was still living there. Slates had been lost from the roof, one of the windows in the upper floor had lost its glass, grass was growing in the gutters, and a sapling protruded from the chimney.

The drive curved around the back of the farmhouse and ended in what I thought was a yard of some kind. There were more buildings around the back, as well. Now that I was closer, I could hear the occasional bleating of a sheep, coming from around the back of the house. Under the glare of the security lights, I could plainly see a short path off the drive to the front of the farmhouse. It went through a small gate and into what was now a very overgrown garden. I stepped off the road onto the path.

Despite my presence causing the exterior lights to flare up, nobody came to twitch back the curtains. I approached the door and assumed my presence there would've set off some kind of alert to the inhabitants. After a few minutes of waiting, with no movement from inside, I stepped up to the door and knocked hard on the wood. There was still no noise from inside.

Around the back of the house was the same. The backdoor itself opened out into the main yard. Opposite the house was a large barn, with two smaller buildings alongside. There was a sharp smell of animal muck. The kitchen windows didn't have any curtains, and peering in, I could see there was nobody inside. I knocked on them gently and called out a loud 'Hello', but nobody came. Looking closer, I could see the layers of dust on the surfaces. Nobody had cleaned the place in years, it seemed.

'Shite,' I muttered, limping up to the back door. I pulled back the hood of my jacket to display my AJC logo more clearly and issued the police command to open the door. The system obeyed immediately and the door clicked open. I went inside.

It seemed nearly every room had a light on. I wasn't sure where it was getting the power from, as I hadn't seen any turbines as I'd approached. Perhaps there was a solar rig on top of the outbuildings. Down south, farmers had diversified by going into solar arrays. They grew crops in summer and dragged out arrays in winter. Just to make ends meet. I'd have been surprised to see this up in the dales. Sunshine wasn't abundant.

I checked the house from top to bottom. Whoever had lived here was no longer there. Although there was some furniture, there were no possessions left. Cupboards were empty of clothes. Hooks on the wall hinted at where pictures had once hung.

It was while looking out through the curtains of one of the back bedrooms that I noticed movement again. I held the curtains back and peered down into the muck-littered yard.

Then I saw it. A drone. A rugged model, designed for rain and snow and hard landings in fields. It looked old but then these sorts of drones were expected to live for years.

I watched it glide across the yard, emitting a series of crackles and beeps. Then it turned towards the house and rose slightly in the air. My heart might've beaten a little faster in any normal situation but I was in a state of drugged indifference now. Things really couldn't get any worse.

Then I heard an animal noise, the bleat of a sheep. The drone disappeared from view and re-appeared, directly behind the ragged mess of an animal. It was directing it towards the main barn. As it neared the large double doors, one of them slid sideways a fraction and let the sheep pass through. Then it slid together again. As it closed, I could just see the forms of other sheep behind it.

In the yard I could see the drone disappear off in the darkness beyond the lights of the yard. It seemed to be heading back out into the fields.

I stared at the closed barn doors for a few minutes. I shook my head, trying to clear it, to get my concentration back. I kept thinking about moments at school. The deeply grooved moments, which don't mean anything, but which always came back to me when I couldn't focus. The pain in my knee finally reminded me why I was there. I turned away from the window and hobbled back down the stairs. It was a matter of minutes before I'd found the main server and spliced myself into a live connection. I managed to get it interfaced to my bead. I was about to put in the call but my mind kept coming back the sight of the sheep in the barn. I stopped the call. Hesitantly, I tried to pull up the screens that controlled the farm's drones. It wouldn't let me. All the physical systems were locked down. This was industrial-grade security. Nobody wanted to lose their livestock because some script-kiddie had been arsing-around with their drones' herding vectors. I gave up on the server and hobbled back to the kitchen. The drone had returned, visible through the window, hustling another sheep about the yard. Its systems weren't bothered by my shape-abstract.

Outside in the yard I found a stack of metal fencing posts. I grabbed the nearest and turned to find the drone. The metal bar felt good in my hand. It felt right. I held it lightly, letting it swing by my side. The drone was fussing around the other end of the yard, trying to get this new sheep to move out from a corner. The sheep wasn't going to come out. It could see me. While the drone wasn't bothered, the sheep was terrified of my shape-abstract.

I moved away from the front of barn, swinging the bar from side-to-side in front of me. The sheep scampered across the yard and straight up to the doors, which were opening too slowly for it. It crashed its head into the partially opened door. The drone followed it closely, making sure it was properly locked in the barn. I walked up behind. With as much speed as I was able to apply, I swung the metal bar up and into the underside of the drone. It flew high into the air, driven upwards by the impact, then fell back down, its prop blades screaming. It failed to correct its fall. It bounced onto the roof of the barn. I thought I was going to lose it up there, but at the final bounce, it toppled over the guttering and fell, smashing onto the concrete of the yard. I hobbled over and smacked the top of it again and again with the bar. Its tiny servos stopped whining after a while.

The double doors were stiff but I managed to heave them apart, pushing against the power of the automated motors. Inside were about fifty sheep. Not that many for the size of the barn. In some distant corners, I could see the fluffy collapsed shapes of more. These didn't move and, somehow, they looked wrong. Then I realised. They were long dead.

After I watched all of the sheep stream out of the shed and away into the darkness of the fells, I twitched my fingers, plugging my bead back into the farm's comms channel. Then I called for an ambulance.

Chapter Twenty-Seven

I slipped out from a side entrance of the hospital, dropping into the levels underneath the Dead Arches. Between the curves of metal and glass above me, it was possible to see the orange glow of Airedale at night. There were no stars.

I'd pinched a bunch of dressings from the room before leaving and was busy stuffing these on my face as I navigated wheeled tubs of bio-waste and other reeking, decomposing matter. Vents from the hospital blew steam – and who knows what else – all over my face and hair. The bandages glued themselves to my cheeks. All this shit was well known to the algorithms. Anybody with multiple bandages on their cheeks would've flagged up to a human handler. I didn't mind this happening now, though. A human handler was better than the alternative; they were slower and they weren't in charge of the cars.

Being careful not to scrape my many sensitive bruises, I pulled the cap down low over my eyes. The light material of the trousers caught on the adhesive wrapping on my knee with every step, forcing me to adjust it every few yards. In between sorting out my knee, I scrolled through my contacts and found Carrie's glum miniature face. An eye-twitch later I was putting in a call. It bounced on the second ring. I tried again. It bounced again. Either she was on a call with someone else or she'd put a block on me. It was nearly midnight on a Monday. I knew which of these two scenarios was the most likely.

'Sod you, then,' I said, as though stuck in an argument with the bins.

In the darkness of the alley, I scrolled through all my other contacts. There was nobody else who would help. Or who could help. I wondered where all my friends had gone.

I hit a main street, noisy with drunks and late shoppers. I could see a south-bound autobus approaching, so I broke into a limping run and made it to the stop in time.

The other people on the autobus pulled the dead-eye in the opposite direction when I stepped on. I found myself a place at the back and started scrolling through the local news postings. There was a particular order I had to do this in. Within reason.

I normally picked up my spores from a guy in Bingley. I knew he could get me other stuff as well. Problem was, he was always on the move and he only let his presence be known through a few message boards. You had to be good at crosswords in order to get his drugs.

My brain was all over the place, still swimming with the painkillers from the hospital. They'd told me I had to rest the knee for at least a day. This was never going to happen. I had to move fast. But my mind wasn't capable of counting in threes, let alone solving cryptic puzzles.

Thankfully, the guy had just tweaked an old pair of posts. He was getting lazy. I'd been to that place before.

The Crown on the Bradford Road.

About an hour later I was hobbling through the door. It was still busy, despite the time. After midnight on a Monday is not a party night. The pub was old and tiny. There were rooms, separated by the bar and linked by a grotty corridor. In the back, it sounded like there were a lot of Brazilians watching some football game. There was a great deal of shouting and laughing. Out front was a more sedate crowd. Somebody a little older than me hunched at the bar, wobbling his way through his tranq-spiked lagers. Two old women were in the window seat, grandly and silently surveying the room.

My man was reading a small roll-up, which he'd laid out carefully on the table. He'd kept it out of the puddles by building a shallow foundation of beer mats. There was a glass of mineral water by his side. As I entered, he looked up and waved expansively at me.

'Good evening, mate,' he said. He spoke with a thick Turkish accent. Although you never asked a person's name in such circumstances, people I knew always called him Karl. I suspected that wasn't his real name.

He waved me to the seat in front of him. 'You look awful, mate.'

'Ta,' I said, sitting.

'Belinda,' Karl called out. 'Can we have some music in here? It's dead, you know.'

The barmaid, who had been serving the Brazilians, came round to the front bar. She glared at Karl but twirled her fingers in the air above her head, flicking a ring-infested middle finger at us when she had finished. The music – cheesy samba cut with Saharan-synth – roared into life.

'Thank you, Belinda,' said Karl.

The two old women exchanged glances, necked their drinks, and started to leave.

'Are you having a drink, my friend?' asked Karl.

I shook my head. 'Not thirsty.'

He grimaced. It was unspoken protocol to have a drink. Although the premises were carrying out the service of acting as his shop front – a service for which he would be paying them generously – there were still expectations. It meant something to play along with the charade.

'Belinda,' he bellowed again.

The barmaid appeared at the bar again and raised her eyebrows at him. 'Aye?'

'A lime and ice for my guest.'

'Aye,' said Belinda.

A glass of slushy green was dumped on the bar and she disappeared.

'You going to get that?' he asked me.

I turned and looked at the glass. 'No.'

He sighed and shook his head. His long, ragged curls flopped around his eyes and he flicked them away. I had always thought Karl was in his sixties but tonight he seemed younger. Perhaps it was only relative.

'You got your pre-load?' he asked.

I slid my card across the table and he lifted it out of the beer, delicately wiped both sides on a mat. After he'd passed it above his roll-up, he nodded and returned it to me.

'That OK?' I asked.

He grimaced. 'You are pissing me around? What else have you got?'

I dug out four other pre-load cards and threw them in the puddle of beer in front of him. He shook them off and checked each in turn, expression not softening. 'This is not enough.'

'I haven't got any–'

'You have credit,' he said. 'I know that for a truth. Go and load yourself up, my friend.'

'Can't do that. I'll get you some next week.'

He squinted and took a sip of his beer. 'You in trouble?'

'A little bit,' I said in neutral tones. 'You know I'll be back. I'm a good customer, yeah.'

He stared at me for a while. Then he nodded. 'OK. This is what we do here. I give you a little credit. You tell me where you live.'

I hardly paused. 'Yeah, whatever.' I gave him my address and he scribbled it down in a little notebook.

'I will be checking,' he said, grinning. 'We're good to go. Whaddya want, eh?'

I told him what I wanted. He listened for a while and then frowned. 'I thought you usually wanted spore?'

'Yeah,' I said, after a short pause. 'I'll have some of that, and all.'

'Any particular variety?'

'I don't care.'

'We have some interesting effects—'

'I don't care.'

He looked at me. 'You used to care, my friend. What happened? And what happened to your face?'

'I was in an accident.'

'A car crash?'

'Yeah.'

'You been to the hospital?'

'Just got out.'

'They let you out? Looking like that?'

I stared at him for a moment.

'Fine,' he said. He waved imperiously towards the bar. 'You drink your drink. I'll make a call.'

An antique mobile phone was fished out of a leather satchel next to him. He dialled a number and, after pulling back the curtains of hair, placed it against his ear.

Whoever he was phoning answered him. He spoke in fast Turkish for a few minutes. During the conversation, he mugged a series of goofy faces in my direction, pretending to be bored by the person on the other end. At a point in the conversation, he became serious and looked down at his roll-out. He nodded a series of curt goodbyes and cut the call.

'All done,' he said to me.

'Yeah,' I said.

'You know,' he said, squinting at me. 'I want to know what you did.'

'Eh?'

'You used to be clean,' he said. 'A good little Justice analyst.'

I frowned. This stretched the multitude of cuts on my face. It hurt. 'I never told you that.'

'I found out,' he said. 'I need to know these things. It's important for the business.'

'I'm still an analyst,' I said wearily.

'Well,' he said. 'That's a matter of opinion. You being here seems to have caused a… what do you call it? A spike of noise. You are a watched man, Hasim.'

I stared at him. 'Have you got what I want?'

'You being watched,' he said. 'Well, that's going to cost you more.'

I sighed. 'I understand. Have you got what I want?'

He nodded, slowly. 'Of course. Have I ever let you down?'

'Where is it?'

He told me where I could pick up the stuff. It would be about five minutes' walk from here.

'And you've got the bike?'

'Well, that's been the tricky part.'

'Have you got the bike?' I repeated.

'My friend, it's a bike…but well, you'll see.'

* * *

The first of the hills nearly killed me. The drugs they'd given me in the hospital were strong and had meant I could do some walking. But sitting on the back of this leaking piece-of-shit moped was probably doing me permanent damage. Not least to my lungs. If they weren't going to pull me over for wearing a balaclava – standard practice for Enforcement – the enviro-operatives were going to stinger me for the fumes the bike was kicking out. And if nobody stopped me for these infractions, somebody was going to do me for failing to wear a helmet.

As bikes went, it wasn't too noisy, which was a blessing. It was ethanol-fuelled, so I knew I could probably drink the contents of the tank. If I were into that kind of thing. There were some mates at school who'd done that since they were twelve. You had to dry-swallow some kind of powder beforehand, or you spent the rest of the day throwing up. And the day after that, in hospital.

Thankfully, none of the good citizens of Cowling Parish were awake at this time of night. A very good neighbourhood. I'd not been up here before. A series of stepped terraces were placed into the hillside, beneath the old towers. These were flood-lit and kept distracting me.

I found the house. I checked it against my bead. It was the right one. There was the logo on the window. I dumped the bike in the street and ran up to the front door. I started hammering and shouting my children's names.

It took about a minute before somebody came downstairs. He was a fattish man, in his early forties. He had a dressing gown on and was struggling with some glasses.

'Excuse me,' he said. Despite the apparent fluster, he knew what he was doing. He'd had training. He'd seen the likes of me a few times before. 'Can I help you?'

'I'm here for Ali and Asha,' I said. 'Service said I can take them home.'

'I'm sorry,' he said. 'I think you must have the wrong house.'

'You're a placement house, yeah,' I said. 'I know you are. I'm here for my kids.'

'I think you must be mistaken,' he said.

I knew he was playing for time. I screamed out past him up the stairs. 'Ali! Asha!'

There were some more noises from inside the house.

'Go back to bed,' the man said over his shoulder. 'This gentlemen was just leaving.'

'I know they're here!'

He spoke quietly. 'Look, man, I know you're upset. I've seen plenty of mums and dads round here. Yes, we're a placement house. But I don't have an Ali or an Asha here. Haven't had a placement for about a month.'

I tried to look past him up the stairs. 'Ali? Asha?'

'If you go now,' he said. 'We'll just forget about this, OK? I won't get Enforcement involved.'

I nodded and retreated down the path to the street. He was still watching me carefully from the door as I started up the bike and set off back down the road.

For the next three hours, I travelled slowly down the dale. If there was anybody hitting the Manchester mountain, watching the progress of this balaclavaed idiot on his joke motorbike, they would've had few patterns to match. Perhaps a busy courier working late. Very late. Perhaps a salesman desperate to empty his suitcase before the month end.

I lost track of the number of houses I stopped at. How often I shouted my children's names. I started to lose my voice by the end. The drugs were wearing off a little. I was sure that some of them had called in Enforcement. As I rode past street cameras I was conscious that some of them moved to track my progress. I knew it was only a matter of time now.

At about three o'clock, I crested a hill that ran down the centre of the southern Shipley residential estates. I stopped and looked through a gap in the buildings. I could see the flames and flares of a major riot further south. Must have been on the Bradford-Airedale border. It was massive. I guessed it'd have drawn operatives from both regions. A number of buildings were already on fire. I could see an old mill lit from within. Its windows were an ordered array of flickering orange-red rectangles. Even at this distance, I could hear the sirens and the shrieks. Something massive went up in a fountain of white-hot flame. A distillery, possibly.

I moved on, down past the crest of the hill, away from the noise. I was nearing the end of my list. The next house was on this street. It was old. Last century. And then some. All the lights were out. I killed the engine in the bike a few hundred metres down the street and walked back. Sitting on the window sill of one the front rooms was a shape I recognised. It was Ali's toy tiger. I could tell it was Ali's, because he'd chewed the ear off it when he was three. The window was open a little, to let in some cooler air. These old places didn't do air-con.

Now that I was here, now that I knew where they were, my original plan seemed ridiculous. I nearly walked away at that point. But I still needed to see their faces. There was no way I was leaving now without seeing them. Speaking to them.

'Ali,' I said, trying to direct my voice up to the window without being too loud.

There was no response.

'Asha,' I said, a little louder. 'You there? Ali? Asha?'

I waited. I thought I could hear some movement. Then Asha's face appeared between the curtains. She looked down.

'Dad?' she asked.

'Yeah, hiya, love. It's me.'

'What's happened to your face, Dad?' she asked.

'Nowt,' I said. I started ripping off the bandages. 'Just for show, in't it.'

'Have you been hurt? You're limping.'

'No,' I said. 'No, I'm fine. Are you OK? Are they looking after you?'

'What've you done, Dad? They said they had to look after us. Because of summat you've done.'

'Nowt,' I said. 'I haven't done owt, me.'

'Why've they taken me and Ali here, then?'

'They looking after you?'

'You must've done summat!'

'I'll get you out of there, I promise.'

Ali's face appeared at the window, squeezing underneath his big sister's elbow. 'Daddy!'

'Hiya, love,' I said.

My eyes caught movement just above the entrance to the door. It was a small security camera. I'd not seen it before. It was moving, directing itself straight at me.

'I've got to go, kids,' I said.

'No,' said Ali, suddenly terrified.

'I'll be coming back, yeah–'

Ali was shrieking now. 'Don't leave us!'

A light came on in the room behind them. Ali was pulled away from the window. His fingers shot out to grab the sill. A woman's voice, gentle but stern, reprimanded him. He clawed his way back to the window.

'I'll be coming back,' I said again, turning for the gate. They were screaming now.

I realised I shouldn't have come. I should have left them.

Chapter Twenty-Eight

———

Although it was considered illegal to download the small patch that cancelled the police override on a flat door lock, I'd done exactly that at about half-past four in the morning. I'd routed it through my gaming cube and dropped it into the apartment's servers in such a way that it would look like the main block server had been responsible. A skilled analyst would've found the link. I didn't care, though. I knew I wanted to protect myself a little more.

Of course, I also knew that Enforcement had alternative means of gaining entrance. These were more direct. They tended to involve kinetic systems. And it was the effect of these same kinetic systems that caused the door to my flat to explode at a little after six o'clock in the morning.

I'd just managed to doze off and was lying on the sofa. The wall-screen in front of me had recognised my lack of attention and had shut itself down. I was a good little citizen. I let all my equipment shut itself down when it wasn't needed.

I woke at the noise. There was a cloud of plaster dust and tiny wood splinters erupting from the hallway. My sofa was positioned in the middle of the room, facing the wall-screen but with its back to the hallway. I heaved myself up, peering over the top of it. There was a calm and optimistic voice in my head, quietly assuring me that this was just a nasty dream and that I would wake up soon.

Then I saw the figures. Masked against any possible chemical or biological counter-attack. Gloved and shielded in dark green polymer. The first two dropped a couple of smoke grenades into the middle of the room and spread out to cover the exits. The second two ran to the sofa and tipped it over backwards, sending me tumbling onto the rug. The last one to enter was thinner than the others. She moved with a sickeningly familiar gait.

I knew all about the theory. They were supposed to enforce the law. They were supposed to encourage you to play by the rules. Before an actual arrest warrant was issued, it was Enforcement's job to make sure we all obeyed the commandments. That long list of little rules that explained how we all lived a contented and comfortable life. Sure, some of the analysts and detectives in Justice could – and did – make use of them to bring in a difficult suspect. It saved us the risk of getting a homemade polymer bullet in the face. We appreciated their work and they enjoyed showing us up for wimps. But this was their territory. This was the kind of job where they simply flew. This was a telling-off, a dressing-down. A caution.

It had been agreed, through some intense negotiations, that Enforcement could make use of the smoke and the masks at their own discretion. They had also complained about the IG implications of having visible ID. There were concerns that some wrong 'uns might trace back their numbers and target some of the operatives' homes. They'd obtained some evidence that this had happened once. In Denver. So they'd managed to operate without the ID, in masks and smoke. They knew this gave them the freedom to work in a stress-free environment. Everybody had the right to work in a stress-free environment.

As the third gloved-finger was shoved in my mouth, I could feel similar digits being shoved up my anus through the material of my pants and trousers. Then one of them emptied a spray into my eyes. This was the usual stuff. A capsicum mix, using the latest gene-tampered varieties. It took a few seconds to take effect. But then it really started to kick in. It felt like a volcano was pissing magma in my eyes. I started to vomit immediately. Tears were spurting out. I couldn't scream past their fingers. And the vomit. But I tried to anyway. At the other end, they had pulled down my pants and inserted something suppository-shaped. These were used by customs, mainly. But Enforcement had got their hands on them as well. It was all part of the routine now. The things were designed to move up your gut until they reached some form of common narcotic. Then they would release a dye and a laxative compound. Drug mules were left in rooms until they dropped a blue shit. It felt alive inside me, like a spiky slug crawling up into my gut. This was standard psychological shit. I could handle this.

But they had new stuff. Some kind of liquid they dropped into my ear. I could feel it slip down. It felt like a burrowing insect. I knew they couldn't actually put a beetle in my ear. But the effect was the same. They held my head tightly as I writhed about. Then the thing reached its destination and burst into a pain fireball. It rippled across the tributaries of my sinuses. I felt it in my brain.

After they had deployed their sprays and gels, the last figure – the one I knew – knelt down and grabbed me by my hair. The voice came out of a distortion machine, metallic, screechy. I couldn't tell whether it was male or female. But I could guess who it was.

'Hasim Edmundson?'

'Piss off!'

'You are Hasim Edmundson?' the voice repeated.

'No,' I said. 'I'm the frigging Tooth Fairy.'

One of the masked figures pressed a discharger into my oesophagus. A different voice, still distorted, barked, 'Confirm your name.'

I hawked up and spat, 'Suck my cock!'

The discharger was activated. I felt like a horse had kicked me in the throat.

The first figure spoke. 'Again?'

I shook my head, beaten. I tried speaking but it took a while, after much dry swallowing. 'Hasim Edmundson. I'm Hasim Edmundson.'

'Hasim Edmundson,' said the thinner figure. 'You have been identified approaching a designated placement house commissioned by the Airedale Family and Child Service–'

'Identified?' I croaked. 'I had my face covered.'

The second prodded me in my ribs. 'You were wearing the same clothes, halfwit!'

The thinner figure interrupted. 'You were identified by a human handler. Do you deny that you were there?'

The second figure waved his discharger in front of my face. I shook my head. 'It were me.'

'That's a confirm,' said the figure. 'We are now issuing you with Enforcement level directive 665-99. From this time onwards, you have a three-kilometre exclusion zone around Asha Edmundson and Ali Edmundson. Infringement of this exclusion zone will result in further visits from operatives like this. We will continue to enforce this zone–'

I spat out some vomit. 'Then bloody-well arrest me!'

The metallic voice laughed. 'No need. As I said, if you continue to break the exclusion zone, we will have to return and continue to enforce appropriate behaviour on your part.'

'You're scared! Arrest me!'

'Any further infringement of the exclusion zone will also be reported to the Family Services.'

'Sod off,' I croaked, spitting out more vomit.

'Those infringements will be recorded against you in any further judgements on the future placement of your children.'

'Get hell out of my house,' I whispered.

They stayed a little longer. Monitored my heart rate. This

was all part of due process. Sometimes the pepper spray could stop a heart. It would never do to actually kill somebody while enforcing the law. That might mean Justice got involved.

They left without saying a word.

The pain in my eyes was easing off a little now, though. I'd ordered some things off take-away that were worse than that spray. I could cope with that. And the thing that was crawling up my insides was just a psychological trick, caused by the material properties of the device. I'd passed out shits that were more alien than that. It was going to be there for a couple of days, mind.

But the thing they'd put in my head was wiping me out. I couldn't think due to the pain. I guessed this must be what a migraine felt like. I had to sit with my eyes closed, shivering on the floor, knees up to my ears.

After a few minutes, I crawled to the bathroom and found some painkillers. After about half an hour, I could contemplate more movement. I sat on the toilet for a few minutes. Nothing blue came out. Still up there. I staggered back through to the lounge and started looking through the cushions that had been scattered over the floor. I found my cap and held it shakily in front of me. Trying to get my bead working was an effort. The projected lights burned into the back of my eyeballs.

I called up the office.

'Sorry, Mafu. Going to have stay at home today, buddy. I'm feeling a bit poorly, OK?'

* * *

I'd cleaned myself up as best I could. There was a massive bruise on my face developing from the crash now. A large swelling on my left eye was making it difficult to look out of that side of my face. My knee still felt like it was going to collapse under me as well. There were few physical injuries on me from the house invasion – this was basic operative training – but my eyes couldn't cope with sunlight. I'd dug out an old pair of sunglasses. The lenses had both been scratched with something sharp. This would've been Ali. Dressing-up.

Outside it was a warm but overcast day. One of those still days where there was no breeze. Where odour hung in the air and choked you. Heading down the hill from my block, I could smell a new summer bloom from the canals. This mixed with the after-tang of a doused bonfire.

I took the bus up the dale. I couldn't force myself down into the heat and clamour of the train. There was no way I was getting in a taxi. As the vehicle edged its way north, through endless residential streets, the scent of rotting meat became stronger and stronger. We left the northern edges of Bingley and drove past a factory. Until a few days ago, it must have been locked up. Another casualty in the commercial battlefield. But now it had been invaded. There were still trails of smoke coming up from a few of the walls. The roof had collapsed. In among the shattered remains of the roof tiles, I could see the vats. Some had been tipped on their side. Huge carcasses, white-green, glistened, half-out of their containers. Although it was too distant to make out the fine details, I could still see the surface of these great haunches writhe. I guessed with supplementary life. The smell here was sickening. Everybody else in the bus averted their eyes. Old people of the dale were not going to witness the death of their city.

At Riddlesden, I tentatively stepped out of the bus and made my way to the Servant's Chambers. These were on the main street. A modern structure built on stilts, placed above the once-protected crumble of a Victorian terrace. The terrace now had metallic shutters glued across its windows and doors. Whoever had been its benefactor had long since lost interest – or died – and it was waiting for some subcontractor to take away its remains and recycle them into road surface.

I took the lift to the Chambers. There was a small vestibule, which led into a large hall. Behind this were further rooms. But it was the hall where we had the action.

Servants were supposed to receive continual feedback on their role and their decisions. I'd done some of the coding to facilitate this in my time. But this was a Town Hall meeting. I never went to these things. They were for voters who liked talking. Who preferred talking over anything else. If there was something more irritating than reading comments from whiny voters on a message board, it was to be sat in a room of them and to listen to their whiny voices up close.

The Servant running this Town Hall meeting was sat in a chair at the front of a loose assembly of local voters. She had a couple of her entourage hovering near the window behind her. I staggered up to the front and slumped down and nodded a greeting at her. Abi Hassan was much smaller than I'd anticipated. Her face was framed by a neatly-folded black headscarf. Her make-up was restrained, her eyes gentle but intelligent. She nodded back at me and smiled. Behind the smile there was an anxious narrowing of the eyes, like she was struggling to recognise me.

'Welcome,' she said. 'I don't... I'm sorry, is this your first meeting here?'

'I guess,' I said. I hadn't spoken since the incident a few hours ago and the action sent jarring shards of pain up into my still-delicate sinuses.

'Are you OK?' Hassan asked. 'I'm sorry... but you look like you've been in an accident.'

'I'm fine,' I lied. 'Took a tumble off my bike, yeah.'

'Right,' she said. 'So... which part of the dale are you from?'

One of the Servant's entourage fluttered forward, his hands making jagged swipes in the air as he worked his way through his projected display. 'Abi, sorry. I'm not sure he's on the roll...'

Hassan nodded. 'I know.'

The assistant nodded and swished his hair, retreating back

to his position by the window.

'Hiya,' I said to the room at large.

'You understand,' said Hassan to me. 'That this is a neighbourhood meeting?'

'Won't be long,' I said.

She smiled. It was a true politician's smile. I even believed it. 'These people are here to discuss neighbourhood matters... sorry, what was your name?'

'Hasim Edmundson,' I said. 'I'm an analyst with the AJC.'

'I can see,' she said, glancing at my cap. 'What can we do for you, Hasim?'

'You chair the Airedale Regionale Board, yeah?'

She nodded. 'That's correct.'

'You have a contract with a company in Newcastle? They manage your Regionale index?'

'It's our Regionale index, Hasim. Assuming you're from the dale as well?'

'I am,' I said. 'I fucking love Airedale, me.'

Her smile disappeared. 'What about the index?'

I leaned forward in my seat. 'I meant, I really, really love Airedale. Do you know what I'm saying, Ms Hassan?'

'I understand you,' she said. 'I can hear you fine, Hasim.'

'Good,' I said. 'Just wanted to be clear, yeah.'

'Let me offer you a deal,' she said brightly. 'We're nearly finished up here. If you allow me to complete my meeting with my electorate, I can spare you half an hour after this. You can have my undivided attention. And we don't need to rush. Yes?'

I was already feeling exhausted. I couldn't bother with arguing. I shrugged. 'Yeah, whatever, love.'

She smiled. 'Good. Now, Jeff, can you please remind me... what was your question again?'

It was only ten minutes more. The room was beginning to heat up. But I didn't want to take off my parka. There were plasters and bandages from the car crash running up my left arm. I didn't mind showing them off – it would've given my story more credence – but I wasn't so sure that they weren't already stuck to the inside of my sleeve. So I sat there, waiting. And starting to sweat.

During the wait, I kept a close eye on the two assistants. The young man with the hair kept glancing in my direction worriedly from his position by the window. The other, an older woman with jowls, was listening intently to the questions from the floor and ignored me. I didn't expect them to call in Enforcement but I was now trying to control repeated waves of paranoia. If they had called it in, I wasn't sure whether I'd have run. Would've been able to run.

I had to speak to Hassan. After the last of the voters had quietly filed out of the chamber, it was time.

We were now in one of the smaller rooms at the back of the building. The assistants had both disappeared, which made me nervous. Though I wasn't sure why.

'Do you know Darren Caines?' I asked.

'Yes,' she said. 'Darren and I are both on the Regionale Board. That's no secret. It's all in the public domain. I can direct you to our minutes–'

'Found them,' I said. 'Has Caines ever contacted your Regionale service in Newcastle?'

'I don't know,' she said. 'I managed the contract directly. Darren is one of the main industry representatives on the Board. He wouldn't get involved with commissioning, with signing off your money, you understand.'

As well as being a neighbourhood Servant, I knew Hassan also represented the region in Durham. She was probably planning to make it to London at some point, possibly even Brussels.

'They tell me he has had meetings with them.'

She frowned. 'Well, if he has, I wasn't aware of it. Is this interview about me or about Darren?'

I shifted in my seat. I was acutely aware of the device that was currently lodged in my gut. It was distracting me. 'Do you have investments pegged against the Airedale Regionale index?'

She laughed. 'Of course! Don't you?'

I was momentarily silenced. I wasn't expecting a confession. 'No... I mean, so you admit it...?'

'Admit it?' she asked. 'There's nothing to admit. Tell me, are you actually an AJC analyst at all? Or are you media?'

I was worried that she might start asking for A-codes. I shrugged. 'Does it matter? I'm a voter, aren't I?'

She raised her immaculate eyebrows. 'True. I have nothing to hide, Hasim. Listen, the purpose of the Regionale index is to reflect our standing in the wider world. It's something that represents us, semantically, to digital interfaces. We should invest based upon it. We should be proud of it, for by investing a stake in its performance, it will make us all work harder at nudging it ever upwards.'

'Falsely nudging it?'

'Oh,' she said, looking annoyed. 'Well, if that's the accusation, please arrest me and we'll have a proper conversation. Our provider is audited to death. They complain about it all the time. If they weren't audited, then the various investment houses wouldn't be linking their own prices to the Regionale at all.'

'So you've done nothing to impact the index?'

'I never said that,' she said. 'Read our minutes! We do a huge amount... but it's real work, not fiddling with numbers. We advertise our growing industries to the world, how skilled our workforce is, what a great quality of life we have. That's how we nudge the figures. By affecting reality! By making the dale the best place in the world to live. You go and write that up in your piece.'

'I'm an analyst,' I mumbled.

She smiled. I was beginning to think this had all been a waste of time. Perhaps it was the exhaustion – or the painkillers wearing off – but I was losing track of why I was here. I tried another tack.

'You spoken about the risk to the Newcastle people, yeah?'

She frowned. 'I don't understand. I understand the concept. But it's not something that I really use... or believe in, to be honest. It's all very abstract.'

'Right,' I said. 'Do other members of the Board have investments linked to the Regionale?'

'Probably,' she said. 'You'll have to ask them.'

'Have you ever discussed methods of influencing the index- '

She interrupted me, a little more briskly this time. '-You're not hearing me, Hasim. Have you read our minutes? The purpose of the Board is to increase the Regionale index rating. That's why we were established. We discuss methods to increase it at every single board meeting. Real methods. Real results.'

'But have you ever discussed risk ratings... you know, and how it affects Regionale?'

She made a face and shook her head. 'No.'

'Right,' I muttered.

'Are you OK, Hasim?' she asked, reaching across and putting her hand on my knee. 'You look in a terrible state. You should get yourself to a medical centre. We have a very good unit down the road. I helped commission it myself.'

'Well done,' I said sarcastically, standing up and stepping away from her. 'Thanks, and that. For answering my questions.'

'You sure you're going to be OK? I can ask Jules to help you down the way?'

'No, ta. I'll be fine.'

I left her office, feeling like I needed to cry. The two assistants ignored my stumbling progress back through the main hall.

Outside the building, it was raining. I hurried a little way along the street, ducking through a few covered alleys. Although the cameras were getting more and more difficult to spot these days, my bead had clocked them all and was providing target icons floating in my vision. I wasn't sure why I even cared now but I was still feeling like I should be careful.

I found myself under an old, stone archway. Through the archway was a garden and a large pond. At one time, this would've been full of ducks and moorhens. Now, like so many expanses of publicly-accessible water, it had been compromised. Spiralling growth of algae and scum sat on its surface and bubbles erupted from the depth every few minutes. Hardly a watercolour, as my dad might have said. Still, it was peaceful to watch the raindrops fall on it.

Visible through the rainfall was some ancient building behind. Funding for its upkeep must have dried up. It was protected by a rusting skeleton of scaffolding and a shredded coat of tarp. The door was a gaping, black hollow.

I twitched my hands and started a search on a public site. I found the name.

'Darren Caines, please,' I said.

'Who is calling, please?'

'My name's Hasim Edmundson. I'm with Justice.'

'Oh, right… of course, please hold, Mr Edmundson.'

I watched the rain and waited. Then a deep voice rumbled in my ear.

'Mr Edmundson?'

'Yeah,' I said. 'Are you Darren Caines?'

'Yes.'

'I want to talk to you about the murder of Meri Fergus.'

There was a long pause. A series of toxic bubbles burst from the surface of the pond. Eventually, the voice replied. Gentle, soft. 'I don't know that name.'

'Yeah,' I said. 'You wouldn't.'

There was another pause. 'Can you get to Stitsils?'

'Yeah, I can manage that.'

'I'll send you the address. End of the day, mind. I'm a busy man.'

Chapter Twenty-Nine

Shortly after graduating from the Bradford training facility, I was sent to work on a job. I was an idiot who didn't have a clue. They realised that pretty quickly, so they gave me a dead-end case of identity fraud. Nobody would've bothered, except the commissioner's daughter had been the target. It seemed they'd been hitting people around the Leeds area. I'd been dumped with a load of names and was told that they'd all had their identities stolen – their irises and fingerprints were now turning up in Madison and Arkansas. It hadn't taken me long to realise that they'd been hawked on the open market. The sellers had cloaked themselves professionally, so I hadn't been able to trace back any leads from the purchase.

The only thing I had to go on was the fact this bunch seemed to live either in Leeds or – I discovered with a bit of help from Louie – in Liverpool. I'd got IG permission to access their movements over the few months in question. When these were mapped, they showed a clear line across the country. They'd all shared the same trains. It was the Leeds-Liverpool express, a busy commuter service. I spent many nights crawling all over the carriages, followed by an amused and endlessly-chattering engineer. I hadn't found any evidence of digital devices, over and above the standard in-service cameras and the like. After a brief detour into the security of the service itself – which really irked their security chief – I came to the conclusion that they must have been ripping people off on the fly.

I had hours and hours of footage from the carriages. But there was no way I was ever going to eyeball that lot and get anything. There was no telling, over a period of a few months, when they'd had their pictures taken. I eventually pulled together a lucky combo – a complicated generic pattern mixing people wearing sunglasses with large satchels in proximity to the victims. This came back with some positive hits. They were relative amateurs, really, as they'd done the job over a single week. A professional would've tried to randomise the timings.

The glasses had hi-def cameras which, when close enough, got the iris no problem. I never worked out how the fingerprints were lifted but the satchels were where the real work took place. These contained the scanners. Known to be physically dangerous, at least in high doses, these bulky machines were capable of reading any digital device, from a distance. They'd been made illegal pretty much as soon as they'd hit the market. Sure, for my work, I had to get into slivers and beads and the like, but I had wires and sockets and a licence.

Possession of a scanner could've landed you a little trip to a remote part of the country. So, it came as something of a thrill to actually hold one of these things in my hand. And with the intention of actually using it. For a digital analyst, it was like being handed an AK-47.

The pockets of my jacket were large enough to contain it but it meant I had to walk a little oddly and it made the other side of my jacket flap a little too frequently. If I'd have zipped it all up, it would've shone out like a proud man in Speedos.

Caines hadn't been able to meet until later in the day, so I'd been back to my flat and half-heartedly choked down some food. As I munched, I'd wandered down the corridor from the kitchen to the bedrooms. It was a rule of our house that we weren't to eat in the bedrooms. This had been one of Dali's rules.

None of that seemed to matter anymore.

In Asha's bedroom, I found her desk heaped up with plastic collectables and sketches in notebooks. She loved to draw. Her special skill was in drawing mice. I'd never understood the mice thing but perhaps that was because I'd never asked her about it before.

Ali's room was busy with stuffed animals, all riding an assortment of toy cars. He'd set them out in some particular pattern, like they were all riding around a bypass of a small town. I wondered whether I should tidy them away but something warned me that he would be very upset if I did.

I tried not to think about what they might be doing right now. How they might be feeling. The look of panic on Ali's face as he had been pulled back from the window the night before rose in my mind. I felt like I'd been punched in the stomach. It had nearly overtaken the other sensation I'd held for so long: the coldness of Dali's forehead as I'd laid my hand across it, the last sight of her.

I sat in Ali's room, amid the tumult, and waited for the hours to pass.

* * *

Caines was a huge, bull-necked man. He had close-cropped reddish hair and beneath his eyes hung heavy folds of freckled flesh. His eyes regarded you, wet and alert, like the bulging monstrosities of a deep sea-creature. Despite his bulk, he looked like he kept fit. There was no spare fat on him. He didn't choke down any of his economy burgers, perhaps.

When he spoke, it was remarkably soft. Deep, but soft.

'You're late, Mr Edmundson.'

'Public transport, in't it.'

'I thought you Justice lot all had cars?'

I shook my head. 'Cuts and that.'

He grunted. 'Come with me.'

Caines had told me to ask for him in the reception of Building Four of his plant. Somebody had been supposed to come and get me and take me through, so I was surprised to meet him in person, impatiently tapping at the desk and sharing some dark joke with the receptionist.

He said he wanted to talk to me on the cutting floor. He had to ensure a new piece of equipment was working properly. I suspected there were other reasons.

In order to get through to the plant itself, we had to pass through the hygiene barrier. Caines handed me the kit in silence. I put on the white poncho and shower cap and walked slowly down a covered passageway. Caines walked along beside me. I noticed that he kept his mouth tightly closed. They were spraying us with something. It smelt a little of jasmine.

Alongside us was another passageway. From here came the loud chatter and laughter of the day-shift leaving the building. There were surprisingly few workers, I thought, for a facility this size.

After making our way through the hygiene barrier, we stepped out into the factory itself. We were in a transportation corridor. It smelt of blood and disinfectant. Automated low-loaders passed by in front of us, following painted lines on the floor. They sensed our human presence and stopped as soon as we started to cross. Some of them carried the meat; there was a mixture of cellophane-wrapped cheap cuts, some frozen boxes, and also a few premium wax-paper wrapped parcels.

We carried on and pushed our way through some sealed doors on the other side. After passing through the airlock, we stepped out into one of the growing-halls. The translucent roof let in what light was available. The warmth was surprising after the chill of the corridor behind us. It smelt terrible in there, like the worst of a hot day on the Aire coupled with the reek of lightly rotting animal. I guessed there were corners of each of these halls where by-product was always going to be missed.

Caines looked up, through the roof, towards the blackening clouds. 'Summer floods are on their way.'

'Yeah?' I said.

'Yes,' he said. 'It's always this time of year.'

'Bloody weather,' I said.

'It's good for us,' he said.

'Yeah?'

'Yes,' he said, turning to face me. 'Floods bring down the water. My vats need to drink.'

He slapped one hard as we passed. Inside, through the translucent material, I could see the lump shake, reacting to the waves of Caines' hand striking its prison.

We passed through more growing-halls until we arrived at the cutting-floor. This was at the centre of this quadrant of the plant. There was a proper roof on this and it was lit by harsh LED arrays. Two technicians were standing by a gleaming device, tapping away at a couple of industrial tablets. As I approached, I could see these were smeared with fat and dried fibres. I'd been dry swallowing for a while now. The sight of these tablets made me dry heave.

'Darren. Hi,' one of them said, as we approached.

'Evening, gentlemen,' said Caines.

Though they were clearly interested in knowing who I was, Caines ignored their questioning glances. He nodded at them and then looked at the machine. 'Come on, I haven't got much time. Mrs Caines has got a baked cod for me at home.'

'Yes, Darren,' said the second technician, swiping at his tablet.

From the corner of the room came a hum of power and a creak of joints. I turned and watched a wheeled robot with an extendable arm and a savage-looking gripper trundle out and across the floor to us.

At the same time, through one of the six doors that led out into the surrounding growing-halls, a vat came trundling through, riding on a low-wheeled platform. The vat came to a stop in front of us. Then the robot with the gripping arm rose into the air and positioned itself over the vat. The claws extended and fell into the opening. There was a nasty noise. A wet noise. Hydraulics squealed. The quivering slab of meat rose from the vat grasped by the savage claw. It was shaped like an irregular cylinder. All meat started off like this, having been forced to grow outwards from a seed stalk, until its outermost cells had been stopped by the walls of the container. Twists and folds of muscle fibre ran up and down the thing, interspersed with the odd jagged lines of fat. The machine let it hang in the air for a few seconds, to allow the dripping growth-fluid fall back into the vat then – with sickening jerks that made the meat swing about beneath it – it moved it towards one of the cutting-machines.

These had immense hoppers on top. The robot positioned its extendable arm above the hopper and then released the huge cylinder of meat. The thing fell, hitting the side of the hopper with a boom and a squelch, and then slowly slid from view.

'We're trying out a new cut,' said Caines.

'Right,' I said.

'It's for the kids,' said one of technicians.

'The kids, yeah,' I said.

We all moved towards a conveyor belt that exited the machine and disappeared into a tunnel at the end of the cutting floor.

'Damn,' said the second technician. He jabbed away at his tablet. The machine stopped purring.

'Is it jammed?' asked the first technician.

The second technician didn't answer. He turned and ran over to the other side of the machine, slotting the tablet into a small charging embrasure on the wall.

'It seems we have a few minutes to wait. We are working with old technology here,' said Caines. 'So, how can I help you, Mr Edmundson?'

I wasn't sure that I wanted to tell him everything at the moment. I was being cautious.

'You sit on the Regionale Board, yeah?'

'Yes, that is correct.'

'With Abi Hassan?'

'Yes, Abi and I are old friends.'

I nodded. I pointed to the bead in my cap brim. 'You don't mind if I record this, do you?'

He smiled. 'I've nothing to hide, young man.'

'And all this,' I pointed at the machinery. 'None of this will be made public… I mean, my recording is for internal Justice use. We'll protect your IP, and that.'

He chuckled. 'You'll have nothing of interest to record from this machine. Competitors have seen it all before. It's old technology here. Those tablets there – control the factory. Been in use for the last fifty years. No need to upgrade if it works, is there? As I said, I've nothing to hide.'

'Good.'

'Although, I'm surprised at your dedication.'

I frowned, 'I'm sorry?'

He smiled again. 'You're no longer employed by Justice, Mr Edmundson. They ended your contract a number of days ago. So, all I'm saying is that you're demonstrating an admirable dedication to the cause of this young lady's death.'

I tried not to react to this news. 'How do you know about my Justice contract?'

'Your contractual status is in the public domain, Mr

Edmundson, I'm afraid. It must be some policy of your agency. All it took was a short search at my end. It's all about transparency, isn't it?'

'So why are you still talking to me?'

'Because I'm interested. In fact, I'm intrigued. The reason that the poor young woman's death has dragged you so far – all the way here – interests me. I want to know why you need to pin blame onto somebody like me, for what is clearly an accident.'

'It wasn't an accident,' I said.

This wasn't going well.

I controlled myself. There was a job I had to do. I couldn't see his bead. Sometimes these things were sewn into the lining of people's clothes. He may have had some glasses somewhere but then he didn't look like somebody who had that affectation.

There was only one way to find out.

I started to weave my hands in the air in front of me. 'Let me get somebody on the line who will help explain the situation–'

'What?'

'Give us a minute,' I stalled, calling up the last few contacts with the twitch of an eye. The receptionist answered. I was stuck. I ended the call. 'Doesn't matter.'

'Mr Edmundson,' said Caines. 'What are you doing?'

The machine whirred back into life. The first technician clapped the other on the shoulder.

'It's ready, Mr Caines.'

'Excuse me,' said Caines, walking back to the conveyor belt. The two technicians also trotted back, clasping their tablets to their chests.

'What do you know about risk ratings, Mr Caines?' I called out, hurriedly following him.

'Not much, lad. Is that your question?' said Caines. The technicians were frowning at me now, from the other side of the conveyor belt.

Small slices of meat started to appear on the belt, initially lumpy and irregular, then gradually taking recognisable shape. They had been cut into the shape of a cow. The horns were problematic. In fact, they were a mess.

'I think you've been talking to some people in Newcastle about risk ratings. In order to boost the Regionale.'

'I think you've been thinking too much,' said Caines. 'What's with the horns?'

'Sorry, Darren,' said the second technician. 'I'll try and sort that now.' He started hurriedly stabbing away at his tablet.

'Meri Fergus died because she were hit by an Enforcement drone,' I blurted. I knew I was giving too much away.

'I knew that,' Caines said. 'What's that got to do with me... or you, in fact? You've been busy in Prevention since you started there?'

'You got the Enforcement Board to lower its acceptable risk envelope... in order to make a quick profit.'

'Listen, Mr Edmundson,' he said, turning to me. 'I've been civil enough to let you in here to talk and ask questions. Please return the courtesy by not throwing wild accusations at me. Or I–'

'Or you're going to call security, yeah?' I jeered.

'I can call them up at any moment,' he said. I watched him carefully. His hand didn't linger anywhere in particular.

'Then do it,' I said. I adopted a tough-guy stance and hissed. 'You wouldn't dare.'

He raised his left wrist towards his mouth. 'You think?' he said.

It was the watch.

'OK, OK,' I said. I had the bugger.

He lowered his arm.

'Sorry, Mr Caines,' I said. 'You're right. I got carried away, yeah? You've answered all my questions. Could you take me back through to reception desk, please?'

'I think I can trust you. Can you find your own way?'

I smiled. 'Don't want to get lost, do I? Won't take a minute, yeah?'

'OK,' he said. 'Happy to oblige.'

Gotcha.

* * *

I was at a fairground ride. It was probably Blackpool. I was a lanky teenager. I had my mates - Kris and Dodgy Pete - with me. Kris had got a high-flying job in Jaipur now. Dodgy Pete had been caught stealing too many beads from old ladies. They'd sent him away. Rumour was it was the Orkneys. When you got Sent Away, you weren't supposed to make any contact with anybody. You were supposed to get a job and settle down and make a new life. Away from all those horrible people who'd made you bad in the first place.

I'd not heard from Dodgy Pete since it had happened. Kris contacted me now and then. But he had gone posh. We had nothing in common now.

The rollercoaster swung around a corner. It had faint audio, so I could hear us screaming swear words. All beneath a jaunty, retro guitar track. The whole cut felt a little too much like one of Memro's regular offerings. It was a bland template. The service was screwing me over tonight. It couldn't read what I wanted.

I pulled myself out of it and re-set the parameters. Tried something different. Using her ID, her credentials.

After a minute, which seemed to last an hour, with the timer shaking away in the display, Dali's face filled the screen. She was a young woman, possibly before I knew her properly. She was in a friend's bedroom. It must have been around the time she was at school. Or just finishing school. She was getting ready for some kind of party. The camera was handheld. This must have been personal footage, possibly from her own camera, or one of her friends'. Memro can't have had much of it, for it was dropping into slo-mo already. A Keralan ballad started up. Usually, these made me shiver. Today, it made me sick. The whole thing made me sick. Peering into these girls' lives, so long ago. The camera cut to a street scene, high angle, grainy. They were getting into a huge car. It looked an off-road vehicle that had been extended. It looked like that event from American culture. I couldn't remember the name.

We were back in the car. The camera zoomed woozily on Dali, close up again. She was drinking champagne.

I turned it off.

The Memro wasn't it. I needed to try something different.

I rose from the sofa and stomped through to the kitchen. The scanner lay in the corner by the door where I had thrown it. As soon as I had got home, I had started sifting the raw data ripped from Caine's watch. It wasn't encrypted, for which I was grateful. Although it took a phenomenal amount of computing power – and sheer space – to encrypt a bead's internal storage, some people still did it. Of course, it immediately made people like me suspicious, which was also why people avoided doing it. As Caines had said, he didn't have anything to hide.

A few minutes later, I had the entire contents of his comms and contact list dropped into a hidden cache on my processing unit and I was flicking through the details on my display. It didn't take long to find what I needed. All the keywords were there. I had found all the conversations between him and the Newcastle people. I found all the posted messages. I found all the videos.

Not one of them mentioned Enforcement risk ratings.

The device had been thrown at the wall a few minutes after this and I had tried to do something else in order to stop the rage.

Spores were distributed in dinky little potato-fibre packets, shaped like long, fattened diamonds. You wet one end and ripped it off, then jammed it up your nose and, after you'd made a small hole in the bottom with a pencil or something, you snorted hard. And hoped for the best.

These packets were a rainbow effect of recycled fibres. They made the whole thing look very wholesome. Like it was good for you.

This batch wasn't good for you. I felt sick immediately. There was a swimmy dizziness that went with it. I felt sick and lay down on the floor. The roof modules merged above me into a queasily shifting game of blocks. I thought I heard somebody laughing in the next room. I got to my feet and ran through to the kitchen, scrabbling at the rug as it rucked up underneath my feet. There was nobody there. The laughter came from beneath the sink. I looked inside. There was just the cleaning bot. Was that laughing? I took it out, suddenly terrified. I flipped it up on its back and found its re-chargeable power source. I needed a screwdriver. I ran through to the lounge and rummaged through the pockets of my coat. I found a screwdriver.

Back in the kitchen, I tried to unscrew the power source from the evil, laughing, cleaning bot. But then I realised the laughing was still coming from under the sink. I took all the bottles of assorted cleaning fluid out and climbed inside. It was warm in here. The laughing was coming from the pipes. I didn't think it was possible that they could listen to me from the pipes.

I had to be sick in the sink. Nothing came out. I dry-heaved and dry-heaved but spat nothing into the black hole shimmering beneath me.

After I had lain on the rug a while, trying to equate the rucks in the material beneath me to the major peaks of the world, I felt a little better. The room had stopped shimmering and I rationalised that the laughing – and the screaming – were just powerful hallucinations.

I still knew I had to get out of the flat, though. They were definitely watching me in the flat.

I went to the balcony and leaned on the railings. It was late evening outside. The air was warm, humid.

I looked out across the rooftops. There seemed to be riots again around the mill. It had been going on for a while. It was just background noise now. I looked down at the street by the front of the block. Without realising it, I started searching for a particular body shape, the same lithe running motion. There was no reason why she should necessarily be here again. But I searched for her anyway.

I stood by the door to my flat. It was open. All I had to do was step out and search. I stood there for about five minutes. I couldn't step through the opening. Yet I was still being watched. What would I have done out there, anyway? Gone up to every person in the street with a flaming bottle? I knew I couldn't find her.

But I knew somebody who could.

I just needed to get through the night, now. And not look rough in the morning.

After Dali had died, they hadn't taken away her medication. I had researched exactly what it was they had given her. What she had worked out would kill her most effectively. What had been the cleanest way to escape.

They were behind a ceiling tile in the bathroom. I wasn't ready to follow her just yet. But I knew that one of the little coloured pills might help me now. I found the wasp-coloured tablet and placed it at the back of my mouth.

Clasping my hand over my mouth, to stop any retching, I dry-swallowed and staggered through to Ali's room. I curled up amid his soft toys and fell asleep.

Chapter Thirty

——

'Head on?'

'Yeah. Proper head on, you know?'

'Whoa. That's sick, man.'

'Yeah. Proper sick, in't it?'

Mafu was only half-looking in my direction. I could tell he was more interested in the game than in my face. His hands were weaving an intricate display above his desk. I was supposed to be feeding back what I'd learned from the professor but my mind didn't seem able to recall much from that meeting. I had all my notes, such as they were, on my display, ready to send them flying across to him.

'You winning, buddy?' I asked Mafu, after a pause. He looked up at me with a confused expression, smiled apologetically, then unfocused his eyes and stared into the distance.

'You want a coffee? A chocolate?' I asked. He shook his head.

Cordan had avoided my eye since I had got back to work. His desk was on the far side of the open plan floor and he had kept his head down at his tablet all morning. I knew he was trying to pluck up the courage to call my agency and tell me to get off the premises. Whatever scraps of work I'd managed to achieve before I went with him to Scarborough might have delayed him pulling up his contacts list. I knew I'd been a dead weight. There was no way I was going to properly update Mafu on the patterns the prof had been talking about. Cordan knew this. I'd known it before I'd even got into his little car.

He knew he'd messed up. That was why he didn't want to speak to me. Probably wouldn't even speak to Mafu. Find some other way out of it. Coward's way out.

In the kitchen zone – a brightly-lit octagonal worktop on the uppermost floor – I found the green-haired pair. They were both in the process of concocting some elaborate chocolate froth, using one of the expensive steam-driven machines. One of them was called Luce but I couldn't remember the other's name.

'Hello,' I said.

'Wow,' said Luce. 'You look terrible. You been in an accident?'

'Yeah. Car crash, in't it.'

The other one was looking closely into my eyes. She looked a little suspicious.

'Car crash? Whereabouts?' asked Luce.

'Up in dale,' I said. 'It were right in the middle of nowhere, yeah.'

'You went with Cordan,' said the other one. 'Were you on the way back, then?'

'Yeah. On my own, though. Went to see some friends.'

'You were on your own?'

'Yeah.'

'That's hard,' said Luce. 'Up dale and all.'

'Yeah.'

She turned back to her chocolate.

'Listen,' I said, trying to act casual. 'Cordan wanted me to start checking out locational models. Do either of you work on those?'

'She does,' said Luce's friend. She leaned in closer to my face. 'What happened to your eyes?'

I shrugged. 'Dunno. They're bad and all, then?'

'Yeah,' she said, nodding. 'Proper bloodshot.'

'Can you get me set up on the locational stuff then, Luce?' I asked, turning to her. I didn't like the way her friend was staring at my eyes.

'No,' said Luce. 'I can show you how to use it, but only Cordan can get you access. You want me to ask him?'

'No, that's alright,' I said. 'I'll ask him myself.'

'OK,' she said, and sipped some of her froth.

I stirred my own chocolate. It looked tame in comparison. 'You could show me how it works, though. Let me test it out on your display, yeah?'

'Yeah, sure,' said Luce. 'You come and find me when you're ready, OK?'

'Will do,' I said, and smiled at them as they left the kitchen.

I perched on one of the high stools and fired up my bead. I logged into the Prevention scheduling system and started searching for public calendars. There was going to be a meeting on the latest update on Prevention comms later on in the morning. I remembered attending one of these before. They only went on for about half an hour but they tended to draw in everybody on the floor.

I nursed my bruises and pretended to be busy for the rest of the morning. Mafu kept dropping in half-hearted suggestions to catch up on the models. He seemed grateful when I suggested pushing it back to the afternoon.

At seventeen minutes before the comms meeting was due to start, I stood up and made my way over to the other side of the office.

'Is now OK?' I asked, standing over Luce's desk. She had a monumental tablet on the table in front of her.

'Now?'

'Yeah? It's not a problem, is it?'

She shook her head hurriedly, checking the time. 'No, it's fine. We should have enough time.'

I nodded at the tablet. 'You don't use a bead?'

'Not for work,' she said. 'They hurt my eyes. I'm old-fashioned. You use a bead?'

'Yeah,' I said. I pointed to my cap.

She squinted at the grubby letters embossed on there. 'Sweet,' she said, laughing.

'Guess I can't use that,' I said, nodding at the tablet.

'For my fingertips only, I'm afraid,' she said. 'I can change the security settings... but it's a pain in the arse.'

I pushed over a chair from another desk. 'No need. You able to share that with my tablet?'

'Sure,' she said. 'View only?'

I made a face and nodded. 'Don't want to break it... not on my first try!'

She laughed. 'You can't break anything, Haz. Don't worry. But, of course, I can make it view-only if you'd like.'

'Nah,' I said. 'I guess you're right. I need to learn. Promise I won't twitch anything, yeah?'

'OK,' she said. I could see her Spidz screen appear on my display. She'd customised it. Its multi-coloured panes obscured the calendar behind.

We spent the next ten minutes sat together, with her showing me where all the various locational models could be found. She dragged in a load of data threads and left them ready for linking. Then we watched as some of the models ran on the display. Outline street maps with hundreds of tiny green dots, moving in seemingly random ways, then clustering, then scattering.

'This is based on real agents, in't it?' I asked.

'Well,' she said. 'It's a generalised pattern from real agents.'

'You ever test the models against the real movements?'

'Oh yeah,' she said. 'Watch this.'

I saw the green dots on the street maps get joined by red dots. If you were being generous, you could say that their movements corresponded to the model's. If you were being right generous.

'Red are real agents at the same location under the same parameters.'

'Right,' I said. 'And their attributes match the models, yeah?'

'Yeah,' she said. 'They're real people.'

A little bell, held by a child's hand, started to ring in the middle of her tablet.

'Sorry,' she said. 'Gotta go.'

'I'll come out,' I said. I moved my hands in rough approximation of the closing signal. This closed the calendar. She seemed to have bought it. The model was still up on my display.

'Great,' she said. 'You coming?'

'Eh?' I asked.

'Wednesday comms update?'

'Think I'll pass,' I laughed.

'Isn't Cordan going to want you at this?' asked Luce.

I shook my head. 'I'm just a temp, yeah? He'll not bother, trust me.'

'What you going to do?'

I leant in close. 'Think I might need to go to the toilet for a while. Had a bad burrito last night.'

'OK,' she said, stepping back and raising her hand. 'I'll see you later, then.'

'Yeah,' I said.

I sauntered off towards the toilets. As I did, I could see everybody else on the floor start to stand up from their desks, chatting, and slowly make their over to Cordan's desk. Nobody seemed bothered that I was heading in the wrong direction. The toilets were at the end of a corridor that ran along one side of the floor. However, as I stepped into the corridor, the image of Luce's Spidz display started to flicker in front of me. I was about to lose the local signal. I stopped.

Shit.

I knew I couldn't stand in the corridor, flinging my hands about in front of me. I turned back towards the desks and hovered by the corner. It seemed the signal dropped off as soon as you started down the corridor. I had to stay in the desks, if I was going to do this.

Everybody was now around Cordan's desk, in one of the far corners. Apart from Cordan himself, who was hidden by the bodies, they all had their backs turned to me. I ducked around the corner into the corridor, dropped onto all fours and crawled back around into the nest of table legs, using the desks as cover. If there had been any latecomers turning the corner of the corridor, I would've looked a very suspicious sight. But I managed to make it to one of the desks near the windows at the opposite side of the building to the comms meeting. I tucked myself up behind some boxes. Looking at the labels on the boxes, it seemed that they contained juggling balls. Geeks.

The Spidz screen was sharp and responsive in front of me. I had total control of the system. If anybody had been looking at Luce's tablet at this moment, they would've seen everything I was seeing. I knew I didn't have long.

I started looking at the attributes of the real agents they had there. I scrolled through the data, looking for forenames.

They'd been anonymised. I swore under my breath. This was rubbish. Then I kicked myself. That was the whole point of wearing the eye-extenders and the masks. If Prevention knew who the rioters were, then Enforcement would know. I should know!

'You twat,' I whispered.

I stared at the display, my stinging eyes about ready to cry.

I felt like somebody had just thrown a bucket of ice in my face. What was I doing here? What was I trying to do? Was she really going to help me?

I was about to shut down the view-only link and leave the building, when I had a thought. The model only worked because they were able to follow real agents and tweak the algorithms based on this. This meant that she was in there somewhere. They may not know her name. They wouldn't know her face. They had nothing close to a solid enough match for a conviction. But they had enough for the model. They had to have followed her. I just needed to find her now.

I started looking for locational maps around my block of flats in Saltaire. There were a few but they were mainly focussed on the mill. If only I could track down that night. I tried to remember when she had appeared.

'Dammit.'

I couldn't remember.

I tried working back through days in my head. I kept losing track. My brain wasn't working. I took a best guess and plugged in a few days either side.

The scenarios came up on-screen. I scrolled through.

There was nothing. I was sweating now. I stank. I only had a few minutes left before people would start coming back to their desks. I went back to the attributes of the model. How did they recognise them? They had height, gender. That wasn't enough. Then I saw 'facial ratio'. They can't have done that? Nobody ever showed their face, did they?

'Eye-extenders,' I breathed. With shaking fingers, I pulled up a shopping site – the kind used by people who paid on pre-load – and looked for eye-extenders. I scrolled through the different types at speed. Found it. I pulled up a drawing app. Loaded up a generic female face. Cut the eye-extenders and dropped them in place. Hand-drew a scarf around the lower-half of the face. Coloured it in by hand, from memory.

It had light brown leaves on a dark blue background. For some reason, this pattern had lodged in my head.

Using my ratio-generating app, I pulled out some numbers. I used these as search criteria on the agents. Nobody was returned.

Over my shoulder, I could hear some laughter from the group. It sounded like they were about to break up.

I created a fuzzy match, going up a level in the ratio. This returned five possibilities. I brought these up. Three were male. I checked the heights of the last two. One was about my height. I discarded that one. There was one left. This was her. I'd found her ID.

I'd found her. Now what?

I copied her ID and dropped it into a locational map of the entirety of the dale. I ran all her movements.

'Hey, dude!'

I looked up. Somebody was standing over me, looking worried.

'What are you doing there?' said the man. He wore a T-shirts that read: Have sex with a Semanticist... it Means Something.

'Feeling a bit poorly,' I said. 'Just going to the toilets, now, yeah?'

'You go, man,' he said, standing back. 'Take it easy.'

I stood and trotted for the corridor. The red dots representing Luana swam in front of my eyes, making me unbalanced. There was a pattern. They tended to start off the night from the one location. I took a note of it and cut the connection to Luce's desktop. Mafu appeared in my vision, from my left. He raised his hand, about to speak, but I cut across him and waved.

'Gotta go, buddy. Tell Cordan I've got another job, and that.'

* * *

I'd had a few friends who'd suggested to go out drinking at The Wall. I'd declined every time. It was a test of your courage. And I'd never been that courageous.

Once, it had been a quarry on the outskirts of Keighley Vale, just off the high road that took the autobuses to Calderdale. Then it had been acquired by a wealthy vat-grower, who'd turned it into some kitsch museum of old Airedale life. Put a roof over the whole quarry and dug out a toy mineshaft. She'd had some holographic displays of wandering sheep installed and piped 'ancient' voices of shepherds. The centrepiece was the drystone wall itself, which bisected the entire ground floor, split with a couple of gates and squeezes. The proper joke of the whole affair was that this wall had been built by some labourers from the Azores, a few months after the place had been turned into a heritage centre. Up here, if you'd wanted to really see a drystone, you didn't need to drive far. But they'd decided to build something anyway.

I had faint memories of being brought there as a child, by the grandparents Edmundson. Even at that age – I must have been about six or seven at most – I could sense the fact that it was tired. Perhaps I was just picking up the signals from my grandparents. Slight sneers, changes in voice tone, changes in behaviour. These burn bright like danger flares to a child at that age.

About a year after I'd visited it, the vat-grower went out of business and had to sell the centre. Keighley Vale, which had once been dotted with new mansionettes and hi-spec apartments, gradually emptied as the work left. The apartments were filled with those surviving on Yellow Contract jobs - the worst terms of employment. The mansionettes were bought up by the Social Housing Collective and converted into separate rooms. The broken people, forever pushed out by local Servant action from one neighbourhood to the next, descended upon Keighley Vale.

In amid this change, the heritage centre had somehow been bought up – nobody knew whether it was one owner or a collective – and been turned into a pub. Rather, it had been turned into a hangar where people drank alcohol. Bamboo scaffolding had been glued into place around the old quarry walls and cheap, polymer moulded seating had been dropped in. The old mineshaft was where they kept the booze. When I'd been in my teens, this had been guarded by a fat American who kept his hands in his pockets all evening. The rumour was he had a pair of sawn-offs up his sleeves. And had made use of them three times in the past.

The fat American had been replaced by a towering Brazilian, who carried his shotgun openly on a shoulder holster. The place was buzzing with noise. It stank of synthetic lime and tequila vomit.

I bought myself a low-alcohol beer – much to the suspicion of the lady at the bar – and tapped off some pre-load on the grubby stump. My cap had been stuffed deep into a pocket, so there was no way I could entertain myself in the normal way. I was thinking about getting some height for a better view and ascending one of the bamboo structures. But I didn't like the way they swayed. Plus, a loner sat at a table by himself was going to attract attention. I stayed by the bar and kept checking my watch every few minutes.

Then I saw a group enter. They looked to be about the right age for post-grad students. She was with them. Short, black haired, dark-skinned. She spotted me within two seconds of entering. At first, she looked terrified. I thought she was going to bolt for the door. I raised my hands in an effort to calm her. One of her friends, a lanky young man with a squashy hat and a bad beard, leaned into her ear and asked her a question. She shook her head at him and walked straight over.

'So,' she said. 'First time I've seen you at The Wall.'

'I've been here before,' I said.

'Really? But you're religious?' she said, looking at my beer.

'I'm not,' I said. 'Really, I'm not. Just get bored by drunks, in't it.'

The man with the squashy hat laughed at me.

She ignored her companion and squinted up at me. 'You're uptight,' she said. 'You need to relax.'

'Are you going out tonight?'

'I'm out, aren't I?'

'I mean,' I said, waving generally in the direction of the basin. 'Out there?'

'Why?' she said. 'You want to come?'

'That's not why I'm here.'

'Oh,' she said, sipping her drink. 'You came to find me?'

'Yeah,' I said.

She stood up and nodded at her companions. They waved her away with grins. We went to find another corner of the room.

'How did you find me?' Although it was asked casually, I could see the tension in her mouth.

'Long story.'

'I've got all night.'

I looked at her for a moment. 'You worried?'

'I take precautions,' she said. 'I want to know why they didn't work.'

I smiled. 'I know. Everybody tries to take precautions... even myself.'

'You? Why you?'

'There's always a way around them.'

'But why you?'

I took a drink. 'That's none of your business.'

'Am I on a Justice database somewhere?'

'Course.'

'But that's not how you found me?'

'No,' I said. 'I've got access to other data mountains now.'

'I'm glad it was you that found me,' she said, and smiled.

I fell into a flummoxed silence. 'Yeah?'

'So,' she said. 'Now that you're here, what do you want to do?'

I took a breath. 'You remember the night you came into my flat?'

'Yes. Of course.'

'You told me something… about the people you're trying to fight, the vat-growers.'

'Probably. I don't talk about much else.'

'You mentioned a name. Darren Caines.'

She made a face. 'Yes. So what?'

'So… what do you know about him? About this Darren Caines?'

'He's a piece of shit,' she said. 'He marketed his business to whole suburbs of Sao Paulo. Told them he was going to make them rich. Whole load of hopefuls arrived on the slow boat at Liverpool. Most of them had invested all their savings – or their parents' savings – in the onboard training programmes. Within a few months of starting in the job, he closed all his operations in Shipley and moved it all back to Keighley Flatts. Hundreds of people laid off.'

'You were one of them?'

'Yes.'

'And you stayed in the dale?'

She looked at me strangely. 'Yes, I stayed. I'm here for the movement, aren't I?'

'The movement?'

She frowned and shook her head. 'Not now. What do you want to know about Caines?'

So I told her everything. About the drone, the risk ratings, the Regionale index, my meetings with Hassan and Caines.

And I told her about Caine's watch and how there was nothing on it.

'He'd have spoken to Abi Hassan,' she said. 'Minute you left her meeting, she'd have trotted right over to his place. She's totally in his pocket. Can't sneeze without his approval. That's the problem with this place. Your Servants can't move without their special interests. You're all screwed.'

'We are? Not you?'

'Yes,' she said. 'I'm just passing through. This is your dale, isn't it?'

'Yeah,' I said.

I wasn't so sure.

'Anyway,' she said. 'I know enough about Caines. Did you know he had a cousin? Wroxeter?'

'I didn't know that.'

'Liam Wroxeter.'

The name was weirdly familiar. I must have read it somewhere. 'OK.'

'The guy's a corporate lawyer or into commercial contracts or something. Lives over in Riddlesden side.' She waved an arm out towards the other side of the dale.

'What's special about him, then?'

'What's special,' she said, putting on a stage whisper. 'Is that he is on the Enforcement Board of Airedale.'

I laughed. 'Bloody hell!'

I remembered where I'd seen the name before. Attendees list.

'Yes,' she said. 'Interesting, isn't it?'

'Absolutely, where can I find him?'

'You can't,' she said. 'He's got tight security. Personal army, nearly. But...'

I watched her smile. 'But what?'

'He's having some kind of party tomorrow night. Along the New Canal. Regular thing, does it every year for his friends,

I think.'

'How do you know all this?'

She shrugged. 'It's just information. We try to share as much information as possible. It helps us all. Information's free, isn't it? We share it around.'

'You know whereabouts on the canal?'

'No,' she said. 'But you can help us out with that, I'm sure.'

I grimaced.

'Is that all you wanted?'

'Yeah.'

'Right.'

Then, without knowing what I was doing, I turned back to her and asked her if she wanted another drink. She said yes. We took it outside and stood on a bamboo platform overlooking the basin. From up here, from such a distance, it looked beautiful. A clustering pattern of lights. For a moment, I was glad that I lived right here. I almost managed to forget everything that was happening around me.

Halfway through the drink, I leaned towards her. She turned and kissed me. She tasted of alcohol and synthetic limes. I wasn't sure why, but it was familiar. I'd kissed somebody, somewhere, in the same context, now forgotten.

After our third drink, we heard the first rumble of thunder. It was distant, from the south of the dale. The warm breeze from the south-west had suddenly turned chilly. The storm was going to cross the Pennines in a few hours.

Chapter Thirty-One

I awoke at two a.m. sunk into a soaking hollow in the sheets. I'd been dreaming of Asha crying in her bed. I stumbled out and tried to find the door, which wasn't where it should be. The left-hand side of the bed was where I always slept, but I'd woken on the right, which confused me. When I tried to walk around the room, I kept treading on things that shouldn't be there. The light coming in from the windows was different. The smell was different.

'Ah, shit.'

I found the door.

'Jeez, man.' There was an old guy with salt-and-pepper hair arranged in two plaited pigtails. He was sat on a sofa. 'You need some of this.'

He offered me the end of a bulbous glass device which exuded a burnt synthetic odour. Leaning against his arm was a younger woman, sleeping, her grubby fingernails clinging onto him. The room was dim, though as I peered around I could see five other people tucked into the corners, far too many for the size of the room.

'Nah,' I grunted. I felt like I was going to be sick. I had to get out of this place somehow. But I didn't know where the door was. Between me and the exit lay a wolf, or at least, it looked like a wolf.

'You've been shouting out, man,' the old guy said.

'Who're you?' I asked, angry with him. I wanted to give him a piece of my mind.

'I'm Joshua,' he said. 'This is my house.'

'Who was crying?'

'Hey?'

'Heard someone crying. Why didn't you do something about it?'

'Nothing in here, man,' he said. It was difficult to understand him. He spoke with a strong Brazilian accent.

He nodded at the smoky device again. 'Take a piece of this. You need this.'

'Don't think so,' I muttered. Need spores.

'Spores?' You don't think you've had enough of that stuff?'

'Have I?' I couldn't remember much. I couldn't remember this room. 'Where am I?'

'This is my place, man.'

'You got spores?'

'Not me, man. But check the pockets of your coat. That's where you were scooping them out from.'

I tried to reach into my pocket before realising I was naked. I suddenly put hands down to cover myself.

Joshua laughed. 'Hey, I'm chilled about the body, man. Don't you go getting today's cold, though. It's 453-56... yeah, that's right, it's back, man. And it's a rough ride this time around.'

I ignored him and turned back into the bedroom. Using the light from the adjoining room, I could see my clothes, dumped in a conical heap near the bottom of the bed. I fished through them, found my underwear, and started to pull them on. From the bed, I could hear somebody stir. I tried to speed up. This didn't work. I fell over attempting to shove a leg into my trousers. I cracked the back of my head of the wall. The pain in my knee and thigh flared. I swore.

'Haz,' Luana called out softly. 'Where're you going?'

'You're dreaming,' I said. 'Go back to sleep.'

There was a pause. 'OK,' she said.

I kicked the rest of my clothes through the door and into the adjoining room. I closed the door behind me as quietly as I could.

The show was amusing the old man. 'You're in a hurry, boy. You need to slow down a little.'

He inhaled deeply and blew out a light smoke.

'I've got two kids,' I said, as though that explained it.

'We know,' said Joshua. 'You talked about them last night.'

'I did?'

He nodded slowly. 'A lot.'

'Uh huh.' I still couldn't remember.

'Seems to me,' he said. 'That they being with the Family Service–'

'I spoke about that?'

'Yeah, you did.'

'Oh.'

'They being with the Service, like they are, means you racing into the night right about now isn't doing anybody any favours, man. You're not getting them back playing The Batman.'

'What? What are you saying, like?'

'Chasing after them on bikes is what I'm saying, man. Hacking into sensitive systems is what I'm saying. That kind of stuff's going to get you into a whole heap more trouble.'

'The bike? I spoke about that? What else did I talk about last night?'

'Plenty of stuff, man,' he said. He paused. 'Your life is… well, it's in a bit of a dip, I'd say.'

'Did I talk about…'

He regarded me sagely for a moment. Then shook his head. 'No. You didn't talk about her.'

I breathed out. 'I don't remember much,' I muttered.

'You went early. You took the first dive.'

'What?'

'You crashed out on Luana's bed. Just as we were getting started, as well.'

'Crashed out? I fell asleep?'

He grinned. 'Yeah, man. You looked knackered.'

I finished dressing in silence. I was ashamed. I'd fallen asleep on her. A little part of me was glad. Being here wasn't right. I still needed to get out. I pulled on my jacket and my cap.

'You going out there, man? In that?'

'I have to get them back,' I said.

He shrugged. 'It's your life, man. You've the right to muck it up as you wish.'

I found the main hall to the house and stepped carefully down the sticky stairs. The door was unlocked. I ran out onto the street. It was raining. A hard, slow, gravelly rain. It hurt to stand underneath the drops.

'Haz!'

I could hear Luana's voice behind me. It was muffled by the sound of rain pummelling the tarmac around me. This had once been an expensive street. Ranks of bespoke mini-mansions ran up the hill behind me. Ahead of me, across the Vale, I could see the dimmed streetlamps of more and more of these streets. This place had once bred accountants and marketing middle managers. They'd all gone now. Escaped back to Chennai or to retirement homes on the flanks of the Corcovado. Before the AI stole all their jobs.

In the distance, a little to right of the Vale, was the brighter glow of the basin. I started trotting down the hill.

'Haz! Where're you going?'

I ignored her.

Already the gutters in the street were flooding. I doubted

the sewers got cleared out in the Vale any more. This place would turn into a river soon. I jumped my way to the middle of the road, in between the two streams. It was driest here, although I was no longer underneath the trees alongside me. The rain drops fell with a dull roar onto the leaves.

Then there came another noise. A strange rattle. High-pitched and intense. Above it all, I could hear the whine of motors. I looked around. Appearing over the abundant foliage of a plane tree, a camdrone was approaching. It sunk in the air. The rattle was the rain bouncing off its ultra-light carapace.

I started to back off, away from the drone. Luana was still calling from the door. I started running down the street, downhill, away from the house, away from the drone. I knew Luana was following me. I could hear her shouts getting closer. I started running faster, sprinting on the concrete. Then my foot got caught in a pothole and I tripped. My elbows caught most of the blow. Even behind the medication and the spores, I could feel the pain jar through my body. I scrambled to my feet and, my trainers skidding in the wet, started to run down the hill once more. Then I noticed the increase in the noise. Ahead of me, coming up the hill, behind me and from all sides, Enforcement camdrones were descending. There must have been close to twenty of them. As was their habit, when they grouped like this, their behaviour in the sky took on that of a flock of birds. They started to bank and roll in virtual unison, splitting their number around larger objects such as streetlamps and parked cars.

A quick glance back up the hill indicated that Luana had given up. But I could see more of the camdrones descending. There was only a small window of time before they sent in a shockdrone. I had to find somewhere to hide. Somewhere down this street would be an empty house, a derelict. I scanned the doors and the windows of the houses. Most of them had rudimentary security. I spotted one that looked like it had been forced already. A quick shoulder-barge and I was inside. I sank behind the cover of the door. There was nobody else in the building. I rocked, holding my knees, keeping low. The rain was cold on my balding head so I pulled on my cap to warm up.

My bead found my eyes and give me a display. A call was pending. It was from an unknown contact. I blinked a command to accept the call.

'Hello, Hasim,' said a sock. It was rather unpleasant-looking grey sock. What looked like badly cut-out circles of paper acted as eyes. A dot had been added to each piece of paper to indicate pupils. Their configuration gave the impression that the sock was cross-eyed.

'The heck?' I muttered. I wondered whether this was some delayed reaction to the spores.

'I need to Red Sea you, Hasim,' said the sock. 'This apparel will delay the algorithms for a while. A human handler will interpret it, no doubt, but that gives us what is held in the arms of a clock. No doubt they are all in bed, or immersed in some grotty little RandoPorno.'

'Who is this?'

'When it rains, the average temperature drops,' said the voice. I could tell now that it had been modulated. It sounded subtly metallic. 'I can't show my face, so just know me as sock puppet. Average temperature between three and four degrees. You've got to track me down, Hasim, I'm afraid. You're a good digital analyst. I've always said that. Hellfire, Captain! You'll manage it.'

'Track you down?'

'Many, many people have not unmanaged the hinted task.'

I laughed. 'It's you, is it? You going to give me another reprimand?'

'Think to your last maritime adventure, Hasim. Don't bring

your plastic friends.'

The call was cut.

Outside the house I could hear the drones hovering. I stood by the window and contemplated making a run for it down the street. They would've followed me, however fast I went. There was no way I could trick them into the house, they were programmed to hover by a door but never enter. They knew they'd be trapped that way.

Then I remembered a feature of the house. Something I'd seen as I ran in, a common feature of these mini-mansions, for those with money.

I staggered down the stairs to the cellar, finding my way by the dim light which came in from the streetlamps. They had some kind of back-up generator attached to the wall. There appeared to be a tiny amount of ethanol remaining in the tank. I fired it up and waited for the LED display to tell me power had started to flow. It took a few seconds but then the numbers started to appear. I could see lights starting to come on upstairs. Wanting to preserve as much of the power as possible, I found the control box and manually pulled all feeds from the upper floors.

There was a door at the other side of the cellar. I picked my way through heaps of excrement-strewn mattresses and linen before making my way to the door. On the other side was an empty garage, save for more bed linen and heaps of rubbish. At one end was the large door, which I saw would raise as a single unit into the ceiling.

I ran back to the cellar and using my processor and bead, spliced myself into the house server. I found the controls, then went back to the garage and, using the house management screens, raised the door. The sound of the rain hitting the outer side of the door filled the room. I stepped out, waving my arms in the direction of the drones, which were clustered around the front door. One-by-one, as if they couldn't help themselves, they charged down the garage entrance, cameras pointed at me. I tucked myself into a corner by the door, trying to encourage them as close as possible.

Then I went back to my display from the bead, hacking into the door's control parameters. I broke past the user limits on the servos, set thing to maximum speed and with an aggressive swipe of the hand, brought the door crashing down, knocking the drones into the garage.

With nimble steps, I ran past the drones to the opposite door and slipped through, slamming it shut behind me. As I ran for the steps, I smashed the back-up generator and all lights went out in the house.

I made my way down the street, casually adjusting my clothes, trying to control my breathing. Inside I was a teenager again, roaring at the departing back of the opening batsman I'd just clean bowled. Outside, I had to look like somebody out for a stroll. I only turned once to check. I could see dozens of little LEDs floating around the garage window. Watching me. I knew they wanted me dead.

* * *

The narrowboat was in the same location. Clive wasn't. He was inside, sheltering from the rain behind his cute little painted doors.

'What happened to Carrie? She's not answering my calls.'

'She's… well, let's say she's a little unhappy about what happened.'

'What do you mean?'

He regarded me for a moment. 'You don't know?'

'What?'

'Her contract was also cancelled.'

I nodded. 'Yeah, guessed that was coming.'

'She's over in Manchester now,' said Clive. 'Working with

Louie on something. She's got a contract. But she doesn't want anything more to do with Airedale.'

'Right,' I said. I looked at him and waited. 'So, what's your point, Clive? Why'd you have to drag me here?'

'Ibrahim wants you to carry on.'

'Don't understand.'

Clive nodded. 'I know. You're in a mess, Hasim. The DI has told me to tell you that he thinks you should continue with the case. The Meri Fergus case.'

'Carry on with the case? For honest?'

'It's true.'

'He's taking me back on?'

Clive made a rueful face. 'Possibly... if you agree to help.'

'You know what, Clive, buddy,' I said. 'I'm shit tired, and that. I can't be bothered with all this. I just want my kids back and to let it all go, you know?'

He narrowed his eyes at me and leaned back. 'Oh, Hasim... you know I don't believe you.'

'I'm sick of it.'

'You need a rest, for sure. You need a shave.' He laughed. 'But then you've needed a shave since as long as I can remember.'

'No, Clive,' I said. 'I'm out, yeah. Straight-up honest. I'm not doing it no more.'

He sighed. 'Are you sure?'

I nodded.

'All that aside,' said Clive, waving his hand in the air in front of his face. 'I know you're still going to do this for Ibrahim.'

'Screw you!'

'Not so fast, Hasim. You forget... I've got all the little infringements of IG. I've got it all recorded. I know what you've been doing. I even know what you've been buying. My bead tells me you've got a scanner in the pocket of that coat over there.'

We both looked over at my coat. The green khaki, now

beyond waterproof, dripped darkly and slowly onto Clive's rug from the kitchen chair where I'd hung it.

'Screw you.'

'Do you know what you'd get for something like this?'

'You've got nothing!'

'Do you know what you'd get?'

'S'all rubbish!'

'You'd get sent away somewhere, Hasim. Probably somewhere south. Away from your family, your friends. You'd be living in a bedsit by yourself in a grotty block of flats in Portsmouth Island or a leaky caravan behind the Canvey Barrier. You'd not get a bead. They wouldn't let you within an arm's length of a terminal. You'd be working on a farm.'

'Screw you.'

'It'd be lonely.'

'You've got nothing.'

'No, Hasim,' he said, turning my name into a roar. 'We have everything on you. You've got a black market scanner. You've used false ID with two significant members of the public.'

'They thought I was media.'

'You've broken into Prevention's system using another person's ID.'

I breathed heavily. 'How'd you know about that?'

'They told us,' said Clive. 'I know Whiley. She's my counterpart. A tablet was recorded in activity while the owner was away. Very clever work, my friend. But you didn't turn off the cameras in the room.'

'I was in a hurry.'

'They're looking at prosecuting. But we can help you.'

'I don't trust any of the bollocks that comes out of your mouth. Sorry.'

'I understand completely, Hasim,' he said. 'You're in a difficult situation. But we're offering you a chance, here. We can clear your name, get you your old job back...'

'Get my kids back?'

'I can't promise that. That's outside our power. But getting you back on the contract would help you in that area.'

'I want my kids!'

'We can't make that happen.'

I folded my arms. 'Then screw you!'

He breathed silently for a moment. I could see he wasn't that emotionally involved in all this. It was a game for him. And he didn't want to lose.

'So, Hasim,' he said. 'You want me to push you out onto the bank now and let you carry on as before?'

'Don't matter, either way.'

He leaned in close and hissed in my face. 'You want to bring these buggers in, don't you?'

I remained tight-lipped for a moment, then slowly nodded. 'Yeah.'

'I can get you back onto Modlee. How does that sound?'

'It's better,' I muttered.

'How about some proper data... some proper ratios?'

'What do you mean?' I asked.

'How about the North-Western?'

I narrowed my eyes. 'You can get me that access?'

'Yes,' he said. 'But you have to bring this home. Otherwise you're out on your own again.'

I sat in the chair. I realised I was very cold. 'What does the DI want? He want Caines?'

'Not really,' said Clive. 'Ibrahim has other concerns.'

I thought for a moment. Then realised what Clive was talking about. 'You maniacs... you're not really going after–'

'Shhh,' said Clive, grinning. 'Don't say it. You know what we need, though, yeah?'

'Yeah. The whole frigging picture, in't it?'

'You'll need to get access somehow.'

I grinned. 'Got that covered, like.'

'How?' asked Clive. He seemed genuinely interested.

'There's a party happening tomorrow night.'

'And how do you know that?'

'Got my contacts,' I said.

'You're going to this? This party?'

'If I can get there without bother, yeah.'

'What do you mean?' asked Clive.

'I'm being watched,' I said. I hoped I wasn't whining. Or sounded too insane. 'Every time I step out of the house, bastard drones follow me. Cameras and that, they're all panning around to find me.'

'It's your ID,' said Clive. 'It's accumulating dirt. That's the problem with this system we've got. You get a blemish and that creates feedback and suddenly the blemish becomes damage and then becomes rot. You know this! This has been your job.'

I shook my head. 'I've just swept rooms for slivers and that... done pattern-matching on encrypted tech. This is out of my league, in't it?'

He grinned. 'Welcome to the next level, Hasim.'

'Eh?'

'Sorry,' said Clive. 'An allusion... a reference, you know? No? Lost to time, clearly.'

I frowned at him for a moment. He was a jerk sometimes. 'How you gonna stop drones and that?'

'I can give you some time,' said Clive. 'I can slow up the algorithms. There are ways to confuse them. But they only work for a short time.'

'How long do I have?' I asked.

'Escalation to human handlers is usually within a few hours. I can feed some confusion into the system that'll give you some extra time. Possibly a couple of hours more.'

'From now?'

'I'm sorry?' he said.

'Does that give me a few hours from now?' I repeated.

'No,' he said, shaking his head. 'Nobody has seen you get here. Or we'd be looking at a camdrone out by the tiller. Your last recorded position will be by that house where you trapped the flock.'

'So, what now?' I asked.

'You've got to wait.'

'It's going to be morning soon, in't it?' I said, looking up at the thin curtains of the boat. Already, it was possible to see the battleship-grey skies lightening.

'You should sleep,' said Clive. 'Keep away from the windows.'

'What are you going to do?'

Clive took a sip of tea. 'Me? I've got to drive the boat, haven't I? Don't want to, of course. But I'm helping you out. Helping you and Ibrahim. Though he's an idiot. Always was.'

'You're going to take me right there?'

'Yes,' he said. 'We're going right into Keighley Basin. Not been there for a while. That will be nice, won't it?'

Chapter Thirty-Two

———

I didn't sleep properly. I drifted in and out of a doze. Eventually, in the early afternoon, I got out of Clive's spare bunk and went and sat in one of his dining chairs. The little double doors that opened out onto the deck with the tiller were closed. Clive had also insisted on keeping all the curtains closed. As I sat there, I could just make out trees and buildings passing by.

Quite often we would disappear under a piece of solid infrastructure or a building. Long sections of the canal that wound their way up the dale were essentially subterranean. Clive had an array of low-power LEDs attached to the front and around the side of the boat. When these came on, they cast finger shadows across the curtains, as if night creatures were trying to get in.

I knew my parents would be trying to contact me, but this was currently impossible. Clive had taken my bead, processor, and the scanner and locked them in a safe. This was for security reasons, he'd said, but I wondered whether it was also insurance. He'd revealed a lot to me the night before – about himself and Ibrahim – which could've been used against him.

However, I'd no intention of running now. There was nowhere to go and it was inevitable that I was going to do what the DI wanted of me. It was my job. I was here to find wrong 'uns.

The rain stopped about mid-morning. The day was still humid. I couldn't see the sky but I could tell, from the brief stretches when we were out in the open, that it wasn't sunny. The warmth and the humidity made me uncomfortable. So I was glad when we finally glided into the tunnels beneath the Basin, where it was properly cool. I liked it in the cold. My injuries had been kept in check with a continual supply of painkillers but the heat was making them itch.

Clive moored up the boat and came down into the cabin. He released a couple of toy camdrones out of the hatch at the middle of the boat and guided one further up the canal, while the other went back down where we'd come from. He used glasses for this, so I couldn't see what the drones' view. Clive didn't talk about them. I guessed he wasn't going to eyeball them all night. He didn't need to. They were programmed to go off like a Himalayan watchtower the moment something suspicious appeared on the towpath.

'You ready?' He asked.

It was around six o'clock. I shrugged. 'Yeah, I guess.'

'Don't come back here,' he said. 'I'll be gone shortly.'

'Back to Bingley?'

He just smiled and handed me my things. I dropped the scanner and the processor back into my pockets before pulling on the cap. It was so cold in the tunnel here, I needed the coat on. The air smelled of garden ponds and old-fashioned diesel fumes.

'That's the way into town,' he said, pointing further on down the tunnel.

I nodded and stepped out onto the deck. 'See you sometime.'

I could still sense him watching me from the back of his boat as I walked off into the gloom of the tunnel. The towpath was supposed to be lit at regular intervals by LED clusters, but a lot of them had been vandalised or stolen, so I picked my way through piles of rubbish in near darkness.

A short while later, after I'd turned sufficient bends to lose sight of Clive, I passed some cavernous opening on the other side of the canal to the towpath. The canal branched off into the unlit tunnel, where I wasn't able to see far but felt a strong breeze. It was colder here, the air smelt of mud and sewage with the faint odour of rotting meat. In the distance, I could hear a low noise, deep, and threatening.

The opening unnerved me, so I walked on for about ten minutes, trying to find a quiet corner where I could fire up my bead. I could see nobody else down there, bar a few boats chugging their way past, but I didn't want to try and work the displays a few feet from toxic water. The problem was, I'd never been down here before, so I wasn't sure where I could go. The hand-drawn map Clive had given me was in my pocket, but only gave directions to Caines' cousin. He'd been insistent that it was hand-drawn as he couldn't afford any digital trails, and even made me write on the key locations. It showed a series of canal locks and junctions where I had to cross the water, take a new towpath, or climb up past another lock. And on and on. It was going to take me an hour or so to get to the marina.

It wasn't long before I came to an ancient concrete bench, set back from the towpath, directly beneath a sunpipe. It cast no natural light now, but there was an urban glow from above. The bench must have been nearly a hundred years old. Kept for its antique status. It was beautiful, in its own way, the rotting cement exposing the aggregate like beads, shining with condensation and a good growth of moss around its base.

I should have kept going. I shouldn't have stopped. I knew it was wasting time, but it had been so long since I'd been in there and I wanted to know what it felt like again.

I sat down and logged into Modlee. It felt like putting on an old, well-shaped glove. I'd missed it.

First thing, I checked out the access. He'd given me everything.

I whistled.

There were ratio trails data, locational trails data, behavioural algorithms, metadata patterns, and above these, further metadata patterns stacked up towards a level of ethereal abstraction. These weren't the kinds of tools Those-Who-You-Don't-Think-About would get access, but they were pretty damn close.

Knowing I almost had full access, I did what any normal person would do. I started looking for myself. A quick shot with the camera and a few seconds of processing later I had the string of numbers that represented my unique facial features. It was strange to see the chunk of digits hanging there in front of me. People had died trying to keep these numbers hidden. People had blown themselves up. Governments had been overturned. Countries divided.

I dropped my ratios into the cute folder in Modlee where all the linked parameters were supposed to live. I liked the way the icon opened when I came near it. It took a few seconds then I got a confirmation that a connection had been found. It wouldn't be the exact string, but it would be close enough. Modlee was now hitting the big room under Louie Daine's office.

Using a temporary locational model, I dragged in the linked ratios. It showed the entirety of the dale. I ran the model for the last twenty-four hours. A bright blue circle appeared up in Keighley Vale. Then it disappeared. It didn't reappear. At least I'd lost them for a bit. As long as I avoided the cameras in the canals, I could appear at this party without Enforcement screwing me over. I set an alert up on Modlee to let me know if my ratios started appearing on the system again.

Then it was back to the case. I started linking Caines and his cousin into the locational models. Then I put in Abi Hassan. There were hundreds of meetings. Too many trees. Not enough wood. I tried looking for any meetings that took place before the night Meri Fergus died. There had been a meeting between the three of them in Hassan's offices in Riddlesden. It was about four hours before the comms flare. I dug out the comms flare model and ran it through a few times. One of those dots was Liam Wroxeter. One of them was Brian Fallin. The rest were willing Servants, all going along with the plan.

Idly, I let the model run on. As the days flickered by, there were occasional recognisable patterns of flaring. Just before the model stopped, there was a final flare. I ran it back through time. This one had been recent. I checked the time.

There had been a comms instance earlier in the evening.

I started pulling all the local media channels. There was a riot in progress in the basin. Enforcement were out in large numbers. Looked like most of the centre was in shutdown. I hadn't heard a thing down here in the canals. I saw a few pictures from people's publicly-shared personal cameras. There were plenty of stillz of smoking shop fronts and fires in the middle of streets. There were vidz, seemingly taken by the rioters, showing them in running battles with Enforcement.

With a scared, thumping rattle in my chest, I checked out any reposts from Violence without Limits. They had nothing from tonight. It was quiet.

Then I tried to find myself a camera. Justice were sometimes allowed temporary access to live feeds. There were plenty of fixed camera views. You could only lurk on these. Like the media channels, they just showed empty streets and some scenes of Enforcement operatives directing flocks of shockdrones around corners. But there was a camera on the roof of the college that had some airtime. Nobody was using it. You could control this one. I guessed it was free because you couldn't see the street level action from up there. It was supposed to show panoramic views of the dale, so that citizens of the PRC and India would realise what a beautiful place it was to visit.

I logged myself in and took control. The view showed the tops of streets with half their lights knocked out. I pointed it upwards. At this resolution, I was never going to find what I was looking for. I got into the control screen for the camera and looked for any pattern recognition functions. There was one for movement. I selected this and set the camera to pan across the whole sky. Then I sat on the wet bench and watched the display. It seemed like the sweeping shots of orange clouds went on without end. Then the panning stopped and we started to zoom in. The camera had picked up on significant movement. Then I saw them.

There they were. Two off-white spots banking in long figures-of-eight. There were two flyers circling in the thermals above the basin.

Clive's carefully drawn and immaculately folded map of the canals lay forgotten in my pocket. I started to run down the canal, looking for an exit.

* * *

Before I stepped out of the door, I dug out the pirate bandana from my pocket and tied it around my face. I kept my AJC cap buried deep in my pocket. Then I stepped through. I came out into an empty street. It was near the centre of town. This was normally a busy shopping street, but now the place was deserted. This time of night was when people started appearing in bars and pubs, trying to find themselves a good time. Nobody was having a good time tonight. Across the street lay the broken wreckage of cars. Burnt-out husks of metal and melted polymer. There was a harsh stink of freshly-burnt vegetable fibre. The air hung heavy with the remains of this smoke.

I stood in the middle of the street and stared directly up at the sky. At this distance, with this level of light, it was too difficult to see. But I thought I could see the two shapes circling.

Holding my cap in my hand, hiding the logo, I fired up my bead. I rolled through my contacts. I tried calling up Lani. He was not answering. I tried Puja. There was no reply. I checked out the reposter - Violence without Limits - again. There was a message on there now. Telling the world that they were going to be above the skies of Keighley Basin that evening. Showing the world how the repressed were being violently attacked by the forces of the state. It didn't say who in the group was going to be up there. But I could guess.

I swore at nobody in particular.

Around the corner of the street came a series of running figures. They were shouting at each other in Brazilian.

'Hey,' I shouted. 'What's going on?'

'Drones,' one of them said, running directly past me.

'Come with us,' said a smaller figure. She wore an unnervingly large mouse mask. She wasn't Brazilian. It sounded like she spoke with a Nigerian accent.

I started trotting after the group. In the distance I could hear distorted directives from an Enforcement drone.

'You with the movement?' one of the men asked.

'No,' I said. 'I'm trying to help somebody, yeah. That's all.'

'What d'you need?' asked one of the men leading the group.

I pointed at the shapes in the sky. 'We need to get them down.'

'Why?'

'They're in danger?'

'Safer than on the ground, man.'

'No,' I said, getting angry. 'They're about to be killed. Trust me. It's happened before. It's going to happen tonight, and all. Need to get them out of the sky.'

'Signal them?' asked balaclava-man.

'With what?'

There was an abandoned mosque set back a couple of streets from where we were. I pointed this out to the man who wanted to help and we broke away from the main group, about five of us. I was bowled along the back streets, around corners, and suddenly found myself outside a fence. The mesh was raised and I was pushed under.

'Can I borrow that?' I asked one of the masked figures. I pointed to the megaphone they had slung from their belt, alongside the torches and the wire-cutters and the smoke grenades and the small containers of ethanol.

'Yeah,' said the figure, who unhooked the megaphone and handed it to me through the fence.

'Is it directional?' I asked.

The figure shrugged. 'I don't know, man. It's not mine, is it?'

This brought much laughter from the other figures. I nodded and said a quick thanks.

It took a few wrong turns before I located the staircase up to the tower. I could hear the skittering of various mice or rats disappearing into distant corners. Then I started to climb. I had to stop halfway and throw up watery liquid.

As I reached the final floor – my lungs going into spasm – I leaned on the sill of the open window and looked out. Below me was the destroyed centre of the basin. Most of it was in darkness. I remember conversations at the office cube for Prevention, on topics such as 'knocking out the lights', and its impact on the behaviour of the crowds. They'd obviously taken to this heart. Enforcement would've killed the lights. I tried to seek out the blue of their vehicles. They were hidden by the taller buildings, it seemed. I could hear commands ordering crowds to disperse, arriving at my ears distorted and alien. They sounded like alien dimensional beings trying to communicate from the other side.

As my eyes looked up, trying to find the white shapes in the near-black sky, I turned slightly and looked further north. I saw the water. This was the worst yet. Whole stretches of the upper dale were silvery orange, reflecting the glow from the clouds above them. Some of these areas were supposed to flood. They had been deliberately set aside for the purpose of catching the high waters – in dry months, they were normally full of solar panel arrays or sun-tube arrays built to grow algae feed. However, I could also see some industrial buildings, and even residential areas were now underwater. I followed the line of water down the dale towards the basin. Beyond the taller buildings that denoted the centre of the basin, I could see the Aire, hugely swollen, disappear underneath us.

Then I saw the specks in the air. There were definitely two of them. I didn't know whether they were in range of the megaphone but I knew they always turned off any comms when they were in the air. This was the only way I was going to get their attention. I seemed to remember reading somewhere that sound carried better up in the sky like that. I just hoped there wasn't too much noise from below.

I found some controls on the megaphone and tried to tighten the angle of the projection. Then I started shouting their names. I didn't know whether it was Lani or Puja or one of the others up there but I thought a familiar name might make them think.

After a few seconds of shouting, the shockdrone arrived. As expected. It rose up from below the line of the handrail and hung in the air directly before me. This one had a belly full of tasers. They were all pointed at me. I slowly put my hands up.

'Police override,' I whispered. 'I'm an operative.'

'Do not move, please,' said the machine. It hadn't adopted

the usual assertive vocal envelope. I must have looked like one of the wimpy ones.

I noticed the alert I'd set up on Modlee started flashing. A load of bleeding use this was now.

'I'm getting my ID,' I said. I started to lower one of my arms. The machine spun in the air and raised one of its taser cannon. I stopped. 'Listen… I'm with Justice. I'm an operative.'

'Do not move, please,' the machine repeated.

'Get me a human,' I said. 'Put me through to a human handler.'

'There is no need,' the machine said. 'We are acquiring facial ratios.'

'I'm getting my ID,' I repeated. Then I started to jabber out words. 'Urgent. Emergency. SOS. Man down. Enforcement man down. Enforcement operative.'

This seemed to have confused it sufficiently for it to pause and seek central confirmation of its task. I took the opportunity to dip my hand into my pocket and retrieve my cricket cap. While my hand was in my pocket, I slipped the scanner inside the cap and closed it up so that it was covered.

'Look,' I said. 'I'm with Justice.' I pulled out the cap and displayed the logo to the machine.

'That's just a hat,' said a new voice. They must have put it through to a human handler. 'Where's your ID?'

'OK,' I said. 'I'll put this down here, then.' I carefully placed the cap on the handrail and started to dip my hand back in my pocket. 'I'm just getting my ID.'

'Careful,' said the voice. 'Very slowly.'

'You're scaring me, buddy,' I said. 'I don't like being threatened.' I started to back away to the stairs.

'Stay still, mate,' said the human voice. It was starting to sound a little agitated.

'Don't like that thing pointing at me, buddy,' I said. I was now near the stairs. The drone had come in closer to the handrail now, trying to keep me in its sights.

'Show me your ID,' said the voice.

I started to back down the steps a little. The drone had to fly over the handrail to keep its tasers aimed at me. It was now in range.

'My ID's in my processor,' I said. 'It's an electronic ID.' This wasn't unreasonable. I hoped the human handler wasn't going to be funny about it.

'OK,' said the handler. 'Very slowly, mate.'

I put my hand in my pocket and brought out my processor. 'Just need to send it across.' I turned on the processor and started to weave my hands in the air. The display was projected onto my eyes. The scanner had lifted everything from the drone. I found its comms channel and A-codes.

'Hurry up, mate,' said the voice. 'Or I'll make this thing shoot you in the face.'

'Just a second, buddy,' I said.

I generated an identical comms channel and logged into the machine remotely. The access screen made no sense to me. It was all military-end acronyms and a noise of options. I ran a screen search on the power switch. There was some typed command for it. I looked for the terminal. Found it. Entered the command. Ran it.

The drone's rotors stopped whining immediately. It fell onto the handrail and fell forward into the tower. The silence was immediate.

Wasting little time, I ran back to the megaphone and put it back to my mouth. I also picked up my cap, pulled it on my head, and pocketed the scanner, starting to shout into the sky again. My ratios would be sending up flares on every Enforcement device from here to the border. And they were going to be sending more shockdrones to the tower any moment now.

After a minute of bellowing the names Lani and Puja, there

still didn't seem to be any response from the flyers. I thought I'd try something else.

'Meri Fergus,' I screamed through the megaphone. I repeated that name a number of times.

A call popped up on my screen. It was Lani.

'Is that you shouting?' he asked. It was voice only. I could hear wind in the background but I wasn't sure whether he was one of the flyers.

'If that's you up there, buddy,' I said. 'Get down now. If it's one of your team, get them down now!'

'No way, man,' said Lani. 'We're doing good work here. Get off our line. You'll get us noticed.'

'Get down,' I said, through gritted teeth. 'You're going to die. Get out of the sky now!'

Lani ended the call. My eyes searched the sky for other objects. It was swarming with them. Always was. Time was when you could look up and see nothing in the sky. Not now.

I could hear the whine of rotors approaching the tower. It was time for me to leave. Just in case it caused me a problem again, I lifted the powered-down shockdrone onto the handrail and pushed it over. I didn't wait to hear the crash.

When I stepped out onto the street and looked up into the skies again, I could see a winged shape, now broken and ragged, plummeting from the air. It fell into the central retail area of Keighley, directly onto the Joyful Shopping Centre.

Swearing without breath, I sprinted back to the entrance to the canals. Somebody was going to the sodding peninsula for this.

Chapter Thirty-Three

___

The party was taking place in one of the few chambered lakes left on the canal system. Normally, these would've been used to turn a narrowboat. I guessed this was the case, anyway. What took place on a canal was about as alien to me as what took place in a golf course bar.

The artificial cavern was vast. The ceiling was low, heavily strengthened with intersecting steel beams. Up above those beams would be buildings and streets. Nobody wanted that lot to end up tumbling into here. Not into this water. Nothing wanted to end up falling into this water. It even moved with unpleasant intent, swirling green and brown, drawn into complex whorls and whirls by the multiple currents acting upon it.

From the ceiling of the chamber had been hung strings of coloured lights, some of which dipped dangerously low towards the canal. These must have been installed for the party. They didn't look like the work of a maintenance subcontractor on a tight budget.

I could see that Liam Wroxeter owned a proper big boat. I guessed it was what they called a barge. It was a good-sized vessel, broad as two narrowboats. Who knows how he'd got it this far inland? He may have just had it built here. The barge was anchored out in the middle of the chamber. It was also draped in the cascades of stringed LEDs. Hung around the prow and the stern there were candle lamps, flickering away in the light breezes.

The whole event was taking place on more than the barge. There was a flotilla of entertainment craft. They'd managed to tie five narrowboats together, end-to-end, forming a large hexagon. There was also something captured in the middle. I couldn't see what this was, but whatever it was they were hiding, it was well-lit. And it was where the party was happening. There was the distant thud of bespoke Dutch house cut with Sri Lankan beach tunes.

I'd come to the chamber from one of the many public towpaths. There were a few others like me on the bank. Some were random walkers, out for the evening, taken aback by the party taking place across the water. Some were media squatters, sat with remote drones, trying to find an opening. I was surprised that there weren't more like Luana and her crew down here. But then I saw the reason why. They were stood leaning in the distant corners of the chamber: Enforcement operatives, armed with long-range darts and tasered-nets.

I walked up to one of the onlookers. He had some cross-breed mongrel on the end of a lead. Guessing his age, I'd say he'd been walking this bank for half a century at least.

'What's happening, buddy?' I asked him.

He glanced briefly at me. 'Party, in't it?'

'Big party.'

'Yeah. Is that.'

We both stood there for a moment, listening to the music.

'You going?' I asked.

He laughed. 'Yeah. I'm sure they'd let us on.' He turned and looked down the bank a short way.

I looked in the same direction. There was a little landing stage set up. A couple of suited heavies stood down there, stopping anybody approaching too close. As I was watching, two women, draped in cloaks and wearing a pair of masks, stepped past the suited men and – giggling and clinging to each other as they struggled above the murky water – stepped down the stones into a little row boat. A woman, unmasked but wearing nothing but a bikini, started to row them back across the lake.

'You could always swim,' I said.

The old man looked down the side of the bank into the water. 'Yeah. Could always swim.'

'Depends how much you wanted to party, don't it?' I said.

'Not that much,' he said and spat again. 'Wouldn't want to go to that kind of party, anyhow. Not for us, if you know what I mean? You know what I'm saying, right?'

I bit my tongue a little. Didn't want to get myself into an argument right now. I hoped his little dog would fall in the water and give him something tropical.

I grunted.

We watched the boat of three women slowly make its way across the water. The bespoke Dutch house shifted its rhythms a little and started booming out a rumbling bass track. The music coming from the barge and the accompanying narrowboats echoed in the vast room. Despite the music, we could still hear the steady chop-chop of the oars of the little rowing boat hitting the water and the almost continuous laughter of the women on board.

A new sound broke. I looked away from the water. Halfway around the other side of the chamber, one of the media squatters' drones started to rise into the air. As it reached head height, it accelerated out across the water towards the rowing boat. I instinctively started checking out the crowd, to see which one of them was trying to control it. Then I spotted her. A woman in her thirties, fat and ill-looking. Your typical media-squatter. She was gently twitching her fingers, her eyes glued to her drone.

There was a muffled thump and then the drone shattered in the air. Bits of polymer and other material spattered into the water.

'What were that?' I said.

The old man pointed to one of the corners of the chamber. 'They've got them sonic cannons over there.'

I could see one of the Enforcement operatives lowering a stubby weapon from her shoulder.

'Surprised they're not up-top,' I said.

'Yeah,' said the old man. 'Heard it were bad tonight. All finishing up though, now.'

I frowned. 'Don't know about that. It was pretty rough a few minutes gone.'

'I'm just walking the dog, me,' he said. 'You wouldn't catch me up there tonight.'

'No,' I said. 'Keep yourself safe, I would.'

'I'll do that,' he said. 'Night.'

Out of the corner of my eye, I could see the Enforcement officer with the sonic cannon peer in my direction. They must have been interested in the old man's pointed arm. Idiot had dropped me in it. I tried to look casually towards the party, while hiding my profile as much as possible.

After a moment, I pulled on my cap and fired up my bead. Checked my personal alert. I'd been recognised on the tower. Then they'd lost me again. There was no further activity. I still had time.

The operative with the cannon had lost interest in me. I turned my attention back to boats. Liam Wroxeter was on there somewhere. I just needed a means of getting to him. I considered the direct approach. Go straight to the heavies down the way and demand access. But this seemed too risky. There were too many opportunities for it to go wrong.

The thought of the flyer, dead in the rubble above me, made me consider simply walking over to the Enforcement people and punching them until they gave me their sonic cannon.

But that wasn't how I did things. Controlling my rage, I logged back into Modlee and created a local model. I was sure that Modlee would give the answer. It knew everything. Using the locational parameters, I started throwing all sorts of data feeds into the mix. It all went in there. I was sweeping the piles of data into the model, my hands high in the air. I was oblivious now to any strange looks I might be getting. I was going to get a warning if I'd been recognised.

The model on my display quickly became a sludgy mess of noise. It was telling me nothing. It meant nothing. I set it to visually scroll through all the datasets. I started seeing patterns. I investigated. But they didn't give me anything: contracts associated with the canal, who was on the boat, the number of recorded crimes on this stretch of towpath. It was still all noise. I realised I was stuck in the past.

I started to look at patterns that were expected to emerge in this chamber over the next thirty minutes. I looked at commercial transactions. I found something.

A few seconds later, I'd ducked back behind the crowds and was making my way towards one of the tributary canals.

* * *

The lights down here flickered, like there was inconsistent power. Like they were dying. Most of the Keighley Basin's municipal power was switched, on a minute-by-minute basis, between the Marrakech pipe and the North Sea Array. It depended on the cost. I wondered whether they'd gone down to second-by-second trading. Assuming they'd got their algorithms correct, it could've saved them a bundle. Well, a bundle by Airedale lighting subcontractor standards.

I tucked myself into a corner by an old redbrick buttress. This was a heritage tunnel. It led from the Leeds-Liverpool into one of the industrial yards of the Basin. As I'd hoped, there was nobody using now. This was getting closer to the troubles. Any sensible member of the public should already be tucked up in bed. Watching RandoPornos of aall the girl and boys they'd fancied at college. And wanking.

This thought would normally have made me a little depressed. But I'd not felt this happy in a long time.

I stared at the flickering lights. I started to recognise their flicker pattern, to understand it. A habit of mine. I was crouched there for at least ten minutes. Then I heard the noise of the outboard engine. It was a proper high-pitched whine. A low-grade ethanol scream. The kind of noise heard across the paddy fields and streets of all the world.

I stepped out from behind the supporting buttress and waved at the little boat. I kept pointing my cap.

'Justice,' I shouted. 'I'm with Justice, buddy.'

The boat slowed and pulled into the side. Sat at the back of it, his hand gripping the tiller, was a boy. He looked to be about fourteen. Even I was surprised. He looked irritated at being stopped but also scared. Scared enough, anyway.

'What d'you want?' he said. 'I've not done owt.'

'I know, buddy,' I said. 'Need to requisition your boat, though, yeah.'

'Fuck you are!'

'I'm with Justice,' I said again. 'I got delegation, in't it.'

'Delegation? That's rubbish!' he spat. 'Means you can arrest me. Nowt to do with thieving my boat.'

'Section 435 has it all,' I lied. 'Look it up, buddy.'

'You're not having my boat!'

'You're going to the party, yeah?'

He nodded. 'Yeah. The Wroxeter boat. That's right.'

'That's why I need it. He's a right wrong 'un, that Wroxeter. You work for him?'

'Nah,' the boy said. 'I'm just delivering booze. They just put in a big order.'

'Let me deliver it for you, then,' I said.

'No way,' he said. 'Boss'll kill us. What is this rubbish, anyhow?'

I started to sweat a little. This wasn't going according to plan. 'You wouldn't want your boss to come under suspicion as well, would you?'

'You threatening us?'

'Just giving you a way out,' I said. 'Wroxeter is one I want. This trouble could be nothing to do with you and your boss.' I paused. 'Then again, if I ask enough questions, it could.'

He fell silent for a moment. Then decided to bluff. 'We're clean, Mr Justice. You'd arrest us if we weren't.'

I started to look back up the towpath where I'd come from. I could hear distant laughter.

'I haven't got long, buddy,' I said. 'Make up your mind sharpish.'

'What you got?'

'Eh?'

'What're you offering? How're you going to make it worth my while, like?'

He was holding out his hand up towards me. I shook my head. 'That'd be corruption, buddy. I'm not into that.'

He shrugged. 'That were my last offer.' He turned back to the starter gear on his outboard.

'Wait,' I said. 'Don't touch that engine.'

He stopped and sighed and spoke very slowly. 'Why the hell not, Mr Justice?'

'Because,' I hissed. 'I don't have much time! You know how many shockdrones there are out on the street tonight? You know how many operatives? You been up there at all?'

He nodded. 'I have, yeah.'

'Well, I can get a dozen of them drones down here in a moment. You ever been tasered in the balls? I can make that happen!'

'Yeah right,' he said. But I could see he was less certain.

'You don't think so?' I said. I stood up and raised my right arm up towards one of the lights. I clicked my fingers. 'Click.' The light went off. 'Click,' I said again. I clicked my fingers once more. The light came back on.

'Hell,' whispered the boy.

I turned around and pointed my arm at another light. I repeated the same performance. The timing was a little out this time so I thought I'd best not risk another.

But it had worked. The boy was already climbing out of his boat.

'You walk along and all,' I said, hopping in. 'I'll leave it at the party.'

The boy muttered a curse at me under his breath.

I hit the starter and flexed the throttle. It was like the boats I'd taken Dali out in, on the lakes and canals of Kerala. She'd shown me how to drive them, of course. The first time she had taught me to do this, we had been out in the moonlight. The light wasn't too different from what I had to navigate by down here. It had been a nearly full moon then. We had taken the boat out to the middle of the lake and let the ripples subside. Then we had thrown prawn bits into the lake and watched the huge catfish rise from the depths to take them. Like the earliest memories of her, this was one of the more vivid ones.

I tried not to think about it. The boat moved fast through the water. I needed to concentrate. I passed the drunken walkers. They tried to wave at me and made a joke. I kept my head low, face hidden by my cap.

When I came out into the cavern, I turned immediately for the barge and the narrowboats and pulled my parka hood up over my cap. Still keeping my head low, I tried to act like I did this on a daily basis. I didn't want any of those Enforcement operatives catching me on their cameras.

Around the back of the flotilla, at the junction between two of the narrowboats, a young woman in a formal outfit appeared, climbing up some steps. She waved at me, so I swung the tiller around and brought the boat up alongside her. It was pleasing how I managed to bring it to a halt at precisely the right place.

'Throw us the rope,' she said. 'You're late.'

'Sorry,' I said, handing her the rope. She tied up the boat and I pulled off the covering from the boxes of bottles.

'How many you got?' she asked.

I shrugged. 'Dunno. Boss just told me where to go, like. Not to count 'em.'

She regarded the pile of boxes. 'That'll do. They'll drink owt, this lot. Been trying to keep them away from ethanol fuel most of the night.'

I laughed. 'That'd mess 'em up!'

'It's not them I'm bothered about,' she said, grinning. 'We got to get back to dry land at some point. I've got a home to go to.'

I started to lift the boxes up and place them on the deck of the narrowboat As I did, she leaned down and lifted them away and down into the cabin of the boat.

'You want any help with these?' I asked.

'Nah,' she said. 'Be alright.'

'S'no bother,' I said. 'I were late, yeah. Only fair!'

She smiled. 'You were, and all. Yeah, you get up here and help me.'

After a few minutes I was staggering through the circle of narrowboats, carrying two boxes in front of me. I'd offered to take them up to the barge. She'd let me out of her sight without too much of a care.

I reached the barge. And I was in the party.

Around me were the corporate courtiers of the very rich.

Fund managers, lawyers, advertising consultants, management consultants, offshore advisers, foreign sales operatives. They were all there. And they were having a night off. They had obviously decided that Keighley was the Venice of the north. It was Carnivale. They all had masks and long cloaks on. And very little else. Some of the men were in swimming trunks, women in bikinis. Some were more modest and had worn light clothing. Some were in their underwear. Some were naked.

As I was in there, striding through in my baggy trousers and parka, I was about as conspicuous as a tramp in a soft-play centre. My only protection was the box of bottles I was carrying. I knew that this was only going to work for a while. I didn't have long.

The centre of the circle of boats was given over to a huge floating swimming pool. It must have been heated, for steam was coming off it, even in the warm stuffiness of the canal chambers. In the pool, I could see five or six people splashing about. More people were simply lounging about the pool side, some with their cloaks on, some without.

It was when I looked about the barge and the pool that I realised my error. Nobody had any forms of communication on them. Never carry a bead to a pool party.

I put down the boxes of bottles on the roof of the barge and poked my head down into the cabin. There were more naked people. Not an even number. And this lot weren't swimming.

Thinking that disturbing them would be unpleasant – for all concerned – I instead started edging my way along the side of the boat, towards another cluster of party-goers who were lounging about on the roof of the barge.

'Where can I find Liam Wroxeter?' I asked the first of them.
'Hmm?'
'I'm here to find Liam Wroxeter,' I said.
'Oh.'
The face behind the mask was half-cut with booze and

spore. They looked a snort short of vomiting over the side of the boat. They pointed down towards the pool.

I could see they were pointing at somebody swimming in the pool. He was a tall, thin man, without much hair. Blond, like his cousin, but simply less of it. Perhaps for safety reasons more than aesthetics, he had decided to avoid the mask this evening. But he was sporting a large fake gold crown, with an arched cobra protruding from the front.

As soon as he looked up at me, I recognised the face as being one of those who had gathered for the Enforcement Board in Shipley. It seemed like a decade ago now.

'Who is this?' he yapped, climbing out of the pool. 'I heard my name.'

'You Liam Wroxeter?' I asked.

'Who are you?' he asked, pulling out a towel from a pile and drying himself off.

'I'm with the AJC,' I said, trying to make myself heard as far across the boat as possible. It had the desired effect of sending some of the guests tumbling for their towels.

Wroxeter noticed this also. Furious, he dragged on a cloak – crimson with ermine trim. Made him look like some sick monarch.

'What the hell are you doing here?' He half-ushered me, half-shoved me into the steering-house of the boat. It had been re-purposed to act as a temporary changing and coat room. Piles of expensive fake fur – and some real fur – coats lay piled, in between shining shoes. I noted a few suit jackets seemed to lay stiffer in their piles than others. Never hurt to have protection when travelling through the basin.

'Well?' he said, when we had got inside cover. Not that it provided much privacy. There were windows all around the walls, through which party guests were trying not to peer.

'I'm here to talk to you,' I said. 'I want to know more about your commissioner business for Airedale Enforcement.'

'You here to arrest me?' he said. 'Is this what you're here for?'

I clamped my teeth tight and took a breath through my nose. After I had his attention I shook my head. 'I want to know about your work with Enforcement.'

'I'll tell you about my work with Enforcement,' he hissed, grabbing my arm.

'Yeah?'

'I sit on the damn Board,' he screamed into my face. 'You can't come here! Into my party and try and arrest me.'

'I'm not arresting, you sir,' I said quietly. 'I just want to ask you some questions. You made any calls tonight?'

'My cousin's been telling me about you,' he said. 'You've been snooping around him and Abi Hassan, haven't you?'

'I've asked him questions,' I said. 'Yeah.'

'Except,' said Wroxeter triumphantly. 'You're not even employed by the Justice anymore! They sacked you! Didn't they?'

'My contract was cancelled, yeah,' I said. 'Temporarily. Back on board now. PO posted this afternoon.'

'You're a liar,' he spat.

As he moved around the room, his cloak kept revealing his saggy body and the grey hairs on his stomach. I tried to stop my eyes drifting downwards. 'Why don't you call your cousin, Caines, to check? I'm sure he's all up-to-speed on this.'

'I'm not calling anybody,' he said, through narrowed eyes. He was on something strong. Probably from Central America. Cooking up that kind of brew was virtually mandatory for a party like this.

'He's not here tonight?' I asked, casually.

'No, he's not,' said Wroxeter. 'He's with his family.'

'Then why don't you call him?' I asked again, a little more desperate this time.

'I have a better idea,' he said, nodding. 'Why don't we go

and see him? Yes.'

I shrugged. This would suffice. Probably. 'Whatever.'

'This party was getting boring anyway.'

'He's not here already?' I asked again. I was sure he must be here somewhere. Ever since I'd arrived, I'd been expecting to see the towering mountain that was Darren Caines blocking out the light somewhere. They would've needed a bigger pool, mind.

'Darren?' spat Wroxeter. 'He doesn't let his hair down at a place like this.'

I felt a presence at my shoulder. 'This man upsetting the atmosphere, Liam?'

I recognised the voice. Damn.

'Hiya, Brian,' I said, not turning around.

'Aye,' said Wroxeter. 'He's really put me off my... you know him?'

'I do,' said Brian Fallin, Head of Enforcement Operations. 'Though why he's here asking you questions, who knows. Right, Mr Edmundson?'

'You can't do anything to me, Brian,' I said, conscious that I was starting to sound shrill. I stepped away from him and turned around. The fat shape of the Head of Enforcement Operations was clear beneath the suit and bow tie. But his face was carefully hidden behind a comedy Guy Fawkes mask. 'I'm not breaking any laws here. You've got business elsewhere, anyway, haven't you, Brian? Up top, yeah? Up top there's a riot going on. Why don't you check that out? Check out a body hit by one of your recon drones? Yes, one of yours! You made a call earlier, didn't you? Somebody's dead because of you. Yet... you're down here, having a drink and... and... and a tumble. What's that about, yeah?'

'I'm just passing through,' said Fallin. 'It's all under control in the basin, mate. Don't you worry about that.'

'Another flyer's dead, Brian!' I yelled. 'You've killed

another flyer.'

'Me?' asked Fallin.

'Your bleeding drones,' I said. 'Your drones. Your risk threshold, Brian. You reset it again. You've killed another one.'

Behind me, I could hear the snickering of Wroxeter. Then something hard was pressed into the small of my back. It felt like a pen. I guessed it wasn't.

Fallin just looked at me and shook his head. 'I think this one's had a little too much to drink. Or was it something you stuffed up your nose? We know all about that, Hasim, don't we?'

'Enforcement not interested in reducing crime anymore?' I asked.

'Oh,' said Fallin. 'We're very interested. You've got a theory we need to hear more about?'

'Yeah.'

'Well, let's go and talk about it, then.'

A few minutes later, I was thrown into a boat with two heavies. Wroxeter, now fully clothed in a gold-trimmed electric blue suit, and Fallin followed in behind. We sped away from the barges and towards one of the tunnels.

From over on the bank, I could hear a voice shouting. I turned my head. It was an Enforcement operative. He was waving his tranq-gun around above his head. My heart sank. Not only kidnapped, I was about to get tranqed again. Then I heard the voice reach us more clearly over the noise of the engine.

'Haz! Haz! What the heck are you doing?'

I squinted. The distance and the dim light were making it difficult to see. Then I recognised the walk. It was Jonah.

I waved at him.

'Are you OK?' I thought I could hear him shout.

'Tell him you're fine,' muttered Fallin. He seemed keen to

keep his mask on.

I gave Jonah the thumbs-up. 'Another party, in't it,' I shouted across to him.

'You OK?' he asked me again.

I nodded. 'I'm fine,' I shouted.

The boat accelerated away from the party and I was thrown backwards onto the floor. It was slopping about with water there and I got soaked. I heaved myself back up onto the little board and pushed my cap out of my eyes. As I did so, I turned to look at the bank. There were about twenty Enforcement operatives streaming into the chamber from a large stairwell. They were armed with close-combat weapons, taser guns, and smart-dart launchers.

'Stop the boat,' muttered Fallin. 'Need to get out. Looks like we're finally doing something about those snoops on the bank. Business up top must have calmed down.'

As the Head of Enforcement Ops walked away, I could already hear the screams. I glanced over my shoulder and saw the first flank of media-squatters getting charged down by a line of Enforcement operatives wielding shockstix.

Chapter Thirty-Four

'Get the damn thing open!'

We were approaching a lock. We had left the main Leeds-Liverpool system now and were deep under the belly of the basin itself. The lock looked like it hadn't been touched for a few years. As one of the heavies swung the gates open, I could see an accumulation of detritus that had gathered in the lock itself. Brought to it through the powers of the wider natural system that dictated that all dark corners of the world like this were supposed to gather shit. There were plastic bottles, rotting branches, children's toys – even the bloated bodies of a pair of brown rats.

The bearded heavy, who was driving the boat, edged us into the lock, sending waves through the rubbish. The rats slowly bobbed into a corner. The clean-shaven heavy had already pushed one half of the gate behind us and was running around, across the bridge above our heads, to close the other gate.

'Get a move on,' muttered Wroxeter. He was sat at the front, huddled in his jacket. Whatever medley of spores and booze he'd been enjoying, its effects were clearly wearing off now. He turned to stare at me, sensing my gaze. 'What are you looking at?'

I shrugged. 'Nowt.'

'Going to get this sorted,' Wroxeter said to himself. 'Darren'll know what to do. We've got to find Darren.'

I nodded and looked up, beyond Wroxeter. The sluices had been opened and water was starting to bubble up into the lock. The water was churned up into black whorls. The stench was unbelievable. I caught Wroxeter hastily clamping a corner of his coat across his mouth.

We started to rise in the lock. Once it had risen to the height of the far stretch of canal, the clean-shaven heavy edged us forward but the other was struggling to get the large swing gate open. Despite pushing his back against it, it wasn't shifting.

'Go and help him,' said Wroxeter, nodding towards the bearded heavy. 'How the heck does anybody get anywhere on one of these things?'

There was a momentary lull in activity as the clean-shaven one hopped out and joined his colleague at the gate. They finally got it moving, with much tutting from an impatient Wroxeter.

At the moment the bearded heavy was stepping back into the boat, I rocked my weight from side-to-side. He lost his footing and fell in between the boat and the bank. Seeing this, the other heavy had started running around the side of the lock, trying to get his shotgun out of his jacket.

'Hey,' grunted Wroxeter, scrabbling on the floor of the boat for his pistol.

I heaved myself off my seat towards the back of the boat. My hands were tightly bound together but there was enough gap between them for me to grip the tiller. I squeezed the release button and twisted the handle. We started to move forward. But the heavy in the water had managed to get a hand on the rail and was pulling it down.

The other heavy had stopped on the little bridge across the lock. He raised his shotgun to his shoulder. I ducked down as much as I could, expecting to hear a shot. But he didn't fire. Wroxeter was covering me, at the front of the boat, directly in line of the shot. The heavy would've taken his master's head off. I was careful to ensure that the boat didn't waver from a straight line.

However, I wasn't clear of danger yet, as Wroxeter had managed to retrieve his stubby pistol. I wasn't sure if it was a firearm or a cigarette lighter. He was pointing it at me with a shaky hand.

'Liam Wroxeter, you're under arrest,' I shouted. 'Through the power of delegation, passed to me through Contract 564863–'

'Shut up!' he screamed. 'I've spoken to Darren. You're not even employed by Justice anymore!'

'Like I told Brian Fallin, I'm back on the books,' I said. 'Look, Mr Wroxeter, don't make this any worse, yeah?'

'I've done nothing wrong,' Wroxeter said. 'Stop the boat or I shoot.'

'With that?' I yelled, trying to bluff. 'That wouldn't stop a mouse, even if you–'

Wroxeter fired. I felt a breeze around the top of my collar. Then a pain.

'Stop the boat,' he screamed again.

I slowed the boat down a little and drifted into the bank. The pain had stopped me from being able to speak. I felt like I was in a dream. A dream where you know you need to run as fast as a cheetah but where your legs are knackered.

He began scrabbling around in his clothes for something. While he did this, he continued to point his gun at me. 'Told you I'd shoot! I warned you, didn't I? You can't arrest me if I warned you I was going to shoot.'

The front of the boat nudged against the bank and came to a stop. I let the engine fall to a sputter. From behind us, I could hear the shouts of the two heavies.

Wroxeter found what he was looking for. It was a retro-phone, about the size of a chocolate bar. It opened up like a little make-up compact. I'd seen them in museums. Didn't know people still used them. Must have cost him a lot of money. They were designer.

He pressed a button on the phone and waited, his right arm still pointing the gun at me. 'Darren,' he said. 'It's me. I've got him... that little Justice goon...what are you doing you idiot?' I started to rise from my seat at the back of the boat. Wroxeter saw me and raised his gun. 'Get back here, you moron! Get back or I'll shoot again... I've shot him Darren, I've shot him...You idiot, get back in your seat... ah hell... gotta sort this first...'

Wroxeter put the phone down, so that he could put both hands on the pistol. I sat down heavily, making the boat bounce violently. Wroxeter put a hand out to steady himself and stood up, trying to make his way back to me. I gripped the tiller and immediately threw us into reverse. With a roar of the engine, we pulled back into the middle of the canal. Wroxeter lost his balance and fell into the water. I twisted the tiller and the boat surged forward. At the last moment, I jammed the tiller across to the right, trying to avoid running him down, and screaming in pain as I did so.

From behind me came an echoing retort. I realised it was one of the shotguns. One of the heavies must have caught up with me. I could feel my back get peppered with fine shot. It stung but I didn't think any had got through my coat. And it was nothing compared to my neck. I still ducked down, careful not to allow my head to stick up too much.

Another shot rang out and the wood of the boat splintered by my right side. Then three more shots. I glanced over my shoulder and could see Wroxeter standing on the bank, firing his toy pistol at me. The heavy had reached him and was re-loading his shotgun. A little further down the towpath, I could see the other heavy. He was staggering with difficulty in his wet clothes.

Then there was another shot. It must have hit the engine. The steady putt-putt of the pistons rose to a screeching, fearful shriek and then they stopped altogether. I could hear the swearing on the bank and the tinkling of ammunition being fed into their weapons.

On the other side of the canal, I saw some sort of access tunnel. It had once been locked, but now stood ajar. I reached over the side of the boat and started paddling with my hands.

The boat touched the far bank just as another shot rang out. I felt it hit the boat. I dived forward, towards the front end of the boat, picking up Wroxeter's discarded phone as I did so and lay down flat as possible in the bottom, the swill soaking into my clothes. Then there was a roar of the shotgun. And again. And again. I could feel the boat shudder with the blasts. It was starting to disintegrate under the onslaught. The water in the bottom of the boat was getting deeper. I was going to sink into the biohazard of the canal if I didn't do anything.

'OK,' I screamed, trying to be heard above the noise of gunfire. 'OK!'

The firing slowed down and then stopped.

'What?' shouted one of the heavies.

'I'm giving myself up,' I shouted. 'Let me stand up, alright?'

'Show us your hands!'

I raised my hands and slowly raised myself up. The door to the access tunnel was about ten metres from me. I leapt from the boat onto the bank. The force of my leap pushed the boat back out into the canal and I landed half in the water. As my stomach hit the side of the canal, my neck was jolted and the pain from the bullet wound seared up into my brain.

'Bastard,' somebody shouted. The shooting resumed.

I kept myself as flat as possible and heaved out of the water. Bits of concrete were flying off the wall in front of my face.

Little gobbets of muck from the bank around me were flying through the air. I crawled as quickly as I could to the door. Just as I was pulling myself through it, I felt a breeze around my ankle blowing the material of my trousers aside followed by stinging pellets.

Despite the shot, I managed to get through and into the access tunnel. It was pitch black. I staggered on, using the wall to guide me. The light from the canal faded behind me.

Finally, I reached another door. This had some emergency release handle, which I managed to heave around. A couple of painful shoulder barges later and I was through. Catching my breath, I slid to the floor and kicked off my trainer. It was so dark, it was almost impossible to see, so trying to get the phone open was a special agent move. I could just about see the catch if I squinted up really close. I clawed at it, almost ripping my fingernails. The back was open. I could see the sliver. I plucked it out - holding it in my teeth - and pulled off my sock. Biting down hard on the sock, I jammed the sliver under the largest toenail. Whimpering in pain, I dragged on my sock and trainer.

I heard a noise and some light coming from the other direction. A sharp whack of the phone on my knee and it was closed. I slid it into my pocket and started to stand. Then something thudded into my neck. I reached up, slapping at it, pulling at it. Small, flighted piece of plastic. Microchip in the middle. Chamber for liquid. Empty.

Smartdart.

A familiar voice rang out, echoing down the dark tunnels, its deep timbre a terrifying rumble: 'Jesus, how wasted are you, Liam? And where the hell is Fallin?'

I lost consciousness.

* * *

We were passing through a long corridor. There were a series of doors to our right. I seemed to be moving close to the ground. Through each door I could see one of the growing-halls. Large tanks bubbling lightly. Pasted low onto the wall of the corridor were old, peeling signs, showing abstracted plans of autonomous handlers.

'He's coming round,' said a squeaky voice. It was Wroxeter. I lifted my head from the hard surface. I was travelling on a low loader. In front of the machine was Caines, a grubby tablet in his hand, controlling where we were going.

Caines turned and looked down at me. 'I'm sorry you've ended up here, Mr Edmundson.'

'Hrrr gah,' I replied.

'There was an accident with an errant Enforcement operative, I believe.'

'Fug,' I said.

'Unfortunately,' said Caines. 'We've also had an alert in our unit here. It appears that there was an unauthorised entry.'

'I'm sorry, Darren,' said Wroxeter. 'I was just freaked, you know.'

'By him?' said Caines, not looking at me. 'Hasim Edmundson here wouldn't hurt a fly, would you, young man? Just trying to do your job, aren't you?'

'Fnrrr,' I croaked.

Caines stepped aside, swiped his hand across the tablet, and directed the loader to the left and into a large growing-hall. This seemed to be a disused part of the factory, for the vats were either empty or contained the remnants of some dead meat that had gone wrong. There was nobody else in the room, bar myself, Caines, and Wroxeter. However, in the distance, out in the corridor somewhere, I could hear other footsteps.

'We need to let you come round, young man,' said Caines.

'My guys can beat it out of him right now,' said Wroxeter.

'They're waiting down there, Darren. I can give them the word.'

'Why?' said Caines. 'For what purpose? I think you've done enough already, Liam. Why go and give him and Justice something to talk about?'

I closed my eyes, screwing them tight, trying to let blood flow back to my muscles. I felt I might be able to move in minute or so.

'He's asking a load of questions, Darren. About Enforcement. About us and Fallin.'

'Brian's a thug,' said Caines, dropping the tablet onto the handrail at the front of the loader. 'Anyway, we've got nothing to hide, Liam. I, especially.'

He was speaking very clearly. Like he wanted to be heard. I realised they had left my cap on the loader as well, dropped down near my head. I could feel the bulkier shape of Wroxeter's phone had been taken out of my jacket pocket, though.

I opened my eyes and watched the two of them move further away from where I was lying. The large breeder tanks loomed above me, their bubbles and grey lumps of meat dimly lit.

I could no longer hear the conversation between Caines and Wroxeter. But they were clearly talking about me. Fingers were being pointed and glances back in my direction. Wroxeter was trying to convince the other of something. No doubt something that involved putting a bullet into a soft part of my face.

I was able to feel my legs now. My fingers burned like needles. The pain of the sliver jammed into my big toe was hotting up as well.

Eventually Wroxeter shouted out. 'Hey, you two! Get in here!'

A decision must have been made. No frigging way they

were going to kill me like this. I tried to stand up. But it wasn't happening. Instead, I reached up and grabbed the tablet off the front of the loader, swiping across the grubby screen. It was locked down by a numeric code. This really was an antique.

'Darren,' shrieked Wroxeter, pointing at me.

'Idiot,' muttered Darren. 'What's he doing? Ah, it doesn't matter. It's all locked down.'

Footsteps were approaching the room from the corridor. Wroxeter now had his phone in his hand. Was trying to dial.

I punched in sequences of the same digits, working my way around the numeric keypad, hoping they'd left it on factory default. None of them worked. I started on ascending sequential numbers. Nothing.

'This phone's had it,' said Wroxeter.

'He's done something to it?' growled Caines.

My legs were responsive now. My balance was still gone. I slid both legs over the side of the loader and scrabbled against the floor. It started to move. Gained more velocity. Fairground ride through a meat hell.

'Shite!' screamed a voice. I couldn't tell if it was Caines or Wroxeter, but it was left behind as I careered away, out of the room and into the next.

'Get him!' screamed another voice, over the whine of the loader moving at maximum speed.

Shots rang out above my head. Bits of plastic and glass exploded in my peripheral vision. Then the loader hit a wall and I was thrown off. Realising that this tablet in my hand was useless unless I got into it, I decided I needed a new plan. I needed to find some weakness in their security. Still stumbling from the tranq, I staggered to my feet, picked up my cap and rammed it on my head and fired up the bead. Taking cover behind one of the larger beef-breeder tanks, I started flickering my way through local points of presence using my bead. Something in here must have had sight of the codes. My bead was showing up an array of security cameras. They were all locked down.

I stumble-ran for the next room. More shots whirred and smacked into the wall in front of me. The door ahead of me slid open as I approached. Which was nice. Always trust an antique. As I skidded through it, I could see the little camera attached to the top. I checked my bead. It wasn't part of the security network. It was unsecured. I hacked in and dumped its temporary footage into my processor.

I was ducking in between tanks now. These were full of grey meat, like the previous chamber. I started running some military-grade code in the footage, code that did a little number recognition – among other things. One of the tanks exploded to my left. Its massive plug of flesh toppled onto the floor with a slap. My trainers skidded and skated on the fluid. The smell of near-rot reached me. I retched. It was the smell of a butcher's cart. Of fridges in long-abandoned houses that I had searched.

Making my way across to the other side of the room, more shots rang out. I tried to put more of the tanks between myself and the men who were chasing me.

My code came back with a few answers. It had found some footage with numbers in it. Been peeking over somebody's shoulder after all. I punched the first six digits I could see into the tablet.

The grubby old slab pinged into life.

A door ahead of me slid open and an arm curled around the corner, presenting a muzzled weapon. They must have doubled-backed along the corridor. Automatic weapon fire shattered the air around my head. The vat behind me splintered into millions of tiny pieces of plastic. There was a wet sputtering as the bullets entered the meat above my head. It toppled forward and I rolled to my side to avoid being squashed underneath it.

Keeping myself low, I scrambled back into the depths of the chamber. I could hear footsteps coming from both ends now. My hands skittered over the tablet. I wasn't sure what I was looking for. Tried plans, schematics, anything. I switched views. I switched floors.

Then I saw it. The controls for this room.

I peered around the corner of the nearest tank. I could see the steps leading up to the spot. But I was going to be out in the open for too long. I needed a diversion. Using the tablet, I found the nearest grappler-bot and sent it whining its way out of its polythene covers and towards the direction of the shots. I could hear a few curses and the sounds of bullets striking plastic casing. Then I stood and started to sprint, not looking back, not feeling the pain in my thigh, knee, neck, and toe. Bullets chipped up bits of floor to my right, cutting into my ankles. A tank exploded to my left. I reached the steps and heaved myself up. I unsteadily stood on the topmost step and jumped.

My legs fell astride the grey steak block. I was half out of the top of the tank. I could see the two heavies now. They were reloading, one at each end of the chamber. They were laughing. I wriggled and slid completely into the tank. This wasn't what I'd planned. Holding my breath, I peered through the murky liquid at the tablet. I had no space. I was rammed up against this pork plug. I could see both the heavies approach the vat. They were giggling and high-fiving each other.

'Well done,' said Wroxeter, entering the room from another door. He was followed by Caines.

'We kill him?' asked one of the heavies.

'He was breaking and entering,' said Caines, turning away. Not wanting to watch.

'Shoot him!' screamed Wroxeter.

The heavies both raised their weapons, directly at the glass.

With one last heave, I stuck a finger out at the tablet wedged into the tank with me. I found my vat's number.

Pressed jettison.

* * *

I had never seen the flood levels in full spate. I understood that this was their purpose. It had been explained to me that the water needed somewhere to go. We had learned about them in school. Diagrams drawn for us. All over Europe, all over the world, they were the same. Large concrete bunkers built to catch the rain, to divert it, to calm it. Beneath some cities, even beneath London, they had sunk huge silo chambers which would simply open their lids and fill up from every guttering system in the area. Here, the intention was to calm the flood by spreading it, slowing it down, catching it in concrete hands for a few minutes longer, just to stop the downstream destruction.

The sight was spectacular. It was also terrifying. Huge, surging currents of muddy, silt-laden water streaming around concrete pillars and over vortex generating mouldings, bubbling around tree trunks, wedged up against the pillars that supported the roof.

It was towards one of these that I swam, dragged, and pushed myself, finally climbing in past the few intact branches and clinging on as the waters tried to pull me downstream.

I must have been in the water for at least an hour. I could feel the cold start to chill my flesh. Then chill my blood. Getting shaky, I could feel my grip start to loosen. A swell appeared unexpectedly and rose up, over my head. I tasted mud and foulness. I felt my cap get torn from my head and swirl away into the darkness. I had to breathe. I let go. The water dragged me away. I felt the bottom of the flood chamber with my right hand. I pushed away hard and burst out of the water, dragging in a lungful of air. I tried swimming to my right, across the direction of the current, but it was pointless. All I could do was barely keep my mouth above the lapping water. I had taken a stomachful now. There was an equilibrium of filth between the waters and me.

Then I felt myself hit something hard. I was immediately pushed beneath the water again. But this time I had something to cling onto. Sharp wire mesh underneath my fingers. I was caught on the Grid. With the sharp metal cutting at me, I climbed up the wire and back out of the water. Beneath my feet, I could feel the debris caught up in the flood. Branches and leaves and mud. I looked about in the dim light, but I couldn't see any sign of the usual heaps of meat. They had been washed clean.

Now that I had a moment to catch my breath, I tried to peer around. The emergency lighting was even more distantly spaced around this section of the level. However, I thought I could recognise some parts of it. I started to edge my way along the line of the Grid. Then I recognised one of the exit points. A few minutes later and I was hauling myself up a metal ladder and into safety.

'Hello,' said the female security guard. 'Look what the cat dragged in!'

'Hiya. You got a processer I can borrow? I lost my bead.'

'That's a shame. It was a nice hat.'

'You got one? A processing block?'

'Of course, for you, Mr AJC. Bring it back, yes?'

* * *

The shopping centre was starting to fill up with the day shift: demonstrators and assistants and trainers from the manufacturing outputs. A few fruit and veg stallholders. A phalanx of strutting baristas, adjusting their black t-shirts carefully.

I got a few stares but most assumed I was somebody else's problem and avoided my eye. As the main doors were still locked I limped through three tiers of galleries, looking for a service exit. I worked my way to the back of the centre, tracing the line of workers entering the place.

Out on the street, it was like nothing had happened the previous night. It was light but still a little while before dawn. Automated cleaning trucks had been through. All broken glass and debris had been cleared away. Armies of window repair subcontractors were busily slotting new panes into grooves up and down the street. There were small groups of people on their way into work. Commuters striding out with their thoughts on the day ahead.

Nobody bothered about the tramp who staggered amid them. I was looking for somewhere to sit down. I eventually slumped down beside a pre-loading kiosk and kicked off my trainer. With all the other injuries, the pain beneath my toenail was just a minor irritation now. It wasn't so mild when I yanked the sliver back out, though.

I let the borrowed processing block flash the sliver for data and slurp it up soft. It was going to be unsecured but I didn't care anymore. The small lump of data pulsed in the display flickering across my eyes. As the phone had been an old one, the data was saved in a weird filetype. But it was all unencrypted. Just needed to know how to get something out of it in proper English. Of course, there was a thriving community of coders who helped out with this kind of stuff. After a bit of searching around, I found a tool that could convert the lump of data into something usable. I fired up the service and dumped the file into it.

I just needed one conversation. One conversation on one night. It wasn't much.

The service pinged back an eighty-three percent success rate. I plugged in the date and the times.

Just one conversation.

I had a hit. He had taken a call from his cousin that night.

'Hi.' The deeper voice. 'You alright?'

'Yeah.' The shakier voice. 'You?'

'Not bad. They meeting tonight?'

'Yeah, we're meeting. You want another favour?'

'Yes, please. Wait, are you recording this? Little insurance policy?'

'No, no, of course not. I wouldn't, Darren. What do you need?'

'Hmm? What you did last time.'

'The numbers, I mean. What do you need it set at?'

'We think... we think a forty-five.'

'OK. I'll make it happen, Darren. And... you know, what are you doing for me?'

'You get what you got last time, Liam. Don't worry about that.'

'The same?' The whining notched up a couple of points.

'You want more?'

'This isn't easy, Darren.' Anger. 'Making sure that Fallin gets his end away is expensive. He's got particular tastes, you understand? I'm spending money here as well.'

'OK, OK. I'll add ten percent.'

'Fifty percent!'

'Twenty. That's all we can do.'

'OK. But we can't keep this up for long. He's getting greedy.'

'We'll stop soon, Liam. Don't worry.'

The sun rose. Its beams fell on me. Although it was bright, I felt like I needed the warmth. I closed my eyes against the brightness.

I must have fallen asleep. The next thing I was aware of was a couple of voices talking.

'Should we wake him up?' It was a man's voice.

'Seems a shame, don't it?' This was a woman. She was also

familiar.

'We can't just carry him like that. He's all covered in muck,' said the man. 'I've got my best clothes on!'

Squinting my eyes against the sunlight, I peered up at the two faces looking down at me.

'Morning, Hazzie,' said Louie. 'You comfy down there?'

'Hiya, Haz,' said Carrie. She was grinning broadly. 'Sorry for waking you up, like.'

'Lazy prick,' said Louie. 'Get yourself up.'

'We need to take you home,' said Carrie.

'Why?' I asked. 'I need to get to the office, I've–'

'No way,' said Louie, holding out his hand. 'Get up.'

I gripped his hand and he helped me to my feet. 'No, Louie, I've got it all–'

'Shh,' said Carrie. 'You need to go home first.'

'How d'you find me, anyway?' I mumbled. 'You been following me, yeah?'

'It were, Jonah,' said Carrie. 'Called me direct.'

'Is he here?'

Louie started to push me towards a car. 'No. He's not. Go home, Hazzie. And put on some clean clothes, pal.'

'Wait,' I said. 'It don't matter about my clothes. I need to talk to the DI. Why are you so keen to get me home?'

Louie touched the peak of my cap. 'You don't pick up your messages, do you?'

'What messages?' I asked. 'I've been busy, Louie, on this case and…'

He silenced me by putting his finger to his lips. 'Shh.'

Carrie opened the door of the car for me. 'Your kids are back at your flat with your mum and dad. Family Services brought them back this morning.'

Chapter Thirty-Five

—

My mother smiled. 'It were strange.'

'Some woman,' said my father.

'Eh?' I said.

'Yeah,' he said. 'Service said she just turned up and explained everything.'

'I hope you're feeling better, now, love,' said my mother. 'She explained everything that's happened to you.'

'Like what?' I said. I was totally confused now.

'You don't need to tell us,' said my father hastily. 'You've got your life, and that.'

'We know it's been difficult for you...' She gripped my arm and nodded.

'What has?' I asked.

I could hear Ali cry out from his room. 'Everything's in the same place!'

'Dad's not tidied up,' said Asha from her room.

My father leaned in closer. He spoke in a quiet voice. 'All the drugs, the going out and that. She's explained it all, how you were helping her. How you helped get her back on track.'

'We're very proud of you,' said Mum.

'And, to be straight-up honest,' said my father. 'I never trusted that Greg from the moment I set eyes on him. He were a nasty piece of work.'

'Well,' said my mother. 'Good at what he did, in his own way. He were better than that Fahd, of course.'

'Fahd?' scoffed my father. 'He were useless. Yeah, at least Greg knew how to look after them. Didn't stop him being a nasty piece of work, mind.'

I frowned. I wasn't listening. 'Did she leave a name?'

'Who, love?'

'The lady?'

'You know who we were talking about, don't you?' said my father. 'Service said she knew all about you. About the kids and that. Where you lived, even what colour curtains you had.'

'Yeah,' I said, laughing.

'I think the Service said it was something like Luna or Liana or some such,' said my mother. 'Did she use a false name, then?'

I shook my head. 'No. No, she didn't.'

* * *

I worked with Louie for a week. He stayed over at my flat and we fought red-eye with cans of Hombre and packets of crispy crickets, fighting our way through the night and the evidence. I had very little contact with the DI over this time. He had sent me a card, though. Told me he hoped I was getting better. I never saw Clive at all or anybody else from the Division.

But they'd posted me a PO.

So I'd asked Louie to stay on for a while. I offered him some of my cut but he said he was sorted. He said he wanted to make sure I was OK. I knew this was bullshit – he had his own PO to work. But I didn't make a fuss. Carrie had been around for the first days as well. She was just tying up her work with the case. She did a bit of forensics stuff on my neck. Had her gecko take a few photos. Confirmed the calibre.

It was tracked back as an illegal weapon to Liam Wroxeter. This went on the evidence stack.

They had offered to post a shockdrone outside, in case Caines or his cousin were tempted to send somebody around. I never got an apology from Enforcement. But Jonah did turn up to see that I was OK.

Louie and I ended up arguing about the case. I told him about the primary model. He wasn't buying it. Not a cent. But I wasn't budging and he could see that it was a waste of time worrying about. So he cranked up his own model – a formal secondary – using the same evidence. I tried telling him not to bother. We both knew that Ibrahim didn't want a secondary.

I worked furiously on the case. I didn't sleep much. The various pains in my battered body were keeping me awake. And I had sworn off any spores. Messages reminding me that it had been a while since I had last used Memro were left unanswered.

* * *

The advocate's offices were in one of the skyscrapers that ran down the middle of Keighley Basin and into the Flatts. Looking out of the window, I could see a fair way both up and down the dale. It was a mild day, with small cotton wool clouds and warm breezes coming up from the south. It was like the summer days I remembered from my childhood. Taking picnics up to the moors and climbing on the rocks. Aunts and uncles around. Somebody producing a bat and ball.

Days that I could probably count on one hand. But that, to a child's memory, feels like eternal summers. Worked deep into my neural patterns. Always there for me to call upon. I wanted to take my children out to the hills and find a stream and try to catch minnows and snails and watch them in a bucket.

'Louie's been telling me about the narrative,' said Ibrahim, appearing at my elbow.

'Oh, yeah?'

'Yeah.' He ran his fingers through his hair. 'Said that you and he hadn't been in the same place over it.'

'You could say that.'

'So, today, are we–' He was interrupted by the sound of the door opening.

Yazmin Ghara, the advocate – and personal friend of Ibrahim – walked in, holding two coffees and trying to fish a processor brooch out of her jacket pocket at the same time.

'Yazmin, let me help you,' said Ibrahim, leaping across the room.

Yazmin was one of our regular Airedale Justice advocates. Although not directly contracted by AJC, the advocates carried our work through to the final conclusion. It was good to see Yazmin here. I liked Yazmin. She was good-looking, about ten years older than me, and she wasn't as disparaging of the cases brought before her as some of the advocates. At least, she didn't swear as much as some of them.

'Let's get started,' she said, settling herself into one of the comfy seats in the narrative room.

'You ready with the primary, Haz?' asked Ibrahim. He sat forward eagerly in his chair, pulling it tight to Yazmin's chair, and reached across her to grab his coffee.

I nodded.

'Well, sir,' he said. 'Illuminate us, please.'

I started talking. I described the sequence of events, the causal links, the conversations, the recordings, the intentions, the desires, and conclusions. Everything that had happened to me. All this was supported by Modlee's whirring displays across the table top and their own processor beads. Louie's help on this had some effect because they were hooked until two-thirds of the way through. Then I could see they were missing something. Like a new convert at a vegan banquet.

I paused. Ibrahim fidgeted in his seat. He tucked a stray strand of his hair behind an ear.

'I still don't get it,' said Yazmin. 'Who are you accusing, Hasim? What's the case?'

'Watch this,' I said.

I finished up by showing them a recording from the professor. I had commissioned it especially, travelling over one afternoon to Scarborough. It explained the case in its entirety. Still a little edgy from our last encounter, I had been forced to use my credentials to even get an audience with Tad. But he had come round to my theory once I'd had a chance to explain it.

The DI and Yazmin both watched the vid carefully. However, as it finished, she was still frowning and chewing on her lip. The DI's face was motionless, unreadable.

'No, I don't understand,' she said eventually. 'This still doesn't tell me who we're prosecuting?'

Ibrahim looked at me.

'All of them,' I said. 'Collectively.'

In the silence that followed, Ibrahim raised a finger. 'Yazmin, may we be excused for a minute?'

'Of course,' said Yazmin, still frowning into space.

'Hasim and I are going to take some air,' said Ibrahim.

The lawyer shrugged and nodded, immediately switching on her news feed with an eye twitch and re-focussing her eyes on something more rewarding. Less messed-up.

'What's up?' I asked innocently, as we stepped along the corridor. 'Something wrong?'

'I just wanted to take a moment, Haz,' said Ibrahim. 'You ever been to the roof here?'

'No,' I said. 'That's not clearance. Not for contractors like me, anyways.'

Ibrahim presented his array of rings and grinned. 'I got myself clearance. Perks of a DI.'

The ride up in the lift was quiet. I knew what was going on. But I wasn't about to open up this conversation myself. Let the DI do that. Normally, this would've been Ibrahim's time to shine, to spout some bollocks about his new house, or his suit, or his kids, and he was keeping quiet for some reason.

We stepped out of the lift into a small, chilly box of reinforced glass and cladding and then ducked through the small door to the roof itself. It looked like a few of the full-timers had been up here having an old-fashioned smoke, or mainly chewing gum, for the place was littered; great heaps of crap were piled up in lead-lined corners.

'Can I have your hat, Haz, just for a minute?' asked Ibrahim.

I shrugged and pulled off the cap, handing it to him. He delicately selected one of his rings and placed it inside the cap, laying both on the floor next to the door.

'There,' he said, nodding. 'Now we can talk.'

What with the mess – and the pigeon shit – Ibrahim had to step lightly, in his gleaming shoes, as he made his way to one of the railings. I followed him to the edge of the roof and stood alongside him, looking out at the dale.

He was silent for a moment, then grunted. 'I love the view from here. It's right in the middle of things. Look, you can even see your house.'

I squinted into the light. 'Yeah, I guess.'

'Right there,' said Ibrahim, pointing. I had to trust him, for the view of the multitude of tower blocks and bridges and cranes was familiar, but new from this angle. Ibrahim hadn't finished, either. 'That's Tarmell's place over there. There's the comms unit on top of the Trench and, just visible, that's the Arches. Beyond that, the dale bends too much and you lose it.'

'Uh huh.'

'You can even see Bhagwat's factory... over there?'

I could. They hadn't repaired the roof, though. I wonder if the ricos had escaped, or if they'd nuked the lot.

Ibrahim turned back to me with a quizzical look. 'You were going off script a little bit down there. Louie told me you'd come to an agreement. Want to tell me about it?'

'I didn't go off script.' I blinked. 'It were all there in the briefing.'

Ibrahim's face didn't move. But he paused long enough. 'Right.'

'You hadn't read it?' The wrong 'un hadn't read it.

'Don't need to,' said Ibrahim. 'If I trust my team.'

'You trust me?'

'Always, Haz. I've always trusted you.'

'Then hear me out, yeah?'

He raised his eyebrows, leaning back expectantly against the railings. I took him through the primary once again. If it had been a firework, there would've been a pause about now and then some bloke in a hi-viz vest running into the darkness.

'I still don't get any motive,' said Ibrahim. 'I don't even know, Haz...'

'She were a threat, what she were doing, it were a threat, to the dale.'

'Posting videos about Enforcement beatings, etc?'

'That's right. It were damaging Airedale, hurting it.' I swept my arm across the view.

'So Caines and Hussain were trying to help? To get it to stop?'

'No, it's not like that. It weren't one of them, it was all of them the processes underneath, and all that. It was all too tightly connected, the professor said, it was tightly-coupled.'

'They were working together?'

'No.' I shook my head. This was getting difficult. 'No, that's not what I'm saying. It's not like joint enterprise. It's different...' I trailed off and turned to him. 'Can't you see it as well? Can't you see what I'm seeing?'

Ibrahim gave a solemn half-smile I'd never seen before.

'Not really, Haz. But I believe you can see it.'

'It were the place, the whole frigging dale.'

'You think Airedale murdered her?'

'That's my case, yeah.'

Ibrahim nodded and turned to stare out at the view. 'It would do that, this place. It's turned dark, it has.'

'I'm not joking.'

'I know,' sighed Ibrahim. 'But you know there's no case, don't you? What you're talking about doesn't exist in law, Haz. It's something completely new. If it's a crime – and I'll trust that you think it is – then how do we prosecute it? We don't have the tools...'

I stood there for a while in silence. The tinkling chimes and pseudo-roars of cars drifted up from below. Somewhere in the distance an alarm started up and was silenced.

'So, that's it, then?' I said.

'We'll go with Louie's secondary. There'll be something in that. We'll do them for fraud. The case is rock solid. Yazmin was biting, when it came up. I could see her twitch. Fraud, the attacks on you, it's all there. Even environmental damage. That'll keep Gilbie happy.'

'Not murder?'

'Not from my perspective, no. But perhaps mine is the wrong perspective, eh?' Ibrahim turned to the door, looking down at my cap and his ring as they rested on the floor. 'Perhaps you need to ask Modlee about it, perhaps it's only Modlee can tell you.'

'What about proper justice, though? It was a crime. You know it and I know.'

Ibrahim raised an eyebrow. 'I genuinely don't know, Haz. Like I said, I think only Modlee can tell us now.' He clasped me on the shoulder. 'But you know what I think? You know how proper justice, like you call it, used to work? It was direct, back in the day, wasn't it? Didn't have Justice Departments, law courts, Enforcement. Before the police, before detectives, there was still justice, wasn't there? It was direct. Chop off their heads. You truly believe there was a crime committed?'

'I do.'

'Then tell me, is it going to happen again? Like this? Is there going to be another Meri Fergus falling from the sky?'

'No,' I said, slowly thinking through the question. 'We've broken the connections. It can't operate anymore.'

'Exactly. You could almost say you've severed its head, the head of this... thing, this monster, that's emerged from the dale. Am I right?'

I looked up to the sky, realising I'd not been bothered by drones in the last few days. Maybe I'd not noticed them as much or maybe they'd really decided to leave me alone. 'I guess...'

'Criminals come in many forms, Haz.' He pointed to his chest. 'I know that.'

I rubbed my eyes, smiling 'That's why you're the DI, in't it?'

'That, Hasim, is why I'm the DI.'

Ibrahim gave my shoulder one last clasp, which I didn't mind so much now, for some reason, and strode to the door. He replaced the ring on his finger and slung my cap over to me.

'Judge, jury and executioner,' said Ibrahim. 'You heard about that?'

'Yeah,' I said. 'I have.'

'That's you, Haz. You're justice.' He pointed to my chest. Then to my cap. 'It says so on your hat.'

Chapter Thirty-Six

——

Memro had cut another good one. Dutch trance segued into Sri Lankan beach beats. Fading up to an early morning scene. Sun creeping over the horizon. A horizon cut with mountains. The view from a personal camera. Hushed chatter, from behind the camera, catching a few words only. Drowned out by the throb of an ancient engine. Movement of the camera suggested the sway of the ocean. Red and white painted railings. The roofs of cars beneath the camera operator. Terminal buildings on a dock. The last cars rolling silently onto the beast.

Dawn was breaking.

The ferry pulled away from the docks. The camera tried to zoom in on the sun about to rise behind the mountains. It missed. It auto-focussed on three figures standing at the stern of the boat. A man and two children. A girl and a boy. Holding hands. The back of the man's head betraying a perfectly circular bald patch. The footage slowed, letting the view linger. The man turned, his face becoming momentarily visible to the camera. Recognised. Logged. Locked in a digital grave, never forgotten. But hidden also, buried beneath a mountain of other faces. A mountain of faces. An ocean of lives.

* * *

The trial took place five months after the case was submitted. Liam Wroxeter was convicted of fraud and was asked to spend time on the Lleyn Peninsula. Darren Caines was fined for his part. Shortly after the trial, the Head of Enforcement Operations, Brian Fallin, resigned his position. Irregularities in process were identified; fraud had been whispered. No case was brought and the story was given out that he'd returned to spend time with his family in Australia.

* * *

Cars roll off the ferry into a small coastal town. Neatly-kept houses amid a wasteland of low heather and rocks. A security camera focuses on the front of a shop. Cars go by, one-by-one, too fast to focus. Then a particular one passes. The footage slows, jerky low-res frame by low-res frame. The girl is in the front passenger seat. The boy in the back, on the far side from the camera. The man in the back seat, closest to the camera, turns and looks up straight into the lens. He starts to smile. A small, secret smile. The car passes from view.

* * *

Kaz Furness, chair of the Enforcement Board, was immediately put under pressure to find a replacement for the Head of Enforcement Operations. Airedale couldn't run without a strong, experienced person in the post. While the recruitment process dragged, Furness recommended – through the Enforcement Commissioning Board – Jaime Ogarde, Chief Inspector of the Justice Division, to act as temporary Head. Three months later, having failed to find a suitable candidate, the Board agreed to make Ogarde's appointment permanent.

* * *

Various intercut shots from dashboard cameras. All turning, all focussing on the same view. All looking at the same vehicle. A car parked on the side of the road. The music gentle. Sun now high in the sky. It was a beautiful day. Blue skies. Clear blue skies. Three figures run from the car. Towards a beach.

The view now from a handheld camera. A cheap camera, bought for a bit of pre-load off a stall in a fun fair. The two children laughing and running. The elder child, the girl, catching herself, when the camera is on her. Conscious of being filmed. Trying to be adult, then forgetting it and whooping. The boy tumbling into the sand. Forward rolls into tufts of sharp marram grass.

Footage of the two children running down a dune towards the sea. The camera operator also running. The view suddenly spinning. Fleeting shots of sky, beach, sky. Then beach with a thump. The man's face reaching down and peering into the lens. He blows into the lens gently. Grains of sand are removed. The camera is handed to the child. The man's filling the screen, crazy zoom, in and out. The man's shaking his head and grinning.

* * *

With Ogarde moving sideways, the Servants now found themselves with another problem. Solved quickly with DI Ibrahim Al-Yahmeni's promotion to Chief Inspector of the Justice Division of the AJC. A temporary position which then became permanent. DI Winters was moved from environmental crime into violent and specialist crime. They recruited a new DI into Winters's position from Sunderland. On her first day in the job, the new DI threw a cup of coffee at one of her analysts, Paully Zappers. Zappers sued her, of course. But he lost the case and she kept her job. Ibrahim could always see the potential in someone. He was loyal like that.

* * *

Shots from the underside of a car. A camera watching the road for obstacles. The car's eyes. This footage is available when a car goes in for scrap. Footage liberators crawling over the mountains of dead tech, scanning for data storage devices. Hacking out the slivers with screwdrivers and penknives. Plugging the footage – raw – into the mountains. Liberating it, they call it. Letting it roam the mountains. Let it swim in the seas. Until somebody finds it.

The car moved smoothly over the road. The view the same ad infinitum. Short grass, rocks, heather, and the odd thorn tree. The footage speeds up. Tempo of the music increases. Ankara hardcore. Cars passing in a blur.

Hitting a causeway. The heat from the summer's sun causing ripples in the road. Ocean on the left. A lake on the right.

Moving north.

* * *

There hadn't been a riot in the dale for months. Although it was always too soon to declare success, the Servants on the Prevention Commissioning Board did so anyway. Head of Prevention Division, Cordan Grene, was commended and awarded a substantial bonus. The Servants approved a request for additional funding. They got money from a tightening in Enforcement's budget.

The Prevention Division grew by approximately twenty-five percent. Specialists from Central States and the East Coast came to understand the models the team had developed. The offices were deemed too small in Skipton. They were offered a floor in the Trench for their growing team.

They declined. They moved to larger premises in Keighley Vale.

* * *

View looking back at a ferry port. A different ferry port. This one a little larger. A little busier. A little cleaner. The shot panning back. The camera mounted on the stern of the departing ferry. Low, ancient hills passing on the side. Buildings of the port being left behind. A few figures waving on the jetty. A row of cars slowly making their up a road behind the port. Cresting the hill. Disappearing.

Centre of the view: a bench. Two figures approach the bench and sit down. One adult. One child.

Now the shots from two different cameras. One a roof-mounted, low-res, monochrome dinosaur. One a hi-def, tourist-trapping, panning, zooming, semi-intelligent operator. Views cut beneath the two. A car pulls up into a car park. It's the ferry port car park. In the distance, at the end of a pair of white lines of foam, is the retreating form of the ferry. Setting off down a long inlet. In the distance, the open sea. Beyond the sea, more mountains.

The music now auto-generated ambient-drone. Very quiet. Synthetic waves lapping at a digital shore pulsed by a distant, ever-so-distant, outboard engine.

Doors to the car open. View cuts to a front-mounted camera on another vehicle leaving the car park. The children get out of the car. They aren't running this time. They are shy. Tired. The man gets out also. He holds the children's hands, one on either side.

Shots now from the tourist-camera, high on a nearby building. It's focussed on the two figures sitting on the bench, watching the boat go. They stand. The hi-res image zooms on them. Memro tricks. The image now low-res. It's a woman and a child, about seven years old. They come round to the side of the bench, facing the man and his children.

The woman waves.

Memro fades to black.

Acknowledgements

I would like to thank all my family who helped me reach this point, especially those to whom this book is dedicated and my mother, my brother and sisters. Without their support and encouragement, I would not have had the will to keep coming back to the keyboard and to keep going.

I would especially like to thank Matt, for being a champion reader of all my work, and for giving me faith in myself as a writer, and in this book in particular. For Andrew, who first read my opening chapters, and who gave me (who always gives me) wise and insightful feedback. I would also like to thank Wanda, who taught me so much when working on my first book, and who gave me confidence that I should continue. Without these three, I would definitely never have got to where I am now.

Finally, I would like to thank the team at Northodox Press for their faith in my book and my world.

NORTHODOX PRESS

HOME OF NORTHERN VOICES

 FACEBOOK.COM/NORTHODOXPRESS

 TWITER.COM/NORTHODOXPRESS

 INSTAGRAM.COM/NORTHODOXPRESS

 NORTHODOX.CO.UK

Printed in Great Britain
by Amazon